CORRUPTED CHAOS

SHAIN ROSE

Corrupted Chaos

Copyright © 2022 by Greene Ink Publishing, LLC

This is a work of fiction and any resemblance to persons, names, characters, places, brands, media, and incidents are either the product of the author's imagination or coincidental.

Cover Design: Books and Moods
Cover Photography: Wander Aguiar
Editing: The Word Faery, KD Proofreading
Proofreading: KD Proofreading, Overbooked PA Services

A NOTE ON CONTENT WARNINGS

As a reader who loves surprises, I enjoy going in blind with each book. Yet, I also want to give my readers the opportunity to know what sensitive content may be in my books. You will find the list of them here for Corrupted Chaos:

https://www.shainrose.com/content-warnings

Blurb

My enemy doesn't make the rules behind closed doors…

Even if he's my boss.

Cade Armanelli might be an infamous hacker with billionaire status who operates better alone, but I earned my spot working alongside him…

Whether he likes it or not.

It's precisely why I'm on the first plane to an undisclosed location for our cybersecurity team retreat. I'm ready to prove to our company that I can handle anything…

Except sharing a cabin and a bed with my meticulous, elusive boss.

He's antisocial.

Ruthless.

Enemy number one.

Unfortunately, he's also number one in tatted, dark, and dangerous.

I quickly come to find that not only are his hacking skills perfection, but so is his performance in the bedroom.

Not that it matters. I have a job to keep, a heart to protect, and our nation's data to secure.

Cade can't help me with any of that.

He's a distraction. One I have to avoid…

Even if it means I'm spray painting a red line down our bed and keeping my boss on his side.

Corrupted Chaos is a light mafia standalone romance with forced proximity, steam, and a tech mogul that will fight and grovel for a HEA with his spitfire woman.

PROLOGUE

Izzy

"Y ou kissed him?" A low voice full of gravel hissed from the side of my parents' house.

Shit. My stomach dropped, my heart leapt, and my thoughts scattered a million different ways at the sound.

Wincing, I shut my eyes and breathed in the smell of wood burning on that cool autumn night as the fire crackled in the center of our Adirondack chair circle. Maybe if I stayed frozen like that I could wish away the man that owned that voice.

Had he just heard our whole conversation?

A moment ago, I'd been teasing my butthurt brother because he couldn't stop complaining about his best friend and my old boss, Dante, marrying our sister. So, I'd told him to get over it because, if anything, I should have been the one crying. I'd actually kissed Dante—but that had been before he professed his love to my twin, Delilah, and proposed.

Welcome to my shit show, right?

As I stared at them curled up together in front of that fire, though, my heart didn't hurt much anymore. I knew he looked at her in a way he'd never look at me. While we were identical in just about every way possible—same wavy brunette hair, facial features, and even curves—I could never hold a candle to the love Dante had for Delilah. Even after I professed my decades-old love for him, I knew it would never be reciprocated because there was no one else for either of them.

I accepted that now after a year of quiet heartbreak. Quiet because I was happy for my sister, quiet because I knew my love for him wasn't that barreling, chaotic love. Quiet because I wanted to keep the peace and didn't want my family to worry.

It took a year of burying myself in work and exposing myself to their relationship to really be over it.

And I *was* over it. But Cade Armanelli, the most judgmental prick I'd ever met, was never supposed to hear about it. This was only supposed to be for family and close friends.

Cade wouldn't bring that. Dante, him, and I all worked undercover together for the government years ago, and he'd always approached me with an undercurrent of disrespect and disdain. The man didn't believe in anyone but himself and thought we all hindered his ability to get the job done.

As he stepped out of the shadows, I swiveled around to stare at him as I ignored his question about who I'd kissed. "Jesus, where did you come from?"

The sharp angles of his face wreaked havoc on my insides. No hacker for the United States of America should look the way he did. Tattoos painted his neck and hands, peeking from beneath the collar and cuffs of his suit. His strong jaw rivaled chiseled Greek gods, and his dark hair was so wavy it looked professionally styled, even though I'd bet it wasn't.

None of it really mattered, though, except for his penetrating dark stare that always held me captive. In the past, he looked right through me, like I was crystal-clear water with no depth at all. Yet, tonight, he studied me like I was a deep ocean, like I was a mystery at the darkest depths of it. His attention, the way he gripped me with that gaze, could haunt even an angel.

"Were you watching us?" I whispered.

I wouldn't put it past him. Dante and Cade were distant cousins, and Cade always seemed to be watching everything going on with his family. And he had the intelligence to do it, considering he was arguably the best hacker in the world. One that I respected, was in awe of, and loathed all at the same time. When we used to work undercover together, he snickered when someone tried to inform him of something, like he already knew, like he had an omniscient power about him.

Then, I moved into the data security department, away from undercover work, and figured I wouldn't have to deal with him. Even if he technically was the head of the cybersecurity workforce within the Department of Homeland Security, Cade worked alone. He didn't need anyone's help, nor did he show up to the office to ask for it.

"I'm always watching, Izzy," Cade said in warning, his ominous stare was as abrasive as his tone. Always watching me? I didn't need him watching what I did or acting as though I couldn't handle myself. I was sure that's what he meant by it, too, because he'd said once or twice before I didn't belong in data security or working for the government in general for that matter.

Still, my body hummed at his confession, as though I was

suddenly turned on and enraged all at the same time by the notion of him watching me.

It was ridiculous. Completely and utterly ridiculous. So, I scoffed at him and picked up a stick to roast a marshmallow. My mom had brought probably a thousand of them, knowing all six of her kids would be back in town to hang out.

As he stalked over to our fire, my four brothers sat up, their radars blaring. They'd finally accepted Dante into the family but trusting anyone else with the last name of Armanelli was difficult. Cade was the brother to one of the most powerful Italian mob bosses in the world, and his hacking skills made him potentially even more dangerous. Yet, no one, not even an Armanelli, could make them back down when it came to their baby sisters.

The fire crackled, and its light danced over him, illuminating his perfect bone structure as he said, "Dante, Delilah. Jet's ready to go."

Them? He'd come for them? Not me. I don't know why that was a surprise and why my ego deflated a bit from the thought.

"Tonight?" My sister's voice sounded shocked but hopeful. Dante must have planned a vacation for them with Cade's help. It made sense considering Cade had the family private jet. For all I knew, it could have been the presidential jet considering the man was in the news for helping the country all the time with cybersecurity.

I stood so fast my knees popped when my sister got up to clear dishes on a tray table near our chairs. I moved to help, then followed her with my own handful to pad through the lush grass into our parents' ranch-style home.

I whisper-yelled over the classical music my mom always played in the kitchen to Delilah. "I can't believe Cade just shows up to our bonfire like this."

"I think Dante probably called him." Delilah shrugged, confused by my frustration. I myself wasn't sure what it was about either. Maybe it was the way he'd confidently told me he was watching, like I was a loose cannon, or maybe it was because every time I saw him, he stirred something in me that he shouldn't. I needed to keep my life like a calm lake, but when Cade came around, it turned into a tumultuous ocean, waves crashing violently on the shore.

I shook my head at my sister, placing a hand on the worn quartz countertop. "He's deliberately acting like my babysitter since I'm still working for the government." I didn't need anyone behind me looking over my shoulder like I was going to mess up. I'd proven myself time and time again over the course of years of undercover work. And now being in cybersecurity, I was determined to stay ahead of the curve. I even took classes to keep up my skills. "I can take care of myself."

"Well, he probably wants to make sure you're safe, considering you're friends." She shrugged and put another dish in the sink.

"Colleagues," I corrected, wrinkling my nose and brushing some of my hair that was frizzing away from my face. "Definitely not friends."

Lilah peered over at me like she was questioning my sanity. I'd probably announced that last part a little too loudly. "Noted," she grumbled, and I turned to the sink to wash the barbecue off a dish, hating that I'd let Cade get to me at all.

Still, I'd had enough people not believe in me over the years. And he was the worst of them. He never gave me more than a glance when he walked into the room, and I knew he'd bad-mouthed me when I'd first started.

Suddenly, my sister stopped and pointed over her shoulder, yelling, "Gotta go to the bathroom, Izzy," as she beelined it out of there.

I spun around, knowing Delilah wouldn't speed off unless she was avoiding something. And sure enough, the reason was standing right in front of me. All six feet plus a good couple of inches of him loomed over me like he was trying to intimidate me.

He wouldn't. I didn't care if he was a whole head taller. The more I thought about it, the more irritated I became that he even attempted to come around me outside of work. I crossed my arms. "Don't sneak up on me in my parents' house, Cade."

He quirked a dark brow like I sounded ridiculous. "Hardly sneaking considering I'm stepping right in front of you."

"Whatever. This is a family party," I pointed out, trying to make one thing clear. "You shouldn't even be here."

There. Now he knew I didn't ever want to see him outside of work, that I didn't like him, that he wasn't wanted.

"Technically, I'm Dante's family." He glanced down at his phone like he didn't even have time to have this conversation. Then he peered back up at me, and his stare held a condescension I wasn't ready for. "Want to go so far as to say we're related too?"

Why did that feel like he was goading me? I turned around to scrub a dish way harder than necessary. "God, you're so annoying."

"If you think I'm annoying, quit your damn job."

Yep. *There* it was. Him being an absolute dick. Cade didn't want me on any team within the government. He'd had it out for me since day one because he thought I couldn't handle the pressure of our work. It didn't bode well for me. We all knew his ties to the president, to the Pentagon, to everyone. The man infiltrated everything because he had access to it all. A few clicks for him, a few hacks, and he'd be raking through my deepest darkest secrets.

"Start working in corporate America."

I stopped my assault on the poor dirty plate and winced at his recommendation. I liked to think I worked as hard as he did. And I had unfinished business with the government. I'd researched enough while undercover to learn that a large Albanian family was breaking laws within our country. We'd caught them once, and I wasn't going to stop until I had them all behind bars. "The Albanians aren't done. You and I both know it." I waved between us like he should understand. He'd seen what they were capable of in the past, and it was our job to make sure it never happened again. As I got better at sifting through the data, I'd found more evidence. "The drugs are a fucking cover for nuclear warfare, and I'm gonna help bring them down."

"You're digging where you shouldn't be. And you may be good, Izzy, but not that good. I've tracked every fucking hack you've done," he said, an arrogant smirk on his face. Then he leaned in and whispered, "It's not warfare, love. It's the laundering of so much money they would control everything. We've built alliances, though. It's fine. You need to back off."

The way his breath felt on my skin, on my neck, so close to me that I could smell him . . . I loved it in a way I shouldn't. My body instantly gravitated toward him as if I should lean in instead of away. "They won't honor that alliance. So either let me do my job or fuck off," I ground out, trying to ignore everything he was doing.

He hummed low, not moving back even an inch. "If you get

kidnapped, I'm leaving your ass with them."

"Great." I peered up into his eyes and turned my face so our lips were just a touch away from each other. "They'll probably be better company than you anyway."

"Say that again, and try to mean it this time," he growled.

Our stares held, his full of something I didn't normally see. Cade was alive right there next to me, his gaze no longer dark and cavernous but wild and full of adrenaline and joy, like a kid ready to play his favorite game. That look mirrored mine when I found something to keep my mind off my own demons. We'd have worked well together in another life.

We heard the bathroom door opening and stepped away from each other. My brother-in-law came in, too, swooping Delilah under his arm, smiles a mile wide as they hurried through saying goodbye to me.

Cade ushered them out of the house without a backward glance.

Well, good riddance to him, too. Except I wasn't proud to say I did flip him off as he exited.

Still, I went to bed with deep-brown eyes threaded with gold in the back of my mind. I tried my best not to slide my hand between my legs, imagining what it would have been like to lean in an inch farther and taste that man's lips.

I hated myself for it the very next week.

The following Monday started terribly with rain pelting down on me as I made my way into work, drenching my navy blouse and pinstripe pencil skirt. I didn't even have time to dry off, though, before HR called me in.

My stilettos squished with the rainwater as I made my way down the hall, hoping they had a simple update for me of some sort. I'd never been summoned like this, not even for a review of my work.

As I turned the corner and knocked on the already open door, though, understanding dawned. Cade in a black three-piece suit sat behind a small elderly woman at her desk with what looked like one outrageously expensive Berluti loafer propped on a bent knee to hold his laptop across his thighs. He was the epitome of a successful and very intimidating businessman.

To add to it, he didn't even look up or greet me as I entered. The woman with wiry white hair whom I had never met before chirped as soon as I shut the door, "Congratulations, Izzy! We have amazing news for you. Take a seat."

I readjusted my pinstripe wool pencil skirt and glanced between both of them with so many questions running through my mind. "I'm sorry. Is he a part of this—"

She cut me off by talking over me. "Oh, Mr. Armanelli sits in on some office procedures. He is a supervisor here. Have you met—"

"We have." My tone gave away precisely how much I despised him.

"Right." She shifted in her chair. "Well, please take a seat."

Chewing on my cheek, my heart beat faster. Thinking over the last conversation I'd had with Cade, I replied, "I'm fine with standing."

"Of course. Of course." She chuckled. "Well, you've been reassigned to Stonewood Enterprises, and it was such a great contract that you'll be starting in the next week. No long waiting period."

"Reassigned?" I stuttered, the air whooshing out of my lungs. I felt like I'd been sucker punched.

"Yes, we've acquired a wonderful contract." She slid it across her pristine white desk while he typed away like no one was in the room.

The fact that he was even there—after having never set foot in this office in all the time I'd been there—was him waving a red flag in my face. Like he wanted to fight.

I cleared my throat and straightened my blouse, not picking up the packet to even appear intrigued. "But what if I don't want to be reassigned?"

"Well, this is within the state's rights, Ms. Hardy. If you check section . . ." She droned on about distance between home and work and where I was needed and a bunch of other crap I knew wasn't true. I just glared at him with his smug expression as he lifted his gaze to smirk at me.

Anger, swift and hot, flew through me faster than I could control. "You requested this, didn't you? The almighty Caden Armanelli." I wrinkled my nose at him in disgust.

Immediately, the woman stood, her blue eyes widened into orbs of concern. People didn't just sneer Cade's full name. Businessman, my ass. We all knew when they threw around the Armanelli mafia name they got what they wanted. "Ms. Hardy, we've talked with a few of your team members, and there is state work you'll still be doing there. It's a great opportunity for you all to be contracted there. Cassie and Braxton will be transferred too. You'll get amazing corporate raises that the state can't compete with. You'll even get to travel for work, and it's good for the team."

"Let me guess." I popped a hip. "If I don't go, my team doesn't either."

The woman stepped between Cade and me, like she wanted to break our eye contact. "You've done fantastic work, and we'd like you all to stay together, yes."

"This can't be protocol."

"Honestly . . ." She sighed and rubbed her eyes like she'd had a long day. Her wrinkles, testaments to the stress she faced, moved with her hands. "I'm going to level with you. It may not be protocol, but if you don't comply, you all will most likely be out of a job."

I leaned to the side enough so that I could see him. "That true, Cade Armanelli?"

One side of his mouth hitched at me sneering his name. "Ms. Hardy, I promise corporate America will suit you."

The lady nodded. "Cade does run most of the data security teams here, Ms. Hardy. I do suggest you take the offer. Your salary—and the salaries of everyone on your team—has been doubled, and you probably have more opportunities there than you do here."

I sighed.

I would have thrown a tantrum, demanded they reconsider, and maybe even thrown a pen or two around. But that was the Izzy of years ago, before I lost myself to passivity. I was better now. I'd reformed. I'd packed my emotions up into a nice, neat box so no one could say I was being a diva or indulging in that personality of mine that got me into trouble.

Everyone said I was such a grown-up now, but most days, it felt like I was simply tired. Keeping a lid on so many emotions would do that to a person. Still, I accepted my lot and hoped I could go home soon for a nap and reset. "Thank you for the opportunity," I told her, the words as sour as limes in my mouth.

Cade's eyebrows raised. "That's it?"

I swear, he wanted a fight, but I wouldn't give him one. The woman hurried on with a nervous chuckle. "I promise, it's for the best. You'll thank me once you're settled into your new position. You'll see. You'll probably have more time on your hands there."

What she didn't understand was that I *wanted* to do all I was doing for the government. I wanted—no, I *needed*—to work hard for them. My mind didn't do well without a goal or something to occupy it. It was how I kept the indulgent side of me, the side that was bottled up, from creeping out.

Cade was ruining everything, and he damn well knew it.

THREE MONTHS LATER

Cade: Stop trying to hack into government property

Me: OMG get a life and stop watching what I'm doing

Cade: Technically, I'm doing my job. It's national security and you're breaching one of our firewalls

Me: Still, you're watching what I'm doing

Cade: Me watching what you're doing is knowing you sold your condo to move to Greene Liberty Apartments where they have a shit security system

Me: Seriously, stop

Cade: Stop sifting through confidential data then

Me: Get over it. It's only for information on the Albanians

Cade: That's not your job

Me: I'm quite aware of your reassigning my job duties

Cade: Yeah, about that ...

Cade: I'm waiting for a "thank you so much, Cade"

Me: Fuck you very much

Cade: You're welcome to come over

Me: I wonder if you think that actually works on women

Cade: I don't have to wonder

Me: You do realize you're my boss. This wouldn't look very good to HR

Cade: I'll take my chances if you're agreeing

Me: I'm not. I have a boyfriend that's actually a good human

Cade: You sure? Want me to hack his data and see?

Me: You better not.

Cade: Yeah, we'll let him have his fun while he's out of the country

Me: How do you know he's gone?

Cade. I know everything ... Stop poking around

Me: Fine. Whatever

THREE MONTHS LATER

Cade: Don't you have anything better to do at 3 am?

Me: Maybe I would have more work to do if you let Stonewood Enterprises give me a promotion

Cade: You're not ready obviously or you wouldn't be doing something reckless like hacking systems in the middle of the night

Me: Leave me alone

Cade: Then turn off your computer and do something else with your time

Me: Nothing else to do right now

Cade: Your boyfriend must be gone again, huh?

Me: So what if he is? Stop watching me

Cade: Get over yourself. I built an alert for when you start digging for Albanian data. Leave it alone

Me: You're seriously the most annoying person I've ever met

SIX MONTHS LATER

Cade: They must not give you enough work over at Stonewood Enterprises.

Me: Well, you're technically my boss, although you're never in the office. You might want to tell the manager who's there every day about it.

Cade: Izzy, I swear to all that's holy, knock this shit off.

Me: Just let me be!

Cade: Go to bed. Fuck your boyfriend. Watch a show. Do anything other than this.

Me: I'm not tired, boyfriend's out of town, and shows are boring.

Cade: Starting to think you need a new fuckboy if he's always gone.

Me: That's none of your business.

Cade: Well, get a new hobby. Go travel with him or is he that dull?

Me: I hate you. LEAVE ME ALONE.

CHAPTER 1

Izzy

"I t's not me. It's you." My boyfriend of almost a year patted my shoulder with his soft, sweaty hand.

I wanted to tell the jerk that someone didn't break up with that line—it was supposed to be the other way around. But all I could do was stare at his phone in shock.

We'd dressed as Harley Quinn and the Joker for my work party. It was an early October Halloween one, and I'd been excited, even put together a really good costume, but as we were about to get out of the car, his phone had beeped with a text.

I didn't think much of it when I grabbed it off the seat for him, but when the screen flashed a pair of completely fake breasts at me, I had to tap the message open.

Who wouldn't?

Text after text after text came up.

Gerald Johnson III was everything I'd wished for. Kind of. The neat box of emotions I'd built for myself really complimented his even-keel attitude. He was your average working man with soft cheeks and blond hair, a quiet demeanor, and was amicable to almost everyone he met. I'd thought everything about him other than his job was perfect. He had work trips that took him around the world. But his father owned a big investment firm, and that's what they had to do—or at least, that's what he told me.

And it's not like I didn't trust him. I'd been on the trips. He'd shown me he was truly working on them.

Or so I'd thought.

His last trip had been two whole months long, and two weeks into him returning home, he wanted nothing to do with me. So much so that I started to question if I was good enough, if something was wrong with me. Had I pushed him away?

Which, now I'd like to say, was absolutely legitimate, considering the texts. But it wasn't my fault. It was his. I held the phone up for him to see, only for him to reply with that line. "It's not me. It's you."

My fault? How was him cheating on me my fault?

"It's me?" I squeaked out, the lid of the jar that kept my dark side locked away turning just a bit. "Let me guess, I drove you to message this Lucy girl your dick on a platter. A platter, Gerald! Really?"

He shook his head full of blond hair and frowned at me with puppy eyes I used to think were cute. "Baby, I didn't want you to find out this way, but honestly, do you think I wanted to come home to this?"

He motioned at me. I peered down at myself, not exactly sure what he meant.

"I told you I needed you to try harder with this workout thing and to let loose a little. Instead, you didn't try at all."

My heart dropped as my blood pressure skyrocketed. Break ups were always a mixed bag of anger and sadness but this time I was clinging to the anger.

I geared up to tell him off, but he kept going instead of letting me talk. "Don't get me wrong—I love how you look. I do. But you know I have a standard to uphold. I need a girl who's going to look the part. Lucy does. And you won't even drink much with me at our charity events. You know that my dad's company really needs me to have a social butterfly on my arm. I think we just need a bit of time apart for you to work on that."

"A bit of time apart?" I sounded like a broken record repeating what he said. Did he think we could get back together after this? Was I dating that much of an idiot?

He'd come home, yet his mind was still far away. I couldn't even get his attention long enough for a good lay, not that he was ever that great in bed. Sleeping with him was trying to scratch an itch that was just a centimeter out of reach. But I'd been celibate for two months and I needed to stop that dry spell.

Now, he was trying to tell *me* I was no fun.

"Look, I don't want things to end this way. Maybe we can work on it." His brow furrowed while he tried to make puppy dog eyes at me.

"Oh really? Should we text Lucy then and tell her you're done with—"

"No!" he yelped and grabbed his phone away. "It's . . . why don't we do this? I'm only breaking up with you for now. Like I said, I've always enjoyed you, Izzy. Just...honestly, I've been talking with my father and some of my friends. We think maybe you need to lose a few pounds before we get married, get into a better place where you don't work so hard and can be on my arm a little more, you know? It'll be good for us to take a break, date around, and circle back—"

"Gerald, I do not want to marry you." I blurted out, my body cringing at the idea. Then, I enunciated each word, trying to make clear that this relationship was over. "And I don't want to work on things."

"Look, I know you're mad. But remember what your therapist said."

My eyes bulged. Was he really going down that road? If so, I think my therapist would have understood if I'd clawed his face apart right then. The jar creaked open a bit farther.

"See. You're getting mad. You do have a temper and a tendency to react when you're hurt. So I have to deal with that too. It's a lot. How do you think it feels for me to be dating an addict, Izzy?"

There it was. The thing he'd always promised me didn't matter. He promised to not use it against me and the motherfucker just did. "But, Gerald, you said—"

"I know what I said. I meant it. It's just really hard to have a good time when I know you can't drink too much or indulge in new things because you're scared of your 'addictive personality.'" He air quoted himself like it wasn't a real thing. "Lucy is a nice breath of fresh air on the side. If you met her, you'd understand. We should all get brunch—it might smooth things over a bit."

Nope.

I'd sort of always known this guy wasn't the one for me. I should have had butterflies when he kissed me, right?

I should have wanted him home early from a work trip rather than for him to stay another day.

I should have, but I never did.

Everything with him was mediocre, but I'd tried. I'd stopped myself from breaking up with him time and time again because I knew that some things weren't meant to be only emotional highs or lows. If I didn't miss him when he was gone, so what? That was me being an adult and handling our separation maturely.

Now, though, it all made sense. "I'm going to go ahead and make this easy for you. We're done."

"Sugar, take a deep breath." He pouted like a child.

"Gerald, don't call me. Don't text me. *This* is over." I opened the car door, but he grabbed my arm.

"Izzy, I do love you." I sort of believed him. He was sweating now and cracking his knuckles with his other hand like he didn't want this to end. "Please, sugar. I really do."

He leaned in to kiss me. I think I was so shocked I didn't react at first, the whiplash of his speech caught me off guard. Then his hand went up my shirt like he was trying to cop a feel.

I jerked away and shoved him. "Are you kidding me right now?"

"We were always good together like this. Let's take some deep breaths and go to brunch with Lucy, baby. It'll all be fine. We need you."

"We?"

"Me," he corrected. "I need you. I love you." His eyes were attempting the hooded, sultry look, but instead he appeared drowsy and stupid.

"The fact that you think we were good together anywhere just proves that this was never a match to begin with." I stopped myself from saying more. I was better at controlling my temper now.

My therapist was right about that.

"Good riddance, Gerald Johnson III." I rolled my eyes and

ripped my arm away from him as I got out of the car.

Of course, the man couldn't let a breakup be clean and easy. He had to roll down his window and make a fool out of us both. "*Good riddance?* I gave you everything. I just needed a little something in return. Not a whore going to a costume party with her big ass out. That should be for me to see only anyway."

Right.

So, this is probably a good time to state that, as a twin, I wasn't the good one. Delilah was. She got the good grades, she was the one who never rebelled, never caused too much of a stir. The one who smoothed over a situation instead of making it worse.

I, on the other hand, barely made it through high school and got sent to juvie when I was so loaded I attempted to shoplift. I don't really remember it. It was a low point for me.

I had my reasons and I kept them locked away in a box under my bed.

This was who I was though. Even though I always had a family that showered me with love throughout my whole life. Addiction can affect anyone.

I didn't need to come from a troubled family or past to have drugs hook their claws into me. Fentanyl worked fast, manmade and potent. It took one time experimenting with a friend, and I was hooked. A few bad occurrences later, and that was it.

But juvie shaped me into one of the lucky ones. I got clean, I went to rehab, I tried not to look back.

Still, I wasn't the good twin. I really tried to be someone like my valedictorian of a sister. But if I was honest with myself, I was the fucking fireball you threw in when you wanted hell, not the angel who'd bring you heaven like my sister.

Quite frankly, I'd dressed as Harley Quinn for a reason. My shirt had Daddy's Lil Monster printed across it, and the red lipstick contrasting against my pale face makeup gave the impression of outrageous behavior.

The costume was all about fun but suddenly, it felt right. I wondered why I was holding back. Why did a woman always have to suppress her emotions so she wouldn't offend anyone else? We were entitled to—no, we *deserved*—the space to feel when we'd been wronged.

My costume fit the bill tonight.

I strode right back up to his car and dug into my purse. I didn't normally carry around spray paint, but earlier that day when I'd been getting the last parts of our costumes, I saw the red spray paint on sale and couldn't resist. It was a vibrant bloodred. The perfect shade to draw the eye for a painting, or a bold color choice for restoring a piece of furniture.

I loved doing both things. They calmed my mind in a way most things couldn't.

The spray paint would serve as such a good part of my next piece, but it was about to serve another purpose.

My steps slowed as I uncapped the can. Had he not been so dense, he could have taken the hint and driven off as I shook it.

"Izzy, what are you do—"

The red spray went right through the window and into his face. "The sex between us was never good," I informed him in a monotone.

He screamed and hit the button to close his window as fast as he could.

I didn't stop spraying. I started to write *asshole* across the sleek black door, but he peeled away, finally realizing his mistake.

That mistake of his wasn't breaking up with me before the early Halloween party at the office. It was dating me at all in the first place.

I sighed a breath that felt fresh, clean, not as heavy as it had been, and looked up at the clouds. A moment of freedom outside my jar, setting free all the frustration and rage, felt freaking fantastic, like I'd been stuffed within small confines and finally got to stretch. I smirked at the sky. Some higher power up there should have known a Gerald the Third wasn't made for an Izzy the First. I was too tweaked underneath it all to deal with someone everyone thought was such a stand-up guy, I guess.

Although, telling my family I'd lost him was going to be a bitch. My mom had smiled the first time she met him, like he was going to solve all her problems with me. "He'll help settle your soul, Izzy," she'd said.

How wrong she'd been.

"So, guess that relationship's over," a deep voice rumbled from the shadows of a side street.

I jumped at the sound and spun around. I knew that voice. I could place it anywhere. I knew it and hated it with every fiber of my being, even though I hadn't heard it all year. "Jesus, Cade. What the hell? Have you been there the whole time?"

Cade sauntered out of the shadows like a man made to be in them. I may have been the only one who thought that though. My whole work team claimed we were lucky to work under Cade because he'd accepted the proposal from Stonewood Enterprises that got them those nice corporate vacations and raises.

I didn't correct anyone, but I knew better. Stonewood

Enterprises, along with Cade's whole Armanelli family, worked with the government. They ran the nation together, and we were simply a part of whatever they wanted us to be doing. Cade wanted me off government work. So, he got his ridiculous way.

Even so, I'd tried to breach the system over the last year time and time again. Every single time, I hit a barrier. And he had the audacity to hack my laptop half the time to tell me to knock it off.

It was a pastime that I slowly started to let go of. I thought I had a good enough life with my boyfriend, and the work at Stonewood Enterprises, although boring, paid the bills nicely.

"Long enough to see you spray paint his face and ruin his car."

"He deserved it."

"Did he though, Harley Quinn?" Cade cocked his head and eyed up my costume. "You want to call the cops and turn yourself in or let him do it?"

Why was he asking me that question? Anyone who'd seen this go down would have stayed hidden, not wanting to be caught in such an awkward moment. Yet, Cade thrived in it. He smiled at me like he was right in his element.

"Are you enjoying yourself?" I threw up my hands. "Why are you even here?"

"Why wouldn't I be?"

It was a ridiculous question. Cade ran cybersecurity teams for the government, the Pentagon, and for Stonewood Enterprises. He flew around the world, worked on top secret projects, and never, not once, had stepped foot into our data security team's office. Even though, technically, he had the biggest office there, he was never seen on our floor. "You haven't been to your office at Stonewood Enterprises since the day I started."

He rubbed his five-o'clock shadow. "Right, and what day was that again?"

I still had the spray paint. "I should spray you in the face too."

He outright laughed at me, and it gave a whole new meaning to fingers itching to press something. My blood boiled even hotter than it had with Gerald. "Are you laughing at getting me moved or me wanting to spray you? Because I assure you neither is a joking matter."

"Why do you have that spray paint anyway?"

"I paint at home when I'm— It's none of your business."

He hummed. "Private about some things, huh? Weren't so concerned about privacy when you were shouting about your sex life a minute ago."

"What you heard between Gerald and me is none of your business."

He shrugged in his three-piece suit. "Everything about you is my business, baby doll."

"Made that pretty clear to me a year ago," I grumbled, ready to let all my demons out of the jar. I'd rehearsed what I'd say to him if I ever saw him again. Without even asking me formally to stop doing something, he'd had me moved instead.

"Ah, the real Izzy's out to play tonight, I see."

My gut clenched at the fact that he noticed, that he saw how I kept something hidden from everyone else. I hated that he so easily perceived what others couldn't, so I acted like I had no idea what he was getting at. "What's that supposed to mean?"

He sighed like he didn't want to be bothered with my antics and started to walk toward the building. "If you want a trip down memory lane from a year ago, go ahead and get your bitching out."

"My bitching?" I stomped my foot. "You deliberately dangled a doubled salary over my whole team—essentially forcing me to agree to move to corporate for a sham of a deal—because you wanted me off the Albanian trail."

"If you say so." He shrugged his shoulders and chuckled, opening one of the large glass doors to Stonewood Tower's entryway for me.

I marched past him, annoyed that he chuckled as if what he'd done was some insignificant inconvenience. "You upended my livelihood to prove a damn point."

His eyes narrowed at my tone. "*Upended*? You got a bonus, more time off, and your team moved with you. I'm still waiting for my thank you.'"

"And you know I'm still going to say, 'fuck you, asshole,'" I said, stepping right up to him and lifting my chin so my words hit home loud and clear.

He rolled his lips between his teeth. And he grew bigger, darker, meaner. Then the smile that spread across his face was wide, showing his teeth as if ready to inflict harm. That was what men in power got: everyone's fear. I could tell he wasn't used to my tone, used to someone pushing back at him. "I really enjoy when you say it with a punch like that. When you really mean it."

I literally growled and brushed past him toward the elevators. "I don't know why you're concerning yourself with anything here at Stonewood Enterprises. We're fine without you."

"Yeah, looks like my employees are doing great things on the street with spray paint." His tone held condescension.

"That was between me and my boyfriend." I wanted to pull out my pigtails, scream, and go home like a big baby. The man could grate on every one of my nerves within seconds and I knew he was trying to.

"Well, ex-boyfriend now," he pointed out.

I couldn't handle him or my emotions anymore. And honestly, that little fact coming from his mouth probably stung more than the whole breakup.

"Whatever, Cade." I scoffed. Now that the lid of my attitude had popped off, I wasn't sure how to put it all back in the jar. "I'm not in the mood tonight."

No one risked talking to him like this. I knew that. A good hacker could dig up dirt, the best one could ruin your life, unearth all your skeletons, or send you to jail.

It was like we all knew Cade had something on everyone. And I knew from the few times in the past I'd been around him, no one crossed him for that very reason.

That wasn't why I despised him though. He'd acted as though I couldn't be trusted, and then he'd literally moved me to a place where I was no risk.

And I was still striving to prove him wrong. I don't know why. Quite frankly, it made this whole situation even more embarrassing.

"My ex-boyfriend won't report me. It would ruin his precious reputation," I sneered, dropping the spray can back in my purse.

"He should report you. That's a criminal offense, ruining the dick's car. Potentially his eyes."

I narrowed my gaze at him. I had expected him to twist the metaphorical knife by telling me I was a fuck-up, but instead he'd called Gerald a dick. Even the slightest display of care from him had me pursing my lips, the rage dissipating. The ball of shame expanded in my gut, and the embarrassment of being caught in my childish act of retaliation was catching up to me. Let's not forget the fact that I'd been dumped too.

I wondered if he'd heard my ex's cruel words before I'd sprayed him.

My vision blurred, and I knew he saw my chin tremble. "Maybe he will, then. Or maybe you can send the security tapes in and file a police report yourself."

He took one step forward and tugged on a lock of my blonde hair before rubbing it between his fingers. "I deleted it from the cameras already."

His admission, the way he touched my hair—it held me captive in a way it shouldn't. "Why would you do that?" I whispered, peering up at him.

"You're my employee. It would look bad for us." He shrugged, and his finger twined around a lock as he stared, like he was trying to crack a code. "You dye your hair for this?"

"It's just temporary spray-in stuff." I waved my red-painted nails in front of my face, attempting to focus on his small talk rather than the terrible start to my night or the fact that my body was reacting to a man I considered my enemy.

"It's too much for a work party." Cade stepped back, taking in my whole outfit. "You tried way too hard for this, dollface."

At least I'd made the effort to dress up and come to this party. The man in front of me didn't put forth an effort for anything. I roved my own gaze over him and tried not to sneer at his suit but the man was coming to a Halloween party without a costume. "'Dollface'?"

"Harley Quinn's a household name after the movies. We all know her nicknames."

I rolled my eyes. Cade would never give us a glimpse into his life; not even if it was only to reveal that he'd read all the comics. He was happy to pry into everyone else's life but would never divulge any small detail about his.

"Whatever. I read the comics, and I like her. And it was supposed to be cute with—"

"Gerald would have been a terrible Joker," Cade said as he scratched at his eyebrow, the streetlight playing over the strong lines of his face. In comparison to Cade, every man would have been a terrible everything. Cade could have played Psycho, Joker, Michael Myers, Batman, Superman, or whatever he wanted and pull it off. He had the height, the sharp, haunted bone structure, and maintained a great physique—although I wasn't sure how. He always seemed to be hunched over a device or computer when I saw him.

Except now.

"You do realize you shouldn't even know his name, right?" I pointed out because Cade had a bad habit of prying into my life.

"I know everything about you," he whispered, and my whole body shivered in a way it never had with Gerald, in a way it only did when Cade talked to me. "Including that you went above and beyond with this costume."

"Well, you can't knock me for trying when you don't try for shit." I snapped my mouth shut. I was still mad. I shouldn't let my emotions control me or make me lash out at my superior. And he was that, even if he was never around.

To my surprise, he pulled a mask from his jacket pocket as he tsked. "So quick to assume I don't do *shit*, huh?" He emphasized my foul language and then stuck it back in the pocket, obviously not ready to put it on.

"A *Scream* mask?" I lifted a brow, not apologizing. "You enjoy Skeet like the rest of us?"

"It's an easy costume if you don't want to participate but have to."

"Of course you don't want to participate," I mumbled, throwing my hands up and turning to walk toward the elevators.

Cade was in charge because he was the best, but his lack of enthusiasm for being a part of the team was quite frankly disrespectful, especially when I'd wanted a team lead position since the moment I joined Stonewood Enterprises' data security group. I'd made it my mission to live and breathe my job. It was what kept me focused, kept my mind from straying to other things, and probably what kept me healthy most days—both physically and mentally.

If I didn't get sleep because I was working on cracking a code or helping another team member with an algorithm, all the better. Half the time, I did it because Cade never answered when a team member called or texted him.

I think most of the team had deleted his number.

"Why would I want to participate when I can do more productive things?" He sounded off behind me, like he couldn't just let the matter be.

Would it be bad if I told him to stop following me and take the stairs up to the top of the building? It was 110 floors. And I knew the scenery would be appealing enough. The building had been designed specifically for the Stonewoods with its shape and silhouette giving the illusion of a wave rising to the sky. On the interior, a cascading waterfall surrounded the elevator, bringing the exterior architectural theme inside. With plush leather lounge chairs in the lobby, marble floors, and crystal chandeliers, it didn't feel like we were ever walking into work. It'd probably take him the whole night to climb to the top floor, then I wouldn't have to see him.

"Oh. I don't know. Maybe because you have a team here that's been working for you all year that you haven't seen and they're all very excited about the costume party," I said.

"Are you?" he asked, and I saw one corner of his full lips lift. There was no way he could know I wasn't actually excited. I put in enough effort to appear so. He waved his key fob in front of the elevator doors.

"Even though Halloween is weeks away and a children's holiday, I dressed up, didn't I?" I placed my hands on my hips.

As the elevator doors slid open, he walked in and replied, "You did dress for the party. Ass hanging out and all."

Cade Armanelli.

He was truly a villain, heartless and cruel.

His words, although just a repeat of my ex's, felt like a sucker punch to the gut coming from him. I told myself it was because of the embarrassment, because my boss had heard it. Still, I gaped and shook my head at him, my blonde pigtails waving back and forth. "Yeah, that'll do it. I'll wait for the next elevator or take the stairs."

His hand shot out and gripped my elbow to yank me in before the doors closed behind us. I stumbled forward on my white heeled boots, almost falling into him. He caught me just an inch from his body.

This close, I had to really crane my neck to look up at him, his height something he'd always had over me. Those eyes of his could have been the same color as honey if he was sweet. Instead, they burned dark into me just like whiskey would have burned going down my throat.

As if he could read my mind, he dragged a finger across my collarbone, up my neck, and then to my chin. "You're too sensitive, Harley Quinn."

"I'm not," I whispered, held captive by how softly he touched me, by how much it affected me. I'd always been drawn to Cade. Even though I hated him, I could never ignore the gravitational pull he had over me.

"You let a man you didn't even care about almost bring you to tears down there. You let him see the fire in you when he didn't deserve it." His finger traced along my jawline as if he were contemplating something.

"The fire?" I squinted at him, trying my best to understand him but knowing my body was taking over. And maybe the same was happening to him, because this man was supposed to be the one who kept his distance, who didn't indulge in idle conversation, and who didn't have time for small events like this one. "Are you okay?"

His jaw ticked. "I'm annoyed that I had to come out tonight for this, and I'm even more frustrated by seeing a member of my team acting foolish. Why waste your anger on him?"

"Your team? You're barely here. You have teams all around the United States. Focus on them. And honestly, should I be madder at him or you for repeating his words?"

"Me?" He let go of my arm and took the mask from his suit jacket, then slid it on slowly. I don't know why my breath caught as I watched him. This wasn't a horror film. I wasn't in danger.

Or maybe I was.

Cade could do more damage to me than anything in *Scream* ever could.

He leaned in near my ear and whispered, "I definitely deserve your anger. And I'd enjoy you throwing it at me, baby doll."

I gasped at his admission and cocked my head to try to get a read on him. Yet, all I saw was that mask as he stepped back and rocked on his heels.

"You don't make any sense." I folded my arms across my chest, not sure I wanted to be anywhere near him, not sure why I was getting turned on by him staring down at me in that mask. He was a mobster underneath the whole businessman façade, and I needed to get out of this elevator and away from him.

He wasn't a neat little box like Gerald. He was a ticking bomb, and I would end up collateral damage if I stayed anywhere near him.

"Does your boss really have to make any sense?" he asked.

"Well, you did just try to tear me down like my ex—"

He cut me off, his voice low and muffled behind the mask. "I said your ass was hanging out. I didn't say if it was a good or bad thing."

The elevator neared the top of the building, voicing the number of each floor we passed. Only ten to go, and I'd get away from him.

I shook my head. We both knew what my ex had screamed at me. "Even if you don't repeat that I should be working out, we both know what he said right before. So if you want to insinuate it too, fine." I shrugged, so over the night. I really didn't care if he saw the tears swimming in my eyes. He wanted me at my breaking point, and now he had me there. I leaned in. "But you know what, I'm done being polite. So fuck you, Cade Armanelli. You can go to hell right along with my ex."

He lifted his mask just to smile at me, as if he'd won, as if he'd pushed his insanity on me. That sinister smile—it was scarier than any Halloween mask could ever be. "You think I'm just like your ex?"

What could I say? Most men were probably like Gerald. They wanted a woman I could never be. Sweet, put together, in shape, without baggage.

Cade held my gaze, and a silent battle waged between us. Did he expect me to admit all my feelings out loud to him? Because I definitely wouldn't.

I shook my head and glanced away. "You're all the same," I grumbled, more to myself than to him.

Our conversation was about to cease—five levels to go. Cade pulled out his phone, obviously he was done talking. Great. I'd go to the party and get the hell out of there fast. This night was proving to be the worst, anyway.

Except the elevator screeched to a stop.

The lights flickered, then went out.

CHAPTER 2

Izzy

My body jerked, and my heart lurched along with it. Never had the elevators stopped suddenly like this. This was a state-of-the-art building with technology that didn't falter.

Just as I swore, one large hand shoved me into the door of the elevator by my neck. I felt his grip on me, tight, in control, and strong enough to crush my windpipe if he wanted to. I don't know if his other arm was around my waist to stop me from falling or if he just wanted full control of me.

I squinted into the dark, trying to see his face. "What the hell, Cade?"

"Now that we have a minute, go on, turn around and let me *feel* how big your ass really is, Ms. Hardy."

I'm embarrassed to admit I got wet right then, his voice filled with gravel and edge against my skin, commanding me in a way I wasn't used to. "What?" I whispered. His tone had already sent sparks through me—so much so I couldn't focus.

"I'll show you I'm nothing like that fuckboy who didn't appreciate what he had in front of him."

In the dark of that elevator, I almost gave in. Cade had avoided me for a whole year. My hate for him had grown and grown but it was rooted in desire. Hate mixed with passion, tangled up with lust. Every woman was attracted to his mystery, his callousness, his dominance in a room.

Yet, I knew better than to be drawn to it when he'd already inverted my life once. "Nothing like him yet so similar. You took from me just like he did. He took my love for granted, you took my passion for my job."

He chuckled near my ear. I felt the heat of his breath, the scrape of his five-o'clock shadow brushing against my skin. "I'll do whatever is needed to keep my team in line."

"I'm not on your team. Your team is you and no one else. You haven't seen any of us in a year."

"I always see you, baby doll." He grazed his teeth over a sensitive part of my neck, and it was like an electric shock zapped through me. My whole body quivered. "Turn around for me."

I lifted my chin, and his thumb instantly rubbed the column of my neck where he held me. Cade wanted me to fall to my knees and crumble; I swear I saw the hunger in his eyes for me to give in to my embarrassment.

Instead, I turned. I wanted him to feel what I did, the desire, the want, the tension. There was no way I was the only one feeling this. He must too.

The growl that came from him was low with appreciation as my ass brushed against his hard length. Then he whispered in my ear, "He wanted you to work it off. Can you tell what I want?"

"Probably the same thing every guy wants. A quick hook up in an elevator to check off your list."

"Nothing about us will ever be quick, Harley Quinn," he admitted. "I've been dealing with your shit for years now, and even having moved you, I'm beginning to think it won't help. So I intend to terrorize you for a very long time."

"Good luck, asshole. I'll quit Stonewood Enterprises." I breathed fast as his hand crept from my waist to my stomach and started to inch up the skin under my shirt. If he touched me for much longer, I wouldn't be able to stop what was about to happen.

"Do you like throwing your anger at me yet? Don't you see I deserve it, and I'll make you feel good while you do it? Gerald could never do that," he murmured as his hand traced my lace bra.

"You're deranged." I shook my head, not sure I could see past anything but him this close to me now, how the adrenaline was pumping through me, how my body wanted him more than I'd ever wanted Gerald.

Forget butterflies—there was thunder and lightning and a goddamn electrical storm pulsing through me.

"I am. Which means you'd better leash your attitude or know I'll be coming for it."

"You show up after a year and expect me to instantly comply with you ordering me around?" I knew I was taunting him, but as I rolled my hips into his hard length, I also knew his cock was so big it'd put most men I'd been with to shame.

It didn't matter—we couldn't do this. We were toeing a dangerous, unspoken line. Tonight, I was too far into my own feelings, barreling toward self-destruction in a new way. And he was . . . well, he was Cade.

"Not like you would listen anyway. You never do."

That pissed me off, because I actually took the team lead's workload half the time. "I always listen to Juda's orders. I'm helping him most of the time."

"Do *your* job, stop doing other people's."

"You have some input all of a sudden? Let's be candid here. Juda tells us what to do, not you."

He hummed low. "You think because I'm not around, I can't make you bend to my will?"

Could he? I felt the pull to him, felt my body surrendering itself even before his hand slid to my lower stomach and hovered over the button of my shorts. I couldn't help my whimper as he waited there, like he was silently hoping I would stop him. I couldn't understand why I didn't.

"You're not around enough to do so. We barely know you, Cade. You can't make someone bend to your will when you don't know a thing about them."

"You think I don't know a thing about you?"

I looked over my shoulder. His eyebrow quirked up a notch. Was I that easy of a study to him? Maybe I'd become boring. Quite frankly, I'd settled for Gerald, and he'd gone and found someone more fun than me.

Maybe I was sick of sitting in my neat little box and not doing what I wanted to. Or maybe tonight, I just lost my mind a little. Because I did the stupidest thing I could imagine next. I let my hand fall from where I'd been bracing myself against the elevator door and unbuttoned my shorts slowly as I tossed a glare over my shoulder, daring him to go there. "You don't know a damn thing about me."

He searched my face, those amber eyes of his staring at my lips, then back to catch my gaze like he was debating something. "Noted, dollface. Guess I'll have to be around more to figure you out." With that, he smiled and dipped his hand into my panties. His fingers slid over my clit fast. He didn't waste time warming me up.

He didn't have to.

His touch was rough, dominant, and wild like he knew exactly what I needed. He sucked on my neck while he pushed his middle finger inside me, and I gasped, letting him, bearing down on him, wanting to feel him more than I should have. "Guess I'll have to be close enough for you to feel me near you, on you, and *in* you, huh?"

I tried to catch my breath as I rode his hand. I'd needed to get laid, sure, but not by him. Not by the man I despised. Yet, he was so different from Gerald; so hard where Gerald was soft, so demanding where Gerald was acquiescent. And so ready to fuck me even though he hated me as much I hated him. We both felt a desire stronger than our hate. Or maybe our hate fueled it.

I wasn't sure anymore.

But the need to have his fingers bring me to the brink was stronger than most highs I'd ever chased in my life. Maybe Cade had always thought I was weak, that I could be pushed around. I'd taken the job without much of a fight last year. I'd stayed in my lane. I hadn't directly rebelled or protested.

I wanted to be good. I did, but something in me needed to be bad with him. He pushed me toward an edge that was raw, jagged, and full of unknown parts of me I'd kept locked away.

So I did what I shouldn't have. I widened my legs, grabbed his wrist, and pushed his fingers farther in me. "I don't need to feel you anywhere after this. I'd rather you go away."

"Really?" His voice held humor. "You don't want me near you but you're dripping all over my hand while my fingers are in you, huh? Is this how wet you got for your ex, dollface, or is it just me?"

"Go to hell, Cade," I whimpered, knowing this was wrong, but his fingers inside me felt more than right. I felt more alive than I had in years, like I was waking up from hibernation, like I'd been locked away and his fingers inside my pussy were the keys unlocking something in me.

"Oh, I'm going to hell, baby. But I'm dragging you with me." He curled his fingers over my G-spot, so fast I heard my pussy purring as I got closer and closer to my climax. He whispered in my ear, "Time to feel the licks of fire and see if you ever want to come back to earth."

Then his other hand gripped my breast over my shirt, pinching the nipple as he pumped his length against my ass. I couldn't grab hold of all the sensations and keep my body from reacting. My climax burned through me, singeing my skin, sending what felt like lava over every sensitive part of my body. I screamed out in ecstasy and pain. I felt rage that he'd brought me to one of the most intense orgasms I'd ever experienced and euphoria all at once. I mumbled that I hated him over and over as he nipped at my neck and milked every ounce of my orgasm out of me.

"Ms. Hardy." He tsked while he brought his fingers to his mouth, sucking them clean. "You can say you hate me all you want but your lies taste so damn sweet."

I sucked in a breath at his vicious words and glanced away because if I didn't, I'd probably try to continue what we'd started. It seemed I didn't have much control when it came to him. Licking me from his fingers, his tongue moving with precision to get every last drop of me, was a turn-on I'd have to forget about.

I buttoned my shorts and stepped back from him, avoiding his gaze while trying to calm my breathing. That moment would have been a great time for the elevator to start working again.

"Now that we've curbed your emotions and given you something to tide you over, let's stop stepping out of line at work for the time being, huh? I don't need the cops called on Stonewood Enterprises because you can't keep your temper in check."

My eyes bulged. "Excuse me? Are you saying you just did that to—"

"To calm you down. Yes." He shrugged and pulled his phone out like what we'd done wasn't an event of epic proportions. "You looked like you were going to walk into that work party blubbering like a miserable Harley Quinn. No one wants to see that."

"Are you fucking kidding me?" I lashed out. "Don't act as if you weren't enjoying yourself, you dickhead."

"I assure you, you enjoyed it more."

"I can't believe you have the audacity to act as though you've done nothing wrong here. You shoved me up against an elevator door the second it stalled. To anyone who watches the tape, you're not exactly the innocent party handing out favors here." I flicked my eyes to the cameras.

When my retort was met with silence, I thought I'd won.

Instead, genuine laughter burst from deep in his chest and vibrated through me. "You're funny sometimes, Izzy. I'll give you that."

"I'm not trying to be funny." I pushed away from the elevator door and pointed to the keypad. "Probably should call elevator maintenance or else HR may receive more evidence to substantiate your screwed-up tendencies toward an employee. I should report you."

He chuckled but pulled his phone up. "Sure, baby. Check that video before you report me. You were moaning and enjoying yourself about as much as me."

I was so sick of him thinking he was above me and my team. Maybe I really would report him. "You know, I deserve a boss who doesn't laugh in my face and act like an asshole every chance he gets. I work hard for this company. Quite frankly, the whole team does."

"Are you saying that's what I do?"

I blew a breath in irritation. "That's definitely what you do."

"Okay." He tilted his head as he thought about it. "I guess I do. And yet, you're going to a damn party because you work for one of the largest corporations in the United States and haven't had a cyberattack or data breach in a whole year."

Stonewood Enterprises threw a couple of extravagant annual parties. I'd heard it was because one of the wives felt it was good for morale, but he was right. We were being rewarded for our expertise.

"Because we're damn good at what we do," I emphasized.

"Yes, and because your boss runs a tight ship. Or would you like to disagree and go back to working for the government?"

I truly hated him, but I couldn't continue pushing my limits. At the end of the day, I couldn't risk losing a job under Cade Armanelli.

His hands were in everything. He controlled the digital world of the United States. If I lost a job here, I'd lose the potential to work anywhere of significance in data security.

That's what his last name meant.

Control. Prestige. Power. And fear.

"I'm not disagreeing with anything you're saying, Mr. Armanelli." I scoffed.

"Glad we got that out of the way." He waited a beat. "Now, are you ready to go to the party or are you planning another outburst?"

My hand itched to use the spray can again, but I couldn't let this night get any worse.

Maybe Gerald was right about some things. Dating someone like me couldn't be easy. Protecting my mental health and sobriety always came first, even when it meant standing up for myself.

I didn't look good on paper. Yet I was proud of the person I'd become.

I sighed as I leaned into the railing of the elevator and tried not to let Gerald's words, or this night, get to me. I turned away from Cade and faced a wall of nothing as I took a couple of deep breaths. "Give me a minute."

Two tears, or maybe three or four, fell before I sniffled softly and wiped them away. I was going to enjoy this damn night, even if these two men had tried their damnedest to ruin it.

Cade didn't give me any time. Suddenly the elevator was moving. He'd swiped the fob, like he'd had control of the elevator the whole time.

"Did you stop the elevator in the first place?"

He smiled and lowered the mask back onto his face.

Hatred wasn't strong enough for what I felt for him.

I hurried out of the elevator, then turned to glare at him again.

But he was gone. He'd vanished into the thick of the crowd, nowhere to be seen amid the bright flashing lights, the glitter flying around, and the thumping rave music.

CHAPTER 3

Izzy

Wall-to-wall windows showcased the city below us and reflected the strobing party lights while the music pumped to a wild, infectious rhythm.

This wasn't your average work party. It was a Stonewood party on top of the tallest building in the United States in an extravagant revolving-restaurant-turned-themed-club. An emcee announced how the next song should get people moving, and a host wearing a fairy costume sauntered up with a tray of drinks that appeared to have mist wafting from them.

"Welcome to Neverland." She glanced at a tablet and then back at me. "You must be doing the twist on superhero costumes with the data team tonight, right?"

I smiled and shrugged, not catching on to what she was saying.

She continued on after looking at her tablet. "Izzy Hardy, your work in cybersecurity this year was phenomenal. You single-handedly avoided numerous data breaches, handled much of the IT, and aided in building JUNIPER."

She definitely had all the details about my job on that device. JUNIPER was a security infrastructure to protect against breaches in Chicago PD's system. I'd worked very hard on it, mostly because my manager, Juda, had no idea how advanced hackers had gotten.

I cleared my throat. "It was a team effort."

She smirked. "Yes, I believe you work with Cade, right? He also always credits a team effort when we try to pay him a compliment. But he's the one who put in this comment about you." I saw her smirk even as she tried to hide it.

That had me looking at her in puzzlement. Was she talking about the same guy who hadn't shown up to his office in nearly a year? Without thought, my gaze searched the party for him, like suddenly I was a sick puppy wanting the attention and praise of a neglectful owner.

"Would you like a fairy dusting?" the lady murmured, holding up the tray.

I shook my head. Alcohol had never been a problem for me, but I didn't indulge when I was at a work event. It wasn't worth the risk. "I'm not drinking tonight."

"Oh, right. We have nonalcoholic beverages at the bar." She scrunched her nose like she didn't have anyone in her life who would pass on the opportunity to have some fun.

I nodded, hoping she'd leave my side soon. I didn't need a rundown of the party events. I was there to be a good team player and then get back to work. "Right."

"And the costume contest, which you have a great shot at winning, will take place at—"

"I won't be participating," I said, trying to smile as I walked past her to find my team.

There were clusters of people everywhere. Considering Stonewood Enterprises ran hundreds of companies, this party was bound to fill the restaurant to capacity. I didn't know many faces at all because working in cybersecurity normally meant we stayed at our computers on our own floor most of the day.

"Izzy Bizzy!" Lucas Cavanaugh bellowed so loud half the restaurant glanced his way.

The smile that flew across my face at hearing his voice was probably the first one I'd had all day. No worries attached to it, no concerns that he didn't want me there. Lucas was a breath of fresh air to anyone who met him.

"Lucas, you're too loud," I grumbled as he pulled me in for a hug. He was dressed as Thor and pulled it off perfectly with his golden hair and strong build.

At his side, Cassie—dressed as Wonder Woman—frowned at me. "Izzy, our team was supposed to be superheroes!"

I glanced around. Sure enough, Braxton was Batman and Penelope was Catwoman. Isaac, who talked to everyone even less than I did because he was always bent over his computer, was dressed as Spiderman.

"How did I miss the memo?" I frowned. "In all fairness, Harley can be a superhero."

Lucas kept his arm around me and squeezed my shoulders. "The memo was entitled Team Costume Party Plan, so you probably didn't read it. Cassie, if you want Izzy to read something, you have to title it Alert: Work Breach or some shit."

I rolled my eyes as everyone laughed. "I'm not that bad."

"Really?" Penelope was the newest on the team, but we didn't talk much. She seemed to be enjoying her nearly empty drink and had the confidence to speak up. "I never talk to you because you seem so driven to get things done."

I opened my mouth to defend myself, but Lucas beat me to it. "She's a workaholic, but she's never let us down. She's always saving our asses when we can't figure out something."

Blushing, I looked down and let my pigtails fall in front of my face. "Everyone's giving me a lot of credit, but we all kicked ass this year."

"Oh my God, right?" Cassie's drink sloshed as she shoved it into the middle of our bar table and held it high. "Cheers to our impenetrable data barrier."

Everyone hooted and hollered, throwing their glasses in too.

Lucas eyed me as he slurped down his drink while our team dispersed to talk amongst themselves feverishly. "Not drinking?"

I shrugged, not sure I wanted to bring down the night by sharing where my head was at.

"Something wrong, Izzy?" Lucas had been on my team since the day I started at Stonewood Enterprises. He'd been in the advertising department but had found me in the work break room one day, scrolling the Narcotics Anonymous program on my phone.

The man asked me to be his sponsor right then and there. I hadn't known if he didn't have many friends or if he was hitting on me. Turned out he just needed a good friend. He worked a lot of hours and had moved from Georgia, fresh out of rehab, after being honorably discharged from active duty when his Humvee was attacked overseas. He'd come to work at Stonewood Enterprises after meeting one of the Stonewood brothers when they'd given a motivational speech at his rehab center.

"Nothing's wrong," I told him. "I just hate parties."

Unlike Lucas, I was good at respecting people's boundaries. He'd told me early on that he'd share his trauma when he was ready. It took him months to confide in me about his PTSD, how he got addicted to prescription meds, and how he fought every day to stay off them.

As for him asking me questions, he had no boundaries whatsoever. "Did your dick of a boyfriend do something?"

"Jesus, Lucas," I groaned and waved my hand about. "Can we not talk about it at the party?"

"Why? You actually want to enjoy yourself tonight?" He took that moment to hold me out at arm's length. "You upped the costume game with this fucking outfit. I always wanted to fuck the shit out of Harley Quinn."

I lifted an eyebrow.

"And I want to even more now that I'm staring at you." He chuckled.

"You're an idiot," I told him. I knew that Lucas was gay, but no one else did. His parents were very strict with their beliefs, and it frustrated me every day that he didn't tell them to shove it. Lucas was perfect in every way to me, his parents be damned. Hiding who you are took a toll, but it wasn't about when I was ready. He had to be ready and accepting his process was most important to me.

"I'm just saying the female form is a beautiful thing . . . especially yours, okay?"

I took the compliment with a shrug. "If you say so."

"Hey, a girl's been eyeing me up from marketing all night. Just play along." He winked at me as he said it quietly. I was practically the man's beard half the time.

"I'm here to be whatever you need," I whispered into his ear and laughed.

"You know how I know that's true?" he asked as he took me by the waist and started walking me to the bar. "Gerald practically foamed at the mouth the last time he saw us together, and you didn't falter once."

"Yeah, well, Gerald and I are no more." I looked toward the ceiling, trying not to make it a bigger deal than it was. Quite frankly, it was nothing compared to what had just happened to me in the elevator.

He glanced at me with his light-blue eyes and didn't even bother hiding the delight in them. "Thank fuck."

"Lucas!" I shoved his massive shoulder, but it didn't move at all. "I'm sad."

"What for?" He waved off the idea and then flashed me a look of concern, his brows furrowing. "Really? Because if you need to get out of here, we can go." Lucas was as much my sponsor as I was his.

"No. No. I want you to enjoy yourself, and it's good for me to be out mingling and networking."

"This isn't a work event, Izzy." He scoffed as we got to the bar and waved over the bartender to ask for a nonalcoholic cocktail for me.

I smiled at him remembering my drink order. "It's the definition of a work event, Lucas. Even if we're supposed to have fun, we showcase our best selves for the corporation. They might not say it, but our bosses are watching us."

"Are they?" He glanced around wildly. "Show me where Cade is then."

"Well, whatever. Juda is the manager. We don't need the boss here."

Lucas laughed. "I don't think Juda has done any work since you relocated."

I rolled my eyes. "Hey, I'm happy he gives me his work so I'm not stuck doing generic IT all day." I'd been assigned that on my first day and been seething mad, but Juda had been more than ready to offload his duties to me when I'd complained.

He chuckled. "You know, if Cade were here, he'd probably thank you for working two jobs instead of one."

That comment had me gulping down my Shirley Temple rather than responding. What annoyed me was that I didn't want to share my encounter with Cade in the elevator just yet. It was as if I was holding on to our ridiculous moment, like it was ours. Why did it feel special when it shouldn't? Why could I tell Lucas about Gerald but not Cade?

I hated that I wondered where he'd gone, why he'd haunted the beginning of my night only to disappear into the shadows when the party was a public display of our accolades. He'd come for that, right? What other reason would he have to be here?

"Well, he chose to not be a part of the night." I shrugged. "We can celebrate ourselves and have a good night without him."

Lucas whooped and dragged me back through the swarms of costumed up employees to our team. Penelope welcomed us back, asked how my family was, and I continued the small talk by saying they were all well. I'd expected questions about them because I'd taken a day off to go visit Dante and Delilah in the hospital as they welcomed their first baby two months ago.

Of course, Cassie, with her dark-brown hair bouncing under the gold Wonder Woman headband, jumped in. "Happy to hear she's doing fine with baby number one, but why don't we talk about your four brothers instead? They all still single?" She'd gleaned this information from me just a week ago as she walked past my desk and caught a recent picture I'd displayed of my siblings surrounding me while I held our new niece.

Penelope looked confused. "You have four brothers?"

"Girl, check out her desk next time you walk by. Everyone in that photo is a sibling. One of them is in the freaking NFL."

"Oh my God. Those are your brothers?" Penelope leaned in, suddenly very invested in talking to me. The funny thing was, that picture of us all was the worst we'd ever taken. After staying up all night worried about Delilah delivering the first child of our family's next generation, we resembled zombies, not humans. Yet, the smiles on our faces were the biggest you'd have ever seen.

"Right? And they look like they're just doting on that baby. Such good brothers and great dating material." Cassie sighed, completely in love with them all.

I chuckled. "Probably only the former considering they are all still single." I could only give them credit for being the best family. They'd been there for me as I struggled to maintain my sobriety, even after nine years. On my worst days, I kept it for them and the rest of my family. To make them proud. To show them I was worthy of their love.

"Okay. Okay. Let's give Izzy a breather." Lucas changed the subject. "Who's coming to Keep Minding our Minds next week?" Lucas asked. "I've got an idea for bringing more people into the group."

I winced. Lucas had taken mental health at Stonewood Enterprises to the next level over the past year, and he dragged me along for some of it. He thrived on helping others, and I wanted to be the same. I wanted to think I could aid others in their healthy recovery, but at the same time, I wondered if the only person I was made to help was Lucas.

"I should probably work while you host all that."

"You're so great though, Izzy. You helped me through my breakup last week when you shared your story about your boyfriend. You and Gerald are goals," Cassie pointed out.

God. Last week I'd gone and shared how being strong when your boyfriend was away could nurture your relationship. I used Gerald and myself as examples to show Cassie she didn't have to worry about someone cheating on her and that, if they did, it was their fault.

Except Gerald had found someone else.

And I was the fool now. And I'd made it even worse by letting Cade get to me in the elevator. I'd been reckless and irresponsible.

Thankfully, Lucas steered the conversation to a different topic. "Hey! Remember when Cassie told her ex she'd just been promoted to data analyst, and he didn't believe her?"

Penelope blurted, "Yeah, what an asshat. Cassie's been killing it."

"In all fairness, I make Izzy help me with half of it." Cassie shrugged and eyed me apologetically. "By the way, I have a work question for you on Monday. I might need your assistance with some coding."

"Of course." I sprang at the chance to help her. "Just put it on my task list, and we'll get on it first thing."

Braxton added that he might need a hand with something too, then Lucas rolled his eyes, grumbling quietly enough for only me to hear, "They'll have you do everything if they can."

I nudged him hard. People needed teachers so they could learn and do it themselves in the future. Plus, I enjoyed the work, even if a certain boss wouldn't give me a promotion and my now ex-boyfriend had complained about my work ethic putting a strain on our relationship. Sighing, I straightened and tried not to dwell on it.

As the small talk continued, Lucas whispered, "Take a break and walk around. Then let's leave. You don't need to be here right now."

I chewed on my cheek. I thought I'd buried my emotions, but Lucas sensed them all better than I ever could. Sometimes good friends knew the limits of your heart better than you knew it yourself.

CHAPTER 4

Izzy

sped off, wanting to get away from it all. Wanting to stop the thoughts. Wanting Gerald and Cade to get out of my head. I weaved through dancers and around tables and got back to the elevator quickly. I hit my floor so I could go back to my desk and decompress. Working was my happy place, even if I had to do it dressed as Harley Quinn.

The lights on our floor should have been off, but the corner office—the one that was never occupied—was brightly lit. My white Harley Quinn boots took me straight to it. I stood in the doorway, waiting for him to look up.

"What the fuck are you doing back here?" Cade grumbled, flicking his gaze up momentarily before focusing on one of the four computer screens in front of him.

"Party's in full swing out there." I motioned behind me, ignoring his attitude.

"Then go enjoy it. I've got work to do," he grumbled as he typed away at something.

Instead of obeying, I pushed off the doorframe and came toward him to see what he was working on. When I rounded his desk, I felt a zing of exhilaration. You didn't go look over a hacker's shoulder or stand behind them unless there was full trust.

He didn't fight me, but I saw his muscles bunch up. I'd gotten a reaction out of him, whether he wanted to give me one or not.

"The party's for you and us. You came with a mask and everything, then disappeared. Sort of missing the point of being on a team."

He turned to give me a stare so cold, it could rival Antarctica. "And what about you? You come back here to tell me that because you want to celebrate with me too?"

"I wanted . . . I needed a second away."

"Because your ex broke your little heart?" He turned back to his screens.

"Or maybe because my boss groped me in an elevator on the way to the party."

"Hardly groping when you unbuttoned your shorts and rode my hand, baby doll," he murmured, clicking away on the computer.

"Harley Quinn's nickname was always *dollface*, not *baby doll*."

"Well, you're acting like a baby, so either suits you," he pointed out.

I rolled my eyes at him and decided to not engage. Instead, I changed the subject. "What are you working on?"

"Nothing of importance to you."

"I could maybe help," I tried.

He shut my offer down immediately. "I don't need help. I assign you all the work that I deem feasible for you."

I tried to peer over his shoulder, but he straightened to block my view.

I crossed my arms in front of me. "You don't need help with anything, but we all help you, don't we? You give Juda work for all of us from some remote location year-round."

"I do that for most teams under my authority."

"Must be isolating to never get to know your employees." I narrowed my eyes at him, trying to see if he cared even the least bit.

He sighed and rubbed his eyes before he continued. "Izzy, I don't want to deal with your shit right now. This is classified information, and I can't have just anyone looking at it."

I nodded and tried to ignore the sting in his words. It was a small dart thrown my way, but I was hyperaware of anyone's potential distrust in me because of my past.

"Okay." I dragged out the word. "If honesty helps prove to you that I'm not here to sling around my shit, I'll try that. I'm not celebratory after being dumped, so I'm not enjoying the festivities. I'm tired, and I want to work, not party. Quite frankly, I probably shouldn't be partaking in something like this anyway."

He straightened and turned to face me. "What do you mean?"

"Well Lucas and I have been sober—"

"Is someone doing illegal drugs up there? Lucas has only been sober for a year and—"

"How do you know that?" I blurted out, confused with how he knew that and also that his tone sounded as if he cared.

He cleared his throat. "I know about the people that work for me, Izzy."

"Well, no one's doing anything illegal." I didn't want anyone getting in trouble with the boss when there was nothing to get in trouble for. "Lucas is fine. He'd call me if he felt he was slipping.

But I know parties always trigger—"

Cade pushed away from his laptop and slammed it shut. "Then our team is done with this party."

"No." I stopped him and studied his approach. Cade didn't know this team. Why would he care if Lucas and I were fine or not? "It won't go over well. Just . . . I came back here to work. It's where I feel most comfortable."

"All you do is work, Izzy." He rolled his eyes like it was bad.

"You have no idea." I narrowed my eyes as I thought of something. "Do you watch our office?"

He didn't deny it. "I watch all my teams."

"You can't possibly be taking in all that information while accomplishing what you have in the last year."

It was well known that he'd stopped nuclear warfare, penetrated enemy systems, and kept adversaries at bay. "I also enjoy working, Izzy. I'm the boss. It's my job to manage you."

"Only because you won't trust people like me to manage some of these employees," I blurted, knowing it wasn't the time nor place to get into this. Juda had told me at my six-month review that it'd be at least two years before Cade would consider giving me a higher position, that Cade had written that in my file.

"You're not ready. You couldn't even handle a breakup today." He stated like it was obvious, before waving me toward the door. "I'll go celebrate just so we don't have to do this."

"Do what? Engage in a normal social interaction?" I scoffed as I stomped toward the door and then out into the hall, him following me. One day he was going to have to come up with a different excuse for not promoting me. "Honestly, a year in, and I think I've proven I'm not a gamble, even if my boyfriend was a dick and needed a new paint job for his car."

"Well, you had a misstep once or twice in your first few years working for the government," he mumbled as we faced off in the darkened hallway. "Let's not forget about that."

My twin sister had been taken because our targets identified her as me. I hadn't been careful enough to make sure she was safe. I wanted to scream in frustration at him bringing that up.

"Technically, I wasn't even working for you back then. Besides, everything turned out fine."

"I still had to watch that train wreck."

I hated that he'd been privy to my undercover work and that not all of it was flawless. But everyone made mistakes when they were starting out. "That was the beginning of my well-decorated career, and Lilah is fine," I spat.

"No thanks to you."

My jaw dropped. "You have the audacity to act like I didn't do what I could—"

"You were a kid trying to make a name for herself and didn't respect the law, the dangers of the job, or the people you dragged into it."

He was right. I'd tried to bring down a drug operation pretty much on my own. I had a chip on my shoulder and wanted to prove myself.

It was stupid.

And I knew that.

But I sure wasn't going to admit as much to him.

"I held my twin sister in my arms while she bled out on my chest. You think I didn't learn from my inexperience or lack of foresight?" I narrowed my eyes at him. This time he wasn't the one backing me up against the wall. Instead, I advanced on him, a finger raised. "Don't ever tell me I don't respect the people I dragged into the operation. I more than respect them. I love them. Lilah and Dante mean everything to me."

"I don't doubt that," he grumbled like he was insinuating something.

"What's that supposed to mean?"

"Well, it's clear you had a thing for Dante. You *kissed* him."

"I loved the idea of him!" I practically screeched, throwing up my hands. I didn't get mad about this anymore. Yet, he pulled out the worst in me, the part I didn't have control over. "I've told everyone this before. Even Lilah knows."

"What *idea* exactly, Izzy? You like the idea of Dante with you instead of your sister?"

I wiped a hand over my face, so furious that I was allowing him to purposely goad me. I knew he was but I couldn't stop myself from feeding into it. "That was so long ago! And if you must know, Dante not only used to be our neighbor, but he was also my friend, Cade. He was a friend like none I've ever had. I had guy friends who tried to hook up with me, get me drunk, or have me try drugs. They enjoyed me acting out and getting wild. But when I really fucked up, Dante was the only one who didn't disappear and still believed in me. He was my *friend*."

Cade crossed his arms and waited. I gave him a second to insult my explanation, but he didn't. It was like he wanted me to confess more.

"He accepted me. He gave me a chance. So yes, I kissed the man. Yes, it was fucking stupid. Yes, I realize I betrayed my sister's trust. I was blinded by the fact that he was there for me, him being a real friend when most were assholes. And then I fell for—" I stopped, almost ready to confess something I never had before. "I fell for a lot of dumb shit. My relationships were unhealthy, but he wasn't. He was the family friend, the rock. He was maybe really my *only* friend—"

"What was I to you then?" His voice suddenly sounded broken and accusatory.

I narrowed my eyes at him. "You? You were . . . you *are* my fucking enemy, Cade! You tear me down every chance you get. The first time I met you, you threw in my face that I was an addict and couldn't be trusted."

"I stand by that assessment back then. You were going into dangerous undercover work."

I couldn't keep my eyes from bulging. I think my hand even twitched because I was ready to smack him. "If you weren't my boss, I'd—" I shook my head, so ready to inflict physical pain upon him.

And then I saw it.

His real smile.

The one nobody ever got to see. Cade in action. Cade in malice. Cade in destruction mode, relishing in the chaos he was about to create.

"Go on, dollface, say it."

"You're unhinged, you know that?" I said, but my heart had picked up speed. My body clenched, my pussy grew wet, and my breath caught in my chest just feeling what was in the air between us.

Even if I knew it was dangerous, pushing Cade to that smile was so enticing that I couldn't help it.

He chuckled. "Oh, really?" He leaned against the wall as he casually eyed me up and down. "If that's the case, you're delusional thinking you could work well with me tonight. I work alone."

"Just because you're ridiculous doesn't mean I can't handle it."

He hummed low before he pushed off the wall, forcing me to move back. He had a look in his eye I hadn't seen before, the look of someone on the hunt, someone ready to capture his prey.

He stopped a centimeter before his body touched mine, and I stared up at him, completely aware that the heat between us wasn't a work-related issue.

"You can handle this?"

"What?" I whispered.

He made a point of looking down between us before he took that last step into my space. Our bodies collided, the sparks flew, my mind scrambled, and my heart jackhammered the blood through my veins.

"This," he murmured into my ear. "We might be enemies, Ms. Hardy, but *this* is where we aren't. *This* is inevitable when we work in the same building."

There was no use denying it, not when my nipples stood to attention as his hard cock pressed into my stomach. I breathed his air, and he breathed mine.

"And do you think we should indulge in it?" I asked softly, as I stared at where our bodies connected because I wanted him to say it, to admit that I affected him the same way I knew he affected me.

"No." His response felt like ice water being poured over my head. "And that's all the more reason for me to have you fired at this point, because I normally do indulge in shit I shouldn't."

And those words felt like fire licking over my body, warming me up again.

"From the reports we get, you've actually done a lot of what you should," I whispered. He'd kept businesses afloat, helped to curb trafficking, money laundering, big drug deals. He'd done so much.

"I've done a lot of bad too."

"Sometimes good requires bad."

He nodded a few times as he stared at me staring at him. I swear he was dissecting me, like he could find every hidden answer. Like the algorithm would show him something nobody else could see.

Then he took a deep breath, and with it, he stepped back, ready to walk away.

Instantly, my body missed the tension and the proximity of him. The closeness of Cade was dangerous. I knew I could end up reliant on someone like him, and that I couldn't afford. Not when I'd come this far on my own.

"You're right." He cracked his knuckles in front of me as if he was readying himself for his next words. "What's the bad in us that will bring the good, Izzy? Is it indulging so we can get it out of our systems? Is it me firing you quickly, which would be bad but end up good for everyone in the end?"

"Don't you dare." I stood up ramrod straight. "I deserve to be here."

He chewed on his cheek before running one tattooed hand over his jawline. I read the letters that were on each of his fingers as he did it.

CHAOS.

And I thought, as his smile creeped up again, I was about to witness it.

"Dare? Is there something else you *do* dare me to do?" He waited for me to give him permission, to step over that line. We'd danced around it for years, and I knew if we took the jump now, it'd change our dynamic forever.

"Would you even take a dare?"

"Try me."

"I dare you to do what you want to me. What I know you've been wanting to do."

He didn't even wait a second before his tattooed hand shot out so fast, I barely saw the blur of ink as it flew to my neck and pushed me up against the wall where he held me captive as his mouth descended on mine.

He didn't kiss me. He consumed me.

He commanded my mouth to open with his, pushed his tongue in and tasted every part he could of me. I met his kiss with the same passion, like I was ravenous for him, like I'd been starved of him for too long. I clawed at his back and moaned into his mouth as his other hand went into my shorts. I didn't care that we were in a hallway where our coworkers might walk in, I didn't care about my job. I didn't care about anything but having him.

He squeezed my neck harder along with my thigh and shoved me high enough up the wall for my pussy to settle against his cock. My legs immediately wrapped around him, and I rocked my hips forward, letting my body take over. He encircled my waist with his arms and walked me back into his office, shutting the door on the way and locking it behind us.

I took my lips from his to say, "Maybe we should leave and—"

"I'm not waiting another minute for you, baby doll. I've had to endure your bad attitude for long enough. Now, I'm going to fuck it out of you."

"Jesus," I murmured. "I shouldn't love your mouth as much as I do."

"You're about to love it more when I taste you."

He slammed me down on the desk, and I moaned at the intensity of it.

No more time was given to me to prepare. He shoved my shorts down and grabbed hold of my panties.

"Hurry," I demanded.

"Hurry?" He cocked his head, and then he straightened, stepping between my legs and towering over me. I pushed up on my elbows to see him taking his sweet time as he slid one hand up from my thigh all the way back to my throat. Leaning close, he whispered, "I'm the boss, remember? I tell you what to do and you listen."

The instinct at this point in our relationship was for me to fight him. I swear he knew it too as I said, "If you're the boss, try to make sure you establish that here tonight, because I might have forgotten."

His hold on my neck increased as he pushed my back flat on the desk, his thick length pressing against my entrance. "Breathe when you're told, dollface or you'll pass out."

"What? Like I'd forget—" His grasp completely cut off my oxygen—he didn't waste time warming me up to the idea—as his other hand worked my clit in earnest.

Instantly, the fear of not breathing kicked my adrenaline into gear while I simultaneously writhed against him. I'd never experienced pleasure with the fear so acutely. I tried to cling to rationality and told myself this wasn't special. It was simply the thrill of hooking up with my boss, the guy I'd lusted over for so long.

I was riding his hand, lost in my desire for him, holding his wrist for leverage, not paying attention to the lifeline that was breathing.

"Breathe, Izzy," he growled. He'd loosened his grip on my throat and I hadn't realized. My eyes flew to his, and I saw a look that wasn't normally there.

Desire and awe.

I didn't have time to consider it much before I gulped in two breaths. Then, the pressure was instantly back on my windpipe, and he was unzipping to pull his cock from his trousers. "Feel just the tip, now, huh?"

I stared at him guiding his hard cock to my center, and my eyes widened when I saw the metal there. If I could have, I would have asked. I would have spent some time assessing the piercing. Instead, he rolled the head of his cock over my wet pussy.

"God, you're already soaked. Next time, I'm going to document this. Make sure we have enough evidence to prove that despite how much you claim to hate me, you paint my cock so well with your arousal."

I couldn't focus on anything as my vision blurred, as my high almost hit, as he looked at me like he was finally about to give me that darkness.

"You on the pill, baby?"

I nodded.

He thrust in and commanded, "Breathe."

I gasped for air. Maybe from the size of him entering me. Or because I needed to breathe. Or because the orgasm ripped through and ravaged me. I couldn't tell which. Clinging to his shirt, I pulled him down as he pumped into me and ground my pussy onto his cock. The feeling of him against my inner walls as I took a breath to bring life back into my body was one I'd never felt.

I'd been high, I'd slept with men, and I'd been in dangerous situations where adrenaline ran through my veins. But this, this was everything wrapped in one. The explosion tore through me and flung me into a stratosphere I didn't know existed.

I screamed his name loudly, and his hand covered my mouth as he continued to fuck me while whispering for me to be quiet. Yet, no part of me was able to cage that feeling as I rode out the best orgasm of my life.

"You're going to make it known that I'm fucking you back here, Izzy. Then I'll probably have to demote you just to keep things fair."

I don't think I responded. I couldn't as I continued to pull in long breaths, trying to come back from another world of pure euphoria.

He slowed his thrusts down. Long and measured, as if he wanted to work me up again. Then, he chuckled. "This is how I like you. No attitude, just gratitude."

That got me to roll my eyes. "Please shut up."

"At least she says please. Want to say please while I fuck another orgasm out of you, baby doll?"

"I don't think you can," I whispered, sure I was done.

The devil danced in his eyes as he pulled his length deliberately from me and let it slide upward so his piercing ran over my bundle of nerves, coated with the slickness of us both.

I shivered at the feeling. "You're playing games, Cade. Fuck me or get off so we can get back to the party."

"I was never at the party to begin with. I was working on calming down one of our best employees in the elevator, and then I came here to handle another situation, but you showed up and distracted me."

I wiggled my hips, trying to get more friction between us. He flexed his cock, and I watched how his length moved out of my pussy's reach. I hated that every part of him was more than perfect, including the size, symmetry, and thickness of him.

"You're staring like you want it again, Izzy." I glared at him as he cocked an eyebrow at me. "Do you? Or should I make you lose your breath by giving you a taste instead? I'm happy to have you gag on my cock tonight too."

"You shouldn't be able to say shit like that." I shook my head at him.

He chuckled as he took a handful of one of my pigtails and started to pull me down the desk. "Knees. I think you need to experience the taste of me coated in your arousal so you can better understand the dynamics of this relationship."

"Me tasting my arousal on your dick won't do that," I shot back, but I was already getting on my knees before him, ready to have him in my mouth. I wanted him at my mercy, if only for a second.

"If I get to come in that mouth of yours, I don't really care what it does, Izzy. Now, open up for your boss. Make sure you take it like a good girl."

Up close, I started to have reservations. I cleared my throat. "You're bigger than I've ever taken, Cade."

"Damn right I am. You'll gag, baby. And you'll love it." He dragged a finger down my jaw to my chin. "Good. Show me you can take it."

CHAPTER 5
Cade

I zzy Hardy shouldn't have been on my team at all. This was reason enough for it. I had my cock so far down her throat, I was sure I could see the indent in the column of her neck. It made my dick pulse harder.

Izzy fucking Hardy: my kryptonite. Curves for days and a fuckable mouth that I'd imagined biting, bruising, and maybe kissing once or twice.

Yet, I had never fucked an employee before, nor did I plan on doing it again. Honestly, I barely fucked any women I talked to more than once. It wasn't worth my time. But Izzy was the exception. This would be a one-time occurrence after years in the making.

And it had been *years*.

After her undercover work with the Albanians, I'd hoped she would leave well enough alone. We busted them for a drug operation, but she'd known there was more to it. Albanians were fighting for power, and it meant they were doing more than one illegal thing. Izzy wanted them on the hook for everything.

They'd mistook her sister for her, and I remember how they'd held one another once Delilah was found. I understood it too. I would have killed for my brother and sought revenge without question.

She wanted justice, and I had to give her credit—she was better than most of the team, or at least stubborn enough to get it. So I'd reassigned her to corporate where she'd be forced to move on. I dealt with rival mob families and threats to our nation, not a little girl from the suburbs who didn't know when to quit.

Yet, I swear even from a remote location, she messed with my mind. Numerous times in the past twelve months, she'd attempted to breach systems I'd specifically told her not to.

But she remained undeterred.

And my dick remained hard for her as if I reveled in her deliberately disobeying me. Nobody deliberately disobeyed me. No one but her. And I was thoroughly enjoying her rebellion.

I made note that I was going to have to erase the security cameras more than once tonight. Especially now that I was fucking her mouth. Goddamn, I was going to catalog this. I wasn't kidding when I said I wanted a picture for evidence. Izzy was beautiful with her mouth wide open, her hazel eyes trained on me, and that jaw slack enough for my length to slide in. I pulled the elastic bands out of her pigtails, so I could undo them and run my hands through her hair, messing it up—just the way I wanted her.

Her plump lips around my dick felt better than I'd imagined, and I was sure every guy who'd met her had imagined it. They were full, like Angelina Jolie's. Her body was so small I almost got concerned I would break her as I fucked her, yet she'd met me thrust for thrust, her curves giving me more to grip as I buried myself in her. The fact that her boyfriend told her to drop weight was a firm reminder that I'd be ruining something in his life soon enough.

I gripped her hair harder as I fucked her mouth, trying my best to control how fast I made her take it. When she gagged and her eyes watered, I smiled down at her. "Damn. I hate how beautiful you look when you're at my mercy." I swiped away a tear trickling down her cheek with my thumb, before pushing further down her throat.

Tonight, I'd gotten her new and untrained, completely willing but not fully ready. I knew Izzy had experience, but she hadn't experienced me. It made me wonder if I could fuck her over and over again until she no longer gagged, until she was used to only me down her throat.

Fuck, I liked the idea of that too much.

When she swirled her tongue around the tip of my cock mid-thrust, I almost lost myself. Maybe I wasn't used to her, not made to last against her, not made to own her like this.

Her nails dug into my ass. She wanted control, but I wasn't going to give her any of it. Izzy wanted that everywhere. In the office, in her life. Even with her emotions. And she really didn't have much of that control.

Every day, I checked the cameras to see who'd made it to work, and she came in wearing these pencil skirts like they'd make her into some prim and proper professional.

"This is how I wanted you. On your knees, begging for more. It suits you."

She narrowed her eyes, probably taking what I said as an insult. The girl always believed I had it out for her which I'd always thought was for the best. Now, with me bottoming out down her throat, probably not. I'd wanted to maintain a professional environment, and I'd done that by not coming to the damn office. I didn't handle corporate life well. Or a social one for that matter.

People didn't want a man around that could unearth all their dirty secrets, and I didn't want to be around people who tried to hide them either. Instead, I worked remote to keep my family, our government, and the Stonewoods in power. I built the systems that allowed us to rule the world, and I'd built them essentially on my own.

"Suck me harder, Izzy." I wanted to feel this, feel her finally do something for me that brought enjoyment rather than irritation. And my cock swelled and throbbed as she did.

Fuck, the woman kneeling before me was going to be a problem. Within a couple hours of occupying the same address at the same time, I couldn't resist her. I groaned as her cheeks hollowed out around my cock, frustrated that she finally listened to me when it came to something like this.

I hadn't expected her submissiveness, and it got me harder just witnessing it. Her tongue rolled over me again, and I knew I had to stop her if I wanted to finish somewhere other than her mouth. I yanked her hair, and my dick popped out from between her lips. I dragged the tip over them and let my pre-cum coat them, glistening like I'd painted my own brand on her. "My cum looks good on your mouth."

She licked it off, eyes holding mine in challenge. "Is that the only place you want it tonight?"

I pulled her up, still a handful of her hair in my fist.

This is why I couldn't be around her. She tested me like she could go up against me and win. I turned her around and bent her over my desk. "I should find a way to mark every part of you," I growled, wanting her to back down.

She laughed and pushed her ass against my length. "Do your worst, Cade. It probably still won't be the best I've had."

The comparison to others pushed me over the edge. I'd thought about Izzy since I'd met her. I practically stalked her digital presence, had notifications on my phone of what she did on the dark web, and checked security cameras every now and then when I was alerted of her facial recognition. She was a nuisance, and I told myself it was to keep her in check, but I realized then and there that she was *my* nuisance.

I thrust into what was mine. "Not when I'm all you've ever had, dollface. Because a person only has what they remember, and I will obliterate your memories of other men."

She gasped as I smacked her ass and then gripped her hip with one hand while my other yanked her hair in sync, bringing her hard down on my length, making her feel every rigid part of me.

She met me thrust for thrust, digging her nails into my oak desk, probably leaving imprints that I would have to stare at later.

"Cade, I'm close. Jesus, so close."

Our bodies moved on their own accord now, smacking against each other loudly, chasing a pleasure that was stronger than the pain we inflicted by ramming into one another. I knew I was bruising her skin with how I held her asscheek, gripping it so tightly that her flesh plumped around each finger. I knew I was too rough, that I'd lost control.

I'd probably lost control the first moment I saw her tonight, standing there in all her glory, spraying her ex. I hadn't expected to talk with her, but I came out of the shadows, ready to carry her off and fuck the anger out of her when I saw it. I wasn't getting the control back either.

Not as I bent down and bit her neck. Not as I craved leaving marks. Not as I coveted seeing how she was mine, the proof visible by her reddened skin.

And then she arched and screamed out my full name. "Cade Armanelli . . . I hate you. I hate you. I hate you."

I love how she breathed those words. Like she needed to believe them. Like I pulled an emotion from her that was so visceral she had to avoid it by covering it with hate.

"Keep telling yourself that, Ms. Hardy." I slammed into her one last time and emptied my seed. "I'm fine with you hating me as long as your pussy loves being wrapped around my cock."

CHAPTER 6

Izzy

I expected the Monday morning after my lapse in judgment to be a dumpster fire of a day. I'd ignored about ten calls from Gerald on Sunday while I obsessed about the night before. And the texts were ridiculous to say the least.

> **Gerald:** We need to talk. I still love you and I'm sorry, okay? Let's meet somewhere and hash it out.
>
> **Gerald:** Izzy, you fucked up my car. At least see me so you can make it up to me.
>
> **Gerald:** I'm breaking things off with Lucy, okay? She wasn't even that good. She wasn't you.
>
> **Gerald:** I miss you. Can I come over tonight?
>
> **Me:** Lose my address. We're done.

That was an easy decision. Dealing with him directly after having the best sex of my life proved we'd never have worked anyway. My feelings for him were nothing like what I felt for Cade.

Which was completely idiotic.

Would I lose my job? Would he tell anyone? Cade had always

been somewhat of an enigma. No one knew anything about his lifestyle. He was the quiet, eccentric brother to the larger-than-life Sebastian Armanelli. But he was still the brother of a mob boss. I knew he had power. I knew he could get rid of me with one command. He'd changed my job with such an order—a mere swipe of a mouse and a few keystrokes. It was nothing to him.

Keeping myself busy was the most important thing I could do now. I canceled Sunday plans with my sister over text and whipped through cleaning my tiny apartment. I blasted Alanis Morissette the whole time in the hopes she would lift my mood.

"Don't look at me like I'm crazy, Bug," I mumbled as I hurried past my black cat, who was perched on the couch. She'd not moved a muscle while I'd been bustling around all morning. "I have to keep busy."

She blinked at me like that was preposterous. To her, it was. The cat didn't move for anything. She even took my favorite spot on the couch sometimes, and when I'd try to shoo her, she'd just meow like I should have the decency not to bother her.

She normally won the argument by glaring at me with those glowing gold eyes. I'd gotten her from a humane society six months ago, and I really couldn't say no to her. I figured she'd lived a hard enough life already. The humane society told me she was a stray someone had brought in after a cat fight. She had a scar above her eye to show for it and only half an ear.

When I saw her alone in her cage, I figured we could be pals. I had scars too, though they were much harder to see.

Gerald had a fit because he was allergic and said he wouldn't be able to stay at my place. I'd felt guilty, but really, my apartment was mine. Plus, I hadn't loved having him there in the first place.

Only Lucas had been privy to my mess when he'd come to hang out over the past six months, otherwise I would go to Gerald's when he was in town.

I pet Bug for another minute as I glanced around my space. "Guess you won't miss Gerald that much, huh?" She didn't even muster a meow for him. "He was nice to my family, though. My mom even said he'd make for a stable husband."

Bug let her head fall onto her paw like she thought the idea was dumb.

"I know. He would have been boring and a total cheater. Plus, I have you. And a great job . . . hopefully."

I sighed and stared at two of my paintings on the wall. I'd taken up painting when I moved out on my own. If I wasn't working, I was painting a canvas or a piece of furniture. My home was filled with reds, pinks, blues and yellows—every color of the rainbow really.

Today, I got up off the couch and chose red. I kept canvases and paint in my spare bedroom. I should have laid down paper around my easel, but I couldn't stop how fast the painting came to me, how fast I wanted it out of me.

A rose this time. With bold and broad strokes, black lines and shadows emerged, and I knew this wouldn't be a piece of perfection. They never were. I twisted my wrist as I painted some of the petals, then grabbed my spray paint to speckle it and mess it up. All my paintings were this way, never perfect. Never clean.

Hours later, I stood back to admire my work and then left quickly, ready to avoid the space for at least a month or two. It was the one place where I didn't keep my emotions buried deep, and that was a hazardous area to visit for me.

I'd think of my sobriety, and I'd consider if it was all worth it. What would be one more hit to ease a feeling? But one time was all it would take to let everyone down, including myself.

When Lilah called that Monday morning after the party, I hit ignore, hoping to avoid her too.

I stuffed my butt into a black pencil skirt and added a light-green blouse which tied into a bow at the neckline. After a swipe of lip gloss, I stepped into my stilettos, grabbed the coffee thermos I'd made for myself, and hurried out, calling an Uber on the way. The fall breeze whipped over my cheeks, and the sounds of Chicago filled my ears. Cars honking, people shuffling by on their cell phones. The bustle here never stopped.

Lilah called again, and I groaned, pressing ignore again. "You know where Stonewood Tower is?" I asked the Uber driver.

She nodded enthusiastically. "I always imagine you all working up there in like a heavenly office, tossing out ideas and having meals catered," the girl said.

I smiled softly at her. "They're always hiring."

She waved me off. "Ah. I'm working on my master's. Maybe one day."

My phone rang again. Now Dante. They weren't going to stop. "Dante, you letting my sister boss you around now?" I answered, wiggling in my skirt.

I heard her mumble in the background, "See. I knew she'd answer your call."

"Just pick up when she calls," he grumbled, sounding like one of my irritated brothers.

"You know, you're not my boss. I don't have to answer her calls just because you say so," I pointed out.

"But I used to be your boss, and that residual training should have you listening every now and then," he chuckled.

"Oh my God. What do you guys want?"

"Well, I wanted you to answer your phone because I got your niece here causing me enough trouble. She won't sleep at night. At all, Izzy. I don't know how babies do it." I chuckled at the sound of his voice mixed with irritation and awe. "I'm serious, Izzy, I don't need Lilah worrying all damn day about you for no good reason."

This is how I knew Dante understood me better than my siblings ever would. He'd grown up near me, worked with me, and become the brother-in-law I needed. He knew I wasn't going to go off the deep end. "To her, it's probably a good reason, Dante."

"I don't get siblings, okay?" he admitted. "She's worrying for nothing."

"To her, I might have OD'd." I shrugged, trying not to hide the hurt in my voice.

"So then answer. That way she won't think that," he replied, like it was that easy.

I sighed because maybe it should have been that easy, maybe I shouldn't have taken her worry for me offensively. "Give her the phone."

I heard rustling and a baby cooing as my sister took over. "If it isn't my elusive sister who needs to come visit very soon."

"Hardly elusive. I just texted you."

"Yeah, yesterday to cancel on me. What were you doing all day that prevented you from driving over?"

We were only thirty minutes apart, but I lived in the city while Lilah had moved to a farm back in our hometown not too far from our parents.

"I know it's not far. I just had a lot to do."

The voice that sounded exactly like mine pushed back with irritation. "I want you to answer when I call, not be busy, Izzy. You weren't even working on Sunday. Now I've got like five minutes till you have to go."

I sighed. Why did I tell her everything? Being honest about my schedule ended in her knowing about all my free time.

"See. You sighed. I knew something was wrong. I could feel it. You had that early Halloween party, then you didn't answer after canceling plans with me and . . ." Her silence spoke volumes. Over the years, her trust in me had been broken. I wouldn't get it back quickly.

Or maybe ever. I wondered if, to them, I was the addict in the family they'd always have to worry about. Maybe I'd need to reassure my sister I wasn't going to be spiraling for the rest of my life.

But wasn't that what I should be thankful for? I was lucky to have someone who would actually care about me like that forever, yet sometimes, I was tired of confirming my health—especially after nine years of sobriety.

"I'm fine, Lilah."

"I know you're fine that way," she scoffed, but I heard the relief in her voice. "Something else is wrong, though. How was the Halloween party?"

"It was good." *I just hooked up with my boss and broke up with my boyfriend on the same night. Quite possibly ruined his car—might need a lawyer for that—and potentially could lose my job if my boss decides I'm too much of a headache.* "Everything's fine. But I have to get to work."

"You've got five minutes. And if you don't give me something,

I'll just sic Mom on you."

"Okay. That's below the belt." I straightened in my seat.

"It's not. I'm staying in her good graces, though, because I gave her a grandkid, so you'd better start talking."

"I should have ruined your relationship with Dante when I had the chance," I grumbled.

That got her laughing at least. "And to think I felt bad for you when he picked me over you."

We laughed and some of her anger dissipated.

"So, you want me to call Mom, then? Have her come to your place and pry into your life?"

I stopped laughing. "You wouldn't. You'd better not. Don't be a bitch."

"I'm a loving bitch, though."

I weighed my options, and as my work building neared, I figured she was going to find out anyway. Cade probably shared things with his family and that included Dante. I really hated that they were cousins now. It's how I'd met him. He'd shown up on my first day on the job with Dante and was introduced as Dante's cousin and the head of cybersecurity.

So, I bit the bullet. "I have a lot going on with Gerald. We broke up, but he keeps texting . . . and then I might have hooked up with Cade." I mumbled it quietly, hoping she would just leave it, but when I heard her gasp, I quickly continued. "But it was like a hate hookup, you know? Like, it won't happen again, and now I have to face him at work, but he's never there usually, so maybe I won't see him. And I just hope to God I don't lose my job."

The line stayed silent. So long that I figured Delilah had hung up.

"You there?"

"What?" she screeched.

"I have to go to work."

"Oh my God. I knew Cade had it bad for you," she squealed. "Remember when you made the joke about kissing Dante at the fire and Cade looked like he was about to blow?"

"He didn't—"

"He did," she said with such conviction, I wasn't going to argue. "And now it all makes sense. You were supposed to kiss an Armanelli man, you just got the wrong one the first time."

I hated that she took what I'd done to her so lightly. "I never should have kissed Dante, Lilah—"

"If you apologize for that one more time, I'm driving over to smack you. It was the push I needed to realize I loved him and you found out he was just your friend anyway. Now, Cade, I bet, is not just a friend."

I heard Dante's voice snap out a "What?"

I was going to kill her. "Do not tell Dante. Or tell him not to say anything to Cade. I don't want to make this a big deal at all."

"Of course it's a big deal."

"You did hear me when I said that I broke up with Gerald, right?" I heaved a sigh and combed my fingers through my hair while sipping on the coffee I'd put in a thermos before running out of the house.

"I did. I bet Cade was a better kisser."

He was. Damn it. "Lilah, stay focused. I really thought Gerald was so good for me and the family."

I hated that I'd let the one thing the family needed to see from me slip away. Gerald was stable. He kept on an even keel. He was what they wanted for me.

Except that he cheated.

"For the family? Like us?" She burst out laughing. "We all hated him. You realize that our brothers were taking bets on when you'd finally break up with him, right? So good riddance."

I choked on my coffee. She'd used the exact same tone that I had before I spray-painted him.

"Are you okay?"

"I'm fine. You all didn't tell me you hated him!"

"Well, we want you to be happy," she admitted, and I wrinkled my nose to keep my emotions at bay. They all coddled me too much.

As my Uber pulled up in front of Stonewood Tower, I sighed. "I really have to go. And don't worry, I'm not at all sad about Gerald, in case you were wondering."

"Well, I wasn't really because he's such a boring doormat."

"Lilah! You said you liked him," I reminded her again.

"Because you were dating him!"

"So, what? Now you like Cade? Because that's not happening," I said with emphasis as I stomped up toward the building in my stilettos.

"I think it's happening. I want to go on a double date."

"You're out of your mind. Like way on another planet if you think that's happening."

"We'll see."

"Goodbye, you freak."

"Takes one to know one!" she singsonged before I hung up on her.

The day was going to be terrible. After my conversation with Lilah, I could feel it.

Although Cade had never showed up at the office before, I knew he'd be there today. Somehow. Some way. Even as I set up my desk and sat down to go through my task list for the day, I knew I was already behind the eight ball.

Especially when my task list was empty.

"Juda, I don't have any tasks listed. You having the same problem?"

"Um, no. My task list is very full. I was going to ask you about it because it seems you've added items back onto my list that I've already assigned you." He scratched his thinning brown hair. "That's unacceptable—"

"Izzy is strictly on IT today, Juda," Cade said from across the hall as he made his way over from the elevators.

Every head in the office whipped toward his voice. I think I even heard Penelope gasp.

Cade Armanelli in a three-piece suit—black and pressed like he'd walked off the set of a photo shoot—was a sight for any fashionable woman, let alone for our motley team who barely attempted to dress anywhere close to business casual for work.

Cassie wore a damn T-shirt most days, and Juda was currently in shorts.

Thank God for my pencil skirt because at least he couldn't look down his nose at me for not putting in the effort. And I needed that boost of confidence to let the furious question fly out of my mouth. "Strictly IT? You're kidding me, right?"

"Why would a boss ever kid about assignments, Izzy? Your job title is IT specialist, isn't it?"

Hands on my hips, I faced off with him. "We all do IT here, and most of us do more than that, including me."

I don't think anyone talked back to Cade, ever. Granted, we mostly communicated through emails or phone calls because he was never in the office, and none of those calls or emails were ever directed at me. Still, I got around my IT title because Juda passed most of his work off to me. He knew I wanted more than technical difficulty problems. I wanted to code and set up security infrastructures. I wanted to use my education, especially considering I was good at what I did.

Cade's attempt to control this was ridiculous, especially since he was never present, and I was shocked that my team didn't jump in immediately to back me up. Cassie and Penelope simply sat there, staring at him with dreamy eyes, and the guys all stood straighter, like they had to compete with his presence.

Didn't anyone remember this was the guy whose office desk was collecting dust? Except for this last weekend when I was spread-eagle across it.

My mind was *not* going there. Even as he smirked at me.

He didn't have an established presence here like he was supposed to. Still, despite that, the moment Cade walked in, this was his floor, and even the Stonewoods knew it.

I chewed on my cheek as I stared at him, but he looked straight through me. His emotion—the pure lust and passion he'd had for me a few nights ago—was gone. It was like his gaze pierced a hole in me, gutted me, and moved right on.

I hated that he had that power over me, that he controlled my job, that he knew exactly how furious I would be about the change.

I flipped my ponytail and continued. "I'm not sure you understand that I help with a lot of the infrastructure that Juda handles."

"I'm sorry, are you saying I don't understand the team, or are you saying that Juda can't handle his own duties?" Cade tilted his head.

"I assure you I can, sir." Juda stepped up and threw me right under the bus. He knew I'd been doing his work for over a year now.

"So I guess Izzy's saying I don't understand this team then."

This guy. He wanted me to snap. If he could make me resign, he wouldn't have to deal with the potential HR hell storm I could cause just from our little elevator fling.

"Is this about—"

He cut me off. "If you'd like to discuss this further, you can see me in my office."

Penelope's eyes bulged, and Cassie's head snapped back to her computer as Cade glanced around. Braxton hadn't even looked up to begin with. Our team didn't want to interact with the boss. Over this past year, we'd gotten the message loud and clear. Cade operated alone. He assigned certain projects, but not the big ones, nuclear ones, ones that could cause destruction if not handled correctly.

Lucas, the freaking best friend anyone could have, cleared his throat. "I'm happy to help Izzy with the team structure if—"

"I'd like to see you in your office," I announced quickly, not willing to have Lucas step in for me. Dude was in advertising and not even supposed to be on this floor. He was the only one ready to walk the plank with me, my ride-or-die. But my loyalty to him was too strong to let him do that.

I was more than ready to face Cade's wrath alone because I had some fury of my own.

CHAPTER 7

Izzy

When Cade motioned for me to lead the way, I tried to hide my eye roll. He appeared to be a gentleman with that suit, its tapered fit, and his gold cuff links that matched the large gold ring he wore. I wondered if it was a family one, not that I'd ever ask. We'd never been the type to exchange life stories and we weren't going to start now.

The Data Security floor of Stonewood Enterprises was sleek. Each large oak office door touted beautiful trim. I knew that trim was hard because of the indentations in my back from when Cade had me pressed up against it. The bruising had faded to the point I thought I could forget how he and I had just fucked in here.

Except as he shut the door behind us, he stepped so close that I had to back up against the door to avoid touching him. One side of his mouth kicked up, like he enjoyed seeing me stumble over myself.

"Scared of something, Izzy?" he whispered against my ear. Instantly, my body reacted, and I shivered before leaning away.

I lifted my chin. "Only that I might have to spend more time with you."

He chuckled, and the sound held menace—like he was determined to bring me to my knees, but this time my mouth wouldn't be wrapped around his cock.

I cleared my throat as he turned to walk over to his desk. "Can you explain why my tasks have been moved back to Juda's list?"

"I can, but I don't need to." He shrugged and then pressed a privacy button that fogged his office windows. I watched as the outside world disappeared around us and he sank down into his leather chair, moving a mouse around to wake up the four monitors in front of him as if he was so comfortable at the office he never visited.

Sitting at those monitors was a direct disregard of my presence. I lost sight of him behind the four screens and then he simply kept quiet. Had he forgotten I was in his office? Could I stand here all day and not be a bother to him?

Almost a whole minute passed as I watched him. I literally counted. Shocked at his lack of elaboration—like, no further explanation whatsoever—the awkward silence grew.

Finally, I threw up my hands. "Cade, I didn't come in here to watch you work."

"Oh, great. Then you should probably leave." He cracked his neck to the side and reached for something on his right.

When I saw they were glasses and he slipped them on effortlessly, I couldn't help but blurt out, "You wear glasses?"

He sighed, closing his eyes for a second before opening them to glare at me. "Izzy, what do you want?"

"You told me to come in here to discuss why you're changing

everything around." I walked toward his desk in irritation. "You're never here, but you're acting like this place doesn't operate perfectly fine without you."

"No." He shook his head, then tapped his temple like I needed to pay attention. "Remember, I said you could come to my office if you wanted to discuss the team further."

"I'm not getting into logistics with you. We both know you're changing everything around when it doesn't need to be changed."

"Based on what? Your expertise?"

"Is that a jab at my education?" I think my mouth nearly hit the floor while my blood pressure skyrocketed. This guy had the audacity to go down that road?

"Izzy, I don't even have the credentials you do. Why you went back to school for a degree in computer analytics is beyond me when you already knew how to hack into government shit in the first place," he grumbled, rubbing his forehead. "Now, doing your assigned IT troubleshooting job, I'm not so sure about—"

"Are you kidding? I handle my job and other tasks. And I'm good at what I do. Stonewood Enterprises literally threw our team a party because we're that good."

"They're always throwing damn parties. Jett's been party happy ever since he got married."

Wow, he had some nerve talking about the guy who owned the company that way. "Look Juda and I have worked in sync—"

"Juda can't handle the job, and you and I both know it." Cade cut me off.

"Well, if you believe that you should let me help him so his projects don't go completely off the rails."

"Do you do everyone's job around here, Izzy? Your task list also included a large project from Cassie and—"

"I like to work," I ground out. "Juda has not once complained about—"

As if on cue, Cade's AI announced that Juda was calling. Cade didn't think I was worth passing up his call, obviously, because he said, "I'll answer." He waited a moment for a beep and then said, "Juda, I'm still talking with Ms. Hardy."

Don't think I didn't roll my eyes as big as I could before I grumbled, "Now it's *Ms. Hardy.*"

"Yes, sir, I'm very aware you're talking things over with Ms. Hardy. I just wanted to make it clear that I've got all this handled. Ms. Hardy has done some great *assisting.*"

Boy, he must have been sweating in his boots out there, because he knew damn well knew he'd done none of the work.

"I know. I know. She's telling me how great you are, Juda, and I'm happy to have you as the team lead." His tone didn't make him very believable. "Please remind me what projects Ms. Hardy was assisting you on so I can be sure her workload isn't too light in IT."

"Oh." Juda cleared his throat.

I tapped one stiletto and noted Cade's eyes were glued to it, like he was absorbing the energy from each tap. He even smiled as Juda tried to brush all my work under the rug.

I didn't correct him. It wasn't my job. I really didn't care if he took credit. I let him finish his ridiculous downplay of my work as I racked my brain for how to navigate this situation. When he mentioned the JUNIPER project, my whole body went rigid.

"She's done well there. We got that algorithm ironed out very quickly. And the infrastructure we set up for the Chicago PD and the voting system for midterms is ideal for combating their ever-evolving cyber threats."

"Juda, I'm happy you brought that up," I said. "I'd love a chance to take that off your plate, if Mr. Armanelli is comfortable with me doing so."

Cade's finger now tapped the desk in about the same rhythm as my foot. "Why do you need to take over?" Cade inquired.

"Because I'd like to continue managing those threats. You know my history in undercover work—"

"Is over," Cade snapped. "You don't need to do that here."

"But I want to," I ground out as I searched his room for the speaker of the phone. "Juda, are you comfortable with that? It will free up some of your time."

"Juda, you realize this is a big opportunity. We intend to mirror some of the setup for the election cybersecurity. We'll fly you out to DC to meet the team and—"

"Oh, I think it's ideal that Izzy takes it, then."

I smirked when Cade's brow furrowed. He didn't get that Juda really had no idea about the project that I'd essentially built from the ground up. JUNIPER was my baby, and I was proud to say it was working out nicely.

Cade's eyes narrowed. "You're not interested in the opportunity for a promotion?"

"I think Izzy's got this one handled," he grumbled.

Cade's tapping stopped. He stood from his chair and made his way over to me as he said, "Great, Juda. I'll iron out the rest of the details with Izzy, then. End call."

The beep overhead signaled Juda was gone. Cade wasn't done yet. He walked around me like a snake, ready to coil me up.

"You think you're winning right now, don't you?" he snarled.

I couldn't help but smile. "You think you can handle a managerial position? If that's the case, why have you been taking all of Juda's work and not standing up for yourself?"

"It's practice, quite frankly. I needed to know I could do his job. Now I know I can handle his duties as well as my own."

"There're calls with management, HR issues, complaints, strategy, not to mention all the other Stonewood bullshit we have to work on."

"I can handle it."

"You saying it doesn't prove it to me." Yet Cade rubbed his chin like he was thinking about it, like he might give me a shot. Then he pulled his cell from his pocket and sent off a text. "Plus, you're going to have to prove it to Jett."

"Jett?" I squeaked. "What does Mr. Stonewood have to do with any of this?"

"He's not going to let an employee run the security of an election."

"But it's your team, and I—"

Of course, it was at that moment that Alice—their version of AI assistant—announced Jett Stonewood calling.

"Either we answer it or we don't, Izzy."

I'd barely graduated high school because of juvie, I'd faced one or two pretty bad drug deals, and I'd been held at gunpoint undercover. My life had been full of extreme choices, but for some reason, this one felt heavy, full of weight, and definitely life changing.

I quirked a brow at him. If I was going to get my feet wet, I might as well jump off the boat into the ocean. "Answer it."

I stood tall as he circled me, and I didn't falter or shrink.

Cade shrugged when I looked over my shoulder at him, and then he pointed to the knot at my neck where my blouse was tied. "This holding your top up?"

"What's it matter?" I sneered.

Then I heard, "Cade, what's going on?" from the man himself. Jett Stonewood had taken over a multibillion-dollar business from his father, invested vastly throughout the world, and partnered with the mob to pretty much rule the United States. I knew that between him and Cade Armanelli, I was about to have probably the most important conversation of my life. He was one of the only trillionaires in the world, and I think he shared half that wealth with the Armanellis.

"I have an employee who's taking over the Chicago PD infrastructure and the election voting cybersecurity."

"Does she know there are holes in it?" Jett shot back.

"I'm sure, since it's her work." Cade lifted a brow at me like he thought I might fold under the embarrassment and pressure.

I chewed my cheek. It hurt to hear the flaws in my work pointed out. But I could fix them. I was going to take care of them. "I'm aware. I'm working diligently to confirm no breaches will happen this year."

"You have the knowledge needed?" Jett asked.

It was a question for me, but I waited a beat for Cade to step in and confirm my credentials.

"She's pretty underqualified," he said instead.

This jerk.

When my jaw dropped, he took that moment to drag a finger across my neckline towards the bow of my blouse, like he was considering untying it. Instead, he leaned close to whisper into my neck, "Sell yourself because I won't. I'm not doing you any favors."

With that, he bit my neck, and I tried my best not to gasp. His hands trailed down my back to my hips, and he pulled me close enough to feel his length—rigid, long, pulsing against me like it had a few nights ago.

He wanted me to fold, to make a fool of myself, to tell his virtual assistant to hang up.

There was no way I was letting him get the best of me.

"Mr. Stonewood, I've worked on the infrastructure from the very first day we changed systems. I think the JUNIPER system is great, but I did tweak it because of the information stored there. With more coding, it will be nearly impenetrable, and I believe it will enable us to mirror that level of security on a larger scale in the future."

"Exactly. This system is linked to the court system of Illinois and the voting—"

"I'm aware they're all interconnected," I blurted out. I hated that I wanted to cut the conversation short, but Cade's tongue was lapping at my neck, and my body quaked with need rather than my mind reacting to the CEO who was addressing something I would have previously given an arm and leg to discuss with him.

Cade grabbed my ponytail and whispered in my ear, "That's my baby doll. Tell him. And untie the neck of your blouse too."

Something was wrong with me. I shouldn't have done it. I shouldn't have even considered it. Yet my hand went right there as I glared at him. I pulled the string. This was a battle of wills, a way to fight him, control my narrative, and win.

My enemy would not have me surrender here. Even if I was wet for him—and damn it, I was so wet—the breath I took quivered through me. Cade must have noticed because he dipped his finger into my cleavage and dragged it to my nipple under my black lace bra.

"Do elaborate, Ms. Hardy," Jett commanded in a tone that indicated he didn't appreciate my bullshit. Like if I had the balls to cut him off, I'd better have the ammunition to back it up.

I did. I was just struggling to breathe and not moan; to pay attention and not spiral into an orgasm. "I set most of them up because Juda had too much on his plate, so I know they are all interconnected." It was a lie, and I caught Cade rolling his eyes, but I wouldn't throw my team under the bus. I couldn't expound further because my pussy was crying out for Cade, so I left it at that.

Cade chuckled, and his hands slid from my breasts to my stomach, then pushed my blouse over my hips to the ground. Next, he was on his knees in front of me. "Ms. Hardy did do most of the setup, Jett. I looked into it," Cade finally confirmed, smiling up at me.

"And you're comfortable working with Cade?" Jett asked. He knew Cade was no walk in the park.

I stared down at my archnemesis, a man ready to fuck me in his office but who didn't believe in me outside of it. This was what I probably couldn't do. The challenge in his eyes was there, telling me to back down now.

"I do work under Cade, but I don't know that I'll need his help on this. Like I said, I just have a few more tweaks for the Illinois—"

"Sure, but we'll use this for the election," Jett stated with authority. "We can mirror this code. Cade, you think it's good enough, right? This is it. If you're working on the Chicago PD infrastructure, I want you on the election team and flying out to meet them in a week."

Cade's hand gripped my nyloned calf tightly all of a sudden. "Not necessary, Jett. I can handle that on my own. Don't even need a team there for it."

Jett sniggered. "My point exactly. You want to do it on your own. It seems Ms. Hardy will be able to at least be a team player if you won't. You two can fly out, meet them, work together to make sure this election doesn't get hacked. That is, if you're on board, Ms. Hardy?"

Cade shook his head no at me, but I didn't have to be told twice to take the opportunity of a lifetime. I glared at Cade and said loudly, "I'd be honored to do that, Mr. Stonewood."

It was like I shifted one block out of place in his perfect setup; I'd put a chink in his armor, a glitch in his perfect system. He ticked his head to the side and flexed his jaw before his hand started to inch up my thigh at an excruciatingly languid pace, with a glare that would bring most people to their knees.

"Cade, make sure she flies to the capital with you to confirm security and operational voting booths too."

"Fine," Cade blurted out. "I'll update you soon. End call."

"You're an asshole." I shoved his shoulders, but he didn't budge an inch as he kneeled there, his eyes glued to his hands crawling up my skirt. "I'll take a separate flight just to be rid of you."

His fingers reached my panty line, and he rubbed back and forth. My nails dug into that tailored suit, and I hoped they ripped into those pressed shoulders as I hissed. "You scared to spend a little time with me, baby doll?"

"I don't really know why we're flying to meet anyone anyway.

It can be done remotely." I whimpered, moving my hips because he was lightly brushing over my pussy, like he wanted to play when I wanted to fuck.

"Jett's old school. Most people don't get the computer world like we do. I wouldn't worry about it. We won't need you there anyway."

"Well, Jett just said you did." I stared down at him.

"Are you always ready to go above and beyond at work?" he asked, perplexed by my work ethic.

I couldn't tell him I had a mind that wandered if it was idle. I couldn't let him judge me. "What's so confusing about a stellar work ethic?"

"Well, for one, I've had to stop your poking around for about a year." He shoved my panties to the side and slid two fingers inside me.

"The fact that you've been tracking what I've been doing for a year means you go above and beyond for work too." I bit my lip to keep from moaning as he brought me closer to climax. Our hatred for one another didn't hold up against my need to get off with him again. I started to think this would be a recurring scenario— something I'd keep going back to if we didn't put a hard stop to it.

"You didn't think you could keep that up and get away with it, did you? I think maybe you wanted me to come for you," he growled.

"Is that why you came back to the office? Because I assure you that didn't need to happen. I'm not even searching for things anymore. I—" He curled his fingers inside me, and I practically fell onto him as I pulled him closer and swore under my breath.

He shook his head at me like he couldn't believe he was here either. "I came back to the office for the end-of-year cleanup. Stonewood Enterprises has an early fall party, then we do annual reviews."

The man had an answer for everything, and this was one that made me feel insignificant and small. Of course we were closing in on the year-end and would need annual reviews. Why hadn't I thought of that? "Right," I grumbled.

"Don't get your panties in a bunch, dollface. You're not that important. Although, I do enjoy your company this way." He chuckled.

"Please shut up," I moaned and pulled my skirt up.

He instantly grabbed my thigh and draped it over his shoulder. "Why? Just want me to fuck you quiet so you can enjoy some good sex finally? It's what you've wanted for a while now, isn't it?"

God, I hated him. "I wanted nothing to do with you. I was with Gerald and—"

"And completely unhappy and fucking bored. So bored you kept searching for Albanian trafficking and drug raids when you shouldn't have been."

"I could help if I had more information regarding—"

"Do *your* job, Izzy. Not someone else's," he murmured before burying his face in my pussy.

"Fine." I dragged out the word. "You know, sometimes it doesn't hurt to exceed expectations." The world kept spinning because people pushed their limits, not because they did the bare minimum.

"Don't try. Just do," he growled as he nipped my thigh, then went back to licking me where I was so wet, I could hear him tasting me.

There was no arguing with a man who took such good care of you, you were about to scream in an office. "Cade, this is really not a place where we should be doing this. Is the door locked?"

Instead of answering, he spun me so my ass hit his desk, then lifted me onto it, never removing his tongue. He lapped at me like he'd been starved and bit my clit when I started to protest again.

It was a futile attempt at best. I wanted that orgasm, was chasing it now. With him, I raced toward a different sort of high. I'd known addiction, known chemical alterations of the mind. This type of adrenaline—the fear of getting caught mixed with primal need—was the human body creating a drug on its own, one of the most highly addictive out there.

I clawed at his scalp, tried to push him further into my center, wanting to feel all of him between my legs. His masterful tongue rolled and flicked over my bundle of nerves. He was the enemy who delivered passion, the one I'd hated for a year now, but who was finally giving me something other than irritation and pain.

"Cade, please. Fuck me. Please, please, please." I'd never begged Gerald like this, never wanted a man more than Cade. The line between loathing and lust had become paper-thin.

He hummed against my folds, and the sound vibrated up my spine, spreading an awareness through me that this man could ruin me if I was this turned on by just this. "I shouldn't give you the satisfaction of fucking you on my desk when you can't follow simple rules."

I'd forgotten what we were talking about and murmured, "What?"

"You won't try to do anything while working directly with me, you understand?" Cade said as he unbuckled his belt and pulled it slowly from his trousers, one loop after another. The leather slid out seamlessly as I watched it, intrigued suddenly by how he wound it up into a ball. "You'll listen, right, dollface?"

I worked my lip between my teeth as we both stared at that ball of leather. He brought it up to my clit and pressed it against me.

I shuddered at the friction as he began to move it there. We both watched as he dipped it low enough to collect my arousal and then brushed it back against my clit, making me moan.

"Izzy, answer the question." The command fell from his lips pointedly. "You'll listen?"

I was past playing games and wanted to get off so bad that I nodded.

"Say 'Yes, Mr. Armanelli.' We need to establish the boss-employee relationship early. If you travel with me, people are going to have to know you're not my fuck toy and that I'd never be with you. They need to know we're only working together."

I didn't ever want to be with him, but why did him not wanting to be seen as my boyfriend hurt? "I highly doubt anyone would think that the recluse genius hacker who's part of a mob family is dating someone like me."

His hand inched up as I talked, like he wasn't listening. His pupils dilated, his gaze changed, his grip on my thigh tightened. "If they did, we'd change the narrative online anyway. The internet writes the news."

"So no worries, then." I rolled my eyes.

"You still haven't said, 'Yes, Mr. Armanelli.'"

"I'm not going to either." I crossed my arms, ready to defy him.

"Good." He smiled, unraveling the belt quickly. With a flick of his wrist, the end of it hit my center, causing a zing to fly through every part of my body.

Pain was subjective, and here it felt more like pleasure. I gasped, "What the fuck, Cade?"

"You listen and you get rewarded. You don't, you get punished. You can ride my belt all you want, but when you don't obey me, I'll discipline you." He leaned forward, mouth so close to mine that I could have taken his lips if I wanted. "Remember that, Izzy."

"I don't think I'll be working for you for long, then," I murmured, getting lost in the way he held my gaze captive. My body ached for him, and I knew that wasn't a good sign. I blamed it on Gerald, on the fact that I'd gone without sex and excitement for months while he traveled and screwed someone else. "And this will be the last time between us. I can scratch an itch like this with someone else."

"Sure you can," he murmured as he finally stood back up, pulled out his cock, and positioned himself between my legs. I felt the head of his cock and that cool metal piercing spreading my folds, reminding me of how big he was and how my body longed to fit around him, to mold to him. "They won't scratch it like I do, though, and you'll come crawling back, begging for me to take your breath away again. But, sure, this will only happen one last time."

"Should I thank you?" I asked him, voice full of condescension.

"You probably are going to want to." He chuckled, then his tone sobered. "Tap my wrist twice if it's too much, got it?"

Before I could even tell him to elaborate, his hand shot out to grip my neck. He cut off my oxygen and made me wheeze for air.

I clawed at his wrist, but I didn't tap. I wouldn't. If this was the game, I was going to win.

He tsked at my futile effort. "This is my breath now, baby doll."

He thrust inside me, bottoming out balls deep on the first one. The large oak desk may have moved. I couldn't even gasp, but he saw how I arched, how I bit my lip in bliss, and he squeezed my neck even harder. "And I get to control when you breathe, when you feel, when you see stars, or when you see darkness."

His other hand worked my clit, rolling it hard and fast as he thrust in and out while ravaging my neck. And I got closer and closer to those stars while nearing the black hole of passing out from lack of air.

Cade wasn't a gentle lover. He wasn't even a lover, really. He was just the guy fucking me into a different sort of universe than I'd ever experienced. His cock alone—so rigid, thick, and long—would have done that on its own. Yet he'd brought in breath play, he'd whipped my clit before working it, and he expected me to take each hard thrust with vigor.

I hated that I did, that I wanted him more than any other man before. My body worked to stay conscious, to meet him thrust for thrust, more concerned with an orgasm than taking another breath.

"Fuck." He swore low as he ripped his hand from my neck and planted both of them on the desk right behind me to give himself more leverage so he could fuck me harder.

Gasping for air, I gripped the front of his shirt and tightened my pussy around him as I came. The rush of oxygen back into my lungs pushed me over the edge. He muffled my scream and let out a string of Italian as he emptied himself into me.

"Fuck, fuck, fuck," he muttered as he hung his dark head of hair onto my shoulder. "You're flirting with passing out, love. You're not careful enough."

I didn't respond, just gulped in more air. We both stayed where we were for what felt like forever. He didn't even pull his cock from me. It was like he wanted it to stay buried there. When he finally lifted his head, those eyes of his weren't burning whiskey this time. They were warm like a light coffee that could wake you up and make you want to plow through the day together.

He searched my face and then traced one finger over my mouth. "You have lips made for sinning, Izzy."

I rolled them between my teeth and gently pushed him away. He didn't fight me but exited my center slowly, pulling my skirt down with him. I shouldn't have let him do even that, but I watched how his hands smoothed the fabric, how he brought his hand underneath to slide my panties back into place, and his touch was as light as a feather.

He took a step back to look me over as he tucked himself into his trousers. "I'm not kidding about the breath play."

I shrugged. "I'm fine." I was better than fine. I was satiated like I'd never been before.

"Next time—"

"There won't be a next time, remember?" I hopped off the desk. We were colleagues, not fuck buddies.

We both needed to draw a line, and this was it. Especially with upcoming trips together, with a team relying on us, with one of the biggest corporations depending on me.

I moved to rush past him, but he caught my elbow, his tattooed hand gripping me tightly. "You intend to have another man with his hand around your neck?" he asked softly.

I stared up at him and saw the fire, the malice, and the dominance. Caden Armanelli stood before me as a man of the Mafia now, not a businessman. I felt it in the way he gripped me, in the way his breath was measured as he waited for my answer.

"So what if I do? You're not my keeper, Cade."

He dragged his other hand over his face as he swore. "Don't go try what we've done with just anyone."

I studied him and saw now that the look of a man flirting with unhinging his monster was gone. Instead, I noted a look of concern, like he thought I couldn't handle myself.

"I'm capable of taking care of myself, Cade," I informed him.

"And I'm capable of breaking every bone in a man's body, but I'd like to refrain from doing that. So don't do it. No one is allowed to hold your life in their hands except me. You understand?"

I ripped my arm from his grip. "Please tell me after year-end reviews you'll go back to being remote, because you uttering that statement is absolutely ridiculous. Do you hear yourself?"

His possessiveness fizzled, and he chuckled while scratching his chin. "After the election, I'll be gone, Ms. Hardy. Don't worry." And then he disappeared into what I imagined was his en suite bathroom.

There was no reason for me to stay. Honestly, I couldn't take him being a gentleman now. It would muddy the waters of our work relationship even more than the murky-ass swamp we found ourselves in now.

Plus, we'd both gotten the sexual tension out of our systems. I was getting a chance to prove myself in a higher position, and I wasn't about to ruin it because Cade and I slept together once or twice.

I grabbed my blouse and pulled it back on, tying the knot extra tight, then got the hell out of there.

CHAPTER 8

Cade

"The answer is no, Jett," I reiterated to the owner of Stonewood Enterprises just a few days later. My blood pressure had definitely risen this week and I couldn't deal with sugarcoating my answer anymore.

Izzy had done this to me. She'd left my office with the smell of her arousal still in the air, her words about seeing other men still echoing in my ears, and the taste of her still in my mouth.

The next day, we didn't even make eye contact, but I still heard her husky voice as I walked past everyone to get to my office. I physically had to restrain myself from checking what she was wearing the past two days.

So, I admittedly didn't have the patience for Jett at the moment. He'd done his best to convince me to do three weeks of teamwork right before the election with a cybersecurity team I hadn't met.

"Fine. Two weeks." He negotiated. "My event coordinators will handle everything, and you can have Izzy do the bulk of the teaching. She built most of JUNIPER anyway, right? She'll be able to handle it—but you *have* to be there. If for no other reason than to confirm we aren't having breaches from a remote location."

"I can confirm that *from* a remote location, Jett. This is bullshit."

"I know that. I'm not an idiot," Jett mumbled. "But it's the team building I need you to do. You're their *boss*. You're the fucking celebrity of the data world or whatever you want to call it. They want to see you. They want to be a part of it."

His wife yelled in the background, "It's for morale. It'll be fun."

That girl was the sun shining into a black hole, I swear. "Tell Vick she's lost her mind since becoming a mother if she thinks this will be fun."

"I've actually found my mind, Cade." She chirped into the phone. "You're an uncle now, aren't you? You gain insight from children even while they drive you crazy. You'd lay down your life for them, right?"

She knew my brother had a kid with his wife. I'd practically staged the two of them getting together.

I pursed my lips and sighed because I couldn't deny I loved that baby. Family was family. "There's something wrong with our makeup." My niece was a monster, but we adored the little tyrant. "I don't know how we can love them when they try to kill us and themselves every chance they get, but, damn, I do."

"It's the best experience in the world." I heard Vick's laugh fading away, but Jett didn't say anything.

"You there, or have you melted into a lovesick puppy from staring at your wife?"

"Fuck you. My wife is perfect," Jett grumbled.

I chuckled because he'd been totally whipped by a pussy, and he admitted it with pride. "You, my cousins, and my brother are all crazy."

"Even so, you're gonna be going crazy in a remote location, swinging around on some obstacle course during team building in a week. So I'll take my life over yours." He laughed at his joke while I groaned.

"You owe me, man," I conceded, knowing I had to do it.

"This is being a boss sometimes, Cade. You can't handle it all on your own. You got to trust someone to manage, and you trust Izzy enough, right? She'll be fine. Let's trickle down some of the control to the team."

"I'm going for two weeks. That's it. And I'm taking my jet."

"Great. Have your team on it. It'll be perfect for bonding and morale." Jett was trying to torture me.

"You're kidding me, right?"

"I'm not."

Fuck me. "I'm not participating in anything when I get there," I warned. "Doing year-end reviews of my colleagues is enough to put me over the edge."

"If I had HR that understood any of the technical shit you guys work on, I'd have them do it. It's just year-end stuff. Once a year, Cade. Once a year, and the election only happens every four years. We need to make sure there will be no hiccups with the voting polls and software. After the next two months, you can disappear off the face of the planet like you're used to."

"Bet your ass I will," I grunted and hung up the phone. Then, I straightened my dumbass tie and stomped out of my office, ready to yell at anyone and everyone because my attitude was abominable after that call.

Seeing the girl who irked the shit out of me by wearing a black pencil skirts that hugged every delicious curve of her ass didn't help. Plus, she was flirting with that Lucas guy who wasn't even supposed to be on our floor. That almost did me in.

As I came to stand in front of the desks, he patted her shoulder and said something about getting a drink after work.

"Izzy, Lucas?" Everyone's gazes snapped my way. "How's your work coming for the day?" Wow. Even to myself I sounded like a jackass.

The little siren's eyes narrowed as she whipped her long brown hair over her shoulder and lifted her chin in a move I now knew was defiance. "Just dandy. We're ahead of schedule," she said, popping a candy cane into her mouth.

Where they got candy canes at the beginning of autumn when only Halloween décor was available was beyond me, but I wasn't about to ask. "Change in schedule, so you'll all be behind. We'll be traveling Monday," I announced loudly. "We're all going to meet the election cybersecurity team. Two weeks of team building, and we'll run tests on JUNIPER in a remote location. It's highly confidential, and the location is classified. Pack for a flight and cabin accommodations. Your itineraries will be emailed with instructions on how to handle workloads starting Monday. Any questions?"

"Should we pack bikinis?" The new girl snickered.

"Clothes suitable for an office environment would be best." I glanced around in irritation. "Or I guess what you're wearing now. Not that any of it is professional attire."

No one seemed at all deterred by my snipe at being casual. Cassie, instead, chirped up, "Everyone getting their own cabin, or should we pick bunkmates?"

I know my jaw flexed because this was all ridiculous. "The Stonewoods' event coordination team will have arrangements figured out. I recommend handling any outstanding tasks you have now as it will be all hands on deck for most of the next two weeks. There will be team building activities like obstacle courses and accessibility to a lake."

Surprisingly, the buzz throughout the office was one of excitement; nobody grumbled like I had. One girl even squealed about how much fun it was going to be.

Juda did offer himself up though. "I'm happy to handle the IT in the office if need be."

How chivalrous of him. Or convenient, considering I knew he didn't know a damn thing about JUNIPER. "Sounds great. Everyone else, we will be flying privately. Make sure to email the coordinators anything that you'd like on hand when you get there."

Everyone except one little glaring Harley Quinn had a smile on their face.

"Any issues with the plan?" I waited a beat. "Ms. Hardy?"

She rubbed her fingers over that red bottom lip, and instantly my dick responded. Her lipstick matched her blouse today and was enough reason for me to send her home to change, but I couldn't do that. I needed to stop looking at her like I could still screw her or bend her over my knee. Especially when she had the audacity to roll her eyes.

"No issues at all. Although IT calls are never-ending, I'll be sure to catch up on the voice mails I have now." Her tone was clipped.

I couldn't stop myself from asking, "And how are those calls going?"

She flipped her ponytail over her shoulder and sighed. "Well, Mr. Rogers was very happy that Stonewood Enterprises could help him turn on his computer this morning."

Her friend choked on his candy cane and then shoved away the box to try to cover up his laughter.

"And what's so bad about that? It's an easy task to walk someone through." Coming from her, it was surprising. She'd stared me down the first time I'd met her, like she could handle anything. And I'd questioned it because a girl from the suburbs going undercover with a mob team wasn't exactly a smart decision.

"You're bringing a novice onto your undercover team?" I asked my cousin, Dante, as we sat in his small office at the state's headquarters. "She's green as hell, Dante. She can't go out in the field and make people believe she's a part of their drug operation."

"Why not? She's young and looks the part."

"She's right out of fucking juvie. Of course she's young. And she was thrown in there for larceny and drug possession, wasn't she?"

He glanced away. "Attempted larceny, and she was with the wrong crowd. Izzy didn't have any weapons on her. She was high and didn't know what was going on. I've known her family a long time. They're my family too. I grew up with them. She needs this. Everyone's treating her like a baby who can't handle herself when she's always been the little engine that could. She just needs someone to believe in her."

"So we're putting Albanian drug trafficking in her hands?"

My cousin shoved away from his metal desk and got up to pace. "It's that or we don't get shit. They know how we operate on our soil. We need someone green. I swear she's good. She's on her way over. You'll see she's got enough experience."

"Yeah, being a drug addict. What if she relapses?" I threw my hands up, concerned that he'd lose someone he considered family by putting her

in this position. She could be killed with one wrong step. "Her brain isn't even fully developed, and we're going to throw her into the lion's den where she's got no tools or experience other than taking a hit when she's down."

Dante's door swung open, and that was the first time I saw her. A small little thing with eyes that popped with gold and green flecks, burning bright with emotion and swimming with anger. Dark waves of hair fell wildly around her face, and she didn't brush them aside to stare me down. She didn't fidget in her black boots and baggy ripped jeans, nor did she try to straighten the wrinkles in her brightly tie-dyed, oversized T-shirt with N'SYNC across it as she popped some gum and followed it up with, "I'm good at taking hits, Mr. Armanelli, but I won't relapse." She shrugged and brushed past me to give my cousin a hug. Then she turned my way, determination in her stance. "Addicts are what the Albanians are looking for. I'm already in their crowd. I'm already vetted. I don't need you to believe in me. I only need you to do your job—which is protecting our data security. Right, Dante?"

"Right." He sighed and grabbed his coat off his chair. "Say what you need to each other now. I'm going out to make a call. By the time I get back, let's all be on the same page."

My cousin didn't give me any time to argue. He beelined it out of there and left me with the girl I knew wasn't ready for the job. "You're making a mistake being here," I told her. "This environment needs stability and people with drive."

"Oh, good. Because I have both." She popped her hip out and placed her hand on it. It drew my attention to her body, so small but filled with curves she'd hidden under the oversized clothes. She even looked a mess.

"Look—Ms. Hardy, right?" She nodded as I confirmed her last name. "I can get you a good job outside of undercover work at a great company—"

"I want this one. Dante says it's for me."

"It's not for an addict."

Something changed in her demeanor. As if I'd hit her across the face by calling her that. She stepped back in what looked like literal pain. Maybe she'd thought I wouldn't say it. Maybe nobody around her did.

I wasn't going to sugarcoat it, though. She had to listen and understand so that she would quit.

"You'll be surrounded by drugs, you realize that, right? You'll be tempted all the time. People will be OD'ing around you, getting themselves killed around you, and you'll have to take it in stride without falling into that world. It's a pressure cooker that you don't want to be in."

She took a deep breath, and her plump lips parted as she did. Jesus, the men would accept her into that lion's den with open arms, I realized, just from the way she looked.

All the more reason for her to get out now.

Yet she squared her shoulders and lowered her eyebrows in determination. "I will *be tempted all the time. And I'll prove over and over again that I'm not going back. What better person to be on the team than one who's already seen an OD, who's already witnessed death, and is still standing here alive. I'm an addict, but I have a lot of reasons to never become one again."*

Determination looked beautiful on that girl. And as Dante walked back into the room, I saw her hate for me in her eyes.

I wouldn't deny that hate looked good on her too.

Izzy was a force.

And she was one I didn't want to reckon with.

CHAPTER 9

Izzy

'd been working through IT problems *and* through the holes of JUNIPER the whole week, trying my best to ignore the man who caused my body to heat up with desire. I was exhausted. And Cade lurking around the office, putting everyone on edge had been even more draining.

No one dressed casually anymore, and everyone sat like they had rods up their asses, typing away with purpose even if they had nothing to do—which was absolutely not the case for me. I'd had numerous calls from various companies umbrellaed under Stonewood Enterprises. Troubleshooting IT issues was the worst position in the office because Stonewood Enterprises was a parent company for hundreds of others, and some of them didn't have their own IT teams, so we took the calls.

Just that morning, I'd helped a Mr. Rogers turn on his computer. I'm not joking. He'd headed into his office after months off and called to tell us he didn't know why it wasn't functioning. I'd actually told Lucas that I felt like my ears were bleeding after that call. He'd patted my shoulder.

Add to that, I had Cade standing over me, announcing we all had to go together to a remote location. Now he had the audacity to question whether or not my duties were too difficult for me. Why did everything he say have to be an insult?

"Well, it's not exactly easy, Mr. Armanelli."

Lucas cleared his throat, and I knew he was gearing up to speak on my behalf.

"I beg to differ. How many calls have you handled this morning?"

My eyes bulged. Lucas even slid the candy canes toward me like I should take another before responding to the asshat in front of us. Candy canes calmed us. It was a bad habit I'd started when I got cravings, and I passed it onto him. Instead of nicotine or a bump of cocaine, he had a candy cane. That'd begun during wintertime last year. Now we both had a problem eating them throughout the year.

We'd been sharing a table in our office space. Most of us had utilized the communal tables near the back because we wanted to lounge together and chitchat while we worked. But since Cade had been around this week, most everyone had migrated back to their desks. The floor wasn't separated by cubicles, but when posted up behind your laptop, it could still feel pretty solitary.

I needed my team—especially when dealing with the terrible IT calls—and Lucas ventured over to the empty tables with me, even if there was some unspoken perception that we might get in trouble.

"Are you getting any work done?" Cade continued, and his eyes flicked between us and narrowed.

"I've taken more than enough IT calls, Mr. Armanelli." I

shouldn't have sneered it. I knew it was wrong. In my defense, it'd been a long week. My boss had fucked me in his office, I'd been recently dumped by a guy who kept calling me, and I'd been given a new position. I was tired. Containing my attitude wasn't on my list of to-dos, and my reflexes to stop it were quite slow.

"You have a problem with IT?" Cade asked quietly. And of course the room was silent. Most of my coworkers had even stopped typing.

"It's just . . ."

"Just what?" He crossed his arms and waited.

No one was going to jump in and help me on this one. "I'm sorry. It's fine. I'm a little stressed."

"With IT work? Because I guarantee you the election security is going to be much more taxing."

I swear I heard Juda snicker. I started to pick at my nails, trying to curb my irritation. Everyone knew IT was shit. Cade himself knew that. Unless, maybe he'd never had to do IT work.

"Have you ever taken an IT call?"

"What?" He appeared perplexed. "Why does that matter?"

"I'm just wondering, since you find it so easy, have you ever done it?"

His eyes narrowed, and then he zeroed in on my nail picking. He tapped his shoe in rhythm with it as he smirked. "I'm sure it's not hard."

My picking got faster, and so did his shoe tapping. Fucker. "Well, why don't you take Jodie here that I have to call back. She's struggling to get her internet up and running for her medical practice."

He cracked his neck, and I saw a little bit of tattoo peek out from his collar. It made me wonder if he was tattooed across his whole chest, all down his arms, everywhere. I'd never ripped his shirt off the way I wanted to.

And I never would, I reminded myself.

"Give me the phone, Izzy."

Of course, now Lucas was smiling and leaning back to watch the show with his candy cane, while Cassie giggled to Penelope.

"Here you go, *boss*." I emphasized his title, and his eyes cut to me.

"You really think this is going to stump me?" He grinned and dialed the number. "Yes, is this Jodie? I'm calling on behalf of Stonewood Enterprises IT. You're having an issue?"

We all waited. I swear it was like we were at the movies. Cade was not personable. Not approachable. And he didn't give directions. He worked alone.

"Okay. Start with checking to see if your Wi-Fi is on." Another pause. "What do you mean what's Wi-Fi?" he practically squeaked.

Lucas nearly spat out his candy cane, and I silently cracked up. Cade glared at both of us.

"I'm sorry. Do you have anyone else in the office with you? They will most likely know where it is on your screen. Wi-Fi connects you to the internet and—"

I watched Cade's jaw get tighter and tighter.

"No. You can't restart your computer. That won't help." Another pause. "Well, if you already pressed *shut down*, then I guess we'll have to wait." Pause. "No. It's not a common occurrence through Stonewood Enterprises, Jodie. It's because your Wi-Fi is probably off. If you could get someone—"

He was cut off again, and I had to get up from my chair to offer it to him while I laughed, tears streaming down my face.

He grabbed my arm and shoved me back into my chair. "No, Jodie. I actually have a great coworker here who's going to help you with all this. My apologies. If you'd just give me a moment." He pressed the hold button and handed me the phone. "I'm not dealing with that."

"Why?" I placed my chin in my hand as I leaned on my elbow on the table and stared up at him with big eyes.

He glanced around at everyone, and I could see that Cade was flustered, like he wasn't sure he belonged in this space all of a sudden. "Who normally handles those calls?"

"We all split them until you assigned them to Izzy," Penelope piped up.

"Are they *all* like that?" His tone was full of disgust.

"I literally had a guy ask me if I could fly in to help him install email last week," Braxton piped up, a soft smile on his face.

Maybe it was that Cade was finally approachable in that moment, or maybe we all bonded over the fact that our tech savviness made dealing with some individuals like pulling teeth.

Either way, we all chuckled when Cade shivered off the thought of the phone calls. "We'll be outsourcing these in the future."

"Okay," I murmured, my heart suddenly beating fast, and he nodded, turned on his heel, and went back to his office, closing the door behind him.

We all glanced at each other like someone had cut the equivalent of Medusa's head off our boss and replaced it with that of an approachable kitten.

"Well, I'm pretty obsessed with him now," Penelope blurted out.

"I know I just went through a breakup, but I'm going to start reading the HR handbook," Cassie laughed.

"Well, I already did, and it's not against the rules. If we get to pick bunkmates, I know who I want." Penelope winked at Cassie, and they giggled to each other.

Lucas elbowed me to get my attention. "You and I are going out for a drink at this remote location."

"Why do you think I need a drink so bad?" I murmured, still not taking my eyes from Cassie and Penelope. Why was I already comparing myself to them and wondering if one of them would really try to screw our boss like I already had?

"Because you look like you're ready to skin a person alive, Izzy Bizzy, and we've got to travel with them for two weeks."

Knowing his tone, I held up a finger to shut it down immediately. "Don't start, Lucas. I don't even want to hear you breathe your next thought into existence. We're not getting drinks. We're going home, we're packing, we're getting our shit together to make sure we kick ass at this team building next week."

"If they don't have alcohol, I'm going to die."

"But not too much, right?" Lucas nodded and we fist bumped because we always noted the limit we could handle. We never wanted to slide back to a place where we didn't have control. Then, I sighed, "But, honestly, me too."

CHAPTER 10

Izzy

They had alcohol at night, thanks to every higher power that may exist. We'd landed early Monday. The drive in was scenic enough with forests and farmland for thirty minutes as we traveled in luxury SUVs from the airport.

As we pulled onto a gravel drive and weaved through thick pines and maples, it opened up to a sparkling lake surrounded by cabins. A bright, bouncy blonde gave us name tags the moment we exited the vehicles along with accommodation instructions and itineraries.

"The election security team is already here, and we've paired you all with them in separate cabins. You'll find food in your fridge, although we will have food stations outside throughout the day. Bars with bartenders are set up between cabins for beverages, and you may call the number at the bottom of your itinerary if something isn't up to par. You each have private Wi-Fi connections with optimum security. We truly think these two weeks will be most enjoyable once you get to know everyone. So please don't switch accommodations."

It was four people to a cabin, and there were five cabins available. Ms. Heather—she'd introduced herself as such—handed over bags for those of us who'd requested items. Mine clinked with the spray cans I'd asked for, considering they were prohibited on the flight.

Eight of us had come from Stonewood Enterprises. Cassie and Penelope seemed pretty disappointed that they couldn't fight over rooming with Cade, but he'd taken his own car, and it appeared his cabin was on the other side of the lake, completely isolated from us.

"Guess Mr. Armanelli gets his own cabin," I grumbled to Lucas as we hauled our luggage to cabins 1 and 2.

"He's probably working on some nuclear warfare stuff that he can't share with anyone else." Lucas laughed and pointed to the literal log cabins ahead of us with what looked like kayaks and paddleboards set up along the shore for us if we wanted. Picnic tables and grills were sprinkled over the grassy areas, and I took note of the zip lines that were attached to some of the taller pine trees.

"Guess this is going to be some real team building, huh?" I murmured, concerned about the height as I stared at the zip line. "I'd rather have someone hold a gun to my head."

"That's morbid as hell, Izzy Bizzy." He nudged me, and my duffel bag and suitcase wobbled, causing the spray cans to clink together.

"Did you request painting supplies?" Lucas sounded appalled.

"It's two weeks! I figured we'd have free time, and I might get inspired."

He pointed to my cabin. "That's your inspiration. Look at your bunkmate. Holy hell."

Cybersecurity for the election was apparently buff, tatted, and dreamy. He had a light-brown man bun and was grabbing a paddleboard in his swim trunks.

"Jesus," I grumbled.

"Goodbye, Gerald. Hello, team building, right?" Lucas grabbed my luggage and hauled it up the porch where a little wooden swing attached to chain-links swayed gently in the wind. "Want to ask him which bed he's in so I can set your suitcase down next to it?"

I laughed. "Shut up, you jackass. He's going to hear."

Right then, the guy turned around and smirked. "Oh, I heard. I'm the first room on the left. Name's Rodney, and I'm fine with you sharing my room if you want." He glanced at Lucas. "Happy to share with you too. I'm pan, and you both seem like my jam." Dude even winked before he turned and ran out to the water.

"Fuuuuuck." Lucas let out a string of curses under his breath. "If I come out of the closet on this trip, it's for him."

"Izzy." Lucas and I jumped about a mile when we heard Cade's low voice behind us. "Heather got the room assignments wrong. We need a private IP address to work out the last kinks of JUNIPER. So you'll be staying with me."

"With you?" I squeaked, and Lucas quite literally gasped, both of us in complete disbelief at Cade's words.

He didn't really give me or Lucas time to digest them either. He just snatched my luggage and strode away as he called out, "Don't make noise at whatever ungodly hour you get back."

My jaw hung open, ready to catch mosquitoes, flies, and any other sort of bugs that might fly by out in the wilderness. After a moment of silence, Lucas practically shoved me. "Why the hell does he want you in his cabin, Izzy?"

Combing a hand through my hair, I shook my head. "I really have no idea. I . . . the IP address thing is . . . I don't know."

This would have been a perfect time to tell Lucas about Cade, except it was one thing to tell my sister who was tucked away in the suburbs and another to tell someone who worked with us. I *couldn't* tell anyone else. I was going to sweep it under the rug and hope the dust stayed put.

"I wonder if he acts normal at home. Can you record him while you stay there?" Lucas asked with a smile on his face.

"That's a hard no. I'm not going to be hanging out in that cabin unless I have to."

Lucas chuckled. "Bizzy, I'd be in there all day. Rodney is chef's kiss, but Cade Armanelli, that's forbidden perfection right there."

It took everything I had not to glance back longingly at the cabin because he was right.

"So, Cade probably knows I'm gay now, huh?" Lucas whispered as we made our way to his cabin instead of mine.

I chuckled and welcomed the change in subject. "That, I have no idea."

"Well, you need to go figure it out. And you need to see if there's room for me to sleep on your floor. I'm grossly intrigued by your new living situation."

I sighed as he shoved me away from his cabin porch. "I really hate you right now."

"Call me if you want to hang out later, but I'll totally understand if you don't." He waggled his eyebrows at me like this was a freaking reality show that I was on.

The walk through the grass, around the lake, and to the isolated cabin on the other side made my heart beat like I was on my way to either be voted off or receive the last rose.

I knocked on the door before I entered, but Cade didn't welcome me in, open the door, or say a thing. After another knock and trying to peer in through the windows, which had closed blinds, I turned the knob.

Cade sat on the living room couch with his feet up and a laptop on his lap, typing away. "You don't need to knock."

"You could have just told me to come in," I huffed and waved a hand in front of myself, already irritated.

When he didn't respond, I decided I wouldn't even bother engaging with him. I deserved someone's full attention, not a half-assed comment here and there without even a look in my direction.

Scanning for my bags, I noticed the furniture was new, the countertops were granite, and the AC was cooling the place even though it was autumn and we could have opened the windows. "Looks like we're actually going to be glamping."

"Yes, the accommodations are fine."

"Where did you put my bags?"

"Next to our bed," he said, like it was nothing out of the ordinary. Like we did this all the time. Like he hadn't made a colossal mistake.

"Our bed?" I whispered. "You mean *my* bed?"

He closed his laptop and met my eyes for the first time since I'd walked into the cabin. "There's one room and one bed in this cabin, Izzy. If you like, you can have the couch, but I figured you'd want a good night's sleep and it's a king size."

"Why would they put me in a cabin with you without two beds?"

"I told you. There was a mistake in the itinerary."

"Well, you can't sleep in a bed with me!" Why did I screech that? I didn't stop there either. I stomped down the hardwood hallway to peer into the one bedroom and growled toward the heavens. The bed appeared plush, soft pastels draped over fluffy pillows with a quilt that looked as smooth as butter. The headboard had solid pine posts stained dark to match the outside feel of the wilderness. "This has to be reason enough for me to call my therapist, text my family, and maybe even fall off the wagon."

"If you do that, it's not going to be on my watch," he murmured from right behind me, and I jumped, not realizing he'd followed me in.

"Oh my God. Personal space, Cade." I stepped back.

He tilted his head, assessing me like a foreign object. "You do realize my dick was so far up your pussy, I almost felt your heartbeat, right, dollface?"

"That was a one and done thing." I held up a finger.

"It was actually two times—three if you count the elevator, though." A corner of his mouth lifted as he took a step back to lean against the doorframe of the room. "I don't think personal space is needed quite as much when I know how you taste."

I grabbed my bags. "I'm staying with Rodney. Or Lucas."

He chuckled and walked up to me to snatch them away. "You're not." He pried them from my hands. "You're going to work with me, and we're going to get shit done because you put work first. Right, Ms. Hardy?"

Someone questioning my work ethic always got me. I'd swear he knew what he was doing, and it made me want to punch him. "I'm only working on JUNIPER, and then I won't be here."

"You scared to spend time alone with me?"

"I'd rather spend time with people who believe in my work ethic, Mr. Armanelli."

He scratched his chin, and before he got a chance to tell me what a shitty worker he thought I was again, I grabbed my laptop from my bag and breezed past him to the living room to go work.

Without his help, I gained access to our private Wi-Fi and dove in. Minutes or hours later, Cade sat down next to me. I felt his heat, even though he didn't say a word while he looked over my shoulder.

"It's been a couple hours, dollface. Why don't you take a nap or eat? You've got to be tired from traveling?"

"I'm proving my work ethic, Cade," I ground out.

"You can't work on these sorts of things when you're tired. You're missing some of the bigger issues." He pointed out one right in front of my face, and I slammed my laptop shut.

"Did you want me in this cabin to micromanage me?" It made sense now. He didn't want to work with me, he wanted to make sure I didn't mess anything up. He thought I wasn't competent enough to handle JUNIPER. And my gut twisted at his lack of confidence in me. "If you feel the need to do that, maybe it's better you get someone else in here to work with you."

"I don't work well with others." He shrugged.

"I don't work well with you!" I screamed. "You have no respect for me, and you don't believe I can do this. And I need—" I stopped abruptly.

To need someone's support, to ask for it, to want their approval, was never a good thing. Especially for someone like me. I could be let down. I knew that. I knew that I didn't want anyone but my family that close. I couldn't afford the risk.

"You need what, Izzy?"

"I need you to find someone else to do this with." I waved at the computer, surrendering some of the work I was most proud of because I wasn't willing to risk the person I'd become. I could stand on my own, be happy on my own, and operate well enough on my own. I didn't need anyone.

It had been that way with Gerald. I'd engaged with him, but I'd never really let him in. Maybe that was why he'd hooked up with someone else, why it didn't hurt me as badly as it should have.

"I'm only working with you." He grabbed my rose gold laptop and opened it back up. "You might miss a few things, but you're capable enough and more tolerable than most."

"Do you even hear yourself? I'm 'tolerable'? 'Capable enough'?"

It was Cade's turn to squirm under my assessment. "Can we just work rather than pass around compliments we don't mean?"

I decided he wasn't worth it and plopped back down in my seat to work in silence.

Making amends wasn't something he was good at either. Or maybe Cade simply didn't care to make amends with me, because he sat at the opposite end of the table and got to work, tapping away at his computer, sending me tasks digitally.

The very last one said *Eat some food.*

I left it unchecked, got up, and called Lucas. "Are we going in the lake today?"

He whooped and said yes.

I left Cade to his devices. We weren't friends, he wasn't social, and I didn't want to engage with him anymore that day anyway. Instead, Lucas and I looked over the itinerary and mingled beside the lake.

"We get three days of no work and all play," Lucas practically sang into the blue sky like he was in heaven.

"I'm already working. Cade wants me revamping JUNIPER for testing."

"Damn. Did you show him the itinerary? Tell him Rodney and I need some alone time with you." Lucas smirked.

"Ha-ha. Not happening. I just want to prove I can do this and that I'm good at—"

"You're good at your job, Izzy. Don't let him make you feel like you aren't. That's a slippery slope."

I nodded, but doubts crept in, like the ones I used to have about not fitting in when my brothers went off to college, like the ones that pushed me into bad habits rather than healthy ones. "I just need to stay occupied and enjoy—"

"The world that this retreat is offering." Lucas pointed to some more very sweaty, very muscular men. "I think they dropped us at a *Temptation Island* experiment or something. How did everyone on our team get so hot? I even stared at Cassie a little too long in her swimsuit today."

"You did?" I turned to study him in disbelief.

Lucas's smile was as bright as the sun setting on his blond hair. He'd put on swim trunks and abandoned his shirt to showcase his abs of steel and biceps that were strong enough to carry anyone into the lake. "Well, that's a lie, but I stared at her flirting with Rodney."

"Now *that* I believe."

He chuckled. "Anyway, tomorrow night there's a mandatory campfire where we should know everyone's name, as there will be a quiz."

"Sounds like we'd better go learn some damn names." I shrugged and Lucas pulled me along like this was his grand adventure.

We met a few at the grill. Rodney, our buff crush, made hamburgers while Melanie, a redhead who was as small as a mouse, flirted with him. Theo was quiet and scared of the lake but nice enough.

Later that night, after enjoying a few drinks and laughing with my new friends, I meandered back to my cabin with Lucas. "You don't have to walk me back to the cabin, Lucas. It's like two hundred yards from yours."

Cade, still in his navy suit and his freaking hot eyeglasses, swung open the door as we stood there, arm in arm.

He laser-focused on where our bodies linked. "Thanks for bringing her back, Lucas."

Lucas didn't say anything for a whole second as he gaped at Cade in glasses. He practically drooled before I elbowed him and he came back from being feral for our boss. He cleared his throat and pointed out, "See, I did need to bring you back. Mr. Armanelli is even thankful for it."

"I'm not going to be mauled on the few steps from one cabin to the other."

"There are bears out here." Cade shrugged and then winked at Lucas, who was smiling like they had some inside joke.

"Bullshit. There are not." I swiveled my head around, though.

"How do you know?" Cade leaned against the doorframe. "We're in their territory now."

"Actually, I think I heard one growling in the forest earlier." Lucas carried on with him.

Still, grizzlies and black bears weren't a joke. "I watched a documentary—they will rip apart a person. So this isn't funny. People have died." I stepped closer to our patio, then hesitated.

"Well, how's Lucas supposed to get back now?"

Cade outright laughed. "Security has us surrounded, Izzy. No bears are getting through. Or people, for that matter."

Did I feel ridiculous for forgetting we were *actually* a national asset working on election cybersecurity? Yes. Was I going to admit it? No.

I waved him off and shoved him aside to walk into the cabin as I yelled over my shoulder, "Love you, Lucas. See you bright and early for a swim."

Cade corrected me. "She'll see you at noon because we need to work first."

Lucas's eyes widened at me, then he mouthed, "Text me," before he spun around and hurried away.

"Great," I grumbled, "so I'm working while everyone else gets to know each other."

"You'd really rather do nothing with everyone than something epic online with me?" Cade stood there in his suit, looking at me with a completely puzzled expression.

"I would rather be with people I enjoy hanging out with and fit in with them." The pull to be a part of the group was about as strong as working hard for me. They were my driving forces as an adult, and I'd accepted them.

"Why fit in when you can stand out?" he asked. "You have more ability than any of those people out there."

"Okay." I whispered the word, not sure how to take his compliment. We threw darts at one another, not positive reinforcement. "Even if you can stand out, sometimes it feels nice to fit in, Cade. Don't you go out and enjoy being with friends every now and then?"

His life was private, but it put the spotlight on his brother and made him out to be a hero, a reformed mobster. Cade was happy to let his brother have the attention while he kept himself buried in his phone. No one knew what he did, but they opted for keeping their distance. Everyone was aware of his brain power, his genius, and how he could snuff out a life—via technology—on a whim.

"I enjoy my family. And I enjoy work. The internet is full of entertainment." He shrugged, turned on his heel, and went into the kitchen. I padded over to the island counter and ignored the buzzing of arriving texts coming from my phone. "You going to answer your phone?"

"Probably not." I shrugged. "It's either my family, Lucas, or my ex. Lilah would call if there was an emergency, and Lucas is probably just letting me know no bears got him."

He hummed. "And Gerald?" He sneered his name, somehow knowing the man didn't deserve our time.

I sighed. "Honestly, at this point, I don't check."

He pulled some milk from the fridge and got two bowls from the cabinet. "If he's bothering you . . ."

"If he is, then what? My boss will give him a call?" I snickered at my comment. "Quite frankly, he'd probably think you stole my phone and hurt me, considering you're an Armanelli."

"As an Armanelli, I don't *call* people that need to be dealt with," He grumbled. "And hurt you? Why would I ever hurt you?"

"Well, you hate me—"

"I don't hate you." His head shot up and his brow furrowed.

"Yes, you do. We've told each other numerous times—"

"You've told me you hate me. I've never said that to you." He opened the pantry door to the left of the stove and grabbed some oat cereal. "Anyway, if he's your ex, tell him to stay that way and stop texting."

He waited expectantly for me to check my phone and, because I didn't want anyone thinking I couldn't handle my own problems, I snatched it up and scrolled to Gerald's messages.

My brow furrowed at what they said. In between all the begging and pleading for him to take me back were questions about his father's company.

> **Gerald:** Izzy, I really need to talk. Things aren't going great with the company.
>
> **Gerald:** I need your support. Investors have been turning down offers left and right, saying our software within the company isn't up to par
>
> **Gerald:** Did you do something?

I scoffed at the notion that he would think I would do anything to him. I was moving on and would never sacrifice my integrity for him.

"Something wrong?" Cade asked as he poured a helping into each bowl.

"It's nothing. Gerald just being ridiculous." I mumbled as I texted him back that he needed to leave me alone. When Cade pushed the cereal my way, I shook my head. "I'm not hungry. I don't eat past eight, anyway. My metabo—"

"Eat the food, Izzy." He placed a spoon next to the bowl and carried his back to the table where his laptop was.

"If you think we're going to live in this place for two weeks with you bossing me around, you're sorely mistaken."

He sighed as he sat down in that three-piece suit to continue working. "I'm sustaining your life because I know you didn't eat outside."

"How would you know that?"

"Aside from the fact I could look out the window? You never eat when you're working or socializing. You didn't eat all last week in the office. Except for candy canes."

"Well, I like candy canes."

"Why? It's not Christmastime."

I guess he wanted to keep talking while he worked. It was an interesting change, even if talking to him while his head was in a laptop sort of felt detached.

I sat down in front of him and took a bite of the cereal because I couldn't ignore my stomach growling. "I started that habit with Lucas. It helps keep our minds from wandering to other habits we used to indulge in."

He did that humming thing again and pushed his glasses up the bridge of his nose as he ate. His brow furrowed, and his earthy brown eyes scanned the screen. When he mumbled out a curse, I couldn't help but ask, "Anything I can help with?"

"No," he answered immediately, but I left my bowl of cereal to round the table, wanting a look at what he was working on.

Just a week ago, Cade would have shifted to block the view of his screen, but now he didn't. He may have said there was nothing I could help with, but he didn't mind me being there. It spoke volumes about the sort of business partnership we were building. I wouldn't venture so far as to say we were friends, or even friendly, but I liked to think his trust in my work skills might have grown slightly.

"Let me see if I can break in. I'm here to test it, right?"

He was eyeing up the Chicago PD security infrastructure, comparing it with codes that had hacked systems in the past. I'd done the research, though, and knew JUNIPER was up to par. Still, I wanted a crack from the other side.

He sighed and didn't move. "You won't be able to do it if I can't, Izzy."

I let him have another scoop of cereal and studied his full head of hair. The back of his profile was almost as good as the front. Full, thick strands just long enough to grab and dig fingers into.

My mind started to wander to other things . . . like had other girls grabbed that hair since me? Did he want me to go to bed so he could call someone else? Did he think of me sometimes like I thought of him?

"Maybe I deserve at least a chance."

"You think you can do this when I can't?" He shoved away from the table, leaving enough space for me to walk between him and where the laptop was located. "Come over here, then." He pointed to his lap. "Sit right here and do it."

He wanted me to cower, to bend to his intimidation. I didn't hesitate, though I knew having him this close would ruin my concentration. I started to think I wasn't ever going to be able to back down from this man, and I also believed he enjoyed challenging me.

This was about to create chaos that I might not be able to overcome. Cade always wanted the upper hand, and instead of allowing me to work while he stared over my shoulder, the man pulled himself back toward the table, sandwiching me between.

My skirt bunched high on my thighs as I gasped. "Cade, what

are you doing?"

His breath was at my neck as he murmured into my ear, "Watching how fast you're able to work while distracted."

He didn't waste a second, pulling up a timer on the computer screen and setting it to five minutes.

I tried to protest by grumbling, "This is stupid—"

But I was cut off by him hitting start on the screen, and my drive for wanting to do it faster and better than him kicked in. I couldn't bear to be worse than he was or to prove him right.

I read through the coding, trying to find patterns as his fingers went to the base of my neck. He swiped away my hair and then inhaled me.

"You're corrupting me, dollface. I tried to avoid you for days, and then I switched accommodations because I saw you look at another man. And I don't know if I can concentrate with the smell of you in every corner of this cabin."

I felt the air being sucked in by him, felt his hand sliding around to the front of my throat, and then his fingers wrapped around my neck. I shifted on him as his cock grew against my ass.

"You wearing panties under that skirt?"

"Shut up," I ground out as I tried to maintain my focus.

But he squeezed my windpipe as his dick twitched. My body didn't belong to me when I was this close to him, and my legs parted a bit as I arched, wanting to feel him, rewarding his ridiculous efforts to distract me.

He hummed as if he approved of my body shifting on him and then whispered, "No, baby. I'm shutting you up." He cut off all my oxygen as his other hand flowed over the curves of my body, taking time to trace the underside of my breasts and then skim over my stomach before kneading one thigh. "You keep pushing like you want me to break you. Don't you know I make the world squirm for a living, that I *enjoy* it?"

His dark confession heated my skin, making me wetter. I rolled into him and dropped my head back onto his shoulder to give him better access to choke me out, to nip at my neck, to consume me.

He lightened his hold. "Breathe, Izzy."

I gasped for the air he gave me and let him push my panties to the side. The codes all blurred together, but I wanted into the system about as much as I wanted that orgasm.

The seconds ticked by. His fingers picked up speed, and I was about to surrender when it all came together, when the numbers finally stood out, and I bypassed what we hoped no one could.

"Fuck," we both said at the same time, though for different reasons.

I gave into the orgasm, and it blinded me, my pussy clenching around him like I needed him there for eternity. He probably swore because I'd decoded and broken into what he couldn't.

He continued the slew of curses and then mumbled, "You're better than I thought. You're better than anyone, Izzy, and that's a damn problem."

I shook my head as I leaned back into him and let his suited arms encircle my waist. It was a firm reminder that I was the mess while he was all buttoned up—still not the least bit unraveled. "This can't keep happening. I don't even like you, and it's a risk to my job. I've worked to prove I belong on this team."

He licked at my neck and murmured, "No one's said you haven't."

"But if they think I'm screwing you, then they'll question it, and I won't be a part of—"

"The team," he sighed, like he finally understood me, or at least knew what my anxieties were, because he then asked, "Did you always want to be a part of something?"

"I grew up in a household full of kids. I was the youngest. I needed them to see me, even if it . . ." I'd never meant to blurt that out to him. Maybe it was the moment or the fact that I'd done something that he couldn't, and I felt like I finally had enough of his respect to share something personal.

"Your family would see you either way. Everyone sees you, even when you're not paying attention."

I sat up and glanced back at him. "What do you mean?"

Cade's eyes were melted chocolate, and his look suddenly felt approachable. Maybe in another world, it would have been. I swear we could have been friends had we met at a different time, in another life.

Here, we couldn't.

Unzipping my suit trousers and fucking my employee in the middle of a work retreat would have been easier than what I was doing with Izzy.

I was giving her a reason to trust me, a reason to like me, and a reason to go down a rabbit hole with me that she couldn't come back from.

It was selfish. I always had a target on my back. I was in the mob even if I was a 'businessman,' and I was no good at any sort of relationship. I didn't enjoy making people feel wanted or important. I enjoyed dismantling them. Consuming all the information about them and then holding the power of their lives in my hands. To see them squirm was a victory for me and my family every time.

So I didn't know why my damn heart beat faster with her in the room and why I wanted to hear everything about her life now. Sure, she was the hottest fuck I'd had in a long time but pushing her past the facade she put up for everyone was becoming something I couldn't stop myself from doing. It was also unavoidable with her sitting on my dick looking at me with those big hazel eyes that held flecks of gold, like she'd captured the sun and dimmed its shine just enough for us to be able to study them.

"I can't look away from you, haven't been able to since the moment I met you."

"Ha-ha." She took my confession as a joke, but I wasn't kidding. "Is that why you moved me to Stonewood Enterprises?" She pursed her lips and rearranged her clothing before scooting off my lap to sit on the table.

"I moved your ass because you were poking around in top secret, confidential records."

"Well, that worked out well. Still breaking into systems, just different ones." She combed a hand through her silky hair.

"That and kissing your boss now, huh?" I looked at her lips and knew I wanted another taste of them as she licked them.

"Don't be an ass." She moved to get up, but I didn't let her. I took her face in my hands and brought her mouth down onto mine. I tasted her, ravaged her, devoured her exactly the way I wanted to. She somehow always tasted sweet, but with a hint of candy canes. Her lush lips moved skillfully with mine as the kiss grew more and more heated, and then she moaned before ripping herself away.

I let her go, my mind swirling with confusion. She wasn't something I could decode, but the way I would rather focus on her than my work was unheard of for me.

She hopped off the table and hurriedly grabbed her glass of water, then paced out of the room and re-entered two minutes later in a big T-shirt that had *As if* written across it with the blonde *Clueless* girl.

She didn't stop moving back and forth in front of me, never taking a sip of the water still in her hand as she raced through her own thoughts. "Don't come near me again on this retreat. We work and then we go our separate ways. This cannot happen."

I stretched before getting up and chuckled, taking a step toward her.

Holding the water between us, she took a quick step back. "I'm not kidding, Cade. This is a bad idea. You know it is. What if we get caught? Then what? We tell the president, 'It's fine, we got your election all set. No one is going to hack the voting systems, even though we were fucking behind closed doors instead of working on it.'" She winced like it killed her to say it. "That sounds so unprofessional."

"You're that nervous about being unprofessional?"

"Coming from the guy standing in front of me in a suit while I'm in pajamas. It's a perfect display of who will get blamed if we don't keep this together."

I shrugged. "I'd take the blame."

"Even if you did, my reputation would be ruined, Cade. And it's already so tarnished, I can't withstand another stain."

She was so hard on herself. "You realize you've gotten over your drug addiction, right? You fought and you won, and people respect you for that." Maybe I'd never told her so, but she had to know from everyone else she surrounded herself with that people thought she was badass.

She'd walked into our office, and her peers had leaned in to be a part of her conversation; she spoke, and they listened.

"No. Nobody respects that. They're scared I'll veer in the wrong direction again." She sighed and turned to the sink. "And if I misstep at all, it will point to me going right down that path again."

"You can take a misstep without going down that path, dollface.

You can have a bad day."

"No. *You* can." She rinsed out her dish, then pointed at me. "You can, and everyone else around here can. Me, Lucas, people who've struggled with addiction and our reputations, we *can't*. We have to set an example and show everyone we have it together. Always. Do you know how tiring that is?" Her shoulders slumped and it was a reminder to me how small she was, how big her personality could be to hide her vulnerability. She sounded exhausted, like she needed a break but knew she'd never get one.

"I can imagine." I answered honestly.

"How can you? You've been—"

"My father was in the mob, I'm a product of the mob. And I have access to causing world destruction because I'm good at my job. People will always think I'm one step away from snapping." I rubbed a hand over my face.

"Does it bother you?" she asked quietly.

"Not much. I know my place. We all have our crosses to bear, right?"

She took a deep breath. "Yep, and mine is okay. It's fair. My family cares about me and loves me. So does this team. I just need to continually prove myself. I can't slide one toe off that straight and narrow line, Cade, or they'll all think I've lost it."

"And I'm 'off that line' for you?"

"You're the damn circle on the other side of the room, Cade!" She slammed her hand down on the island countertop, and her confession—the way her eyes blazed, the way she thought avoiding me would keep her sane—had me doing what I did best.

"You've been over on that side, jumping in and out of my circle, for a long time, Izzy. Problem is, you don't see that you can indulge without going back to using. You can be you without that. Who you are isn't a bad thing."

"You don't know what you're talking about. I am me, and I don't want to indulge in you." She shook her head at me, tears suddenly in her eyes.

"You can hide it and avoid it, but there's no real use fighting it."

"I'm not avoiding anything. I just like it over here on my side." She said it loud, as if to make us both believe it.

I put my hands on the counter, facing her, and leaned in. "Yeah, well, I'm here waiting on the other side when you want to put your pussy where it belongs—on me."

I saw the blush rise over her neck, saw how her breathing picked up, how her lips parted. It was how I knew Izzy needed the adrenaline, the close calls, the risk in her life, just like I did. She would never be able to put herself in a two-story box with a white picket fence and live a normal life.

She just needed to figure that out for herself. And as her hand fisted, I knew it wouldn't be tonight.

"Did you hear a word I said? I'm one of your best employees, and that's all I'm going to be from now on. We're not sleeping with each other while we're working on national security. It's irresponsible."

"That right? Even if you're in a cabin with Rodney?" I shouldn't have said it. I should have left it alone, but I'd watched her eye him up and I'd seen red.

"Yeah and about Rodney. You can't go around changing accommodations, Cade. That's so unprofessional."

I didn't deny it.

She pulled at her hair and growled. "The fact that you moved me to this cabin just because of Rodney is ridiculous, Cade. You realize that?"

"I do need you here to work. It's easier that way. And now you won't have to deal with Rodney either."

"*Deal with Rodney? Deal* with him?" Her voice got higher and higher. "What if I *wanted* to deal with him?"

"You just said we shouldn't be fucking around."

"Yeah, me and you. You're my boss. Rodney isn't even on our team!" She started to storm off to the bedroom, but then she came back to point her finger in my face. "You don't get to dictate my accommodations and manage my personal life."

"Well, actually I do." I was just stating a fact.

Her eyes widened like she couldn't believe I'd double down on that. Clearly, she didn't understand that I'd go round and round with her all day. That I loved seeing how her hair got messier and messier as she combed her hands through it, how her clothes became more rumpled, and how she raised her voice after working so hard all day to speak softly.

"You're an entitled dick, you know that? I don't care if you're in the mob, and I don't care if you're my boss. I'm getting through this election, then I'm going over your head to Jett to get a different position. This"—she motioned between us—"toxic back-and-forth is over."

"If you say so," I murmured just to rile her further.

Izzy Hardy didn't disappoint. When she got pissed, I practically saw steam come out of her ears. She stomped back to the bedroom. I wasn't stupid enough to think that we'd ever be more than fuck buddies, but I'd at least teach her that she didn't have to worry about other people's expectations of her. It was probably hindering her life in some way; she'd thank me later.

Or so I thought.

Until I heard a rattle and then a hiss that sounded a lot like spray paint. And there she was.

Izzy fucking Hardy. Not disappointing for a second as she sprayed a big-ass red line along the center of our room, up the bed, over the comforter, across the middle of the frame, ending on the wall as high as she could reach.

Whipping her head my way, she had a smile that was genuine on her face, and her eyes shined a more vivid green and gold than I'd ever seen, sparkling with so much life that I knew this was the phoenix in her—the version of her I wanted to see always. She looked like she did when I took her breath away, like she was dancing with death, and it turned her on more than bumbling around aimlessly living.

"You're going to stay on that side, and I'm on this side, Cade. Want to know why? Because I *do* say so." She lifted her chin in triumph.

A normal person would have called the event coordinator and sent her insubordinate ass home. I chuckled, though, and leaned on the doorframe, putting my hands in my pockets. "Maybe you should put my name above the headboard so we're clear. I don't think the big-ass red line is enough."

She stomped over to my side and painted *Entitled Dick*.

Then she grabbed her bag and went to the spare bathroom in the living room, most likely because the en suite bathroom was on my side.

I let her fume for the rest of the night, went back to my computer, and got to work on the code she'd used to break through JUNIPER.

A few hours in, the silence of the wilderness closed in on me. My mind wandered to her. I was losing my edge, and I wasn't sure I wanted it back.

While she slept soundly, I rummaged through her luggage and found her spray paint. I put *Dollface* above her head. She woke on the last letter and squinted up at me, leaning on her side to do it. Then she smiled like I'd made her whole life, like this was normal behavior.

No words were spoken between us. She rolled over under the comforter on her side of the damn red line and snuggled in.

I stared at her for far too long before I growled and went into the bathroom to get ready for bed. If I was going to indulge the red line down the bed and across the room, I was happy that the bathroom was on my side. I knew I'd be jacking off to her more than once on this retreat. My dumbass split-second decision to have her stay with me was already backfiring. Indulging the jealousy that coiled through me at seeing her with someone else should have been an indicator to back off.

I turned out the lights as I entered the room and pulled the blankets up over her shoulder, staring at how her dark hair fanned out across the light pillow, how her lips parted with a breath, how her small neck was so delicate that I could steal her life in a second and make sure she enjoyed the feeling the whole damn time. And I fucking wanted to do the latter instead of the former more often than not now.

I swore before rolling over to my side.

The red line wasn't going to last, but I'd give her tonight. She wouldn't get much more than that.

CHAPTER 12

Izzy

O f course I'd gone to bed before Cade. He'd disappeared into the living room as if he wasn't at all perturbed by my spray paint outburst.

Damn, that was going to cost me some money. I knew I'd need to comp them for that, but it felt good to let go, to make it known that I wasn't here to take anyone's crap, that I could toss it right back at him.

I'd felt like me for a moment, acting out and embracing the spark that flared to life. Well into the night, though, I'd woken to see him smiling as he spray-painted *Dollface* over my headboard too.

Something was wrong with us.

We definitely had issues, but when I cracked my eyes open the next morning to sheets rumpled on his side and no Cade in bed, I chuckled to myself. He'd actually slept on his side of the line, he'd indulged me when he didn't need to.

I stretched and grabbed my makeup bag to go shower. I didn't bother with avoiding the painted barrier now. It was the principle of the matter, quite frankly. So I took my time brushing my teeth in the en suite bathroom and stared at myself in the mirror. I ran my finger across the bite marks on my neck.

I hadn't realized how rough we'd been the night before when he got me off at the table. My nipples tightened as I stripped off my T-shirt and underwear to get into the shower. My skin reddened with the thoughts of last night.

No man but Cade could irk me so much *and* turn me on at the same time. He pushed me so close to the brink of my emotions that I wasn't sure how I'd survive keeping a lid on them throughout the rest of this retreat.

I turned on the water and let the water droplets run over my head until they were so hot, they nearly scalded my skin. I needed the heat, the pressure, and the privacy now. I needed to get the vision of Cade working my pussy, biting my neck, and sliding his hands over my body out of my head.

My fingers dove into my folds, and I moaned softly at how wet I already was. I needed the release to focus. The water heated my skin, dampening it along with the sweat as I worked myself up.

I imagined his cock, how hard it got when he stared at me, how the metal would rub against my most sensitive spot exactly the way I wanted, how he knew I wanted him to take control, to steal my breath so long I'd almost panic.

I rolled a finger over my clit, and it was right then that the shower curtain flew open. I jerked my hand away from my center and gasped, "Cade!"

"Don't stop on account of me. No reason to when you were imagining me fucking you anyway."

"I'm in the shower, you asshole!" I tried to jerk the curtain away from him, but he didn't let it go. So I stood back and crossed my arms over my breasts, standing tall. Gerald might have said I needed to lose weight, but I knew Cade enjoyed how I looked, and I did too. I wasn't ashamed of my body.

"You're in the shower on my side, right?" he pointed out.

"Are you kidding me right now?"

"Nope. You started this game."

"Whatever. So what? I'm on your side." I shrugged.

"New rule—when you're on my side, you do what *I* want." He held my gaze, and that look told me he wasn't going to let me leave.

"And if I don't?" I left one arm over my breasts and cocked a hip to prop up my other hand.

"You know I enjoy punishing you, Izzy. I have no problem doing that now. I think this retreat will serve a couple new purposes."

"Like what?"

"Like teaching you who's in charge. Maybe a way for us to get each other out of our systems too." His tone lowered, his eyes darkened, his demeanor changed. Cade wanted me to rebel, and my pussy responded. I could feel how much I wanted to be a brat and not listen.

"Get real," I whispered, challenging him. He was right, though. I needed him out of my system. My response was breathless, excited, and a little too eager.

He stepped back with one side of his full lips rising up. That smirk told me the cat was out to play and he wanted me to be his mouse. "Go ahead then, dollface. Try to leave."

I glanced at the doorway, knowing I could try to make a run for it, but I'd have to move past him. Cade was an immovable tower—a

suited-up, dark-haired, very good-looking, very muscular tower—
that I eyed up and down.

Him and his stupid three-piece suit was starting to get
infuriating even if I saw the outline of his hard cock. I wanted to
see the skin underneath as I stood there naked with water droplets
rolling down my body. And the only way to get it was to push him
like he pushed me. "You wouldn't know how to punish me the right
way if you tried."

I turned the water off and stepped out of the shower. He
didn't move a muscle other than the one in his jaw, which ticked
rhythmically.

Maybe I'd read him wrong. Maybe he would let me walk right
by him and he didn't really care.

But as I took one more step toward the door, his hand slammed
down on the frame. "You came to my side to play, didn't you?" he
asked quietly. His eyes focused on only my center then. "Face the
mirror and play with that pussy. Matter of fact, let me help you."

He grabbed my hair and turned me roughly toward our
reflection, standing behind me and forcing me to bend at the waist.
I caught myself on the counter, but he shoved me down farther until
my ass was out for him to grind his cock against. I couldn't stop
myself from moaning.

He tsked over and over as he rolled his suited cock against
my pussy, and I arched my back trying to create more friction by
moving my hips with him. "You're going to ruin my suit, baby.
That pussy of yours can't even handle my cock this close to it. It's
weeping for me, crying for its owner to come home."

"Funny. I was pretty wet before you got here," I said just to piss
him off.

He chuckled, but when he pulled his cock away, I whimpered, not ready to be done with it. Using my hair, he turned me to face him and grabbed my hip with his other hand, scooting me onto the counter. "Why don't you spread your legs and show me how well you play with yourself, then?"

He let go of me, took a step back, and stared expectantly. My hand crept toward my center, skimming my wet thigh and letting the air between us cool me. His eyes raked over my body, though, and it heated me up instead, like he was holding a fire to my skin. My hair clung to my chest, my breathing made my breasts rise and fall quickly, and I knew that, to him, I probably looked wild, wanton, and ready to burst with an orgasm.

I hovered over my pussy, but instead of going right for that, I rolled a finger over my clit and moaned, holding eye contact.

He swore fluently and unbuckled his trousers. My core immediately clenched as his strong hand dove into them to pull out his long cock. He pumped it as I rolled my clit between my fingers. He matched my rhythm with me like he did when I was tapping my stiletto, as if he wanted to be in sync with me and could feel my movement before I even made it.

"Slide a finger in, Izzy. Show me how well you listen to your boss when he gives you a command."

My whole body shuddered in pleasure when he used his position of power on me. "You're not my boss here, Cade." I got off on the fact that I could defy him, that he wanted me to rebel as much as I wanted to.

He took a step closer, pumping his dick a bit harder as he rolled a thumb over that piercing. I practically salivated for him. I wanted my mouth, my pussy, and my body wrapped around him.

"I'm the boss of you everywhere. Especially here. You're on my side, Izzy. You do as I say or . . ." He waited for me to finish his sentence.

"You'll punish me?" I asked, my eyes almost rolling back at having him this close while I worked my clit faster and faster, my nipples tightening as I approached an orgasm that would probably knock me right off the counter I sat on.

His hand shot from his cock to my wrist and yanked my hand away from my clit just as I was about to hit my high. He pulled me forward so fast, I wobbled off the counter, but he used my momentum to turn me to the mirror again, shoving me in the back so that my stomach was against the counter and my ass was at his mercy.

He didn't waste time, smacking my ass hard—so hard I cried out— and I arched my back for more as my cry turned into a moan. He took his cock and wet the tip in my arousal. Then he ran a thumb over it like he wanted us mixed together on his hand before he placed that thumb between my ass cheeks right on my other hole. "I should take your ass for a ride right now for the way you talk to me."

I gasped as he flirted with my only virgin hole, teasing it and working it so much that I forgot about the sting of my ass cheek as I started to pant and beg him. "I want to feel it. I want to feel you."

He laughed like I was ridiculous, pulled the belt from his trousers as he bent down close to my ear and said, "Next time, if you listen, maybe I'll indulge you."

Instead, he folded the belt and whipped my ass. Once, twice, three times.

He stepped back to do it. Like he wanted to see his work.

Like the tears in my eyes and the red on my skin was his freaking masterpiece.

He put the folded area of the belt at my clit, the leather teasing the sensitive spot, and grabbed a fistful of my hair. "Move your hips, baby. Ride my belt like a good girl."

Some would have been embarrassed, but I felt his cock against me, saw the hunger in his eyes, and more importantly, I felt the urge to get off so deep in my bones, I didn't care.

I rolled my hips and arched my spine, taking what was mine. The orgasm was the whole reason I'd come to the bathroom, and I snatched it by letting him work that belt against me. Embracing the wave of euphoria felt like toppling into a dream. And he moved the leather just right for me to revel in it too.

"Your pussy is so wet, Izzy, it's dripping down your thigh." He admired his handiwork as I gasped for breath and came back to reality.

A part of me would always see Cade as the man I wanted to overcome, as he stood over me with my hair wrapped in his fist like he had complete control. Maybe it was my personality, my way of maintaining my control, but I pushed him like I knew I could. "Guess your punishment wasn't good enough. I'm not feeling much pain, just pleasure."

His gaze cut to mine, and he must have picked up on how I wanted to undermine his power. The world was afraid of him, but I wasn't. I don't know if that bothered him or aroused him, but he didn't hesitate to give me another lashing to show me who held the cards.

I endured it. I practically embraced it as my body started to quiver from the pain and the pleasure with each whip. He'd done it twice and hesitated on his third, hand pulled back, ready, but suddenly, he murmured, "Jesus, we need to stop. Why don't you tell me to stop?"

"Do we, though?" I couldn't hold my tongue, couldn't stop myself from wanting more.

"We need a safe word, and you actually need to use it if it becomes too much." He shook his head.

"It's just *stop*." I shrugged. "And I don't need it with you." But I think we both knew I should have used it, that I was focusing on the pleasure and not the pain.

"You'd push me and yourself past the point of breaking, baby doll." He heaved a sigh as he stepped closer to rub the redness on my ass cheek, holding my gaze in the mirror like he wanted me to understand something. "You're a menace to our sanity, and I can't fucking deny you. I'm obsessed with how you resist me and then square up to me. We have to know when to stop."

I was braced on my elbows, watching him watch me in that mirror. His hands kneaded me like I was suddenly a treasure he couldn't quite figure out but knew was valuable all the same. "I don't want to stop, Cade."

He hummed, not saying whether he agreed with me or not. Then he kneeled behind me and lowered his head. Cade wasn't going to give me his cock, and I swear it was like he was saving it. Instead, his tongue licked my thigh softly. He took his time bringing his lips to it and tasting what must have been my arousal there as he murmured, "So sweet. So damn sweet. I'm going to dream about this pussy forever."

It didn't matter what he was saying to me at that point. My elbows gave out, and my chest fell to the granite as his mouth crept up to my center. He worked his thumb over my clit before he spread my folds wide enough for his tongue to dive in.

He licked me, devoured me, then slowed down like he wanted me to last, like he thought I could, like his mouth wasn't a damn expert at what it was doing. I was already so far gone after him reddening my ass that I probably would have come on his tongue quickly either way.

The orgasm that had been building in me sliced through my soul, cutting open my heart and putting Cade right at the center of it. I screamed his name, whimpered it, moaned it, and then whispered it.

I knew tears ran down my face as he milked every last drop of my climax from me.

Then he stood over me, and just when I thought we were done, the head of his cock nudged a little into my opening. "Cade, oh my God, I don't know if I can."

My body practically shook from exhaustion as he smiled at me. "One more, baby doll. I'm taking one more from you, and then you can leave my side of the red line, huh?"

He thrust into me like he belonged there, and he squeezed my thighs and brought my ass in close like he needed to be surrounded by me. I gasped as I watched him fuck me with that damn suit on.

He lost control under it, his neck flexing, his chest heaving, and his dark eyes watching me in that mirror. "Don't come to my side unless you can handle me fucking you sore, Izzy. Don't come near me unless you're ready for me to wreck you, because it's all I want. All I dreamed about."

His words, that piercing against my inner walls, the way he clung to me, digging those calloused fingers in so hard there would be bruises, pushed me toward my third climax.

I begged for him to go faster, to fuck me harder.

Caden Armanelli didn't disappoint.

CHAPTER 13

Izzy

C ade put me in the lukewarm shower with him afterwards. He practically had to carry me because I honestly felt like my legs might give out. His hands were suddenly gentle, his touch light as a feather, as he washed me off and then told me to go lie on my side of the bed.

"My side, really?"

"If you don't, I'll fuck you again so hard you truly won't be able to walk. I'm sparing you. Do as you're told."

I'd seen this coming. I enjoyed hearing him tell me what to do, I enjoyed pushing his buttons, and I enjoyed the consequences of my actions. I felt more alive than I had in a long time, like I could be myself with him the way I couldn't with anyone else.

I slipped on a green bikini and short flowy skirt before he came out of the bathroom, buttoned up in his suit again.

He eyed my outfit but didn't say a word about it. "Lie down on your stomach."

I probably needed a nap, so I listened. He grabbed a tube of aloe vera and pointed to my butt. "It'll soothe your skin."

I shrugged. "I'll be fine."

"Sure you will," he said softly, but he had already lifted my skirt and pushed my bikini aside to rub the cool substance over one cheek. Thankfully, I could tell that the bottoms would cover most of the red marks as I stared over my shoulder at his tenderness. When he pulled the waist of my skirt to the side to see where his fingerprints were already bruising certain areas, he tsked. "Should have been gentler."

His demeanor was such a juxtaposition to what I was used to from him. We were supposed to be enemies. We were at each other's throats usually. And then he rubbed aloe vera on me like I meant something to him, like he didn't only want to fuck me into oblivion and leave it at that. It got me wondering if he was like this with everyone. If he fucked all the women he was with this way.

As he put my swimsuit back in place, I sat up and blurted out the question. "Do you always carry around all the tools needed for a good ass reddening?"

"That your way of asking if I'm sleeping around?" He lifted a brow.

I narrowed my eyes at him even as my heart clenched at the idea. "Of course not. I don't care who you sleep with. We're just getting each other out of our systems, right?" I threw his initial reason for hooking up with me in the bathroom back in his face.

I only did it to have him correct me, though, because when I imagined Penelope and Cassie eyeing him up, I saw red.

"That's good. Because I packed this aloe vera for anyone who'd bend over for me. Not specifically for you." I swear he said it to get a rise out of me, and when I wrinkled my nose at him in disgust to cover my hurt, he full-on laughed. "Go have fun out there. Supposedly, we have to know everyone's names for the damn campfire tonight. Come back for lunch."

"Or I'll come back to sleep, and you can eat lunch with whoever will bend over for you." I stomped to my purse, grabbed lip gloss and a towel, and left him. I swayed my hips a little more than usual, hoping he was watching me the whole way.

When I heard him growl out a curse and mutter, "That outfit is a damn joke. Barely covers your ass," I smirked to myself and flipped him off before turning the corner to get the hell out of that cabin.

The sun on my skin and the sparkle of the lake brought me back to the real world. I texted my sister on the way to Lucas's cabin to check in on Bug. She was driving in every now and then to check on my cat, while my apartment building staff fed him twice a day.

Me: Bug still alive?

Lilah: The cat still lives.

Dom: Why the hell are we group chatting about this?

Declan: They wanted to make us feel bad that we didn't offer to take care of her pet even though we live across the country.

Lilah: Well maybe you should all live closer.

Declan: Yeah, my job would allow for that.

Me: Doesn't the NFL only last a season.

Declan: I'm kicking your ass when I see you, Izzy.

Me: I'd love to see you try.

Lilah: Does that mean everyone's coming home soon?

Dimitri: I'm never coming home. Mom's putting something in the water back there. I don't want to be the next one giving her grandkids.

 Lilah: Come on. My baby does need cousins.

Me: Oh no. She got to Lilah too. We might need to kick her out of the group chat.

Dom: I've sworn off women for this very reason. Izzy, you're the only one I'm talking to from now on.

Lilah: Oh please. Izzy's about to go down the same rabbit hole as me anyway.

Declan: What's that supposed to mean?

Dom: Is she dating someone?

Dimitri: She'd better not be fucking around with someone dangerous like you were, Lilah. Izzy, are you being careful?

Each of my siblings, but especially my brothers, were so damn overprotective I couldn't fathom telling them that their baby sister was screwing around with her boss, a mobster.

Especially not after Lilah married an Armanelli and they punched Dante square in the face.

Me: Lilah, look what you started. For NOTHING. I'm on a work retreat. Leave me alone, Hardy boys. Your baby sister is fine.

Declan called me as I trekked up Lucas's porch stairs. His deep voice cut me off before I could even say hello. "You're not doing something dumb, are you?"

"Well, hi, asshat. Nice of you to call and see how I'm doing."

"I'm in the middle of my workout, and Lilah is dropping silent clues like I don't pick up on that shit."

Of course Dom called right then. I rolled my eyes. "Now Dom's calling. Literally nothing is happening. She's just taking the heat off herself. You guys are so overprotective. Please stop."

He sighed like he didn't want to worry about me, but he did.

All of them did. Because I'd made them worry too much before. "So you're good?" he asked, and my heart squeezed. Declan was the closest to me in age other than Lilah. And he would have got on a plane immediately if he thought something was wrong.

"I'm fine, Dec. Go back to your workout. Tell the fam you talked to me, too, so they don't all keep calling."

He agreed that he would, and I heard some texts go through as I hung up.

Lucas was at his door, smiling like he hadn't seen me in ages. "No bears ate you!" he exclaimed.

I punched him in the arm, and he pulled me under his shoulder. "I'm not working at all today. Cade told me he'd see me at the campfire, so I say we take today to have some fun."

"Our itinerary literally says to do so and there's food and drinks all day."

I scoffed at how easygoing it seemed. "I'm surprised this isn't more by the book."

"I think Mrs. Stonewood is in charge of these events, and she believes people work best with a team they trust, positive reinforcement, and low stress levels. I've talked with her a few times because I host the mindfulness group."

"She sounds like she has the right idea." I shrugged as we meandered over to my original cabin and Rodney waved us in. We met with his bunkmates, Melanie and Lorenzo. We all sipped the coffee Rodney made, and he told us he was excited for the rest of the day.

We went swimming and paddleboarding, met more of the team, and enjoyed what felt like a vacation. There were sixteen of us, so we could hang with some in the cabin if we didn't want to swim, grill with others if we didn't want to sunbathe, or catch up with old friends if we didn't want to engage with new ones.

Cade texted once to tell me to come eat, and I rolled my eyes because it was probably a reminder that I hadn't gone to have lunch with him. Was he watching me out here with everyone? Was he at all interested in coming out to be part of the fun?

Lucas caught me staring at our cabin while we sat in the sand, munching on a few leftovers from the grill. He nudged me. "How's living with the infamous Cade?"

What did I say to that? "He's definitely different from what I thought he would be."

"I want more than that and you know it." Lucas nodded as a few people passed us and waved.

"I don't know. He works a lot, obviously. He's mostly on his computer. But he eats cereal, which . . . I didn't exactly expect."

"You know, when he's with his brother and Dante, they seem different," Lucas muttered, pulling up pictures on his phone. That was the life Cade lived. He'd be photographed with his family because they were the Armanellis, but when he was alone, people let him be.

I shrugged as I looked at a picture of him laughing with a little girl, security surrounding them. The headline read, "Rare Spotting: Billionaire Tech Mogul and Alleged Mobster Caden Armanelli Enjoys Day with His Niece, Ivy, Heiress to the Bratva."

"So, he loves his infamous family," I murmured, but the words and the picture stirred something in me. Something a lot like insecurity started as a tiny snowball and rolled down the hill, growing and growing in size. He had this big life, this family that he never talked about but obviously enjoyed, and I wanted to know more about it. More about him.

The feeling scared me. We were supposed to just be having fun.

"Right? He looks so damn human here other than the men in suits around him. Seeing him every day, the concepts of tech billionaire and mobster fit, but he's not as happy as this picture shows. Unless he's with his niece, maybe."

To most of the world, though, he wasn't human. He was like a mutant that could hack into all their data, and everyone feared him for that.

"I wonder if it's hard for him to know everyone's secrets and be normal?" I pondered out loud, thinking of the conversation I'd had with him in the cabin. We all had our crosses to bear.

"Maybe if we get him to participate in some of the trust exercises later this week, we can ask him." Lucas chuckled, like the idea was ludicrous.

Quite frankly, it was. Seeing that picture of him had reminded me how out of my depth I was with him. I was fooling around with a mobster, a billionaire, and a man who could cause destruction to just about anyone he wanted.

Instead of going back to my cabin, I avoided him. I avoided the situation. I reminded myself that indulging in my stupid desires was what had gotten me into trouble in the first place years ago.

I wouldn't do that again.

I was here to showcase my work on JUNIPER, to teach people

how effective we could be as a team. This was what the retreat was supposed to be about—getting to know one another so we could trust each other when the time came to learn JUNIPER, to implement it, and to be the best team we could be, for the good of the country.

Rodney came to hang out with us just as the sun set. Right before the bonfire, I told Lucas I had to go back to my cabin to change.

"Change for what? We love you in your bikini top and skirt," Rodney joked, his innocent flirting a welcome distraction in the latter part of the day. Not that he was the only one, I'd seen a few people doing the same today. We were all having a good time.

It was probably not the smartest professional move, but again, everyone had come from different states to learn about JUNIPER to prepare for the election. We weren't going to see each other again, so there was really no HR protocol, and with most everyone being single, except for one or two people, hookups were bound to happen.

I was single, aside from my very hot boss whom I was sharing a cabin and a bed with, even though I'd never wanted to. The boss whose hands I thought about every chance I got. The boss who was a billionaire tech mogul that I needed to stay away from.

I was single, I repeated to myself as I smiled at Rodney. Very single. "I'll get bit by mosquitos and be freezing if I wear this all night."

Rodney chuckled, yanked his hoodie over his head, and pushed it over mine. The warmth of it wrapped around me fast as he pulled my arms through and stood back to look at me in his clothes. "There. You're all set now."

I rolled my eyes but smiled at his wink, while Lucas whistled. "Rodney knows a good-looking woman dressed nice when he sees one."

We made our way to the campfire and found Adirondack chairs to lounge in. I silenced my phone, knowing this was going to be more of an intimate setting, and ignored the numerous texts I had from Gerald, my family, and even Cade.

I couldn't avoid glancing over at his cabin, though. It glowed bright even as the horizon dimmed behind it. He hadn't come out to socialize all day, and it was a good reminder that he wasn't one of us. I probably wouldn't see him all night until I went back to our cabin.

The bubbly blonde event coordinator, Ms. Heather, practically skipped over to the sixteen of us in our Adirondack chairs as the moon showed its face. "I'm so happy you've all made it. I believe Mr. Armanelli should be on his way soon. He's informed me"— she waited a beat as if to make sure we had all noted that she was speaking directly with him—"that he's made some tweaks to JUNIPER and has been working on other classified projects so far this week."

I caught the grunt before it flew out my mouth. If my pussy were classified, he'd worked on it very well.

"He's sorry for his absence but is so excited to meet everyone tonight. There will be a bartender, and food stations are set up for dinner, which we'll have after we go over introductions. Because this is team building, we'd like everyone to introduce the person to the right of them, and from there, please tell us how you got into cybersecurity."

Everyone went around the circle. We'd all already met and had a great day, so the introductions felt like cheesy formalities.

Rodney and I were the very last people to go. "Yep, so, Lucas is right," I said. "I'm Izzy Hardy, and he calls me Izzy Bizzy. I got into data security while I was working undercover for the government . . . before I got transferred." I shrugged.

Melanie didn't let my short answer suffice, though. "What got you into undercover work?"

"Honestly, a family friend pulled me in." I took a deep breath. This was about team building. So, I tried my best. "He thought I needed redirection after getting out of juvie."

I waited for a gasp or two but none came.

"The first day on the job, someone on his team called me an addict. They said I wouldn't be able to hack it. Most of you probably saw that tattoo on my ribs today—the one that reads *addict*. I got it because I *am* one. I'll always be even if I'm not using, but I wanted to remember to be more than that too."

A few of the people glanced at my drink. I didn't explain that my addiction was to opioids and that I'd monitored my alcohol intake since day one of my recovery. I knew the risks of a drinking induced relapse. I also trusted myself enough after nine years, but the lack of confidence in me still stung.

"I'm also a recovering addict," Lucas chimed in.

And then two others joined in, along with Rodney. "I'm seven years sober, so I won't be drinking. Thanks for sharing, Izzy. Good to know we all have struggles, whether it's addiction, mental health, or something else. No one gets through life unscathed, right?"

Something about Rodney's acceptance of the world made me envy him. "Well, without further ado, the last man of the evening— Rodney." I waved a hand in front of him. My tone lightened the mood, and as the fire crackled in front of us, I described him. "Rodney's an excellent paddleboarder, decent at the game of chicken, and can probably beat me in pull-ups. I also enjoyed how he made me and Lucas a mean cup of coffee with extra sugar just the way I like it this morning."

"I'm hoping she'll enjoy more than that soon." He waggled his eyebrows at me, and my only response was a blush staining my cheeks. Harmless flirting. Without any sort of depth. That's what I should have been pursuing. Rodney gave me butterflies but didn't knock my socks off. Cade, though, he'd corrupted the butterflies, scared them away, and brought lightning in as a replacement.

Handbook be damned when it came to people hooking up on team-building work retreats. I had a feeling most were thinking about the same thing because we were all around the same age, intelligent, and very good-looking.

Rodney went on to tell the team why he was involved in data security, but I didn't really hear him because my eyes were on the corner cabin. Would he want one of these women? Would he indulge if he got the opportunity? It made me hope he wouldn't leave those walls, and I hated the way my jealousy flared when I realized Cade's light was off.

And from the wooded shadows, I felt him before I saw him. Close.

Hovering.

Listening and analyzing everything we said.

Rodney finished up by looking at the event coordinator. "And since I'm the last to introduce himself—"

"Not quite the last." Cade stepped out from where I'd felt him, and some of the girls gasped when they saw him.

Most of the guys were dressed in sweats and hoodies, so it shouldn't have been a shock to see him dressed in that too. Even I was in Rodney's baggy hoodie. But Cade in black jogger sweats and a hoodie to match hit different. His athletic build filled them out perfectly, and he looked almost approachable.

He rocked back on his heels and introduced himself. "Cade Armanelli. Head of data security for the United States government, the Pentagon, and Stonewood Enterprises."

Heather cleared her throat. She didn't want to prompt anything from him, I could tell. Instead, she shuffled her papers around. "Well, I'm so happy to have you all introduced. Like I said, please feel free to eat at any of the grilling stations or have a beverage. My number is located on your itineraries under *Ms. Heather* if any of you need anything at all."

She walked up to Cade and gave him a hug, murmuring she was glad he made it. The freaking man smiled at her, and I swear it was more genuine than when he looked at anyone else.

Jealousy unfurled inside me. I figured Heather, as our event coordinator, would hurry away, but she took a seat right next to Cade, like she'd saved those last two chairs across from me for them. No one knew we were hooking up, but damn, in that moment, I could have sworn the whole thing had been orchestrated to push every button on my emotional panel, a ploy to get me to blow a gasket. The bartender brought them glasses filled with amber liquid. It was like Cade had them all trained already, like he was being catered to above all of us.

With a beautiful blonde as his right-hand woman.

Predictably so, I guess. He was a billionaire mogul and our boss, after all.

The very one I'd told myself I hated only a few days ago. He was an enemy, not a friend.

Still, if we had to answer the questions, then so should he. The fire snapped, and the bugs buzzed around me as I got up to grab another drink. "So, what made you get into data security, Mr. Armanelli?" I asked. "Heather made all of us answer the question. You should too."

He smirked at me as if calling him by his last name was ridiculous. Then, as I grabbed my beer and marched back to my seat, Rodney swept me up and pulled me into his lap.

Cade's smile died. It dropped off his face like a weight falling from a skyscraper. That lightning in my stomach, the one he commanded, struck as I saw his glare take over.

"Ms. Hardy, I'm so glad you asked," he murmured as his eyes watched Rodney's hand on my thigh. My legs were bare except for the small skirt I'd thrown on, but that was basically covered by Rodney's sweatshirt. "Data controls us all. When I was younger, it was a way to escape. Now, I make sure *nobody* can escape it."

Melanie combed a hand through her long hair and flicked it over her shoulder, smiling at him. "I love that. It's so heroic, all the work you've done."

She did know he was a mobster, right?

Heather laid a hand on his forearm, and I saw her move her wrist back and forth, wiggling it enough that we all saw how the diamonds on a bracelet she wore sparkled in the night. "Cade's done so much good for the nation." She giggled then. "And for us. Cade? Remember when you got me this bracelet?"

I thought I saw Cade's jaw tick and his amber eyes seemed to avoid mine in that moment. "I recall."

"Cade, are you shy?" She smirked and I swear she met every single one of the women's eyes as if to stake her claim on him. "This is what I mean. He won't say that he gifted me a bracelet after we hung out a few times and he knew I would be able to set up events well for him." She poked him. "You never give yourself enough credit."

"How generous of him," I blurted out and almost slapped a hand over my mouth. But Cade's eyes caught mine and held me hostage, as though he was ready for me to lash out.

Cade hummed, not responding to my barb as he laser-focused on Rodney's hold around my waist. "Izzy, I heard your story as I was walking over from my cabin. You ever prove to that specific someone that you weren't what you had tattooed on yourself?"

He had to know that story was about him. The first time he'd seen me, he hadn't realized how broken I still was.

No one knew the reason behind it. I'd hidden it away and pretended my actions were just the terrible choices of a dumb child.

That *was* part of the story. Just not the whole thing.

Yet that day, he'd called me an addict and I'd been gutted in a way I wasn't used to. My friends were addicts, the person I'd loved had been an addict, but not me. My parents babied me, my siblings tiptoed around me, and my friends enabled me. No one outright called me on my shit by digging a verbal knife in and then twisting it when I wasn't ready.

No one but Cade.

"I'm not sure there's anything to prove. I am what I am. It's why I got it tattooed on me. You have tattoos also." I pointed to his hand, the lettering and black ink snaking up toward his forearm. "I'm sure they mean something to you too."

He dragged his thumb over the letters and nodded. "I either enact the chaos on my hand or I leash it. We control the data, right? So, we make the rules."

Rodney chuckled. Heather leaned in and whispered something to Cade.

Did she think he was available? That he'd be interested in a woman like her? Was he? To me, that woman had no demons, had no rebellion locked inside for him to push out. But maybe I was just a plaything, and she was more his style.

For some reason, the thought wreaked havoc on my heart.

After more chitchat, and Rodney rubbing my arms up and down as the fire got dimmer and dimmer, people started to retire to their cabins. I heard Heather whisper to Cade, "I'll see you later, then." She kissed his cheek, and he let her.

He even nodded like he intended to go meet her somewhere in the woods for a rendezvous. If he brought her back to the cabin, I would truly lose it. The jealousy that slithered through me was fierce as it wrapped around my lungs and stole my breath.

"Want to go to bed?" Rodney whispered, and I glanced at Lucas as he yawned.

"You two keep it PG tonight." Lucas hugged me and whispered, "Text me if you need anything." Then he headed off, and the dominos kept falling. The last few people stood and stretched, not willing to go too far with drinking or staying up late since Cade was in our presence.

Cassie and Penelope said good night, but I saw Penelope slip Cade a note before she walked down the darkened dirt path that led to our cabins.

"Yes," I jumped up. "I definitely think it's time to go to bed,

Rodney. Walk me?"

With only Cade still sitting and Rodney getting up from behind me, I took in the man I'd avoided the whole day.

The fire illuminated his skin, licked at the Italian tones of it, and highlighted the jagged edges of his cheekbones. "Ms. Hardy, I'll walk you back to our cabin. I need a word before you turn in for the night."

Rodney stopped and turned, his eyes studying Cade and then me. Cade didn't hide the way he stared at me, how his gaze tracked up and down my body slowly, like he wanted Rodney to know he was staking a claim.

"I got her, Cade." Rodney's arm was around my neck, insinuating he was going to hold me through the night, implying we were a couple used to this stance.

Cade nodded once, then twice, before he got up.

He walked slowly over to us, then his hand went to my waist. Both Rodney and I watched how he slid it around me. Then he jerked me forward so hard I stumbled into his chest. I would have stopped him, but the look in his eye told me now wasn't the time to fuck with him.

I could practically feel the stare down happening over my head. "*I've* got her." Cade made it clear.

"I'm down to stay if you two are into that," Rodney offered, but his arm had fallen from me, willing to give me up. Most people would with Cade's dark glare on them.

"I'm not into sharing her. Ever," Cade growled.

"Okay. Izzy, you got my number, right?" he murmured, and that was the moment I could have taken the out and gone with him, not stayed with a man nobody really understood, who a lot of people either feared or revered.

"It's in my phone, Rodney," I replied.

As Rodney walked off, we let the silence stretch between us. Finally, I stepped back and put my hands on my hips. He didn't address what had just happened. Instead, the man dug through his sweatpants pocket and pulled out a pocketknife. He grabbed a marshmallow from a food station and stuck it on the tip of the blade.

I widened my eyes at his lack of attention. "Um, hello? Do you feel good about that?"

He held the marshmallow near the flames, and we watched the sugar sizzle, the white of it burn. A moment before it would have caught fire, he pulled it back sharply. Him standing over the fire with that knife reminded me how he could dominate a space, how tall he was, how he owned all of us in one capacity or another.

"What did you eat today, Izzy?" His tone was measured.

"Food," I shot back, annoyed that he wasn't giving my question an answer.

He hummed. "Want a taste of the marshmallow?" He held it out to me.

"No." I stepped back. "It's after eight."

"What's one marshmallow after eight when you eat at least five candy canes a day?" he asked in mock shock.

I scratched my forehead, giving myself a second to cool off, trying to make sure he didn't get a rise out of me. "Were you watching me out your window today?"

"Anyone could guess you and Lucas were still eating those things all day, woman."

I waved off his explanation. "Answer me. Do you feel good

about staking a stupid claim on me with Rodney when you're supposed to be my boss? I don't want that getting around."

"Why? You that into Mr. Rodney?" he asked because he, like all men, was completely dense in that category.

"This isn't about Rodney!" I stomped right up to him and his stupid marshmallow knife. "You're jeopardizing my reputation with this team by walking around claiming me as your fuck toy. Which I'm not. I'm not hooking up with you anymore."

"Really?" he said, spinning the knife with the marshmallow still attached. "So instead, Rodney's going to be the man you let choke you out?"

My eyes narrowed, and then I remembered he'd told me back in the office not to let other men touch my neck. But Rodney had. "You're being insanely territorial for a guy who took a girl's number tonight *and* promised to meet Heather later. Sounds like you and your event assistant have a lot to catch up on too considering you bought her a bracelet."

"You watching me like I watch you, huh, dollface?" He chuckled and took the piece of paper with the number on it from his pocket.

"I'm just saying, you're being irrational for a man who seems available enough that women hand out their numbers."

He nodded and then I stepped back as he stepped forward to turn toward the fire. He threw the number into it.

We both watched as it burned. "Better?" he said softly.

I took a breath. "You still bought Heather a bracelet. Seems you know each other."

"I fucked her once, didn't happen again. I wouldn't have chosen for her to be here either, but she's obviously good at her job."

I took a breath at his admission, and jealousy cut so deep into me I felt it in my bones. Cade was becoming mine even though I tried to avoid it.

"Dollface, are you jealous of a little bracelet?" He tilted his head like he was confused.

"It's a very expensive, beautiful bracelet!" I blurted out. I bit my lip. "I think this is where we end. I'm . . ." I glanced away from him. "There's something wrong with me when I'm around you. I feel a little bit of everything too much."

"And how do you feel with Rodney?" Cade wasn't letting go of the fact that he'd seen another man touch me. I saw it in his eyes.

"Okay, that's none of your business," I told him. "It's beyond what this relationship is capable of."

He hummed and then took the marshmallow from the knife and set it on a piece of chocolate. "You know . . . I think people sometimes forget who I am."

"If you say so." I shrugged, confused by him pondering such a thing right now.

"Does it feel like sometimes people forget who you are? That they forget you're not just an addict or an IT specialist or a hot piece of ass?"

He studied the marshmallow on his blade. Then he set it on a stone on the ground and cut it in half before he attached one half back to the tip. The blade was long, one that could do real damage. I wondered if he always carried it on him, just in case.

"With me, I think you forget that I'm not just your boss, Izzy. And they forget that I'm not just this tech genius." He met my eyes and walked up, his blade held in front of him, pointing at me with the marshmallow on the end. "I'm not just the guy who stops nuclear warfare from touching this nation."

He took my chin in his other hand and held my jaw. I stood taller, staring up at him. Even if the man held a knife to me now, I wouldn't cower.

"I'm also Cade Armanelli, a man who can *cause* nuclear warfare, a member of the most powerful mafia family in the world. A man who's more than happy to shed blood when someone tampers with what's his. Do you get that?"

My heart pounded, and I knew he felt it—his finger was right on my pulse point. "If I say I don't?"

His stare pierced my soul, and the fire cackled in time with his jaw popping. "Open your mouth, Izzy."

"I don't want it. It's a lot of sugar for someone who's—"

"Open. Your. Mouth."

That adrenaline flowed through me again, my body responding like it knew the man I got wet for was near me, demanding that I listen to him. Defying him was a craving I couldn't deny myself as I ignored his command for a second time.

He grabbed my neck and yanked me to him. "The fact that I enjoy dealing with your shit is going to cause me a lot of problems in the future. I already know it. Don't make me pry it open, woman. Because I will."

This time I did. The knife was on my lips already, and his eyes looked so wild that I wouldn't have been surprised if he shoved the sharp blade into my mouth if I didn't comply. He took his time dragging the blade full of marshmallow across my tongue. "Suck it clean."

Daring. Dangerous. Him. It was all I wanted now. It was what my body was ready to beg for.

I licked it carefully, then closed my lips around it, avoiding the sharp edge while holding eye contact with him. I wanted him to know that even here, he didn't scare me, that he never would.

When I pulled back, he let me go and I murmured, "You could be all those things, Cade, but it doesn't really matter because you are who you are to me."

"Is who I am better than Rodney?"

"Are you concerned about him?"

"You sat on his lap for damn near an hour."

"And? It's not like I was screwing him in the chair or anything."

His jaw flexed up and down, up and down. Then he spun away from me and went to sit back in that Adirondack chair. He let the fire fill the silence, and I didn't move an inch.

Cade in sweats and a hoodie at the fire was enough to hold me captive for the night, even if it was in silence. He was probably the most beautiful man I'd ever seen. I knew how his hands felt on me, how his lips commanded a kiss, how his cock got me to submit even if I didn't want to.

"Well, I can guarantee you that's all he was thinking about with your ass on his dick."

"Probably. Considering I thought about it too."

He growled low and his eyes changed. I saw how his neck tensed, how he seemed to grow in size. "You want to fuck Rodney, Ms. Hardy?"

"Maybe." I shrugged because that was the honest truth. "He's fun, no strings, single, and so am I. He's open to a lot and doesn't come with much baggage."

"Compared to who?"

"Well, compared to most people."

"Including me?" He didn't glance away. He just tapped his knee with that blade still out, glinting in the night.

"Yeah, I think our baggage is about full."

He hummed. "Why don't you come sit on my lap like you did his and see how much baggage I have. Then you can get a good comparison."

I couldn't stop my immediate reaction of biting my lip and glancing down at his lap. But then I eyed the caterers still taking care of the food and drinks.

"Thank you for the services tonight," Cade called out over his shoulder to them. "You're dismissed. Leave. Now."

I'd never seen grown men scurry away so fast.

"Better?" He quirked a brow. "Come sit now." I saw the indent of his hard cock and how it flexed under my attention as my eyes traveled down. "Come on, Izzy. If it's about fun, no strings, and being single, we might as well take advantage of it."

"You can bother Heather for that." I chewed on my lip, trying to put up a fight even though I wanted to give in.

Instead of him giving me a chance to make the decision, his hand shot out and grabbed my elbow to yank me down onto his lap.

"Jesus, Cade," I chastised him, but he was busy rearranging me so my ass fit right against his cock, so my back was against his chest, so that my hair was being pulled away by his hand to expose my neck.

"This hoodie his?"

It was a simple question, but then I felt the metal of that blade. It'd cooled in the fall air and sent goose bumps along my neck where it lay, right at the V of the material. When I didn't answer fast enough, Cade swiftly pulled one side of the fabric up and brought his blade down the middle of it. It cut fast, almost effortlessly.

He'd sliced it all the way down so it hung on me like a cardigan. "Cade! What the hell?" I grabbed both sides of it and wrapped it around myself.

"Do you enjoy messing with my head?"

"I'm not messing with your head," I practically stuttered, confused.

"I'm not going to stare at a woman I fuck on another man's lap."

"You fucked me. Past tense."

"Wanna bet, dollface?" he growled in my ear. "Lose the skirt."

"I only have a bikini on under this."

"You'll be losing that too."

CHAPTER 14

Cade

I'd started to believe there would never be a last time with Izzy.

I'd watched her all day instead of working. I'd tried to call my brother so he could talk me off the ledge and get me back to work. Instead, he'd told me to go mingle with the damn employees. No one understood I was trying to remain the last single Armanelli. I was trying to do us a favor.

Because I wasn't a good man unleashed.

Rodney had looked her way more than once that afternoon. I'd peeked out of the window to see her sucking on candy canes with her best friend, whom I also envied, even though I could tell their relationship was only friendly. I didn't want any man around her now.

Especially not one who'd put his sweatshirt on her. Fuck me.

She'd sat there in another man's dark hoodie, and I knew right then and there I'd destroy it. I ripped it from her body and threw it into the dirt.

"I want to see that green on you while I fuck you next to this fire," I murmured, trying to cover up that I hated his clothes on her.

It was more than obvious, though. She knew that. It was fucking personal and sexual and territorial when you slipped your clothing on someone else. I was also aware that another woman wearing jewelry around her that I'd bought was unacceptable if she felt for me how I felt for her. It'd be something I'd have to remedy later.

"Cade, if someone comes out here—"

"They'll know you belong to me on this retreat. They need to know that anyway." I wiggled her ass so that my cock was between her cheeks and took my time dragging my knife over her bikini. "As a matter of fact, maybe we lose the bikini, huh?"

Her skin was damp, and so close to the fire, she glowed with a sheen of sweat. I watched goose bumps form on her skin as I trailed my knife to the edge of her green bottoms.

"You lose my bikini, I walk back to the cabin nude," she pointed out.

"Good point," I murmured before I slid the tip of the knife along her bikini line before pushing the fabric to the side, letting the metal come to rest right next to her clit. My blade was sharp, the point dangerous. I made sure to sharpen it every year, not because I ever thought I would need it, but because I liked it.

It was even more rewarding seeing the use I had for it here and now. The metal glinted in the moonlight as I moved it inch by inch back up her stomach to her bikini top and then I moved those little triangles to the sides too, letting her nipples pop out, erect, ready to be pinched and sucked by only me.

"Perfect," I murmured before dragging the knife to her neck. Her hazel eyes held fire as she glanced up at me. "Now, you're at my complete mercy."

She smiled, and it reached all the way to her eyes, like this was where she belonged, and she'd never say otherwise. "Do you like what you see, Cade? Feel free to enjoy the view. If someone comes out here, though, everyone's going to enjoy the view of my pussy too."

She thought I cared about my job, about our reputations, as I growled and stuck my knife in the dirt next to us. I only cared that people would get to see her vulnerable, see what I was starting to think was mine.

I ran my hands up to her breasts. Then I pulled her back into my chest so she could rest her body over me while I took in the woman who was on the cusp of bringing me to my knees. "Why did you share that story with everyone tonight?"

"My tattoo story?" She shrugged like she didn't want to talk about it, a nonverbal indicator that she wanted to indulge in an easy fuck with me again. Then her hands were over mine, kneading her tits through them. "I don't know, Cade. Who cares?"

This one wouldn't be as easy.

I'd listened to her honest answer as I walked toward the fire, and it stopped me cold in my tracks. God himself couldn't have made me move as I listened, as I heard she'd tattooed my callous words on her ribs. Didn't she know I'd said them to protect her? And now, she must have realized I respected her work ethic and who she was more than I did most. Right?

Getting lost in the trance of my words on her skin, I sought out the writing. My hand dragged to her side to find the ink, and I rubbed back and forth over the lettering. "I didn't say it to hurt you, Izzy."

She sighed. "Yes you did. You wanted me off the team. And it's fine—"

"It was true I wanted you off the team because I wanted you safe. You were young. And you were getting involved with people who didn't value a fucking life." I tried to explain it.

"Right. Well." She sighed. "What you said is true. I'm an addict. I'd just never heard it before, and I'd dealt with so much . . ." She stopped like she had more to share but didn't want to.

"Tell me."

Instead, she rolled her hips. "There's nothing to tell. I fucked up when I was a kid, and I'll pay for the consequences the rest of my life. I've tried to keep it together since then, and I'm proud that I have."

"Keeping it together like you do, dollface, it's a waste." I leaned in and angled her rib cage close to me so I could graze my teeth over that tattoo. "I should carve this tattoo out of you."

"Why?" She was breathless as I rubbed it and sucked my way to her back, up her shoulder blade and then to her neck. "I like it now. It reminds me of how far I've come."

"How far you've come from what?"

"I used to indulge in my emotions, Cade. I used to dwell on every stupid thing. It's what got me to where I was. The dwelling, only focusing on my pain."

"Pain from what?" I slid a hand from her tattoo down to her pussy. I needed to work her, to feel her, to know that her arousal was mine to drown in as she shared herself with me.

She paused and then her words came out painfully. "I lost someone."

"Who?" How had I not known this?

"Why do you have to know, Cade? It doesn't matter."

Everything about her mattered to me; I'd just started to see that. "Maybe it matters to me."

"I was just young and dumb. Drop it." Her voice cracked, and I filed it away to explore later. I wasn't going to drop anything about Izzy Hardy any time soon.

It was a filler answer. And suddenly I wanted to decode her. I wanted it all. I rubbed her clit as I massaged one of her breasts and murmured, "You're not telling me the whole truth."

She rolled into me and whimpered. "What do you need my whole truth for when we're not doing anything after this re—"

I curled my fingers into her to stop her words. I didn't want to hear them anymore. "You want to get rid of me so badly, huh?"

Instead of answering, she gripped my wrists for leverage to ride my hand. She was so wet, it sounded like my own little personal waterfall instead of her denying that we had something outside of fucking on this trip. That's what I wanted to hear, all I wanted to hear.

"Knees, baby doll. Right in front of the fire."

She was so close she couldn't deny me as she slid to the ground and kneeled before it. I stood, shoving the chair back, and then stepped between her calves, spreading her knees farther into the dirt. Instead of telling her how good her ass looked or how someone could paint a damn masterpiece of her back alone, I took one step back, kneeled behind her, and yanked her ass back against my sweatpants.

She yelped and fell forward, catching herself just inches from the flame, her hands in the dirt now too. "Cade, this is too close."

She was talking about the fire, but I wanted her dripping sweat, so hot and close to burning up inside that she'd never forget who put her there. I pulled my sweatpants down and didn't hesitate as

I said, "Make sure you brace, then, baby. Or the fire will get you."

It wasn't a real threat. I grabbed her hair to pull her back when I thrust in. Hard. Her whole body, the curves, the ass, the tits, moved in perfection. I let my cock rail her, and she met me thrust for thrust. The fire danced around us, the only light of the night, with the moon and the smoke curled around her body like she was fucking the devil.

Maybe I was him.

I felt like the devil as I held her so close to the fire's edge and fucked her with all my might. It was a damn beautiful sight, the green of the bikini on her almost luminescent skin, the way her dark waves fell over her shoulder, and the way her muscles flexed to meet with mine.

"Nobody gets me but me," she murmured into the fire, and I was unsure whether she was talking to it or to me. I always knew Izzy struggled with something, she fought with letting go like she had to keep herself bottled up for the rest of her life. But she was wrong, because I was coming for her. I wouldn't stop until I got her either.

"I get the real you, baby doll. Me. Because I fuck it out of you every chance I get." My cock hardened more at the words. The world faded away around us. All I saw was her. All I wanted and needed was her.

And she must have felt it too because her pussy clenched, and she screamed my name into the fire like I owned her. I truly wanted to believe I did.

It'd have been a lie, though. When she flipped that dark hair over her shoulder and stared at me with a glint in her eye and said, "Anybody can fuck an orgasm out of someone, Cade. Doesn't mean you're getting a damn thing other than that," I knew she owned me.

My blood pressure rose, and the need to control her for a moment, to make her see that she was mine, took over. I grabbed the front of her neck and flipped her so she lay on her back in the dirt, hair spread in the dust. Her hands went to my wrists, and her eyes sparkled like she didn't fear me at all. I held her down and pumped my cock above her body with the other. "I'm marking the you that you think no one wants to see, Izzy. It's mine, right here, right now."

With my words, I came over her breasts and stomach. We both watched my cum shoot out in ribbons over her, marking her for me alone.

She let me pump myself until every last drop was gone, and she held my gaze the whole time. When I was spent and breathing hard over her, she smiled up at me softly and said, "Happy with yourself, Cade?"

I cataloged her under me, the dirt in her hair, the rumpled bikini, the way her sweat beaded randomly over her beautiful skin and mixed with my cum. "You're damn near perfect in the dirt, Izzy Hardy. I'm struggling not to take a picture of you."

"I'm an absolute mess."

"And that's exactly how I want you," I murmured to her as I rolled from her body to sit next to her. She moved to get up, but I stopped her. "Give me a second."

She lifted a brow like she was going to argue.

"Please." I didn't beg, but I would with her. I'd have done just about anything to have her there with me for another moment. I reached for Rodney's sweatshirt and took my time wiping myself from her body. "I used to clean up a lot of messes back in the day, but this one I'm enjoying cleaning up most."

I smiled to myself as I threw that sweatshirt into the fire.

"You're ridiculous if that brings you joy, Cade," she mumbled as she pushed her bikini back into the right position and sat up, dusting the dirt from herself. "And I'm sure the messes you cleaned up were much worse than this."

I hummed. "If you're talking about my days as a part of the old Armanelli family, sure." I shrugged, thinking about that part of my life, how I suddenly wanted her to understand. "We've tried to be a cleaner, more productive family."

She picked at nothing on the ground, avoiding eye contact. "I know that. The world knows that. Even Heather is proud of your accolades." She sighed. "Everyone has embraced and accepted who you are."

I thought about my life. Growing up a son to a powerful mafia boss had shown me a lot of the ugly world. Not that my brother, who was first born, didn't see more. "They've either embraced who I am or learned to fear who I am."

"Do you get tired of people fearing you?"

"No," I answered honestly, "because they should. If anything, I get tired of acting as if I'm not a threat, like I enjoy mingling with all of you for the sake of whatever this retreat is."

She laughed. "It's called building trust. Team building."

"I don't work well with others."

"Probably because you don't care if people fear you rather than respect you. And I think everyone wants to. You're a freaking god when it comes to hacking."

"Is that all I'm a god at?" I threw a small joke her way.

She rewarded me with a genuine smile. "So Cade has a sense of humor. Maybe you should show your team that more often."

I tugged on a strand of her hair. "Maybe you should show your fire, your emotion, and the real you more too."

Narrowing her eyes, she argued. "Nobody likes all that. That's like saying you want to show the world the Armanelli mobster in you."

"Sometimes I do." I shrugged and threw a small piece of a twig from the ground into the fire. "But I save that for the days the world really needs a reminder." She rolled her eyes like I didn't make any sense. "You realize I gave the go-ahead to have my father killed, right?" I blurted, like she needed to know that the man she'd just fucked was essentially a murderer.

My father deserved his fate, and my brother and I had taken him down. He'd been a ruthless killer that hurt the nation over and over. Still, losing a father and being the one to cause that loss made many wary of me. She had to understand I'd be ruthless, that I wasn't just a sweet man who delved into cybersecurity. I did it for the country, for my family.

And I'd kill again for them too if need be.

"I'm aware that it was rumored, yes." She nodded, not recoiling at all. "But according to your fans, like Heather, it was for the greater good."

I dug the heel of my shoe in the dirt, trying to play off her explanation. It was a good one. "I'll admit it's a brilliant twist on the story. My mother was an Italian woman with a lot of love in her heart. She told us to make decisions with love. I made the decision to have him killed for the greater good, sure, but I was also angry. I acted in anger. And I'd act in anger again if I felt a man took his power too far."

"You have a lot of power too," she reminded me quietly.

"Yep, and I'm happy to piss off, rile up, and fuck with anyone in the world, Izzy. I enjoy doing it. I like the control and believe I'm capable of handling how far I push everyone. My father liked it too, but I never thought he was capable of handling it."

She considered that for a moment as we stared at the fire that was slowly dying in the cool air. "I bet your mother would have been proud of you then."

"My mom would have been proud of a serial killer." I laughed thinking back to her making cannoli for my father even after he came home from getting rid of a few guys. "Quite frankly, she married one. My father was a mean son of a bitch who trafficked women and drugs and laundered money."

"Then you did the good the world claims by getting rid of him," she murmured, and for some reason, her acceptance lifted a weight from my shoulders that I didn't know I'd been carrying.

"Maybe. Or maybe I did it to piss some people off," I countered. "It's what I enjoy most, right?"

"I don't know. I've never felt riled by you at all," she said with mock certainty. Then she leaned in and bumped my shoulder, a sparkle in her eyes as she smiled at me.

I hummed low, just imagining the way her body vibrated when she wanted to lash out at me. "You, I might enjoy riling most, Ms. Hardy." I saw goose bumps rise on her skin and pulled my sweatshirt over my head. "Why the hell you'd go to a damn campfire in a bikini is beyond me."

"I didn't," she huffed, but she snuggled into my sweatshirt like she was trying to absorb my warmth. "I said I would go back to the cabin to get into some warmer clothes, and Rodney offered his hoodie instead."

"Next time another man tries to put their clothing on you, consider that I'm going to cut it off and burn it. Got it, dollface?"

"I'm not really sure I do get it." She tapped her chin.

Fuck, that woman had a knack for aggravating me too. "What's not to get?"

"I can't be in any sort of relationship with my boss, Cade. And quite frankly, we don't like each other enough to be in one." She always said that like it was some mutual thing.

"I like you just fine. I especially enjoy your pussy—"

"No." She cut me off with a hand in the air and then stood up from the ground. "Aside from sleeping together, this isn't a match made in heaven. And we don't need the drama right now."

I stood up too and dusted off my pants before pulling her close and starting the walk back to our cabin. "I'd argue that it's less drama to fuck you silent when you're bickering with me about something ridiculous."

"I really don't bicker. You haven't been around me long enough to say that I do."

I chuckled at the fact that she couldn't see she was doing exactly that. "So, what? You want us to stay on our sides and work real nice without me bending you over the counter to fuck you while you're walking around in your baggy T-shirts?"

"I can get a pencil skirt out if that helps," she offered.

"I'll take fucking you in either."

She slid a hand over her face as she tried to act unaffected. Yet I felt her body heat against mine and noted how her breathing had picked up. Izzy Hardy was just as obsessed with screwing me as I was with screwing her. "If we sleep together again—and that's a big if—we don't tell anyone and it ends after the freaking retreat. And we need to get JUNIPER squared away first, which means you need to team build with us."

"I don't need to team build—"

"Team build or no cabin fucking, Cade," she ground out.

I mumbled, "Like you make all the rules . . ."

I was starting to think she did.

CHAPTER 15

Izzy

T he next day flew by because Cade and I actually worked together in unison. He wanted JUNIPER to be a freaking breeze, same as I did, and he seemed to want it done ASAP. I wasn't sure if it was because I said no screwing around until then or if it was because we were getting closer to this retreat being over.

Still, I texted Lucas that I had to work, then sat down across from Cade. Of course Lucas asked for a pic of our boss in the morning, and I smirked as I silently tried to sneak one. Even if my whole work team was spending the day out in a wilderness paradise, frolicking around while I worked, I really had nothing to complain about. My view was just as good.

Or bad if I was trying to keep my hands to myself. Which I was.

I chanted in my head that I really was. But Cade wore those damn glasses as he worked, and every now and then, he'd push them up the bridge of his nose like a drop-dead gorgeous geek I wanted to lick for the rest of the day.

Not only that, he'd had breakfast delivered before I woke up, and because he wasn't sure of what I wanted, he had them bring waffles and pancakes and doughnuts and eggs and freaking fruit.

When I sent off my picture to Lucas, Cade immediately said, "If you get to take pictures of me, don't be mad when I take some of you."

My face heated. "I don't know what you're talking about."

"You hold your phone at a very different angle when you're taking pictures, dollface."

"Whatever," I grumbled and eyed the feast between us on the table. "I don't need to eat any of this." I normally drank coffee and counted calories for breakfast.

"Eat some of it, or I'll force-feed it to you," he replied without looking up from his laptop.

I chose some fruit and a waffle, so as not to appear ungrateful. Then, as I started to cut a doughnut in half, he grabbed the whole thing, put it on my plate, and firmly placed it right by my laptop.

"Eat your food," he repeated.

I rolled my eyes, but complied, because it wasn't worth the argument. Plus, I wanted the food anyway. The chefs at this retreat were outstanding, but I had no idea where they were even making the food. "Where do you think they get this food? Is someone cooking in a cabin around the corner?"

"Probably." Cade shrugged, completely bored with the topic of conversation. "Coffee is on the counter for you."

"Oh! Thank you." I hopped up to grab it and search for the sugar.

"Already added the sugar, Izzy. I bet it'll taste as good as Rodney's."

So, he'd been listening to everything I said the night before. I took a sip and let him have this one. "Tastes even better."

He couldn't hide the way the corners of his mouth lifted a bit as I sat back down. Then, he sent me a file to work on, and we typed away for the next hour in silence. At some point, my back started to hurt from sitting on the wooden bench, so I grabbed my laptop to go work in bed.

First, I changed into some jean shorts and a blouse for team building later. I wasn't sure if they'd have me talk about JUNIPER, and I wanted to appear semi-professional.

After a minute or two of diving into more emails, I got a message on my computer screen.

Cade: Why did you leave the table?

Me: I had to change, and it's more comfortable in bed.

Cade: You're going to fall asleep instead of work.

Me: I'm not. I work in bed sometimes. I feel like it gives me a different perspective.

Cade: Seems like a dangerous place to be.

Me: Why?

Cade: Because it only takes a second for your cabin partner to slide between your legs or for your hand to wander where it shouldn't.

Me: Don't start. We have work to do.

Cade: I stopped working the moment you told me you were in our bed.

Me: Technically, one half of the bed is yours. The other half is mine. It's very clear from the spray-painted line.

Cade: Line seems a bit blurry to me.

Me: Leave me alone.

Cade: Why did you change?

Me: Because we have a team-building event in ONE hour.

Cade: What are you wearing?

Me: Just a blouse and shorts.

Cade: Can your hand slip into those shorts easily?

Cade: If it can, be sure to let me know how wet that pussy is for me.

Sexting and digital play was something I thought would never turn me on but having Cade message me from the other room had me pretty much soaked. Especially when I pictured him sitting at that table with those strong fingers typing away, black ink under his rolled-up sleeves, and the veins protruding from his forearms.

I pressed the ignore button on my messenger app and tried to stay on task. But I couldn't help myself once he'd put the idea there. My hand roved over my jean shorts, and I pushed the seam of the fabric back and forth between my legs.

He caught me like that, my eyes closed and a soft gasp escaping my lips. I jumped, and my laptop almost went flying. Cade had padded quietly down the hallway and leaned on the doorframe with those fucking glasses. "No need to stay quiet, Izzy. I like the sound you make when your pussy is being played with."

"Jesus, I was not doing that!" When I chanced a look at him, he was smiling at me like we were breaking all the rules and he was going to bask in every second of it.

"Did you check your daily tasks yet?"

I chewed on my cheek and went to the daily tasks. There were a few left—one of which was to call Stonewood Enterprises and update the owner on our progress, and the last was what he wanted me to see.

Task: Unbutton your shorts.

"Hand in the shorts is going to feel better anyway, right?" He lifted a brow, not letting go of the fact that he'd caught me in the act.

"Unfortunately, I have to call the freaking owner of Stonewood Enterprises to tell him we are minutes away from finishing up JUNIPER for testing with the team. So I guess I won't be doing that."

"Izzy, the call can wait. Your orgasm can't. Play with yourself for me," he commanded, the last words low, an unspoken threat.

I waited, like I was going to defy him. I wanted to know my punishment.

"You wait another minute, and I'll corrupt your whole computer, dollface. Then you won't be able to work at all."

Shit, he was good. It was the only thing I didn't want. I would have taken him smacking my ass or getting his belt. It meant he wanted this; he was practically begging for it by actually threatening me with something.

That had my heart galloping with the rush of pleasing him, of seeing his desire for me, of him at my mercy.

Taking my time, I closed my laptop and set it aside. "Fine. You want this so bad, Mr. Armanelli. Let's give you what you came for. Tell me what you want."

He didn't even hesitate. "Unbutton your shorts and push them down."

I slowly pulled the button open on my shorts but stopped there. I wasn't about to give him all of me by discarding my clothing simply because he asked. "This will have to do, Cade," I snarked, and then I shoved my hand into my panties and moaned, feeling the nerves on my clit singing from receiving attention so quickly. This was me. I wanted it fast, raw, and with my clothes still on, like I could get it anywhere just thinking about it. He'd see how fast I could barrel into an emotion, into an orgasm, how fast I could be consumed. My eyes rolled back as I rolled my hips, but Cade didn't let me get lost that quickly.

"Open your eyes, Izzy. And slow down."

My eyes shot open, but I didn't slow down. I went faster, my breath, my heartbeat, the heat rising on my body. "I'm taking it how I want it, Cade."

I worked my clit, rolling it between my fingertips, and I watched as he fisted his hands at his sides, as his neck tensed, as he licked his lips. He was holding back, not coming to me, leaving me to chase the orgasm on my own. I loved how he stared at me with desire, how he wore those glasses still—like he was researching me, analyzing me, decoding me.

I slid a finger inside and moaned. There was no lasting when he watched me like this, when I felt like I was doing everything wrong, but it felt so right. I screamed his name when I orgasmed, and my whole body convulsed as I saw stars.

He pushed himself from the doorway and strode over to his side of the bed where he sat before grabbing the wrist at my shorts. He pulled my hand from my panties and sucked my fingers clean. "Jesus Christ, you taste so damn good when you're being bad, baby doll."

And before I knew what he was doing, he stuck his phone in my face and snapped a picture. "What the hell, Cade?"

"One for one, doll. You took mine, and now I took yours." He slid his phone back into his pocket, and then his dark eyes, warm as molasses, roved over me.

"Oh no." I shoved him back. "Stay on your side. We have a team-building exercise in twenty minutes. Heather said we'll be doing a paddleboard relay race before I assign teams to work on the different parts of JUNIPER."

"Well, you can be late."

"No. *You* and I are not going to be late." I poked him in the chest. "You have to come."

"For what?"

"For people to see you and trust you and want to work with you," I said as I grabbed my pink bikini.

He eyed it. "You're wearing that for a paddleboard relay?"

"Yep. And I'm hoping it falls all the way off," I threw back because I knew he was going to say something about it being too skimpy.

He groaned, padded over to his suitcase, and grabbed swim trunks, surprisingly without saying a word. Then, he went to his bathroom to change. I thought I was winning as I threw on my bathing suit and sucked on a candy cane in the living room, waiting for him.

My plan went completely off the rails when he walked down the hallway in nothing but dark swim trunks. I'd never seen the way his tattoos wrapped around his chest, how the black snaked over his skin. When he moved, each of his muscles flexed.

Caden Armanelli hid that perfect body under those tailored suits he wore, but not today. He had two towels hanging off one arm, and he grabbed some sunglasses from the counter to put on before he said, "You ready?"

The answer was no.

I leaned against the table for support. I knew I was drooling too.

How had I never considered that he'd look so good without a shirt on in the sunlight? "I don't think . . ." How was I going to get around this? "Why don't you have a shirt on?"

His brow furrowed. "What? Why don't *you* have a shirt on, dollface?"

I glanced down at myself, completely forgetting what I had on. "I have a bathing suit on."

"So do I."

"But you are . . . You look . . . You're the boss."

"I don't care what I am. If you're getting in that water wearing a swimsuit you might lose, I'm getting in it with you. Now, let's go."

"Instead of focusing on what might be happening with my swimsuit, focus on being the boss, Cade. The team needs to see you." I was telling him as much myself, goddamn it.

"The team has a boss. Me. Whether they like me or not doesn't matter."

"It always matters. Respect makes a person work harder. Just because you're their boss and they might fear losing their jobs doesn't mean they are going to do the job well. Haven't you ever heard that?"

He stared at me for a second too long, and his eyes changed. "I used to think the same about my father, about my family. We didn't need fear; we needed respect. My brother and I made friends rather than enemies."

"See?" I pointed out and shrugged as I walked past him through the doorway. At least maybe now we'd get somewhere, even if I had to look at how hot my boss was throughout the whole day.

I stomped out to the paddleboard relay and tried to hide my frown and irritation when basically every girl swarmed Cade. Lucas was by my side in a hot second, too, telling me exactly what he would do if he got Cade alone. It definitely wasn't subtle, or professional, but I didn't blame him. That body and those tattoos had everyone drooling.

Then, I was even more frustrated when Cade did exactly what he was supposed to do. He freaking interacted and swam and engaged with everyone on the team. He joked with them. He laughed. An outsider would assume he belonged there, like he was a part of us, like he wasn't the callous boss everyone made him out to be.

The fucker won the paddleboard relay for his team too. All of a sudden, the billionaire tech mogul was an avid paddleboarder? I swear I almost shoved him off the damn thing.

And after, everyone was more than willing to accept job tasks for JUNIPER. They even complimented us on a great team retreat, as if I had something to do with it.

Cade nearly knocked me off my feet when he told everyone that none of it would have been possible had I not built the system.

I went to bed that night hoping he would roll over onto my side of the spray-painted line and tell me it was all overrated, that we should screw until the sun came up.

He didn't.

Suddenly, he was the perfect boss, and I was the one who wanted to step over the line.

CHAPTER 16

Cade

A week in, I was still showing Izzy what a good boss looked like. Her words had stuck with me, made me realize I'd neglected a large part of my job. I'd treated the teams I'd worked with like employees rather than family.

My team was a part of my family, in a way. They protected the world I wanted to keep living in. One where I was in charge, where the president trusted me, where my brother and my family were safe. JUNIPER and this team helped with that. Sure, I could do it alone, but with people I trusted, it was much easier.

And over the past few days, Izzy had taught seamless sessions at the luxury private conference center down the road. I particularly enjoyed how it looked like a large log cabin on the outside but the inside was equipped with every high-end piece of technology we needed.

Izzy stood at the podium, answering questions about how each voting system could be handled in different states and explaining what to do in the event of a security breach. She didn't falter when they questioned whether our setup was good enough to hold against other countries.

She spoke with confidence, with passion, and with a respect for all of them. She believed in her team, and I think that's why they believed in her.

The lesson she was teaching me shined through in the way she portrayed herself. I found a higher respect for her and everyone there.

Well, everyone except Rodney.

Rodney would eye her up and try to help her onto her paddleboard or tell her a joke that she would laugh at. There were moments I thought I was going to drag her back to the cabin to have my way with her.

I didn't but, damn, I'd considered it.

I couldn't continue down the road of purity much longer even if I tried, and for some reason, she was holding out too. When I'd put on my swim trunks, I'd thought she was going to claw her way up my body, but she hadn't.

We remained professional, except for the visit I'd scheduled earlier that morning when she'd been away from the cabin. I'd tasked Heather with buying another bracelet, this one worth millions, with diamonds lining the inside of the wrist because I knew Izzy wasn't flashy. There were other stipulations to the jewelry, but it was quite an easy find when we had contacts around the nation for diamonds and jewelers. The Armanelli family's wealth extended everything. When Heather brought it over, I saw the disdain on her face, but I sent her away immediately after explaining she could keep the bracelet, but it was not significant to me other than it being a thank you gift.

When Izzy got back to the cabin each night, she worked hard

and didn't take any time to rest. I saw how, without me antagonizing her, Izzy worked herself to the bone. Other than the candy canes she ate, the woman would constantly forget to eat. If I didn't put food in front of her, she'd skip meal after meal.

So, on day seven, we meandered back to the cabin, and I cooked up some pasta as she sat typing away on her laptop. When I placed the plate down in front of her, she practically cried tears of joy when she tasted it. "Who taught you to cook like this? Is it homemade alfredo or something?"

I laughed at the joy in her face. "My mother, bless her soul, would have been livid if she saw how you didn't eat throughout the day. Thankfully, she taught me and my brother to cook a little."

"I literally can't talk to you right now. Please let me enjoy this in silence."

The silence was agonizing though because she moaned the whole damn time and made my dick twitch.

"You staying up to work?" I asked her after she shoved the last bite in her mouth.

She held up a finger as she finished chewing. "That was quite possibly the perfect meal. So, I guess I have to say thank you first."

As she licked her lips, I tried but failed not to watch. "Want to thank me another way?"

"Cade ..." She sighed, rubbing her eyes. "I have more work to get done."

"Like?"

"Rodney needed me to send him a training, and Juda wanted me to send a few emails. I have a few more things to get accomplished."

"You can give it a rest. You don't have to do a million jobs at once. They all think you're doing great out there, Izzy." Didn't she see that she worked herself to the bone? That everyone else's requests of her didn't need to come before sleep?

"They do. Sure. What about you, though?" She glanced over at me for a second before going back to her laptop.

"Does it matter what I think?" I wanted her to admit it did, that I meant something more to her than everyone else.

The woman glanced up, but then avoided my gaze and shrugged. It was the avoidance I pinpointed, the way she stopped for a nanosecond too long. I wanted her full attention now. I wanted the story she held back.

Even though she kept typing away, as if we weren't having a conversation, as if I didn't need her full attention, I shouldn't have cared. I did the same to everyone else all the time. With her, though, that shit was infuriating.

She didn't think I was worth her time? Was the damn job always more important, even after she'd worked a full twelve-hour day?

"Izzy, I'm talking to you," I murmured, giving her an opportunity to adjust her approach.

She sighed in exasperation. "I'm aware. And I'm listening and working. Juda stayed back to help with everything in the office, and he—"

I walked over and slowly but firmly closed her laptop. "And he can do his damn job for once. Now, answer my question honestly this time. Why do you care what I think?"

"You're the boss, Cade. Everyone cares what you think."

I dragged a hand across her jawline and to her lips to trace them. "You never really did, though. You work hard under the guise of wanting a promotion, but that's not it."

"Then what is it?"

"I don't know. That's why I'm asking."

She looked out the window before saying, "Maybe I'm proving to you, and to everyone, I'm not just the addict you said I was. I'm a hard worker too."

"You've proved that for nine years to everyone—including me the first day you were on the job," I reminded her.

"Maybe." She chewed her cheek as I kept rubbing those soft lips. Her mouth dropped open, and I became mesmerized beyond our work relationship, beyond the new boss-employee line I'd drawn for myself.

I couldn't stop myself from sliding the bracelet from my pocket, then grabbing her wrist. She stared at it, completely puzzled as I took a small key to twist on the inside of the bracelet. It snapped open, and she gasped when she saw its inner walls lined with large diamonds. Her eyes sparkled in question as I clamped it around her wrist and used the key on the other side to lock it. I pulled it once to make sure it would stay, the gold of it glinting against the lamp light in the dining room.

"What is this?" she whispered.

"A gift for the woman who's proven herself to me always."

"I can't accept this. It's too much." She shook her head and tried to pull it from her wrist.

"I thought you might say that. But it's locked on you now. So deal with it."

"Are you kidding me, Cade?" Her eyes widened. "I can't wear this around. It probably costs more than my life savings and—"

"You're wearing it until I take it off of you," I snapped, glaring at her glaring at me. Didn't she get that I wouldn't have it any other way? She deserved this more than any other woman. I wanted her to see that she meant more than just a woman I'd slept with once. She was something to me although I couldn't quite pinpoint what yet.

We both jumped when her phone buzzed between us. "Are you going to answer it?"

She shrugged and didn't reach for it immediately. "Probably just my family or Gerald."

"Why the fuck is he still messaging you?"

"Yesterday, he whined about something happening with his company. I think he wants my sympathy and then he wanted me to know he'd sent lilies—not that I even like them."

I knew exactly what had occurred with the company. I wasn't going to admit a damn thing about it though. "Why don't you like lilies?"

"They remind me of my time in juvie. Someone brought them to me after I got out." She shook her head. "Anyway, aren't you supposed to send roses for love?"

"Is he saying he still loves you?" I asked, shocked.

"Sure." She glanced away. "Anyway, roses are a girl's favorite. You can't beat that deep red."

I hummed as I snatched her phone to see if it was Gerald this time. It was Rodney asking for a nightcap. I considered throwing her phone into the sink and turning on the garbage disposal. Instead, I showed her his message.

She didn't try to hide any sort of embarrassment or guilt as she straightened the silly *Titanic* T-shirt she'd been wearing all day and pulled away from my touch. "We should get to bed."

"You going to text your friend back?"

She narrowed her eyes. "I don't think it's any of your business who I text."

"Even if it isn't, I still expect you to answer the question, dollface."

"So what if I do text him back, Cade?" She got up from her seat and put her hands on her hips in an effort to show she was perturbed. All I saw, though, was that the T-shirt inched up her milky thighs.

"What type of nightcap could he possibly give you that I can't provide?" I didn't attempt to stop myself from asking the question, from goading her into answering me, even though we'd been keeping things PG for the past few nights.

"I could ask you about the women handing out their numbers to you or texting your phone."

"They don't have my number."

"Why's that?"

"Because I don't give out my number to random women like you obviously do to random men."

"I've been hanging out with Rodney for days, and he's a coworker. That's hardly random."

"Define *hanging out*, because if you're doing more than I think you are with him, Izzy, I swear to God . . ."

"Are you serious? You haven't looked at me twice for days. You're being all five-star boss professional now." She sneered the whole damn thing, like she couldn't stand me like this.

I held back a laugh and looked at this beautiful woman who'd unexpectedly secured a death grip on my soul. I think we were so sexually frustrated that we could fight about anything. "Are you complaining? Because you specifically told me to be that."

"That's right. I did." She nodded hard, as if trying to convince herself. "I also told you I wanted no-strings-attached fun and that I'm single. Rodney checks the boxes, Cade."

"If he's what you want"—I leaned in, and my next words held menace—"tell him to come over."

Her hazel eyes, with their warm mix of green and gold, widened in shock. "For . . . for what?"

"For your nightcap. You want some fun. I'm sure Rodney can give it to you. Matter of fact, tell him to find a fucking toy and bring that too. I'm happy to watch, Izzy. I'll enjoy seeing that he can't bring you to the high I can."

She lifted her chin and snatched up her phone. I saw the way her body shook, how her breathing got fast like it had all the times before. Izzy was turned on beyond her wildest dreams thinking of the new fantasy I'd planted in her head.

The problem was, I didn't know if I could handle having some fun with her.

That firecracker of a woman was quickly becoming mine, even though we had a spray-painted line down the middle of our bed. Even though I'd avoided the idea for a few days. It didn't matter.

Izzy Hardy, standing there in her mess of a *Titanic* shirt, now with my gold bracelet on her wrist, was going to be my downfall.

She tapped her screen and brought the phone to her ear. "Yeah, want to come to my and Cade's cabin?" She paused as she stared at me. "I think he'd enjoy us doing that here." Then she held the phone out to me. "He wants to make sure."

I didn't even want to hear the man's voice. Still, I clutched the phone to my ear as he asked if he could bring one or two toys. "If they'll make her feel good. That's what this is about."

He explained and I agreed. Without so much as a goodbye, I ended the call before throwing her phone on the couch and pulling her to me to devour her mouth.

When I drew back to glare at her, I said, "Remember the taste of me when your fuckboy comes over to make you feel good. And know that I'm in charge. If he veers even one iota off the scheduled programming, I'm throwing him off our porch."

She smirked. "I'm not even sure I want this, Cade."

I nipped at her collarbone and murmured, "Let's check," before I slid my hand under her shirt and into her panties. "Fucking soaked."

She purred like she might not be able to wait to get off, like my fingers would do the job just fine. I wanted to give in for a split second. It'd be a way for me to keep her all to myself. But I saw the hunger in her eyes, saw how she wanted to explore something new, and I had confidence enough that she'd end up where she truly belonged in the end—on my cock and not his.

I pulled my hand from her panties and licked my fingers. "I'm only going to allow him in our place for so long with you tasting this good. But let's enjoy it, huh? See how loud another man can make you scream."

It was the approval she must have needed from me because her shoulders relaxed a little, and she smirked. "Fun with the single men on the retreat . . . I guess I deserve that after Gerald."

I chuckled. "Well, you did say the sex with him wasn't that good. With me, it's always going to be, Izzy."

CHAPTER 17

Izzy

My heart thumped way too fast inside my chest to make small talk with Cade and Rodney. They'd both had no problem shooting the shit over glasses of water because Cade hadn't offered anything else. I'm assuming that was because Rodney was sober, but I contemplated grabbing a shot of whiskey for myself.

Two very hot men had agreed to do things with me.

Sexually.

Completely willing. On a damn work retreat.

And I'd practically initiated it. Or been goaded into it after Cade had offered.

I excused myself to go to the bathroom and freshen up. Instead, I tried to cool the anxious sweats as I stared at the bracelet on my wrist. He was showing me I meant something to him, right? I twisted it on my wrist and my heart leapt at the feeling of his jewelry being locked on me.

Was this too wild? Was I stepping way out of the comfort zone

I'd lived in all these years?

The answer was a big yes.

Did I feel alive, though? Like I didn't have to hide myself with Cade?

The answer was again a great big freaking yes.

I felt like this when I was about to accomplish something big, like completing JUNIPER. Like I'd earned it. Like this was the life I wanted to live.

And Cade had pushed me there again; he'd seen the need in me and felt inclined to make my day.

"Okay," I murmured to myself, "calm down."

I waved my hands under my armpits before spritzing some perfume on my neck and between my thighs.

I needed to make sure I smelled the part, okay? I even did a couple lunges for good measure. It was actually time to amp up, not calm down.

I could do this. I wanted to do this. My nipples tightened just thinking about them both eyeing me up.

And when I opened the bathroom door, they were standing there—Cade in his suit, except he'd lost the jacket and had his top button undone with his sleeves rolled up, and Rodney laid back in gym shorts and a black T-shirt.

"Ready, baby doll?" my freaking orchestrator asked me.

"I don't know." I nervously laughed. "You guys want me to change?"

Rodney shook his head. "You don't get more beautiful than you look now, Izzy. You're perfection."

I blushed at his compliment as Cade waved us into the room.

He'd brought in a leather lounge chair from the living room

and sat—like this was his show, like he was about to get the entertainment of his life.

Real-life porn would have been great entertainment for me too. And Cade knew exactly what he wanted with it. But he eyed me one last time as I stood before him, Rodney right by my side, his hand around my waist. "If either of you don't listen for even a second, I throw Rodney out on his ass. We clear?"

Our friend chuckled and nodded. "I'm here only to enjoy and obey. Not cause havoc." He hesitated. "And I'm guessing you both could cause some pretty insane havoc, considering the looks of this room."

One side of Cade's mouth kicked up. "The red paint was all Izzy's idea."

I rolled my eyes and took that moment to set my own ground rules as I lifted my T-shirt over my head. Both of them watched, both of them didn't move, both of them ate me up with their stares.

"I'm somewhat impulsive, I admit. But my only rule is if I say *stop*, we stop. It's my safe word, and I mean it."

Both of them nodded, and Cade looked at Rodney. "Anything you need to add?"

Rodney pulled his shirt off with a smile and said, "Hell no."

Cade gave one swift nod, then his voice got low. "Sit on the bed, Izzy. And Rodney, close our door so she can see herself in the mirror."

We both listened. I was surprised to see how full my breasts looked in my bra, like they were swollen with need, and how fast they rose and fell. I knew I was more than ready. My pink panties showed a darkened spot where my arousal had already soaked through.

I crossed my legs and hung them off the bed in the hopes neither of them would see. Cade caught it though and immediately said, "Spread your legs, dollface. Let us see how wet this makes you."

I glared at him, already wanting to defy him.

He growled. "Listen, Izzy. Or we're done."

Jesus. I loved when he commanded me in that tone. My legs listened immediately and spread for them to see.

They both hummed in approval, and Cade took it a step further. "See how wet she gets for us, Rodney? Like she can't keep herself bottled up."

Rodney cracked his knuckles. His eyes sized me up, reminding me of a bull scraping his hooves on the ground, gearing up to run at a target.

The man I knew I was falling for leaned back in his chair with a tent near the zipper of his trousers. The other man in front of me was hard underneath his gym shorts too. I licked my lips and placed the palms of my hands behind my back, pushing my breasts out a little farther.

"You told me to enjoy myself, Cade, so I'm going to try." It was something I never would have done before. Yet, with Cade watching, I knew he'd make sure nothing went too far. I also knew he planned to pull every emotion from me and still make sure I didn't tumble over a damn edge into some oblivion.

"Rodney, touch my girl's panties, huh? Let's see how wet we can make them."

Rodney stalked up to me and murmured that it would be his pleasure before his rough hand descended, pressing one finger's pad onto my clit. He stood to the side of me and combed his other hand through my hair as he did. We both watched each other in the mirror as he moved his finger back and forth, back and forth over my clit.

It only took seconds for the light pink of my panties to become dark, for my arousal to mark his hand with slickness.

As my breathing picked up, I glanced at Cade. The man sat there rubbing his chin, studying us, like he wanted something more. "Take her panties off now."

Rodney's hand left my hair and slid over the curve of my breast to dip down into my cleavage as he knelt in front of me. "That okay with you, baby?" he asked, staring right into my eyes. He was still rubbing my clit, still keeping up our rhythm as he waited for my response.

I nodded fervently, needing more than this, craving everything they could give me. I was letting go. I was taking what I wanted.

Silence filled the room other than our heavy breathing and the howling wind of the night air outside. Rodney pulled me down toward his face by hooking a finger at the middle of my bra. His eyes were focused on my lips, and I swear they tingled with anticipation of having his mouth on mine.

Yet, right as we were a hair away from tasting one another, Cade murmured, "Don't touch *my* mouth, Rodney."

Like the red line I'd sprayed on the damn bed, Cade drew his in the sand. Instead, Rodney let his hand fall from the lace of my bra and sat back on his haunches as he almost seamlessly moved to take off my panties.

I raised my hips while rolling my lips between my teeth, trying not to whimper at the lost opportunity of kissing someone right then. My body shook with need. I wanted either of their touches at this point.

My eyes held Cade's as he growled low in approval at the sight of my lower half completely bare to them both. I'd shaved earlier that day, and I think they both approved of how I'd tidied up.

"Well, if that isn't a golden pussy on a platter, I don't know what is," Cade murmured. Then he asked the man kneeling before me. "Ready?"

Rodney nodded and leaned in to smell me. When I looked down, shocked, he was staring up at me with a smile. "She smells fucking divine, Cade."

"I know," Cade replied before he told him, "Bring her to orgasm without tasting her, though, Rodney."

"What?" I breathed out, almost choking on him denying me Rodney's mouth. "He can taste me now, Cade."

Cade chuckled as if I were too eager. "Dollface, I make the rules, right?"

"It's a dumb rule, though."

Rodney didn't seem to mind us going back and forth. He pushed his thumb against my bundle of nerves and slid two fingers inside me while Cade responded, "What's dumb is you wanting to argue with me when I'm giving you everything you want right now."

"I wanted that," I whined, but I was already riding Rodney's hand, letting his fingers move inside me.

"Maybe our boss will do the honors and take that hot-as-sin mouth of yours instead," Rodney prompted Cade. He was a man after my heart, bless him.

Cade sighed as if we were two of his employees acting out and giving him trouble. Even though we'd inconvenienced him, he stood up to his full height and walked over. His fingers threaded through my waves, and he tipped my head back. Even a second of his touch had me whimpering, and then his other hand went around my neck as he took my mouth in his.

His tongue tangled with mine for dominance, forcing me to feel everything he was. Desire, passion, and what I wanted to imagine might have been something other than hate.

When he pulled back to take me in, he held my gaze and said, "Come, dollface. We want to see you let go."

I closed my eyes and let what was inside me out. Like a wrecking ball, my orgasm smashed through any wall of embarrassment or reservation I had about this hookup, about having two men pleasure me at once, about being ashamed of anything I wanted in the bedroom.

We were consenting adults, trusting of one another, and, well, they were both very, very hot.

But both were greedy because they didn't give me much time to recoup from hitting my high. Instead, Cade sat on the bed and asked Rodney, "You bring it?"

He didn't specify what, and so I was surprised when Rodney pulled a small device from his pocket. It looked like a black rubber teardrop with a cufflink on the bottom of it. "What's that?"

Cade leaned over and growled in my ear, "It's what I'm putting in your ass, baby."

He probably saw my eyes widen. "That's not going to fit."

He hummed. "Rodney, make sure she's ready, huh? Get it nice and wet."

I swear Rodney probably did this way too often. He didn't even hesitate. Why would he? He'd brought the toy over to the cabin in the first place. He held it at my folds as he continued to kneel before me and smirked when he pressed a little red button on the cuff link. The device buzzed right at my entrance, and I gasped, slamming both of my hands down onto his shoulders to steady myself and keep from falling right off the bed.

"I'm ninety-nine percent sure this is going to be too much for me, guys," I admitted.

Both of them laughed and shook their heads. "I'm convinced you can handle the world if I gave it to you all fucked up, Izzy," Cade murmured to me. Rodney removed the device, now shiny and almost dripping with my arousal. Cade grabbed my hips immediately and lifted me up to stand, then pressed a hand to my back. "Bend forward, baby."

Rodney scooted just a few inches forward so that I could bend at a ninety-degree angle, my hands on his shoulders, and ass back, out to the world. The device was handed over to Cade, who took it without so much as a thank you.

"Now"—he slid behind me, still seated, and rolled out the next word—"relax."

I felt how cool my arousal had become on the device, how it started at the tip of the teardrop, then, as I breathed out, Cade pushed it in slowly, firmly, right into my puckered asshole. "Holy shit," I whimpered when it felt like he'd pushed the whole thing in.

"We got another half of the plug to go, Izzy. Relax."

I whipped my head up to look in the mirror and saw Cade's gaze on my ass, saw how he stared with what looked like awe, and it made me want to take it all—to show him he could hand me the fucking world and I'd conquer it.

Yet, I was so full, so tight. He must have felt that too because he glanced up to catch my gaze, and those dark eyes held me captive as he sucked one of his fingers before bringing it down to rim my hole around the plug.

I moaned. He pushed it further. Then, suddenly, the vibration started. And I lost my mind to another place in the galaxy. "It's in, dollface," I heard from far away, even though it was Cade right next to my ear. He pulled me down as he said, "It's going to shock you, too, baby. I'm turning on the electricity."

I gasped right then because it happened at that moment, vibrating and then sending a zing of pleasure or pain through me that was so close to all my most sensitive nerve endings that it practically sent an orgasm up my spine. "Oh my God. God. God. God."

Cade chuckled. "I think she likes the toy," he said as he held me over his length, preparing to have me sit on him. "You like what we've done for you, Izzy?"

The question sliced through my heart as Cade stared at me with those amber eyes. He was accepting me, giving me this, pushing boundaries for my pleasure. "*You* did this for me," I whispered.

The way his hand roved over my chest to feel my heart beating as he held my gaze had tears forming in my eyes, had the world fading away where I could only see him, and had me convinced I could fall hard for him.

I bit my lip and tried to shake the feeling but Cade must have felt our connection too because as Rodney leaned forward, Cade growled, "No more, Rodney."

Rodney halted and waited for further instructions, Cade's voice too full of warning to disobey.

"Stay and watch or leave. I don't care which. Your mouth isn't allowed to touch her pussy though." With that, Cade brought me down hard on his dick.

I tried not to cry out, but the feeling was too much. Cade's hands slid to my bra and yanked it down so he could play with my tits and pinch my nipples. He didn't simply kiss my neck, he bit it as Rodney slowly stroked his own cock, watching me rock on Cade's length.

The picture we made in the mirror, a man with his eyes between my legs, jacking himself off and Cade behind me, fucking me exactly the way I liked, had me flying toward what couldn't be just an orgasm. It was probably death and heaven. Or hell. Or both mixed in one.

"You feel all this?" Cade asked as he bit my ear and squeezed a breast while thrusting in extra hard one time. "It's what I give you. You want a little good time, dollface, and you get the best fucking of your life. With me. Always with me."

He was trying to tell me something. I knew that. He said it with conviction, his cock pulsed with purpose, and his hands owned my tits with demand, but I was too far gone.

As another vibrating shock zapped my inner folds, I shivered, my whole body building toward something so monumental that tears started streaming down my face. I heard Rodney moan as he emptied his seed in his shorts and felt Cade thrust in me harder and faster. He lost control—his neck flexed, his hands gripped me tight, and those tattooed forearms bulged with veins moving to avoid his muscles.

I only saw him and felt him, how his cum shot into my walls, how he softened within me. I only saw the man that agreed to all this solely for my pleasure, and it pushed me over the edge. Blinded by an orgasm from both heaven and hell, and I was sure it had to be both at this point.

It took Cade a minute to wrap his arms around me and remove the plug from my behind. He glanced at Rodney and tossed it his way. "Time for you to go, Rodney."

"Fuck." Rodney slowly stood. He eyed me and then Cade with a sort of awe. "Call me if you want—"

"We won't want." Cade cut him off, his tone hard and definitive.

Grabbing his shirt, Rodney mumbled that he had to try before he left the room. Neither of us moved until we heard the front door open and close. Then Cade was pulling me back toward the headboard and situating me on the pillows. He disappeared for only a moment to return with neck ties.

"What are you doing?" I asked him.

"Haven't you looked down lately, dollface?"

Confused, I peered around me.

"You're over the red line, which means you're on my side of the bed and have to obey my rules."

"We just obeyed your rules," I pointed out, turning to my side and propping my head on my elbow. He didn't let me lounge there, though; he pushed me onto my back, dragged his hand down my arm, and took my wrist.

"Give me your other wrist," he murmured.

I laughed nervously. "I'm spent, Cade. You just had a man finger me and then you fucked me. I don't need to be tied up."

He'd stopped listening and grabbed my other wrist to fasten the silk tie. Once done, he lifted my hands above my head and tied me to the headboard. "My side, my rules."

"I think this whole 'your side, my side' thing is a little bit on the nose."

"It was your idea to begin with."

"I did it based on the principle of the matter—"

"Right." He disappeared into the bathroom, and I heard running water before he came back with a warm washcloth. Instead of continuing to argue with me, he dragged the towel over my cleavage and across my nipples, back and forth, back and forth. "Tell me, dollface, what was that principle again?"

He asked me only after a minute of standing over me, working my breasts, and quite frankly, I couldn't talk, let alone remember what the principle was. "Are you going to stand over me all night?"

"I'm cleaning you up. As you said, another man's hands were on you." He slid the towel down my stomach, to my hips, over my clit, and then between my folds.

"You invited him here, Cade," I reminded him, because suddenly I saw his real emotion. He was letting it unfurl around us as he took his time wiping every spot Rodney had touched like he needed to make sure I'd be washed of him. "It was fun, right? You enjoyed yourself."

"I always enjoy hearing you get off and fucking your pussy, Izzy. Admittedly, I think I enjoy it more when it's just me."

"Okay." I dragged out the word.

Cade slid one finger all the way up in me slowly and curled it into my G-spot without further discussion. "You're wet again, Ms. Hardy. Should we stop messing with fuck boys and give you what you really need?"

He slid it all the way out and let his cock drag over my clit, lubricating me with arousal. Yet, his movements were agonizingly languid. "Jesus." I arched on the bed, rolling my hips as I tried to get more friction between us, to speed him along.

He went in again slowly as his eyes held mine. In them, I saw the menace now, the jealousy, the way he looked when I wanted to call him Mr. Armanelli. "Was it him or me that pushed you over the edge? Was it his fingers in you or my *cock*?"

My pussy convulsed and tightened around him at the words. And he snatched that finger back. I whimpered, "Please, Cade." He smiled at me darkly, and I yanked on the ties to see if they'd give. "If you don't want to get me off, untie me so I can do it myself."

"Of course I want to get you off. It's what I've aimed to do the whole night. What do you think I'm doing now?" He took a full minute to roll his thumb over my clit . . . just once.

"It's too slow, Cade. You know it is. I need more. Please." I was so close again.

"Please what? Tell me what you want this time: me, or for me to call Rodney up again."

I rolled my hips and looked down at his strong hand between my legs. "If this is how fast we're moving, we can call Rodney again."

He narrowed his eyes in malice. "Really? And tell me, baby doll, who's the one who makes you cry out always?"

My mouth lifted as the need to piss him off and defy him barreled through me. "Rodney?"

The growl that came from him was so primal and so low it traveled straight up my spine. "You like being a fucking brat, Izzy, I swear. Tell me really. Or I'll bring you to the edge all night without letting you get off."

Him staring at me, with his jealousy bleeding through his tone, the way he antagonized me with such slow foreplay, it made every part of me vibrate with frustration, with need, with more emotions than I'd ever let myself feel. And as they barreled through me, I realized I wanted them all. I wanted to feel everything while he fucked me to either heaven or hell. But I wanted to go with him. Only him.

"I want you. Now."

His touch became powerful, fast, and completely what I needed. He slid three fingers in and fucked me, letting me ride him as fast as I wanted. I unraveled in seconds as I screamed his name and convulsed around him.

He smiled at my wetness, how I practically gushed out my arousal. "Such a pretty, messy brat, aren't you?" he said as he unbuttoned his shirt. "You know what I like for brats to do?"

"What's that, Cade?" I whispered, still trying to catch my breath.

He unbuckled his pants and pushed them off. A naked Cade was a masterpiece to witness. He towered over me, his cock straining with that piercing as it stood to attention again, thicker and bigger than I kept thinking I could take. Yet, I'd just had him, and my mouth watered to do it all over again.

"I like for brats to be quiet and listen. We have a much better use for your mouth than to have you be talking right now."

He didn't give me much time to respond before he climbed over me and tilted his dick to my lips. He placed his hands on the wall above the headboard and said, "Open."

"I—"

He thrust in. He really did want me to shut up. He fucked my mouth hard and fast like he needed it to sustain life. I took every thrust with pleasure and rocked my hips as I did. I loved seeing him coming undone, loved how he needed me in the moment, and loved the words he growled as he did. "I'm going to fuck you all night, dollface. Fuck you till you can't walk, can't breathe, can't talk—unless it's to scream my name. And it will be only my name you're screaming."

He pushed himself off me fast before he came in my mouth, and then he was down by my lower half, putting a pillow under my ass. "No more men near my pussy, you understand?"

"Cade," I pulled at the tie again. "It was just f—"

"No more fun unless it's with *me*." He parted my folds again. "You're mine."

"Cade, there's no way I can get there again," I murmured because I felt my body shaking, not sure I could handle another.

He smiled with confidence. "I get one more. And then I'm still going to fuck you, baby. You're on my side. My side, my rules."

He lowered his head, and his tongue ravished me.

I screamed his name the whole night. I blacked out screaming it, I think. And I didn't regret it, not even for a moment.

What this man orchestrated, what he gave me, what he let me do without shame, it was dangerous, because I realized I didn't want to bottle up my emotions and desire anymore.

I felt free.

I felt alive and indestructible.

But I wasn't.

CHAPTER 18

Cade

I woke to the faint buzz of Izzy's phone vibrating from the living room. Someone was texting her again, and with it being so damn early, I needed to know who. Not wanting to move from her side, though, I grabbed my phone and did what I did best.

I hacked hers.

It was a complete invasion of her privacy, something a man should never do, and yet I did it with no remorse. The woman wasn't going to have any secrets from me for too much longer if we kept going at this pace anyway.

I took over her system so I could operate her phone as if I were holding it and accessed her new messages. Over thirteen new ones, all from her ex.

I clicked into the inbox and saw red—hot, deep, anger. The man had been texting her nonstop. Berating her. Threatening her. Complaining to her about his stupid daddy's company. Loving her. Hating her. Coaxing her. Sending her pictures. And now there were pictures of the flowers he said he'd left at her doorstep.

He was a goddamn stalker. Said me, the guy scrolling through her phone without permission. But Izzy was mine to fuck with. Not someone else's. She did the same to me time and time again.

With Gerald, she didn't answer him or engage with him. He'd fucked with her long enough.

I petted the waves of her hair before I curled up next to her and extended my arm to snap a picture. When I was satisfied with the outcome, I sent it his way with a text.

> **Me:** She's fine. She's asleep with me. And she doesn't like lilies, dipshit. Stop sending them.
>
> **Gerald:** Is that Cade Armanelli?

Good. He knew who I was. I knew I was photographed sometimes in the news and that Izzy had spoken to him about me. When I didn't respond, my phone rang. And I answered with a smile on my face. "Don't call her when she's sleeping, Gerald. She needs her rest."

"What are you doing in bed with her?"

"What's it look like I'm doing?" I asked putting a hand behind my head on the pillow and smirking at her as she stretched with the bracelet on her wrist. It looked good there, like it belonged, like maybe something of mine had always belonged on her.

"If you're screwing my girlfriend, I swear to God, you'll be sorry."

"Let's say she *was* still your girlfriend," I continued down his stupid-ass line of thinking. "What exactly would you do to me, knowing I was fucking her? Knowing who I am."

Silence stretched over the phone. I think his brain had finally kicked in.

"Text her again, and you'll lose your fingers." I meant every word.

"What?" He whispered as if he was daring me to repeat myself and couldn't believe me.

I had every threat locked and loaded though. "Don't text her again. Don't even think about her again. Focus on that job of yours or you'll find yourself without it, without money, without fucking electricity. Do you understand? I can take everything away from you in seconds."

"Are you… are you messing with my company?" He stuttered out.

So, the imbecile did actually have a few brain cells. "Hacking an idiot's life isn't something I enjoy doing. It's much too easy, but if you bother her again, I'll take pleasure in it."

I actually was already finding quite a bit of pleasure in it, but I kept that to myself for now.

As I hung up on him, Izzy narrowed her eyes at me while she tucked the sheets in close to her body. "Someone bothering a person who's close to you?" she inquired, having no idea it was Gerald.

I moved closer to her with a smile on my face, and she shoved me back. "Um, no. Stay on your side. We had fun last night, but if you're that serious with someone else, we probably shouldn't—"

I cut her off by rolling on top of her and devouring her mouth. She met me with the same fervor, clawing at my back and sucking my tongue until she yanked my hair to pull me away. "Cade, I'm not into other women—"

"That was Gerald. He now understands you don't like lilies and that you're sleeping with me." I showed her my phone.

"You hacked my phone?" she squeaked and then glared.

"You're welcome."

"Oh my God." She rolled her eyes, laughing.

I laughed with her, and then I fucked her until we had to get to work. She made a half-assed attempt to get me to remove the bracelet before we went out to work. She told me she wouldn't know how to explain it.

"It's a gold bracelet." I shrugged. "No one is going to ask about it."

"It's lined with huge diamonds!" She stuck her wrist in my face. "Remove it."

I burst out laughing and refused. She didn't fight me much after that.

I heard her deflect when one woman asked her about it, and I'd already dismissed Heather for the rest of the trip. So, no one was any the wiser. And it was a damn near perfect setup to be in the same cabin as her after that night. We worked hard in silence, and then I made her orgasm loud later on.

The itinerary had more team building and working on systems, but JUNIPER was proving to be effective, and testing with everyone was going extremely well.

I found myself enjoying not only her but the whole team. I only took two calls from my brother to handle confidential projects, and Izzy completely understood and gave me space without hesitation.

"Is she always in your cabin?" Bastian asked the third time he called to check in.

"Are you always so up in my shit? Don't you have a wife to bother?" I responded back.

Bastian laughed like he enjoyed giving me hell. "She just yelled that she needs me to go pick up some essential oils for God knows what, and that you should buy your girl something nice. If you want to keep her around, you might want to try doing something different instead of burying your head in your phone like you normally do . . . or are you only fucking her?"

"I didn't say I was doing any of those things with her. She's my employee."

"Right. So, question still stands. Are you only fucking her?"

"None of your damn business." I hung up.

And then I called the florist.

CHAPTER 19

Izzy

We were twelve days in with just two days left of glamping, and I was surprised to admit that things were going well. We tested new breaches on JUNIPER daily and brainstormed different scenarios. We worked on our day-to-day tasks and did some zip-lining, campfires, and swimming in between.

Cade was on a first-name basis with everyone, and he and Rodney were practically pals—except when Rodney stared too long at me in my bikini and Cade whacked him over the head.

Lucas didn't ask me questions, but I knew they were flying around in his mind. He'd pried about my gold bracelet that I now twisted more than I should on my wrist all the time. I didn't disclose anything. I couldn't. We were in a safe little bubble for now with Cade staying too close, hovering too much, and staring too long.

I told him so that night, and he laughed, not giving a shit.

"It's not funny. We have to go back to work after this where you're the boss."

"I'm your boss right now," he murmured, typing away on his computer at our table while I watered the fifth bouquet of roses that'd been brought in the days since Cade had hacked my phone. He'd murmured they were sent to match my red spray paint.

And I couldn't stop myself from bringing out a tiny linen-wrapped canvas I'd packed in my suitcase. While he worked, I set it down on the table, folded up a piece of paper to use for edging, and started to spray paint. It took some time to move the paper and get the angles perfect before I went to grab a brush and my paints. All I needed was black and white, and I shaded it quicker than I normally would because the art flowed freely through me now.

Everything was freer. I didn't hesitate to show what I was feeling as much. I was more comfortable in my own skin. I even embraced the emotions I'd long since bottled up. My heart and my soul were liberated because they were toppling head over heels in love with Cade.

This rose turned out jagged, but with a bright white background, it appeared as though it was growing in the sun, in the light, and not succumbing to any darkness. Would I grow in our love too? Or would there be darkness?

"You hone your talents in things outside the digital world, I see," Cade murmured as he stared at my picture, my hands, and then my face. "You're truly a beautiful specimen, Izzy Hardy."

It would have been a precious moment, one in which we could have talked about what this relationship was starting to look like, had my sister not called.

Lilah's name popped up on my phone, and when I swiped to pick up the video chat, her frown made me immediately ask, "What's wrong, Lilah?"

"Well, I thought Bug got out, but she's fine." She followed up with that right away, knowing panic raced through me immediately. "But I was looking for her everywhere . . ." Her face fell and she glanced down.

"Okay, well, what? What's wrong?"

She held up a crinkled note. The writing was almost illegible. But it didn't have to be well-written for me to know every word. Every curve of the *w*'s, every period and punctuation mark.

"What is this, Izzy?" Her question came out scratchy, like she'd been crying. "This isn't your handwriting."

My heart dropped; the blood drained from my body.

"Whose is it?" she whispered.

Everyone had a secret, right? Everyone wants to keep one thing hidden in their life. Maybe more. People thought the skeleton in my closet was that I was an addict. They didn't know the whole truth.

They wouldn't want to. Life was ugly. It was unkind. It was unforgiving at times too. To keep living, though, a person has to take the ugly and find the beautiful, take the wretched and search for the blessed.

Maybe I hadn't done that. Maybe I'd just buried it all deep down and tried to hide it instead.

Vincent was ugly. He was the ugly sort of love that shaped me, that molded me, that made me the person I was today.

"Please don't leave me. Please. You can't. You can't die," I sobbed as I cradled him.

His buddy was already standing over me, tapping his dirty tennis shoe on the ground. "You gotta go, Izzy."

"I'm not leaving." I fisted the paper in my hand. His letter to me. It said goodbye. It said he was leaving, but he couldn't.

"You're going to stay? For what?" he asked, his voice cracking with fury. "You're sixteen. He's twenty-one. Do you know what that looks like? He should have never been with you, and now he's gone."

"No." I said desperately. He couldn't be.

"Yes." His friend pushed back, trying to grab my elbow to pull me from the floor where we'd slept that night, but I ripped my elbow back. "And he didn't leave a letter to his mom or his family. He left it to you."

Jonny never had approved with us being together. No one had. And his words pelted me like a hailstorm that I couldn't see through.

"We love each other," I murmured.

"He didn't love anybody but the drugs," he grumbled and swiped the mess off the floor. Needles and powder and . . . God, had we done all that? "How much of this did he give you?"

I was sobbing, the tears pooling so high before I blinked them away that I could barely see my lover's blue lips. Could I drown in them? Could I get lost in my own tears so I didn't have to wake up either? Because without him, I didn't want to.

"How could this happen? I was right here the whole night. I was right—"

"He gave you more than you asked for, and you passed out." He shook his head in disgust. "He's known for—"

"Don't you dare talk bad about him right now."

"He's been cheating on you this whole time!" his friend bellowed at me. The words cut through me, trying their best to cause damage.

I shook my head in denial. I would ask him when he got up. "He needs our help, Jonny. He's not fucking breathing, Jonny. Call someone. Call someone, please."

He pursed his lips, and his chin shook but no tears came. "You gotta get out of here, or he's going to be charged with statutory rape and dealing to minors before they pronounce him dead. You'll cause the family a shit storm. Disappear. Don't come to the funeral, and don't mention his damn name."

"But . . ." I glanced down at him, "He's not dead, Jonny."

He grumbled "Fuck me," before he came for me. He didn't hesitate to swoop me up and carry me to his car kicking and screaming.

"How can you do this? I love him! Don't you love him? He needs help."

As he threw me in his pickup and slammed the passenger door, I scrambled for my purse to look for my phone. By the time he rounded the hood and got in, he held his up to his ear and said, "Yeah, my friend OD'd. I'm pretty sure he's gone, but we need an ambulance."

Whatever he said after that, I didn't hear. I was bawling, begging, pleading with God. I needed my first love back, even if he was a secret. Even if I was his dirty little plaything.

At sixteen, everyone would have said I'd been groomed, coerced, pushed into loving him.

They'd have been right. I learned that much later. Jonny called me to say our drugs had been laced with fentanyl. I'd been lucky. Vincent hadn't.

Yet, it didn't negate the pain. It didn't make this any less hard. He'd gave me my first kiss, my first falling in love, my first time letting go of my innocence. He'd also shared my first high, and now I'd shared his last. We were connected. He'd told me I was his forever, that he'd love and take care of me to infinity and beyond.

I crumpled up that paper and stuck it in my pocket. His last communication with the world had been for me. For only me.

That had to mean something, right?

"Get rid of that note, Izzy," Jonny warned as he dropped me off two blocks from my house. "And here, take a few bars. If you're feeling down, they'll pick you up."

I snatched them, my body already scouring for a way to avoid the sadness, the agony, and the trauma I would have to endure on my own. "Jonny, I don't think I can do this."

That first heartbreak, it was like a meteor flew from the sky and landed right on the one thing that pumped love through my veins.

"You can. Do it for him, Izzy. For us. We're your friends. We can't have this on our records. Don't tell anyone. Don't tell anyone, or you'll ruin the memory of him."

My mother and sister greeted me as I walked in that day. I told them I was sick from my sleepover, that my girlfriend had been the worst kind of friend and I needed space.

They knew something was wrong.

Lilah knocked on my door for much longer than normal. She probably somehow felt my grief. So I covered it up with a pill.

And I did that for days, weeks, months. I did it until juvie, and I read that letter over and over again.

Burying emotions took time, practice, effort, and training.

I buried that emotion so deep I could barely access it.

I hoped I would never have to again.

"Izzy." She shook the paper in front of the phone again, but this time there were tears in her eyes. "Tell me who wrote this to you right now."

"It doesn't matter," I whispered. My therapist told me over and over that I should talk with someone whom I trusted about what I'd been through. The secret was between my therapist and me alone. I didn't want to get anyone in trouble, even if Vincent was gone, even if I didn't talk to any of those people anymore.

Now, I struggled with the embarrassment that I'd been taken advantage of, that I'd fallen for so much when I should have been smarter.

My therapist said I needed to share this with my family. But why? For them to worry even more, to be even more disappointed? My therapist had told me over and over that I'd been young, drugs were involved, I shouldn't blame myself.

I still did.

"It does matter!" she screamed, and Cade took that moment to stop staring at his laptop.

When I hustled out of the room and down the hall to our bedroom, the man followed. His stupid sharp eyes behind his stupid hot eyeglasses read my every move as he leaned on the doorframe, watching us both like he was ready for the destruction.

The man loved to see people uncomfortable—I knew that about him now. "Get out." I motioned for him to leave.

He shook his head no, but the look of concern on his face caught me off guard. He should have been smiling, should have relished my sister unearthing my secret.

"Izzy, I'll make Dante call Cade and have him send you home right now if you don't tell me. This is . . . this is a suicide note from someone! Izzy, who wrote this?"

"It doesn't matter," I whispered, but I remembered the words and, although I hadn't read it in maybe a year, they flashed before me now. The hand that held my phone shook as I thought of her rummaging through my things. "You shouldn't have been looking through my stuff. Put it back now."

"I was looking for your damn cat, and I came across the box."

"You didn't have to look in it." I raised my voice and then took a breath before I tried to rush past Cade into the living room.

He stopped me with a hand on my arm and took the phone from me.

Lilah gasped and stuttered, "Are you two working?"

"Something like that. Put her stuff away, and she'll call you back."

"Cade, this is serious."

"Do as you're told." He hung up and stared at me.

Curling up and crying in the bathroom was what I wanted to do, but instead I stood there with my chin raised. "You already know part of the story from the campfire. The rest is I was involved with a guy before juvie. I loved him, and he was too old for me."

I waited for his recoil, for him to frown upon my actions, but there was none whatsoever from him. He waited, like he wanted the whole story.

I took a deep breath, turning the bracelet that I wondered if he would want me to keep after I admitted this. "It was wrong and stupid and reckless. But he was my first love. He'd have been charged with statutory rape had anyone found out about us. I was sixteen and now I know he'd probably preyed upon me, groomed me, and changed me." I shrugged, trying to shake away the heat of embarrassment I felt rising to my cheeks. "Therapy taught me all that. Yet, even still, a heart can break quickly and soundly. Mine shattered when I realized he chose to leave me, that he didn't love me like I thought I loved him. I was embarrassed and in pain. It broke me, was big enough to destroy me."

Cade tsked. "You haven't been destroyed yet, baby doll."

I let out a small laugh that held no joy. "Cade, I've hidden this for a long time. It's embarrassing and wrong and . . . heartbreak and embarrassment hurt. That pain wrenches at your soul. Shakes you awake with the weight of the reminders and the pain. I couldn't handle it at first and used drugs as a crutch. It's how I know that love broke me, that I'm wrecked for all others."

"Why would it wreck you for others?"

"I try to find . . ." I hesitated, looking for the right words. Cade was messy, my boss, and my weakness. Falling for him was like jumping out of a damn airplane, not knowing if the parachute would open. "I try to find love that won't hurt, that's safe and comfortable at best. That way, if I lose someone like I did him, I won't go back to what I did then."

He studied me for a moment before asking, "What did his letter say?"

Would he look at me differently if I told him?

CHAPTER 20

Izzy

My gut wrenched, my heart breaking all over again at the thought of telling the man I was falling for about the first man I'd ever loved.

"It was just a way of him saying goodbye to me." I tried to brush it off even though my body shook with the pain of remembering that day, his written words, his lifeless form.

"That all it said?" He stepped close, caging me in against the hallway wall.

"I can't say it out loud," I whispered, about to break. My body shook from trying to hold in my sobs, trying to overcome the emotion that fought to escape. "I don't want to talk about it."

This could have been the moment Cade broke me. He could have told me to buck up or said this was why he didn't trust me with more at work.

He could have said so many things. But he didn't.

As he stared at me, his hand came up to rub my cheek. He didn't look through me or glance away from me. He held my gaze like he wanted more. He wanted everything. He wanted my soul, and he couldn't hack into my mind to get it. Here, he had to ask if he wanted this side of me.

And I had to say yes.

He held out his phone. "If you can't talk about it, put it in writing on a screen and let me read it."

I took my time typing in his Notes app, tears streaming down my face. Yet, Cade wiped them away, one by one, over and over again. Patiently, softly, caringly.

Line 1: I won't say this is a love letter, because it's not.
Line 2: But if I were to have written one, it would have been about you.
Line 3: So, don't blame yourself.
Line 4: You're too good for this place by me.
Line 5: I probably should have let you go before all this.
Line 6: But I couldn't. You were the only one who loved me.
Line 7: All that love around you. I just wanted a sliver.
Line 8: It fucked with my head and made me weak, so weak I held onto you.
Line 9: You think I'm strong to do this? Or a coward?
Line 10: Maybe if I tell you to move on, I'll be strong but . . .
Line 11: I'm too jealous and our love ain't healthy
Line 12: Get a love that isn't dangerous like ours
Line 13: I'm sorry for the mess.
Line 14: But I'm letting you go now.

"He was dramatic and poetic," I whispered as I handed him the phone. "I've memorized every line, and sometimes I just scramble them all up in hopes that it will mean something different."

He did what he always did when he was avoiding words: he hummed to give us both a moment to digest what was happening.

I showed him my darkest secret, trusted him with a part of me I didn't want anybody to see. He had the power now. I'd given it all to him.

"Will you delete it?" I asked quietly as he continued to stare at the phone.

"Am I a dangerous love or a safe one, Izzy?" he asked without answering me.

"I—" His dark gaze held mine, expecting me to know the answer. He wanted to know where we were going, as if we had anywhere to go at all. I knew my heart was lost to him, but I still tried to ignore it. "Aren't we just having fun, Cade? You let Rodney in here because—"

"I let Rodney in here for your enjoyment. Not mine." He immediately cut me off. "Don't confuse my willingness to make you happy with how serious I am about you. I would've never have done that before."

"We're serious now?" He'd lost his mind. "What do you mean you wouldn't have done that before?"

"Because I don't share . . . except for you. For some reason, I'm inclined to make you feel good, even if it fucks with my head. I loved seeing you look alive with another man between your legs while I watched, but don't think for a second I'd let it happen again. You and I are done with others from this point on."

"You don't control that. If I want to go grab Rodney for a quickie—"

"It'll be the last quickie he has before he dies a slow, excruciating death." The threat rumbled out of him, so menacing I believed him.

"What are we doing?" I whispered, I asked, my heart beating so fast I swear my blood couldn't keep up. "You're talking like this is serious."

"Is it not?" he asked, making me suddenly feel like I was the crazy one.

"What the hell would I tell our team out there?"

"The truth?" He shrugged.

"Didn't you just hear me? I slept with an older man when I was sixteen, Cade." I winced as I said it out loud. "The first time you met me, you called me an addict. Now I'm sleeping with my freaking boss. That doesn't look real great for you."

"I'm not too worried about my reputation." He chuckled and leaned back against the wall to take me in. "What are you really scared of, Izzy?"

Did he not realize I could fall for him so fast and so hard that I'd never make it back to the surface? "Why do I have to be scared of anything? Why can't it just be that this was fun and now we need to stop fucking around?"

"You ready to go back to bottling up everything you're feeling?" He lifted his stupid dark brow.

"I've done it just fine over the years," I blurted out, then I gasped at the words, slapping a hand over my mouth.

And there was that genuine smile of his when he pulled discomfort from someone, or when he cracked a fucking code or finished a stupid confidential project that he wouldn't let me help him work on. "Exactly. And why do that another second when you've been fine letting it all go here?"

"Am I some sort of experiment to you?" I yelled. "I can't gamble with this, with us, with any of it. I lost my first love because I was being reckless with my emotions and my behavior."

"You lost him because he OD'd. He chose his own fate."

"I could have stopped it," I whispered.

"You can't think like that. It's like saying I could have stopped all the lives lost because my father. I could have stopped him."

"But you did." I pointed out.

"I could have done it sooner."

"Do you really think like that?" I wondered if he took blame like so many children took on their parents' sins.

"No." He shook his head. "We can't change someone's path once their mind is made up. You can't go back and rewrite his story or think of the what-ifs. It's why you shouldn't try to scramble that letter into something it's not. You accept what people have done and respond to it in the way that's best for you."

"Is that what you did with your father?" I asked quietly, trying to understand him maybe like he was trying to understand me.

"Yes. We gave him what he deserved." He stopped for a second to glance at his phone. "With Vincent, it seems you can only respond by writing him back, huh?"

"Like a letter?" I squinted at him.

He shrugged. "Maybe."

I shook my head. "Look, I can't. I can't do any of this, okay? Let's forget we talked this over. It's just... I should have been able to stop him . . ." I took a deep breath.

"No, love." His voice was soft, but firm. "You can't blame yourself for a decision he made, Izzy." He tried to pull me into his arms but I didn't let him. He was saying what I'd probably needed to hear for a very long time but hadn't gotten to.

Yet, I wanted to hide from him. I wanted to disappear. I wanted a damn hit or pick-me-up of a drug I couldn't go back to.

That was the moment.

That feeling. It could consume me.

I knew I had to step away. I was lost in the depths of my own ocean of sorrow and embarrassment with another wave about to drown me. And it could have been the opposite; I could have been flying in a cloud of my own happiness, crazy in love and not seeing that the sun was about to blind me. I got too close to it all, and then I wanted to indulge in what could ruin me.

It was a sign. A stark reminder. "We shouldn't be talking about this."

"Why?" He frowned and then searched my face.

"Why? Because I haven't told anyone this. You shouldn't know this, Cade! Why would you even want to?" I poked him to shove him back, but he didn't move an inch.

"Because I want to know everything about you. I'm trying to figure you out, to understand you."

"I don't want you to," I exclaimed and combed my hands through my messy hair. God, I should have had it up in a ponytail. I shouldn't have been prancing around in my wrinkled mess of clothes, head full of waves and face free of makeup. I'd unraveled and let myself go free when I shouldn't have been. "I'm not a fucking algorithm to decode. I'm a screwup. That's it."

I held my arms out and waved them in front of myself like I was presenting. I'd lost the mask. I'd lost the facade. I was standing in front of him, vulnerable, and I didn't know if my heart could handle someone loving the real me again, someone breaking my heart and leaving again.

"Funny that you're more attractive as a screwup than a well-put-together doll. I mean, don't get me wrong. I'd take you either way, but this you is what I want." He didn't even say it as a joke.

My heart squeezed at his words, how he looked at me with genuine affection in his gaze. My body responded, but I *couldn't*. "This was a fun cabin retreat, Cade. Not a relationship. I have to go back to being put together after this."

He pulled a lock of my hair and stepped close. "Should I fight you for your mess, baby doll?"

"You wouldn't win." I chuckled sadly and glanced away. Why was my heart already breaking?

But he turned my chin up and made me stare into those whiskey eyes of his. They held determination and domination. "I always win, Ms. Hardy."

"Well, it's not a game we're playing. We can't do this anymore. The red line of spray paint is being reinforced."

He shook his head. "What are you so scared of? Losing someone you care about again? You care about me?" The man was smiling as if he'd been given some type of award.

I rolled my eyes. "If I cared about you, we'd have a hell of an uphill battle. Don't you get that? I've had therapy for my addiction, Cade." I paced down the hallway to the living room, and he followed to watch me walk back and forth. "I've studied it and researched it—like I do with the fucking systems we dig into. I know what's good for me. Relationships like this . . . how can they be? You're still part of the mob, even if it's a business now. And I'm still an addict, even if I'm recovered for now. We can't sit here and say that how we bump heads . . ."

He narrowed his eyes, then went to take a seat at the table where he opened his laptop. "You're avoiding the real conversation, Izzy."

"What's the real conversation, then?" I stopped to place my

hands on my hips and glare at him and his stupid computer.

He didn't even look up from it. "You're using a man's suicide to cage you in. It's keeping you away from really living the beautiful chaos you would be if you'd let go and talk about it. So I'll indulge you for now, and when you're ready, I'll be here to talk."

"Are you kidding? Our relationship is—"

"Nonexistent. This is all fun. I get it," he mumbled, shifting his focus to work. The man even started typing away on his keyboard.

I strode over the laptop, snatched it from his fingers, and shut it angrily. "I'm talking to you."

"And I'm working"—he shrugged—"because you're saying nothing of real importance right now. Might as well work."

This fucking guy.

I held the laptop out in front of me and then slammed it down onto the ground.

When he smiled, I fucking stomped on it like a child. "So much for working, you jackass."

A full-on grin spread across his face. "There she is. Now, do you need to say anything else before I take you to the bedroom and fuck you silent? I can't stand the bullshit you're spewing today about not being with me. I have other things to do."

"Do you hear yourself? I just told you I was dating an older man at sixteen and he was my first love. He committed suicide, and I spiraled, and now you're working me up into a fucking frenzy as if I might not spiral again?" My voice was well above a normal volume as I got in his face, my emotions out of control.

I felt as though my life was out of control. I'd let all my emotions run wild on this trip, and now everything felt like it was all unraveling, and I couldn't stop it.

He rubbed his jaw, and I heard the scratch from his five-o'clock shadow, imagined the way it would feel against my skin. "You feel like you're losing it, Izzy? You don't want to trust yourself? Why not? Have you looked at your life in the past nine years?"

I hesitated, though it didn't matter since he was ready to dive in anyway.

"Because I have. I've seen how you operate over the past year. You stay up late working, you walk a tightrope of restrictions, you don't let your hair down like you need to, and you don't let that little Harley Quinn inside you breathe."

"That's not true—"

"And she needs to breathe, dollface. Or else you'll never be happy."

"What if my happy isn't healthy, Cade?" I chewed my lip and glared at him.

"I'd be happier with a toxic mess of a girlfriend anyway."

"Don't call me that." I stepped back. Fear slithered through me at the same time my heart soared. "I just wrecked your freaking laptop."

"I know." He stared down at it. "Want to apologize?"

I crossed my arms because I really didn't. Our relationship had always entailed me giving him attitude—that was our touchstone—and even here, when I was saying we couldn't have anything between us at all anymore, my soul was still connected to him. I wanted to be a brat, but I ground out, "Sorry. I shouldn't have done that."

"Such a good girl. Does it feel as nice as holding back?" he murmured as he got up and slid a finger down my arm. I shivered as he meandered out of the room while I stared at the red roses, the beautiful bloodred roses, still so alive because I'd watered them every day. So many of them the whole island counter was full of glass vases. That's where the thorns were hidden though, tucked away, pretending they weren't there at all.

I saw how my little canvas had been propped up against one vase. Cade must have done it . . . he enjoyed the part of me that was artistic, like he could enjoy my beauty and my thorns, all my problems and my strengths.

He walked back in with a new laptop and sat back down.

"You had another laptop that whole time?"

"Even if I didn't, the staff would have gotten me one." He was back to typing.

I threw up my hands. "This is why we can never date."

He chuckled and then took his glasses off to rub between his eyes. "You know what, Izzy? Fine. How about we entertain your idea for a week or two. Have a weekend to yourself when we get back. Sleep on your side of the bed. See how you feel, huh?"

"I'll feel damn good about it," I concluded and nodded my head with a jerk. "Come take this bracelet off."

He tsked at me. "That's not happening. It's a gift that stays on you. Forever."

"Even if I don't want anything with you."

He shrugged. "Seems you don't right now. So, you're getting what you want."

I don't know why I felt like I was going to cry, but tears formed in my eyes. So I spun around and stomped out of the room.

And that was the end of it.

Cutting off the relationship before there ever was one.

I had to deal with my family. Lilah had called me about ten

times in the last ten minutes.

So I did.

I called her back, I shared my story, and she listened without judgment. It was what a sister did. And then she got super pissed that I'd never told her in the first place. I wasn't sure why that was such a relief, why she didn't coddle me through the whole thing, but I needed it.

She even laughed as I asked her if she was worried. "Worried about my sister? Sure. But I'm not as worried now that you've let it out and shared it all."

It was a gentle revelation that she believed I could be okay, that she believed in me and my sobriety. And she'd wanted my reality, not my façade.

The structure I had was falling apart. And the change scared me. I just needed to work, needed time to myself, so I took it.

I went back to the job, and I avoided Cade for the last two days of the retreat. I avoided everything, the calls from the team, from the rest of my family, and even from Cade.

But avoiding life and the feelings inside of a soul always has a way of coming out.

CHAPTER 21

Izzy

We'd celebrated our achievements on the last day of the retreat. JUNIPER was sent out to all the cybersecurity teams in every state, and we were assigned regions to make sure they would be taken care of. I set up protocols and trained the team to handle breaches, planning with all of them to have weekly video chat meetings up until the election.

Our last night, once I'd brushed my teeth in the guest bathroom and slipped into a Beethoven the dog T-shirt, I saw Cade lying on his side of the bed reading a comic book. Dressed only in sweatpants, tattoos painting his chest, and those glasses still on, my heart hurt not being able to climb on top of him.

I sighed and crawled into my side, then pulled my Kindle app up. I needed a good romance to live vicariously through.

"What are you reading?" he murmured, sparking the first conversation we'd had that day.

"Not sure yet. I should study some—"

"You should read for pleasure," he immediately corrected me.

If only he knew about the types of books I read. The blush that stained my cheeks with his wording probably gave me away though.

He chuckled. "The look on your face tells me what I need to know."

I scoffed. "What are you reading?"

"I'm reading for pleasure too. I can't get the Harley Quinn out of you right now, so I'm reading the comics instead."

Why did my throat instantly feel dry with his confession, like I couldn't swallow down the pain of losing him that had started to grow in me? I had no control over the next words that came out of my mouth. "Can I read it with you?"

"Sure, dollface. Sure," he murmured. Then he pulled me close, let me lay my head on his shoulder, and he read to me. The night stayed platonic, but somehow it felt more intimate than anything I'd ever experienced.

The next morning, we didn't discuss anything. Instead, we said our farewells. I gave Rodney a hug goodbye, along with a few other people from different teams, then we all flew home.

Back in the office that Monday should have been fine, but I'd spent a weekend on my own. I'd stared at that terrible note longer than I should have. I cried in my bedroom and then in my spare room and then contemplated calling the man I felt I should be living without.

I painted picture after picture, and all of them reminded me of roses. I sat at my computer, ready to work, but couldn't find the drive to do it. Bug purred around my legs most of the day, consoling me, which obviously meant I was in a funk. She wasn't a loving cat.

When I saw him saunter in Monday morning, I avoided his gaze but felt the heat of it on me. He welcomed everyone back and congratulated us all, but especially me, on a feat not many in our industry could accomplish. He said it in front of everyone, and I blushed without looking up. The compliment coming from him was a fucking accolade that I would think about for the rest of my life.

Yet, I didn't care about it right then. I cared about the way his voice slid over me, the way it felt like it was rubbing all the best parts of me, and how I wanted him all over again.

The rest of the week wasn't any better. I was back in pencil skirts and stilettos with my high ponytail even though every day I yearned to wear a T-shirt to work, to abandon the professional look, and let my hair down. I instead worked quietly on tasks Juda assigned to me from Cade because Cade wouldn't come talk to me. We'd all gone back to way it was. I even stayed and worked late every night since I had nothing else to do with my life.

I really didn't. At least Gerald had stopped texting me. Except I had Cade to thank for that, too, which depressed me even more. And my sister was being more than a little annoying with her group texts—like I needed more on my plate.

> **Lilah:** So, I feel like you need to tell our brothers what you told me over your work trip.
>
> **Dom:** I think you need to tell us too, Izzy. What's up?
>
> **Declan:** Don't leave us hanging.
>
> **Me:** I'll tell you all in good time.

Probably. Maybe.

> **Lilah:** She won't. She's hoping you'll all forget. I have super twin powers and can read her mind.

Dimitri: Get over yourself, Lilah. Everyone can read Izzy's mind.

Me: You can't.

Lilah: Okay well they should at least know who you're sleeping with.

Declan: What the fuck. I don't want to know that. Don't sleep with anyone, Izzy.

Lilah: Too late. She slept with Caden Armanelli and thinks she can keep it from everyone.

Me: Why are you the worst, Lilah?

Dimitri: What in the actual fuck? I'm at work ... I'm calling you in ten minutes, Izzy. You'd better pick up.

Declan called me first. I ignored him.

Me: No. All of you better stop calling. It was only a few times, and it's over now.

Then Lilah called. I wanted to scream. Siblings were the worst humans in the world, even if I did love them and would die for them. Some days I wanted to kill them myself.

Me: I have to work.

Lilah: It's 6 p.m. there.

Me: And I'm still working. We'll talk soon. It's over, it's fine. Please drop it.

Then Lucas texted me too.

Lucas: Something's wrong with you. We're going to this mask party near Stonewood Tower tomorrow, so you can have a drink and tell me.

Me: I'm not in the mood, and I have a lot of work to do. Go without me.

Lucas: Just bring a hot dress if you intend to work late, and I'll get you a mask. You're going.

Me: I'm really not.

Lucas: If you don't, I'll literally follow you around all weekend like a sad puppy who needs their fun friend back. I can't handle your sad hazel eyes all day.

Me: Fine.

I was such a good friend that I did what I was told. I picked a hot black dress and grabbed a makeup bag for after work. I knew I'd work late because I'd seen a hiccup in my region of JUNIPER the day before and wanted to dig in deeper.

The workday went the same as all the others, except that Cassie and Penelope breezed out early and most everyone else meandered out after them.

Lucas kissed me on the cheek and handed me a mask. "Text me when you get there. I sent you the address."

I nodded, still focused on tinkering with my work. We were a week and a half out from the election, and I wanted everything to be perfect. My firewall was stable, withstanding various normal attempts of breaching, but this one small attempt was different.

"That's odd," I murmured as I dug into it. Thankfully I'd set up a system that alerted us to these weird site visitors because this one appeared to have a foreign setup.

One I recognized.

I followed the coding onto another site and hit the dark web for another ten minutes. It didn't take me long as I hurried through codes and algorithms designed to distract most.

Months ago, Cade would have seen me digging, but now I didn't think he bothered. Honestly, I only researched things for the election. I was past my undercover days, I realized. Maybe it'd happened at the retreat when I was distracted in a way I shouldn't have been.

The thought made me work harder. I coded quickly and set up a hacking algorithm to break down the firewall. I grabbed my bag and went to the bathroom to change while it ran. I straightened the black dress I'd put on and eyed myself in the mirror. I'd probably put on a few extra pounds on my hips over the retreat. I smoothed my hand down the flowy silk of the dress.

It hugged the curves of my body and left little to the imagination. I loved the buttery silk of the dress because it was soft, comfortable, and sexy. I loved that when I moved, it let my curves sway, making me feel like I was embracing my feminine energy. With the lace at my cleavage and the open back, I knew I'd fit right in at the club.

I sat back down and applied smoky eyeliner, then red lipstick, as I waited for the firewall to break down. My screen moved quickly through codes that I knew had to mean something.

"What are you doing?" I heard his voice from far behind me.

Shit. I jumped and slammed my laptop closed.

His eyes were on me, my dress, my red lips.

I shot up from my desk and grabbed my bag. I didn't want him to see that I'd been tinkering with old data and think maybe I'd stumbled onto something with the Albanians, that I was back to my old habits.

We were past them, right? Or maybe we weren't, because if they were trying to hack our systems, Cade would need to be told. Better yet, Jett Stonewood and the president had to be told.

I would have to make sure later, though. I couldn't tell him now or it would look like I had a vendetta. Not after the praise at the end of the retreat. I didn't want him to look at me like I was a reckless person, not cut out for the job again, I realized.

After all we'd done on that retreat, I couldn't handle being that to him again, even if I didn't know what I was now. Sometimes the unknown in the dark, where a person can't find a damn thing, is better than seeing the reality of it all.

"I was finishing up for the night."

"Dressed like that?" I glanced down as I saw him eye my body like a starved animal.

"We're going to the Halloween party at the club down the street."

"Again, dare I ask, dressed like that?" His voice dropped a few octaves, and I had to clench my thighs to keep from spreading them for him.

I crossed my arms, and he growled when my cleavage bulged. "Yes, dressed like this. Got a problem with it?"

One of those large, tattooed hands shot out to drag one finger over the gold on my wrist. "Since we're entertaining your damn idea that what was between us was a good time and done, the answer is no."

"And if we weren't entertaining my idea?" I whispered because I wanted to torture myself, obviously.

"If you were with me? Wanting to go out dressed like that? We wouldn't leave the fucking building."

"Someone is a bit territorial over a little skin showing, huh?"

"No, dollface. I know how to fight. I'm not worried about a guy looking at you wrong. I've slit enough throats to combat that." His tone held menace as he threw around that Armanelli power. He didn't do it often. It was how I knew Cade still felt something for me. Felt something deep and dark and dangerous. "We wouldn't leave the building because I'd rip the dress off and bend you over your desk."

"Cade," I whispered, taking a step back, knowing I couldn't resist him if he pushed me much further. And I had to because I felt the heartache of losing him already.

Losing him when I didn't even quite have him was gut-wrenching. Depressing. And staggeringly more difficult than I'd thought.

"Want me to show you, baby doll? Or are we still playing your silly game?"

"No," I blurted out and swiped my makeup and purse off my desk. "Find someone else to fuck over a desk."

He straightened my chair and then leaned on it. "You think I can replace that sinful mouth of yours? Or find a girl who gives as good as she gets and can rival me in hacking, Ms. Hardy?"

"I'm sure you could find someone." I shrugged, but the idea tore my heart out.

He nodded once, a frown appearing on his face, and he stepped back. Maybe he was letting me go; maybe he'd finally decided I was replaceable. "Yes, Izzy. Maybe I could, but I wouldn't want to."

He waved me past him, and I walked out toward the elevators. I tried not to look back, tried not to catch one last glimpse of my heart being left there, bleeding out on the floor.

When I turned, he was still leaning on my chair, his hands fisted around the back of it.

Did he feel it too? The way we were losing something we never really had?

CHAPTER 22

Izzy

I texted Lucas as soon as I got to the club, then I disappeared into the crowd. It was dim enough for people to lose their identities under their masks, but I still found my friend at the bar in all white with a feathered white mask around his eyes.

He handed me the black one and said, "White and black swans. Somehow, I think it's poetic."

I chuckled as I slid mine on. "Probably not."

"Let's get Izzy Bizzy a drink," he murmured. "I want that look on your face gone."

"I should probably just let you have fun and take one for the team. I'm not in the mood."

"This is what I mean." His shoulder bumped mine as we took a seat at the bar. "Something's up with you. I should have brought the damn candy canes so we could talk it out."

I pulled my hair from the tight ponytail I normally wore to work and shook it loose around my mask. Then I leaned over and unbuttoned his white suit. "We're not at the office. Candy canes don't work now."

His lips pinched at the corners as they thinned, while his blue eyes bored into me. "They work about as good as we're going to get, considering we don't have the real thing."

I studied him. "Are you good?"

He sighed and wiped a hand over his face. "You know you don't always have to be my sponsor, right? And I'd tell you if I was at my breaking point."

I picked at a nail. "I'm not saying that you wouldn't. I'm just—"

"You're not sure you'd tell anyone if you were about to go off the deep end? So you're projecting your own hypothetical actions onto me?"

Scratching my forehead, I looked around the bar. A blonde bartender with a peacock mask carried over a mojito for me and stared at Lucas with lust in her big green eyes. Poor girl had no idea that Lucas would never sleep with her, but I had to admit, Lucas in a white suit was a sight to see. Even so, he liked brunettes with beards, and she didn't have either of those attributes. "You want a drink now? On the house?"

He chuckled and pulled my stool close like he wanted her to believe we were together. I knew the drill. I laid my head on his shoulder and saw her face fall almost immediately. "I'll have an old-fashioned."

"Great." She hurried away to make his drink.

I gazed up at him lovingly. "Would you like me to act like your girlfriend all night or just for the next minute?"

He pinched my side, and I yelped. He laughed as he said, "If I did like women, you'd be the perfect one."

"Yeah, yeah. Well, I'm a mess according to . . ." I almost said

Cade but then cleared my throat. "Gerald."

"You finally get hit by the sad bus and are depressed you lost your shit boyfriend now?" He pushed his lip out, and I flicked it. "Fuck, Izzy. That hurt. I'm only teasing you because you're not sad about that and you know it."

"Well, technically I am sad," I admitted but waited for the bartender to drop off his drink before I continued. "Am I sad about Gerald?" I hummed for a second like I was thinking about it. "Probably not. He's finally stopped texting."

"No shit. Do you know why he stopped now?"

"Not really." I glanced away.

"What aren't you telling me? You came back from that trip like you had a broken heart, but . . ." The freaking lightbulb in his head must have gone off. "Do you have a broken heart, Izzy?"

I took a swig of my mojito, staring into my drink. He paused so long that I glanced up.

The thing about Lucas was he knew my quirks, my tells, my everything. That's what you got when you worked so closely with someone. It was funny, my twin sister may not have been able to pick up on them, but someone I worked with forty hours a week and then hung out with on the side certainly knew me best. Perceptive colleagues who spent the majority of their time with one another could easily learn more than was intended for them.

"You're fucking Cade? Is he the one who broke your heart?" my friend bellowed.

"Jesus! Be quiet." I smacked his arm. "I'm not fucking him. Not anymore. And it was mostly hate fucking. Honestly, most of the time, I really despised him . . . except when I didn't."

"That doesn't even make sense, Izzy Bizzy." His tone sounded soothing and concerned.

"No. Don't do that." I hated being coddled. "Don't get all big brother on me. I already have four of them."

"Each and every one of them are hot too. Please tell me that one day, one of them will swing my way."

"Not as of yet, but I can't have you as another overprotective brother-in-law. So you're going to have to steer your spear not so near."

He choked on his drink as he laughed. "The fuck are you talking about? I'm not trying to marry anyone."

"Right. I know. But my sister wasn't trying to get married either, yet here I am with a brother-in-law."

"True. True. I think we need shots." He rubbed his jaw. "And another drink. Damn, Izzy. I was not expecting you to tell me you fucked our boss."

I groaned. If I was laying it all on the table, I should confess to the rest that was bothering me. "And quite frankly, I can handle that. But I . . ." I took a breath and said what I needed to. "I can't handle losing someone else because I lost someone when I was really young."

Lucas sat up straight, in disbelief, like he was a dog who'd heard a suspicious sound. His ears were perked, ready to attack or protect his best friend. Me.

That's why I decided to tell him. Why I knew he'd be the one to understand.

So as people danced around in masks and had the time of their lives, I told my best friend everything. And he listened. His jaw may have dropped when I told him about the cabin retreat and about my first love, but he didn't judge me. He didn't even wrinkle his nose at me.

And at the end of my story, he leaned in. "Was he at least good?" Lucas whispered close to my ear, and I threw up my hands before dropping my head on the bar.

"You're a terrible friend, you know that?" I asked without picking up my head.

"I'm your best friend," he growled before pulling my hair so I would sit up. I glanced at him. "And I ask the questions that matter. Because you know what will happen if he's good?"

I rested my elbow on the bar and set my chin in my hand to give him the full attention he wanted as he dragged out his point. "What will happen, dear Lucas?"

"You won't get over him. You'll find your way back again and again."

"I told you it was mostly hate fucking."

"Hate fucking is the best fucking, and we all know it." He held up a shot of rum and ticked his head at mine. "Cheers to you and the dumpster fire that your life is about to be."

"I'm not cheers-ing to that." I had lifted my shot glass but pulled it back.

"Fine. Cheers to me pulling you from the dumpster fire that you're inevitably about to fall into."

I rolled my eyes but clinked my glass against his before I downed it. "I hate that you're probably right." I took a deep breath. "I already told him we're going our separate ways."

"Ri-i-ight." He dragged out the word. "Cade Armanelli doesn't let go of something he wants."

"We don't know that he wants anything more from me," I said quietly.

"He does. And I've read that the man could have single-handedly managed the hacking of this election, Izzy. He's a freaking god amongst us, even if we want to pretend he's not. He won't let you go."

I rubbed my eyes and then swore because of the makeup I'd put on. "Get more shots, Lucas. We're going to need them."

————

Our night should have progressed into a blurry fun mess, but instead, Lucas told me he was going to the bathroom and that I should stay put.

Instead, I decided to wander around and see if I knew anyone. Most of our team hadn't mentioned coming out to the Halloween party, but I knew people had to let off a little steam.

It was only minutes later that I saw that mask.

It was in the corner of the club, hidden so well that most people just passed by him. But I felt his eyes. His dark stare. My whole stomach clenched in fear, anticipation, and hunger.

Cade Armanelli had shown up in that same *Scream* mask from our last pre-Halloween event at Stonewood Enterprises.

Not even a second later, the lights cut out in the whole club.

Screams rang out, and I gasped when, a second later, someone grabbed me. I jerked away, ready to fight until I heard the gravel in his voice close to my ear. "Fight me, dollface. We'll both enjoy this more if you do."

"Are you kidding me right now, Cade?"

He shoved me up against the club wall as people milled around, trying to get their bearings in the dark. "Why would I kid about fucking that pussy? The lights are out for a reason."

"Jesus, that was you?" I glared at him and then hit his dark shoulder.

His head lowered in the mask, and I think I shivered as adrenaline coursed through my veins. He leaned in and whispered against my ear. "You like the mask, baby doll? Want to fuck a stranger instead of the guy you're trying your best not to love?"

Love.

I knew I loved him. It was the reason my soul felt alive right then, why my skin felt the shock of his touch. His hand was at my thigh, and I whimpered. "People are going to notice, Cade. There's no music or anything. We can't do this."

It only took a moment of him sliding his phone out and pressing a few buttons for the music to blast on with a few of the strobe lights. People screamed in celebration, and then his hand dropped his phone back into his pocket, only to pull out that switchblade he always carried with him. "Now, I'm pretty sure I can do what I want to the woman in black."

"I thought we weren't playing my silly game?" I lifted a brow.

"Aren't we? You're at the club, showing off half a dress, talking to any guy who holds you hostage, in a mask."

"Hardly showing it off when the lights are out."

He chuckled. "Exactly."

The fucker had done it for that very reason, I bet.

"I'm done." I tried to push past him, tried to play it off as him being ridiculous. It was my best excuse to avoid my heart beating so fast that it might jump out of my chest and into his hand where he'd have control of it, where I'd never get it back.

Yet, Cade wasn't done with me. And Caden Armanelli had come to play. He grabbed my hair and shoved me against the wall, then put his knife at my neck. "Did I say you could be done? Do you think you get to walk around swaying that nice ass for someone other than me?"

My nipples pricked and my breathing hitched as I felt my heart jump into his hands and saw how he held my life in them too.

"Look at how hot you look when someone threatens your life. How wet are you, dollface?"

I chewed my cheek, not wanting to answer but knowing it may be the wettest I'd ever been.

He pushed the knife farther into my neck. How people just walked by with no concern for a woman up against the wall was beyond me. "Answer me. Or say stop, Izzy. Tell me now if you're ready to play."

I lifted my chin. "Not wet enough," I answered and smirked at how the grip in my hair tightened.

"You'll pay for that," he growled. "Unzip me, baby. And work my cock into you. I want to feel your pussy milking me, strangling me, squeezing me."

Social etiquette was gone. The fact that we were in public meant nothing. All I saw was him. This man knew how I wanted it, how I would beg for him to take me in the most fucked-up ways, and how it would turn me on. He accepted the twisted part of me and knew when to grab hold of it and not let it go.

I unbuckled his pants and drew him close. He took one step toward me like he was shielding us from the world. With his big hoodie on and his back to everyone, he practically was.

I pushed my panties to the side and guided that thick length to me. I rimmed my folds with his pre-cum, and he let out a low hum while I whimpered. Then I whispered, "I missed you, Cade."

And he dug that knife just a bit deeper. I felt the pinch and the skin break. A beautiful dark crimson ribbon of blood dripped down, down, down into my cleavage and he took that moment to lift his mask. Cade watched the red, his eyes full of possession and darkness before he dipped his head low to lick it from my chest. My whole body quaked at the feeling, completely hypnotized by the way he expertly lapped it away. Then, he pulled the mask back in place and I couldn't refuse myself anymore. Giving in to what I wanted, I wrapped one leg around him and mounted his cock.

He thrust in immediately too, fucking me with that mask in my face—haunting me, consuming me, owning me with a goddamn knife to my throat. I was lost to him, and I wanted to be. It was wrong and I didn't want to be right.

We both moaned and reached our orgasms fast, him coming inside me like it was the only place to be and me clenching around him like I needed his fucking dick to survive.

After a moment, he stepped back, and I gasped at him taking away his cock and the knife. It was a monumental loss.

I stared as he readjusted the bottom half of my dress and then zipped up. "You're mine, Izzy Hardy. Even if I have to mask up to have you." He left me then.

I didn't know what to do other than stare after him.

It took me a good five minutes to make myself move. When I found Lucas, he'd been drinking without me, and I was about ready to catch up.

CHAPTER 23

Cade

I'd just fucked up on a royal level.

It was why I didn't deal with bullshit and relationships outside of a close circle of family and friends. I could fuck a woman, sure. Hell, I'd done that countless times. I'd told myself I wouldn't get serious with her. My brother and my cousins were already married off. One of us had to stay sane. It was supposed to be me.

Yet, making love to Izzy in that cabin was asking for a shit storm, because I couldn't see into the future without her now. Somehow my clothes still smelled like her, my mind still heard her, and my body still damn near ached for her.

In the office today, I'd considered messing up her prim-and-proper pencil skirt. It had my cock twitching just thinking about it. And when I saw that she'd changed into that sinful dress that swayed with her hips and showcased her tits and nipples when she was aroused, I was a goner.

I'd have followed her off a cliff. And going to that damn club was the equivalent. I shouldn't have fucked with the electricity of a club for anything. Normally, I was controlled, efficient, and didn't mess with regular society if they weren't a sever threat. It was a line I didn't need to cross.

Yet, men seeing the way she looked would have had me blacking out a whole city block.

I didn't know why. I could get pussy anywhere. But this one was golden.

Goddamn, I was stupid to have thought I'd be able to quit her cold turkey after the retreat. Quite frankly, I didn't want to quit her at all. After seeing her pain and the way she'd carried it all on her own, I found for the first time I didn't want to see someone squirm. I didn't want her to be uncomfortable. I wanted to shoulder the weight with her, to show her that she could handle it all.

And if she couldn't, I'd be there to handle it with her. Because I saw how impulsive she could be, how she dealt with her feelings around me, how she needed an outlet. I gave her that. And it kept her sane while she kept me humane. Without her, I would watch the world burn and not give a single fuck so long as my family wasn't involved.

She made me want to see our world succeed and thrive. It wasn't just a job to me now.

But without me, she was chaos. She needed me to push her, to pull out the real her. Without the real Izzy, the world was less brilliant, less crazy, and so fucking boring.

Even if she hid it from the world, she couldn't quite hide it from me. Izzy was a mess.

Dirty.

Filthy.

Chaotic.

Beautiful mess.

And I enjoyed the shit out of it.

Except for tonight. Because after I left that club, I went back to my office and stayed there until I got a notification at three in the morning from a damn street security camera. It alerted me to Izzy walking back to her apartment with Lucas. And they were both tanked. I considered whether she'd make it. Lucas was barely standing with his arm over her shoulder.

And fuck if I wasn't going to look. Was she taking him home?

Because she couldn't. She wouldn't. We'd just agreed she was mine. Hadn't we?

And my brain glitched there. It broke down.

I couldn't love her.

I couldn't.

I rubbed my hand across my oak desk and wondered if Izzy's arousal still coated it. I growled at my mind wandering and woke up my computer screens.

Work. Not play. That's what I needed to do.

JUNIPER was in everyone's best interests. I dove into that instead of worrying about her. Until I checked her region and saw what she must have.

And she'd seen it hours ago. Izzy Hardy was a genius at finding information. I'd give her that. But she was a damn slob about what she left behind. Breadcrumbs led me right to her, which meant the Albanians were on her ass too.

Fury barreled through me like a bullet. And it got stuck in my flesh, burned at the skin, and spread like fear and blood would have had I really been shot.

They'd tracked her immediately, and they could move fast. The

Albanians were ruthless and hungry for power. This was a perfect example of why I couldn't want her, couldn't have her tied to me. I couldn't.

We couldn't afford messes now. We were clean. We were businessmen.

I slammed my calloused hand on the desk and pulled up her apartment security. Of course, the cameras of her apartment were down. I kept tabs on most of my team in some capacity, but I'd be lying if I said I didn't check hers most.

I eyed the camera system of Liberty Greene Apartments on my phone. Beside the other squares on my screen, the inky black block mocked me. It'd been black for hours now, it seemed, considering I'd rewound the damn recording.

Fuck me. The responsibility of having data at your fingertips was sometimes all-consuming, tiring, and worrisome.

Apartment security systems were old and frustrating enough that I decided it made more sense to just drive over there. She lived within five minutes of my place anyway.

Even if I called Dante or Bastian, they'd tell me to handle it or dig through the security system to see whether it was just a squirrel chewing through something or it was a tactical move. I was betting the former, but I couldn't be too sure. I'd have been a fool to rely solely on probabilities.

I jumped into my Tesla and hit the self-drive feature. I'd been given the new version of the vehicle because I'd helped the owner build the software. Living a great life, right? But I had to be sure my security was up to par—that no one could hack that system.

I was the best at what I did because I focused on it continuously. I didn't have time to spare for driving when I could be figuring shit out for the company.

Or figuring out why Izzy's system was down.

The problem was, the more I dug, the more something didn't seem right.

So I did what any hacker would do. I breached her phone camera system. This wasn't stalking, it was checking up on my employee. Of course, there was no sound and her phone must have been buried in her fucking purse.

The fact that she and Lucas had left together gave me enough reason to make my way over there instead of leaving it until Monday morning.

Call it intuition or call it plain old stupid luck.

She'd have been dead otherwise.

CHAPTER 24

Izzy

"Get up, Izzy," I heard Cade's voice growl, venom in it. I jostled awake, not at all sure how Cade could be in my apartment.

Had I called him here? Please, God, I hoped to all that was holy that I hadn't.

Fuck, my head hurt. And my mouth tasted like cotton and rum and maybe Cheetos after a whole night of rotting in my mouth. God, that was gross.

How I was still on the couch and Lucas was still under me not stirring was beyond me.

I jerked back to look at him and shook his shoulder. His strong chest shifted back and forth as I did, but he didn't open his eyes. "Lucas."

My first thought was *no*. My second thought was *please, God, not again*.

Déjà vu.

Cade sighed behind me, then rounded the corner to check

Lucas's pupils. "You guys enjoy yourselves? Because it looks like he's not responding."

My vision narrowed, the blood in my veins rushed, and the beat of my heart quickened.

"Lucas!" I screamed, grabbing his arm and vigorously shaking him. "We didn't have that much to drink."

I squinted, trying to remember. It'd been maybe two drinks and a shot. Lucas had consumed that much more than once with me, but I'd practically had to carry him down my hallway.

"He must have done something while you weren't looking." Cade wasn't doing much other than dialing numbers on his phone, totally calm, as if this was normal.

My heart dropped, my breath shook, and my mind filled with what-ifs. "He couldn't have. Lucas, you wouldn't have, right?" I asked him, hoping he would answer. Hoping like hell my best friend could hear me and would pop out of his sleep and laugh. It would have been a cruel joke, but I'd have welcomed it.

Instead, he didn't move, and my soul, my being, my mind, sloshed around in a river of disbelief. This had to be a dream. This couldn't be happening.

As I tried to lay Lucas back down on the couch so I could do something, I screamed at Cade, "Call 911! God, what are you doi—"

Cade's monotone voice cut me off. "Calm down." And then he lifted the phone to his ear. "Yeah, we need an ambulance. One of my employees OD'd."

"He didn't do this," I hissed at Cade. How dare he accuse him of it? My friend was sober; my friend was clean. We'd done the work, we'd put in the time, we'd had the meetings, the talks, the exchanging of promises.

I rubbed Lucas's face, his strong jaw, his lips. Every part of him that was normally so full of life held death right at his doorstep.

My throat closed, and my gut twisted in fear. I couldn't lose him to our shared weakness, not when we were this close to being stronger than it.

"Please, please, please. Please be okay. Just stay with me, Lucas. Do you hear me? I need you. We all need you."

I broke, and the tears spilled from my eyes as I pulled him close, his head falling to my shoulders.

"Yes, I'm aware. He's alive. But I need an ambulance here immediately. We're at Liberty Greene Apartments, number 307." That fucker's monotone voice as he said the words grated on my every nerve. I wanted to kill him, my rage at the world directed at him and anyone if they thought they could be above us, if they thought this wasn't an emergency.

He didn't understand.

Even if Lucas had slipped, this wasn't his fault. It could never be his fault. Didn't people get that? That we struggled *every day* to come back from something that clawed within us to get out.

Cade's boot tapped as he glared at us while he waited for whatever the dispatcher was saying. "I can check for a pulse, but he's alive." He waited a moment. "Because he hasn't yet turned the color I know so well."

His admission was a reminder I needed for later, one I'd filed away. Cade had seen dead bodies before—he'd killed before. I knew from working undercover what the Armanelli name meant. And even if they were reformed, even if he and his brother didn't want to do anything bad, they still could.

"Well, I'm not going to be in the ambulance, that's for sure," he said like he was affronted. "His friend is here. She'll need to be checked also. They were together, and she's hyperventilating."

I wouldn't correct him about anything.

"I'm not sure what she's done." Cade eyed me suspiciously, and I accepted the fact that not even he would ever consider me as anything but a flight risk. Even if I believed in myself, I'd always be the first one they looked at as an addict, the one who may have grabbed the drugs and risked her life. "But I'm sure she's not on drugs. Just her friend."

His assessment had my jaw dropping.

He continued, "Also, this won't be logged. I need to talk with the chief. You can tell him it's Cade Armanelli."

"What are you doing?" I whisper-yelled at him. "Just hang up. I need your help."

"There's nothing to help with. He's out cold right now." Cade lifted a brow like I was stupid.

"He could die!" I screeched.

"Dollface, your friend will be fine." He pulled a lock of my hair. "His breathing isn't shallow enough for death. A coma at the most. It's not your fault, and we'll get through this, but I have to talk with the chief." He shrugged like it was no big deal and then turned around to speak with the chief of police for some unknown reason. "Yeah. It's Cade. You need to check the cameras of this building. They're not secure anymore."

I held my friend as Cade walked out of the room. I rocked him back and forth, back and forth. I cried as I sang a song my mom used to sing to me as a kid. Maybe he'd be comforted by it, or maybe it was a comfort for me, I wasn't sure.

As the paramedics rushed in, I held his hand until they wouldn't let me anymore. I rode in the ambulance because Cade demanded I be let in after he threw his name around.

The shift in treatment was immediate. They administered Narcan to reverse the drug overdose as I stared on and they took him back to the ICU, but the doctor came and gave me information on him immediately. There were no wait times, no brush-offs, and no checking of my credentials. This was the Armanelli treatment, and I was very aware that it was different from what a normal person walking in would experience.

But Cade was gone. He didn't ride in the ambulance with me. Instead, two men in suits walked up as I left the ambulance. One introduced himself as a friend of Cade's and said he would be staying with me until Cade returned.

"What do you mean?" I huffed. "I don't need someone here with me."

"Tough, Ms. Hardy. We will be with you for the near future."

A nurse told me they would give him fluids and run tests and that I could wait in the lobby. So I sat in the waiting room, staring at a screen, not sure who to call or what to do. Lucas didn't have much family that he kept in contact with, and I didn't want to tell anyone he'd OD'd. He could do that when he was ready.

And he would be ready. Because he was going to wake up.

The only person I could think to text was Cade and not for any other reason than to get rid of his goons.

Me: Your men here are unnecessary.

Cade: Look at them as company.

Me: I don't want company. Lucas wouldn't either. We need privacy.

Cade: Privacy for what?

Me: He's fighting for his life in there. Do you even care?

Cade: Well, I sent my men there, didn't I?

I scoffed. He didn't understand that sending a stranger to witness someone's private agony wasn't helping.

Me: You saw him lying there lifeless and didn't even come to the hospital.

Cade: His vitals are strong. They're running bloodwork to see what happened with the drugs. He'll be fine. The doctor's charts say so.

Me: Did they call you?

Cade: No.

Me: Then how do you know?

Cade didn't respond to the question, and he didn't have to. He'd probably breached the hospital system to find that out. I envied how good he was, and my heart melted a little that he'd checked.

Me: If you want to see how someone is doing, you can come to the hospital to see, Cade. You don't have to hack the hospital system.

Cade: I'm working.

Me: Fine. I'll see you at work on Monday, then.

I silenced my phone and shoved it back in my pocket. I needed to be present for my friend.

Not more than an hour later, though, I heard a voice I wasn't expecting. "Here," Cade grumbled as he shoved a box of candy canes in my face.

"What?" I whispered, my heart racing even as my eyes started to tear up. "What's this?"

I knew what it was. It was Cade making a freaking gesture.

It was him bringing what he knew both Lucas and I needed most of the time. He acted like he didn't watch us, like he didn't care about others, but there was so much in him that was good, and this was proof of it.

"What's it look like? They're candy canes," he said as if I were the most dense person he'd ever come across. Then he shook them in front of me, an invitation to take them.

I grabbed them and hugged them close. I was still in my black dress and felt ridiculous in that moment. My hair was a wavy mess, and my clothes were utterly wrinkled from a night out and sleeping on a couch.

My jaw dropped when Cade lifted a bag he had in his other hand and pulled out a baggy T-shirt of mine that had Boyz II Men on it, my favorite mom jeans, and flip-flops. "You should go change."

"How did you get my clothes?" I murmured.

"Do you really want to know?" He rolled his eyes and then rubbed them like he was tired of everything. "Go change, dollface."

I snatched the clothes from him and ran to the bathroom before I could burst into tears in front of him.

Cade was quickly becoming the person who wasn't the enemy

and instead the man who saved me from my burning dumpster fire of a day. And as I got changed in the hospital bathroom stall, I realized that my heart squeezed and almost fell apart whenever I saw him. People didn't break down in tough situations unless someone else was there whom they trusted, whom they could lean on, whom they knew would have their back as they broke. It scared me that my soul trusted him, that I was happy he was here instead of anyone else.

How could I avoid that anymore? I loved him. Wildly. Passionately. Uninhibitedly.

I splashed some water on my face and wiped away as much of the mascara as I could. My hair was a wavy mess, and my face was free of most of my makeup. In flip flops and baggy clothes, I felt comfortable and like maybe I'd be able to get through this without crumbling.

When I returned to the lobby, I found him sitting there, typing away on his phone as always.

I cleared my throat. "Thanks for bringing a change of clothes and candy for me." Should I tell him? Blurt out my love for him and see if he reciprocated it?

He waved away my thank you. "What do you want to eat?"

"Huh?" I asked.

"You haven't eaten, have you?" He threw a pointed look at my stomach.

"I'm not very hungry at the moment, Cade."

He just rolled his eyes and then went back to his phone.

We didn't talk for a good five minutes as I stared up at the TV, not watching it at all. What could I talk to him about? We didn't really get along except when we got along much too well without our clothes on.

"You don't have to stay here, you know? I can send you updates on Lucas when I get them."

"I don't need updates," he grumbled.

"Oh, right. Because you just hack into systems to get all your information." I grumbled back. Then I ground my teeth together because he'd just been nice enough to bring me clothes. "I'm sorry."

That got him to put his phone down and peer over at me. As he studied me, I wiggled in the uncomfortable plastic seat next to him. I swear he enjoyed making people sweat because a smile whipped across his face, pure and utter joy filled it, and I was shocked at how young and innocent it made him look. "Izzy, you apologize to me for your anger as if it's not the thing I like most about you."

"You like me being a bitch to you?" I curled my lip. "Get real."

"I do. It's who you are."

"You're saying I'm a bitch."

"I'm saying you're fiery and a little off sometimes. I enjoy it. It's why I almost fucked you in an elevator after spraying your boyfriend in the face. It's why I fucked you when you spray-painted our bed and when you broke my laptop, and why I'll probably continue to think of fucking you forever."

"Can we not bring up my outbursts?"

His smile grew even bigger. "How is Gerald, by the way?"

"I don't know. He hasn't texted me since . . ." I threw up my hands. "None of this matters. Lucas matters, and I wish they'd let me back there to see him."

He sighed, glanced at his phone, and then got up from his seat. "Food's here for you."

Confused, I glanced up. A delivery guy was bringing two bags of sandwiches and chips our way.

"Jesus, are you actually a thoughtful person?" I couldn't stop myself from asking.

He shrugged. "I'm taking care of my employees." He emphasized the last word and kept his eyes on me.

Pursing my lips, I nodded and took the bag. "Right. Let me go get some cash . . ."

As I moved to walk past him, he gripped my elbow and leaned in. "I'm not that nice, Izzy. You try to pay me back, and I'll take you to a hospital closet and gag you with the money."

His touch on my arm sent sparks all through my body. I ripped it away because I didn't want to feel anything for him. I couldn't. This wasn't the place or the time. "You should go."

He shook his head no.

"Cade, Lucas and I need this," I said, but really *I* needed it. I needed him to leave, to leave me with my thoughts and my feelings, and to get a moment to sort through all of them. Love would shatter me, and I think I knew that this was exactly where it was headed. I rubbed at the scrape on my neck that was left from our activities the night before.

We'd done that.

And how was I to know that I could survive when my best friend lay in a hospital bed not surviving what we'd both fought so hard for.

Sobriety meant making healthy choices, even when they felt like the most painful ones.

"I don't trust myself with you, Cade. I need this. I need time," I whispered.

His stare was full of frustration. "I'm not good at waiting, Izzy."

I rolled my lips between my teeth, not sure I could hold out much longer away from him anyway.

He sighed and ran a hand through his thick hair. "Do you have anyone you can call to be here with you?"

"Other than security for no good reason?" I pointed at some of the men in suits. What could I say? I couldn't bring myself to call my family. Delilah would be concerned. They'd worry, and their worry would bring the weighted guilt of what I'd already done to them. "I'm fine here on my own. I'd like Lucas to have his privacy."

"It's still good to have support," he pointed out.

I wondered if he believed that, if he ever had support. "Would you call your family if they worried constantly about you relapsing?"

He tilted his head like he was considering it. "Sure. Bastian would be there."

I gulped as he said his brother's name. Sebastian Armanelli. It should have brought a lot more fear than it did. "You love your brother?"

He smiled like he knew the real question I was asking. "I will always love my brother, dollface. And I stand by everything he's done and does, even all the mistakes he's made. Just like I'm sure your brothers and sister would do for you. Family doesn't shrink from your mistakes and disappear; they just sink their roots in deeper to get you out."

I bit my lip because I wanted to believe what he was saying, because I wanted to think that my family didn't want to rid themselves of their bad wolf, but I couldn't. Instead, I just shrugged.

"Ah, it's something that's learned, Izzy. We'll have you figure it out one day." Cade motioned to the food. "Now, sit and eat your sandwich."

I sighed. Even if I was hungry, eating anything right now felt ridiculous. "I wish he'd wake up to eat with me. He loves subs. Or that they'd at least let me in to see him."

"They will soon enough. Now eat. I made it a priority to feed you on that retreat. You'll have to do it on your own now while you make me wait to be a part of your life for God only knows what reason that is today."

I grumbled that he might be waiting a long time and then asked, "Why is it a priority that I eat?"

"We can't give Gerald the satisfaction of you losing your ass, now, can we?"

It was an insult or a joke or maybe a compliment. Either way, he got the first smile pulled from me that day as I listened to him and sat down.

Before he left, the man strode up to me and tipped my face up to his. "It'll be okay, baby doll. I promise."

Then he kissed my forehead and walked over to the nurse's station.

Cade wasn't a god. He wasn't a doctor. He wasn't even a nurse. Yet I believed him. Maybe because I wanted to or maybe because amongst the men in our world, Cade really was a higher power of some sort.

Further proof of it showed when, not a minute later, a nurse came to usher me back to Lucas's room and I saw Cade standing down the hallway, giving us a final nod like he'd orchestrated getting me into his room.

I didn't have time to read into it. I was focused on Lucas as I hurried into the sterile, overly clean room. The white curtain was pulled back and the monitors were beeping as my big lug of a friend lay there, quiet, peaceful, and without a smile on his ever happy face.

Lucas looked like he was resting, and I hoped he felt like it too. I hoped he was putting his demons to bed as he slept in between the world of life and the one of death.

Crying for him wouldn't do him any good, but I did it anyway. Then I tucked in his sheets just right and rearranged his tray table to make sure the tissues were set up there with a cup of water for when he woke. I ordered food that wasn't perishable, and I turned the TV on low and found BRAVO.

"Look, Lucas, it's your favorite housewife. Kyle's about to host another extravagant party. I swear, one day, they'll realize none of the parties matter. It's about who you spend your time with instead, huh?"

I hated that tears were running down my face again.

"I used to think it was all about just a guy and the parties I went to with him. Can you believe that? Then, he left me and I realized his love was gone and I hadn't taken the time to figure out how to love myself. Or how to love my family and the people who were really there for me, you know?"

It was a good reminder that I needed to go see them. That I needed to hug the ones I loved and cherish them every single second of every single day. They deserved that and so much more from me. Self-loathing after addiction was a bitch to get over, especially when I could recall the way they all cried for me, how my mother's face broke when she saw me high. It's funny how black-out gone I could be but the hardest glimpses of my reality were still etched in stone.

Now I just wanted to make them proud, do something better

for the world than be an addict. The world deserved the good, not the bad, especially my family.

"Lucas, I found out some information, and I'm going to find out more. I'm going to show you we can be more than just this. You get that we can, right? We don't have to fall back into the same patterns. We're stronger."

Maybe I was telling myself, maybe I was close to relapsing, maybe all this stress and emotion wasn't good for me.

Or maybe I was right.

Without great risk, there's no great reward, right?

I left the hospital quietly, rounding a corner and leaving Cade's security behind. I didn't want a tail or anyone to witness that I was going to dig and dig deep into the Albanians. I had a new mission.

One I was going to take care of on my own.

CHAPTER 25
Cade

I was well aware that Lucas wouldn't be coming into the office, but Izzy flat out didn't show. I'd called my security for the last time Sunday night, and they'd confirmed her whereabouts. I'd received no update other than that she was safe. So I'd tried not to check my security on her.

Truth be told, I had fucking facial recognition notifications set up everywhere for her, I could hack her computer or her phone, and I contemplated doing all of it.

But she'd asked for time. She wanted privacy for her and her friend. I tried to understand it. I tried to give her that.

She deserved that after I saw the way she held her friend, after I saw the look of terror on her face. Babying her wouldn't help. She didn't want it anyway. She needed and wanted to feel like I trusted her to handle it.

I did. I had to. Or at least I was going to try to.

Except now she hadn't shown up to work, and it was half past her normal start time.

I grumbled to my brother on the phone about it.

"Wait. You went to the hospital to drop off candy canes?" my brother asked again.

"You want me to hang up on you or finish the story?" I shoved away from my desk and wondered what the hell I was doing in a corporate office anyway. I could be at home where I had five screens set up instead of four and be getting much more done.

Especially considering all I was doing was walking out my damn office door to check to see if she'd shown up.

"Well, did you call her?"

"No." I wasn't going to either. I was becoming a goddamn stalker. I'd checked the fucking hospital records just to make sure I could ease the pain in her eyes instead of having her wait for the nurses to give her the update. Let's be honest, those nurses weren't giving updates fast enough in my opinion, anyway.

She needed time to digest her feelings for me, and I probably needed the same.

Bastian snickered over the phone, and then I heard him repeat everything to his wife.

"Why are you telling Morina about the candy canes?" I asked, my voice laced with anger. He was purposely trying to piss me off.

"Because you got it bad. Haven't you been following Izzy around for years?" Then he muffled the phone again to tell Morina that indeed it was Izzy. I hated that everyone knew her from her undercover work, and now she was working directly under me, making my life a living hell.

"I haven't followed anything she's been doing." That was a bald-faced lie. I was literally going cold turkey on checking her shit. "I don't know why I told you any of this."

"Because I'm your big brother and you've got no one else to tell."

"I could have called Dante." I threw out our cousin's name

because he would have listened to me be a pussy too.

"Yeah, but he would have told you the same thing I'm about to tell you, and it's that you'd better stop fucking around if you like her. Which you do if you brought her candy canes, dumbass."

"I'm going."

"Morina says Izzy wouldn't just miss work. Call her," Bastian demanded, authority in his voice now. "Don't be an idiot, Cade."

We'd been businessmen a long time, but the feelings we got sometimes, they had us breaking protocol, breaking the rules, and following our gut.

I hung up and gave in to calling her.

Of course, her phone was off.

I had half a mind to hack it and see what she was doing before it went dead. Instead, I went into my security monitoring system to check Liberty Greene Apartments. I'd been so damn proud when I turned her alert off after finding that indeed one of the wires for the apartment building had been frayed. The chief confirmed it with me, and it'd been a firm reminder that I didn't need to stalk any girl, that I was getting too twisted up with her.

Yet, the black screen was there again.

This time, I swore fluidly at myself for ever being fooled. I called the security team I had following Izzy. "What's the deal with Liberty Greene Apartments' cameras?"

"Huh, boss?" He sounded half asleep.

What the fuck?

"Are you doing your job right now? Because it sounds like you're just getting out of bed."

The silence that stretched over the phone was too long.

"What the hell is going on?"

"So, we were going to tell you this morning that we lost her last night. She snuck out of the hospital, but we saw her in her apartment later that night, so we thought we'd get some rest with the cameras working and all, but now we're noticing—"

It's the fear that strikes lightning fast through a body when they realize they've potentially lost the one they care about that's stifling. I'd had it before with family.

With Izzy, it was different. More fierce, more brutal, like a damn wrecking ball flying in and knocking the breath from me.

"You're dead if she's gone." I hung up on him, not having the time to spare on the idiots that should have taken this job more seriously.

I only had myself to blame, though. I'd let someone do the job that should have only been mine. I'd let her sway me away from her when I should have been making the rules. She could have space from everyone else but not me.

That's what I should have told her. There was no more privacy when it came to me.

I was her person from now on. I should have known that from the very beginning and I cursed myself for not getting my head right in the first place. I knew better than to listen to her, but she was my glitch, my downfall, and she spread like a virus and corrupted every part of me.

Love made a person stupid. And I loved her.

I'd been a damn fool the night before, turning off all my devices and trying to rid myself of my newest addiction of checking up on her. I went to work out. I didn't bother going to my penthouse's gym but instead ran through the streets without my phone. I didn't need a distraction, and sometimes that was what all my devices were.

I enjoyed the fresh cool air and let the breeze clear my head and fill my lungs.

Now, as I sat there, I couldn't seem to get any air at all.

If she'd been taken, it'd be on me.

Fuck.

I called her phone again. No answer. All bets were off then. It only took me five minutes to see that she'd gone back into her files. That someone was watching her every move. Cameras in her apartment building had been hacked, this time much faster and not as clean.

Lucas's OD made sense now. Her cameras going out made sense.

Everything made too much damn sense.

And I'd been too focused on my emotions for her that I hadn't noticed. Been too busy fucking her to see what was right in front of my face.

In another life, I would have welcomed the threat to our power. Albanians wanted to take over—as if they stood a chance. And they were deliberately moving that way in confidence behind our backs, like we wouldn't be ready.

I called my brother and Dante as I skirted around my desk and sped out of the building. Both of them needed to know what was about to happen.

I informed them of the Albanians trying to hack the election and pushed the data as fast as I could through a secure text to them.

I commanded both of them on the phone. "I'm on my way to Izzy's. You two need to work with the Stonewoods and the bratva to make sure the Albanians keep their shit in line for this election."

Dante added, "What's Izzy have to do with it?"

"She's the one who found it."

"Before you?" Bastian's attention was piqued now.

"Fuck off. The cybersecurity was already in place. We'd have caught the issue, but Izzy stumbled upon it last week. For some reason, she didn't inform me. And they're watching her. Her friend OD'd, but it had to have been a hit."

"Shit. Get over to her house and protect your girl then," Bastian grumbled.

Dante halted the conversation. "His girl? What the hell does that mean? If you're fucking around with Izzy, Cade—"

"Then what?" I got in my car and slammed the door harder than necessary. No one was going to warn me off my girl.

My girl? When had she become that?

"That's my sister-in-law," he bellowed into the phone. "Wet your dick somewhere else."

"Watch your mouth. It's not just that with her."

"Jesus fucking Christ," Dante swore while Bastian mumbled in Italian.

"I don't have time for either of your shit. I just told you we have an election on the line and Albanians going against our alliance. She's not safe until we set it straight. Especially because they think she's the only one who knows."

"I'll need the records," Bastian sighed. "They aren't going to admit it right away. We'll need a few days and—"

"If they have her, Bastian, they aren't getting shit. Fuck." I smacked the seat of the car as my Tesla drove me to Liberty Greene Apartments. "Give me a second. I'm here. I'll call you back."

I took the stairs two at a time and cursed the cameras as I ran down her hall.

Her door was wide open.

Her phone had been smashed and left on the floor.

No Izzy.

No sign of her anywhere.

The place wasn't trashed, but the knocked-over table and crushed phone on the ground told me everything I needed to know.

I got back into my car as I hacked the data from her phone. I was able to pull up the last moments on there before it had been destroyed, and thank God she'd had training.

It was her begging. And every second I listened, I lost a little more of my control.

"Please. Please. I'll come willingly." I heard the whimper and closed my eyes as I felt the true pain in her voice. "I've been sober nine years. I don't need you to drug me."

Izzy was strong. She went toe-to-toe with me and spat fire when she needed to. Here, she was broken. And when they laughed at her and spoke in Albanian, I saw red.

Black.

Fury I'd never felt.

One man shushed her and said, "It'll be easier this way."

And then I heard her crying, screaming, fighting. Then silence and rustling.

Silence.

It was probably a sound that would never comfort me again.

I remember how I let it seep in. I remember how I knew it changed me right there, right then.

That girl had been a nuisance and an enemy of mine. I'd embarrassed her and probably tortured her a little.

But no one made her beg or tortured her except me.

The bellow that ripped through me was loud and feral before I dialed my brother's number back.

"Got an update on—"

I blurted it out. "The Albanians have her."

"What?" he whispered. "That's not possible. They've got to know she's with us—"

"They don't know she's really with me, Bastian."

"Is she?"

"Don't fuck with me right now."

"I'm not, brother. I'm not." He sighed.

"They drugged her. She's a recovered addict, Bastian." I couldn't hold back the shake of emotion in my voice.

My brother tried to calm me down. "Okay, look, we'll handle—"

"*I* will handle it," I corrected. "They're mine now."

"Cade, we agreed to be allies—"

"*I* didn't agree to anything. You did. I never agree," I reminded him. "And in my world, details matter. They didn't want to figure out the details before they drugged the girl I love—"

"You're in love with her now?" Bastian's tone changed.

"Figure out how you want to cover up the chaos, brother. Because I'm about to unleash it."

"Jesus Christ, Cade. I can't cover up your shit. Can't we wait a second and—"

"I'm not waiting. And get ahold of Dante and Lilah. They need to swing by my place and pick up Izzy's cat."

"I'm not dealing with a cat when you're about to fuck up everything, Cade. You need to chill."

"I am. And you better deal with it."

I didn't wait for him to respond as I hung up and pet the cat's head. "You'll see your mom soon. I promise you that."

No one had authority over the world like I did.

And I intended to exercise that authority to the fullest in the next few days.

CHAPTER 26

Izzy

fought when the needle hit my arm. I'd survived opiate addiction, and I was sure whatever they had in that syringe, my body was going to suck it up and feel a high I never wanted to feel again.

So I fought. I fought hard.

It wasn't the fear of experiencing a drug. I'd done that already. It was the fear of losing my sobriety, of losing to the addiction I'd fought so hard to overcome.

When two men had rushed into my apartment as I sat there decoding, my instincts kicked in immediately. I'd been trained years ago for undercover work. I knew the basics in self-defense.

I scrambled for my phone and hit record because it was the first thing I could reach before they knocked it from my hands. I kicked one of them in the balls and tried to shake the other free from my arms.

Two large men against me wasn't really a fair fight, though. And I was out of practice.

I got a good claw across his face before he hit me hard in mine, and the other guy pulled my arms back and locked me there while his friend pulled a needle from his jacket.

Fear hadn't really hit me until that point.

I'm not proud to say I begged. As I struggled in their arms, I hated how desperate I sounded. "Please. Please. I'll go with you willingly. I've been sober nine years." I choked on a sob. "Please."

"It'll be easier this way," he murmured in my ear. He said it softly, like he was doing me a favor.

I screamed, I cried, I struggled.

I lost.

One prick of the needle, and it only took half a minute to feel it. The one I'd tried so long to avoid.

It was faster, stronger, and more potent than the last time.

I could lie and say it didn't feel good. Hitting that high always felt good, though. It was a drug for a reason. Still, tears slid down my face at the loss before the weight of my head felt like too much.

"Fuck, dude. She's not going to OD, right? If she's sober, it's going to hit her harder, right?" The man spoke English and then switched to Albanian. Back and forth, back and forth.

Nothing mattered anyway. I'd floated off.

I was gone.

Their questions faded away. The question of whether I would survive this faded away. My worries faded away.

Everything faded away.

The rough scrape of cement on my cheek wasn't a welcoming wake-up call at all.

Even as my body woke, I didn't move a muscle. My brain was foggy, my heartbeat erratic, and my concern for my well-being was on high alert.

It didn't take long for the effects of the drug to roll through me. I dry-heaved and curled into myself as the shivering started. I'd promised myself I'd never go through this again. I'd believed it too.

What do you do when your choice is stolen from you and leaves you with nothing but the aftermath?

Tears wouldn't help me now, but they still fell over my cheeks. I tried to shake off the turmoil I felt, but defeat could be suffocating. It held my breath and light and hope for another day hostage as it weighed down my soul.

But I wasn't a victim of addiction. I was a survivor. Lucas always said it took him and the drug to succumb, not just the drug. I tried to remember that now.

It would take me giving up and not moving for me to surrender to the fate they wanted for me now.

I wiped my eyes and scoped out the space. I was on dirty cement, and they'd left me alone with four walls surrounding me and a metal door.

No windows. No light except what came from under the door. A toilet in the corner. And that was it.

As my stomach cramped and my body shook, I embraced the symptoms. Withdrawal was a bitch, but it meant the drug was leaving my system. It meant I'd survived the blackout.

Those moments on my own lasted for hours, maybe for a whole day. I know I went to the bathroom, that I crawled around the four walls to confirm my surroundings, that I moaned in pain as I rubbed at the injection site.

Still, I tried not to dwell. Coping with my failures gave my mind something I could control. I focused on the kidnapping, on how they spoke Albanian, on how they came for me. It proved I was close to something; it proved they were doing something illegal, and the only thing I'd found lately was what I'd dug into on my computer at work.

Albanians were rigging the election, and this confirmed it.

Now I had to determine exactly how they were doing it, then get the hell out of there before they killed me. I didn't know which part would be harder.

Yet, when the first guy walked in hours later, I figured I might actually be able to pull it off.

Alteo wasn't a very smart man, although he was massive. He smiled, showing crooked teeth, as he saw me sitting up in the corner. "Oh, good. You woke up, huh? My boss was very nervous you would die."

I lifted an eyebrow. That was confirmation they didn't want me dead. "Yes. You could have killed me. Why didn't you?"

He waved away the question and brought me a plate of food. It was just chips and a hot dog, but even though my stomach growled, I didn't take it.

"Oh, please eat." He shoved the plate my way after he placed it on the ground. "If we wanted you dead, you would be, right? So what would I put in your food?"

I pointed to the injection site on my arm. And a wave of sadness hit. Nine years was a long time to earn back. No one knew how proud I was of it, but I did. It was a painful thing to think about. Painful and unfair. I'd thought about relapsing before, but at least then it would have been my own choice.

"So." He cleared his throat like he was embarrassed. "That was to help. To calm you down, huh? My friend shouldn't have done that. Let's forget about it."

The man looked ashamed, and I instantly wanted to smack him. "Forget about it? Do you know it took me nine years to get clean?"

He winced and curled up in a big meaty, muscle ball, like he was more wounded than I was. "Look, don't tell my dad. If you do, we're going to get into serious trouble, okay? We're already getting too many questions."

So, he was reporting to his father. I was back in undercover mode, back to surviving, even if I had to bury every emotion I felt right then.

He sighed. "Can you just tell me—are you an Untouchable? We weren't given that information. And we've received a call. We thought you were just a Stonewood employee and it would be a quick fix to get rid of you."

An Untouchable. It was a high status within the mob. In the Armanelli family. When a woman married in, no other family— Albanian, Russian, Italian, Serbian—could touch them. It meant death. It meant war and pain and wrath from every other family.

I chewed on my cheek and rubbed at the injection site. I needed a plan, and the plan was going to be what he'd just given me.

"You know my sister became an Untouchable not too long ago. She's my twin. You must have known that. And you must know how quickly things happen when families are intertwined . . ."

His eyes widened. "I don't keep track. This was my first big job. I needed to eliminate election threats, and we've been doing that all over the country. And now we got someone hacking our systems—I can't be responsible for that." He looked panicked, like he'd been saddled with the worst luck.

Hope blossomed when he said there was hacking going on. Cade had to know I was here. But was I worth the risk? I shrugged at the man sitting next to me, not willing to give anything away.

"Damn it," he grumbled before leaving the room. The door slammed shut, and I stared at the food.

My hand twisted over the bracelet Cade had bought me, still clean and shiny on my wrist. Did he care for me enough to come? To look for me? I felt a desperation for him then that I hadn't before. I wanted to see him one last time, tell him how I cared for him, how it wasn't just fun. Life and death situations would do that to a person.

I wanted to be reckless even if I was afraid to be. Recklessness had got me in trouble before. It was how I got my first taste of drugs. And then, because with them, my mind didn't worry, didn't stray into feeling like I was doing anything wrong. Then Vincent found me and told me he loved me.

So, I found myself doing anything and everything for him. Therapy would show me later that I was young, easily coerced, easily preyed upon. So many young girls had suffered the same fate, but it didn't mean we were to blame, it didn't mean I had to let my relationship with Vincent define me.

Guilt and shame can envelope and suffocate a soul, but we don't have to let it. Cade showed me that. He let me breathe, let me be myself. I promised myself if I got out of here, I'd thank him for that.

I growled in frustration at my predicament and grabbed the water they'd given me with the food. I chugged half of it, and my body rejoiced at getting something.

Another man walked in and I scrambled up to face him. He'd been the one who'd stuck me with a needle. His dirty jeans and ripped shirt showed how well he took care of himself. He hadn't even washed his face where I'd scratched him because the blood was still caked under it.

"My boss isn't sure what to do with you." His meaty hand dragged across my jawline as he got within a few feet of me. "I told him I could get answers out of you quick."

"I'm not sure what answers you want." I shrugged, not shrinking back at his touch.

"You intercepted data, and we need to know what you found, little girl. We need to make sure you don't talk."

Hate is ugly and unkind, boiling in a soul for years and years—like hell itself is heating it. It can be endless and toxic, but it can keep someone going. I hated this man for taking my sobriety, and I felt the hate bubble out of me when I spoke to him. "How do you intend to keep me from talking? I'm an Untouchable, after all."

He narrowed his eyes and searched my hand for a ring. They were all confused. And I confused them more with my fake admission. Yet, if acting like I was tied to Cade kept me alive, I was going to do that.

"Living alone, without Armanelli? That doesn't sound like an Untouchable to me."

"Want to find out?" I lifted a brow, taunting him.

"You're so brave, huh?" He didn't like me testing him. I saw it in the way his neck flexed. Then he stomped over to the door and yelled out of it, "Alteo, bring in the bucket."

His friend heaved in a white plastic bucket filled with water sloshing from it with each step he took. There was a look of anguish on his face. "Dion, I don't think we should do anything to—"

"Tie her hands behind her back," Dion commanded.

Fighting would do me no good. So, instead, I aided Alteo by placing my wrists behind me. If I worked with at least Alteo, I might get out of this alive.

"I say we just wait for my dad to get here and—"

Dion shoved Alteo away and took his place behind me. He whispered in my ear, "Get on your knees."

My stomach curdled at him this close, at how he said the words with a slimy innuendo. But I listened. I couldn't do anything else but that at this point.

His hand grabbed my hair and dunked me fast, holding me under long enough for my body to have survival instinct kick in. I inhaled. I choked. I coughed. And I fought. I pulled my arms as far apart as I could, fighting the zip tie to no avail.

He pulled me up and whispered in my ear, "Want to talk now?"

I either embraced the rage or the helplessness or the defeat. All my emotions were there, though. Bright. Powerful. And vengeful.

"Talk to you, Dion? I'd rather die," I murmured, and turned to look over my shoulder, catching his gaze.

He roared before he dunked me again.

I fought him again as he held me under until I thought I might pass out, might die from drowning.

I crumbled to the floor, choking, as he let me go while he laughed. His laughter was enough to show me I could kill, that I would relish taking his life. A new hatred grew in me right then, and I embraced it. Embraced that my emotions could bring pain, could bring destruction, could ruin someone. A life-and-death situation that does that makes you accept who you are.

I pulled myself up from the ground. As his smile widened and he dragged his gaze up and down my body, I lifted my chin. He wouldn't make me cower, even if his eyes hovered at the edge of my baggy T-shirt. I was so thankful I wore shorts, but I knew they wouldn't hold anyone off for long if they wanted me.

"Are you really an Untouchable? What do you know?" he asked through clenched teeth.

"You won't get any answers without letting me speak with your boss."

He struck me hard across the face, and I tasted blood in my mouth as I fell to the cement floor.

"Man, we're supposed to give her good accommodations," Alteo grumbled.

"Sure. Sure." Dion shrugged. "You both realize I get her after your dad meets her, though. I'm going to teach you some manners too." He bent over me. "I will start by telling you I like a nice woman, one who doesn't talk back. Until then, you don't eat."

He took the food off the ground, like he'd won.

"Wouldn't have taken the food you offered anyway," I grumbled. It was petty, dumb, and asking for a beating.

He didn't disappoint. His boot hit me right in the stomach. The second kick I was ready for, but the wind had already been knocked out of me. I wheezed for air, for life, and scrambled on the floor as he tried to land a few more blows.

When he finally had me cowering in a corner, he chortled. "Good. I see the fear in you now. Next time"—he leaned close, and I smelled stale tobacco on his breath—"don't make me work for that fear, and it'll be a lot nicer in here."

Before he left, he cut my zip ties, pulled a needle from his pocket and dropped it on the floor.

The clink of the metal door sounded like the metal of my own personal jail in hell closing.

"Maybe, she's rethought that sobriety, huh, Alteo?" He waved at his friend in the corner who looked disgusted by what he had witnessed. "And look, I accidentally dropped this on the way out. That'll help you make all our lives less miserable. Maybe just another hit. It's even stronger than the dose I gave you. Then I'll come check on you."

He turned away, and Alteo walked out after him, eyebrows scrunched together like he felt some sort of guilt. I ran my hands along the dirt of the floor, avoiding that capsule of death.

Ending my life now would have been an easy out. Vincent had shown me that. Succumbing to any sort of anguish by wiping yourself out is less painful than having to live through it. I knew that. It was like going through the coldest winter in the hopes you'd see summer on the other side, drowning but still clawing to the surface in the hopes you'd make it to the sunlight, to air, to living.

I wanted to live. I wanted to unstrap the burden of my addiction and throw it out.

But I grabbed that needle after an hour of sitting there and finally faced it. I held it in my hands the way I used to; I held it to my arm the way I used to.

I teetered on the edge.

I lay down on that dirty cement floor and stared at it. I wondered if Lucas would have told me to fuck it and go for one last high or if he would have told me to fight.

I knew the answer. He believed in my fight.

Still, there in that room, I came to terms with death, I think. I let the dirt mix with my hair and my tears as I struggled with the fact that I wasn't solving anything locked in a room. I wasn't going to get to see Lucas.

I wasn't going to get to tell Cade I loved him.

I wasn't going to solve any election rigging and make my family proud.

And that's how he found me.

Cade Armanelli walked right into the room my kidnappers held me in like we weren't in some undisclosed location, like he had the authority to, like he freaking owned the place.

I took in his stupid suit. It looked unruffled, as if he'd just come from work, and the only thing that showed anything different was his face. He came up to me but stopped abruptly and frowned when he saw what was in my hands.

"What are you doing here?" I whispered, not hiding that I was fighting for my life down here- not just at the hands of the men that kidnapped me, but at my own hand. I was fighting against the need to just end it all.

He gave me a look like I was a complete imbecile. "What the fuck do you mean what am I doing here? Give me that. Now." He pointed to it.

"Are you saving me?" My voice shook, ignoring his command. "Are we safe? Because Dion—"

"We're safe. Alteo gave me access to you after I leveraged his bank account and his father's. His father is coming here now to have a word with me regarding this whole mix-up."

"Mix-up?" I squeezed the needle tight. "This isn't a fucking mix-up."

He cut me off with a hard tone and a look of fury. "I'm aware, Izzy." He stuck his hand out. "Give me the needle."

"Why?" I stared at the dirt on the ground and licked my cracked lips. "I'm only one day sober at this point—"

"Eight years and thirty days."

My eyes whipped up at him—how did he know the exact number? He glared back at me.

"No." I shook my head, my dirty matted hair waving back and forth as I sat there. "They stole that."

"I know you think that, dollface." His words sounded like coddling, but the tears sprang to my eyes anyway. "I hacked your phone. You did good recording something. But I heard you. And I'm so fucking sorry." His voice cracked, and then he cleared his throat, like he might cry, like he was broken up about all this, like he cared. "But no one gets to steal that from you. Your sobriety is yours. If someone takes it, it doesn't count."

"Who says?" I whispered, my heart splintering at his rationality.

A small smile formed on his lips. "Me. And I can write it in anything across the fucking globe if you like. I'll put it on every website and into every book printed because I believe it and you should too. It'll be the damn 'Izzy clause.'"

I pushed myself up off the floor and continued to let the tears fall as I gripped the syringe. "I'm furious, so fucking mad, I want to tear them all apart, and I'm sad too. And I don't do well with all these emotions."

"Then start over. And start over from the very beginning." Cade held my gaze, carved through the mess of my broken soul, and got to the root of the matter. "Your first heartbreak you felt deeply. It doesn't make that emotion wrong, Izzy. You need to feel it. Start over and feel everything this time." Cade waited a beat. "They did this to Lucas too. You can't let them win. Just give me the needle."

Jerking from his statement, I think he saw the rage, the fury, the madness in me. I wanted blood. "Who did this to him?"

"Needle." His hand was out, and I practically punched him with my closed fist, letting him pry it from my grip. He pushed the needle, and the liquid in it squirted out onto the floor immediately. Then he was rushing me, lifting my chin, checking my neck, my cheeks, my lips. His hands smoothed over every bruise, every cut, with a gentleness I didn't know he had in him. There was fury in his eyes but a frown on his face as he said, "They hurt you, dollface."

It wasn't a question but a statement.

"I'm fine." I took a steadying breath and gripped his wrists to pull them away from my skin. I couldn't have him baby me now. I wouldn't survive it if he did. "Please tell me who did this to Lucas. What happened?"

"I think they meant it for your drink. I searched the security footage. It's why there was Rohypnol in his system. We're figuring it out. I'm getting you out of here, and we'll figure it out once we're gone. Alteo let me in, but it's a quick in and out. I have a team outside that'll take you—"

"I'm staying," I blurted out, shocking myself. But the words rooted themselves deep in me and I couldn't let the idea go. "They hurt me and my friend. They stole our sobriety and they've been at this for years, Cade. I wasn't digging for nothing. They're rigging the election. And they want something more—"

"It doesn't matter." He gripped the back of my neck and pulled me close. Every touch of his was softer, though, like he was scared I would break even as he pointed a tattooed finger at me. "You shouldn't have been on that computer, and you shouldn't have been hacking without my knowledge, Izzy. You're leaving."

I put my hands on my hips. "I'm not. We need to find—"

He eyed my baggy T-shirt and let me go so that he could pace back and forth, pulling at his hair. "We don't need to find anything. Izzy, you're out of your mind."

I narrowed my eyes. "I found their hacking, Cade. And they hurt my friend."

"You went flying into the dark web like a kid who was let off their leash at the zoo. I tracked your IP address. You tapped information and touched every single thing you could. Had I been paying more attention to what you were doing and less attention to—" He stared at my lips as he stopped talking. "Damn, your mouth is bleeding. We need to get you out of here. They want to know what you know. They think you're the only one who knows."

"But now you do too."

He nodded darkly. "I'll deal with them. I need to walk you out now, or I'll fucking carry you."

But we were too late. In filed five men, and I saw the way Cade's jaw flexed, how he walked over to me and put himself in front of me. He may have been my enemy once, but now I knew he was my protector.

Alteo mouthed, "Sorry," to him, and Dion glared at both of us. But the other men who'd walked in didn't acknowledge us at all.

They kept their eyes forward with hands on their firearms.

The last one to walk in must have been in charge. I knew it by the way the men fanned out around him, and he looked down at me as if I were a puzzle he was trying to figure out.

He straightened his suit and tsked at the sight. He was clean-cut—some might even have called him attractive with his strong jaw and dark hair with silver highlighting his temples.

He extended his hand to Cade, and I was surprised when Cade stared down at it but made no movement to take it in his own. The man's brow furrowed. "Cade Armanelli, I'm sorry we're meeting this way. My associates let you in without a proper introduction. I'm Aleks Mustafa. I'm sure you've heard—"

"I don't need an introduction, Aleks. I didn't come here for one," Cade said loud enough for all the men to grip their weapons tighter. His voice held malice and frustration. It wasn't a tone to have when one was in a small room loaded with guns.

"I understand." Aleks's voice was consoling. "I didn't mean disrespect."

"Didn't you, though?" Cade murmured quietly. "These accommodations the best you could do for a woman you took?"

Aleks smiled and nodded as he turned to his men. "Alteo, I said to get her accommodations."

"We did, Dad," the other man murmured.

One deep breath was all that was needed for the men to take a step back, like they were scared he would lash out. "Alteo, you're my son. Would you expect my accommodations for you to be in the dirt?"

"No, of course not, sir." He shook his head rapidly. "We thought she was just an employee at Stonewood. Not an Armanelli tie, I swear."

"And why would an employee of Stonewood need to have a stay with you in the first place?" Cade inquired.

"Well . . ." Alteo's eyes darted from his father to Cade, his father to Cade. When he realized his own father wouldn't vouch for him, he scrambled. "She shouldn't have tried to pull information from us. We have nuclear weapon locations, confidential files tied to—"

"You were trying to rig an election," I blurted out.

All their eyes flew my way. Dion's narrowed, Alteo's widened, but Aleks's were the ones I held. I saw the hunger in them, the need to shut me up, and the coldness there too. He'd do anything to get out of this.

"Sweetheart, you know not what you found." He chuckled. He was a snake circling his prey, ready to kill with a venomous bite. He sought out my weakness.

"I know what I saw."

He glanced at Cade. "I haven't properly met her. I was on my way. I'm sorry for this whole mix-up, but we had to be sure she wasn't going to spread such an accusation. You understand?"

Cade didn't respond. I only saw his muscles tense.

"Alteo informed me she's been in cybersecurity a while. A little paranoid bird, huh?" He waved me off, smiling at Cade as though they could be friends. "I've looked into her history, and we saw indications that she indulges in drugs, has a record—"

"'A record'?" I whispered. "'Sorry for the mix-up'? I was drugged and beaten when I got here. I—"

The man didn't let me finish. He acted surprised and appalled with a gasp. "Alteo, is this true?"

"Father, but you said—"

"No." Aleks looked at another large man and shook his head in disappointment. "Take him away."

"Sir, please. Wait—" Alteo struggled against the other man, yelling as they dragged him out. Aleks and Dion remained.

Aleks's sharp gaze shifted to me. "I'm sorry for the poor arrangements. Please accept my apologies."

I chewed on my cheek. This wasn't my place. Cade would have to side with me or this man. He knew the truth. He had to. We all stood there in silence so tense a knife wouldn't have been able to cut it.

Was I supposed to forgive him? Is that what they wanted?

"Izzy, the man would like you to accept his apologies," Cade said softly but firmly as he slid his phone out.

My heart stuttered, and then I was sure it crumbled right there in that room at his words. He expected me to do the one thing I thought he was always pushing me not to do. Bury my damn emotions, bury my anger, just take it.

I cleared my throat as I felt the tears pricking my eyes. "You're forgiven."

"Oh, good. Good. I thought—" Aleks never finished.

The lights went out, and with no sunlight in the room or the hall, we drowned in darkness.

And screams. Painful, wretched, torturous screams. I fell to the ground as gun shots went off and I heard men running in.

It was only a matter of fifteen seconds, then the lights were back.

In front of me stood a man who strongly resembled Cade. He looked calmer, though, at ease. My brother-in-law stood with him.

Dante Armanelli nodded at me with those green eyes full of

concern. "You okay?"

I nodded back.

Yet, Cade was the one who held all my attention, his knife at Aleks's throat.

Aleks had his hands in the air. "Please. Let's calm down. I didn't know she was your Untouchable. If that's what this is about . . ." He chuckled nervously.

"I'll nuke your whole goddamn country if any of you come near her again. How about that for her being an Untouchable?" Cade growled, and I saw the way his whole body shook in rage, veins popping on his forearms, like a pressure cooker about to blow.

Aleks didn't move a muscle, beads of sweat forming on his forehead. "Bastian, your brother." He gave Bastian a look like Cade was insane. "Let's be reasonable now, huh? We didn't know her and—"

Cade didn't give him time to finish. He stepped close and shoved the knife harder into his throat to break skin. "You're talking to my brother as if I'm not here, Aleks. You think he can stop me? You think if I really want to, I won't just slit your throat? That I don't rule whatever the fuck I want?"

"Mr. Armanelli, please—"

"Yes. Start with begging," Cade commanded and shoved him back. "Get on your knees to do it too."

He chuckled like he thought Cade was joking, but the beautiful man who I knew I loved right there and then, in all his crazy glory, in his madness, his fury, lifted a brow.

Aleks nodded fast then. "Of course." He got on his knees. "I really meant no harm, and my country is innocent. I have a wife."

"What if I gave her a dose of what you gave my Untouchable, a dose that was almost lethal?"

The man started to sob. He knew he wouldn't live, that he probably wouldn't be spared. "She's just a woman."

"Don't women rule us? She owns my soul. I can control every computer you log into, the technology that protects your country, and I can control if you live or die. But she controls me. She says kill you, and I ask how she'd like it done. Do you understand? Take a look around you."

We all glanced around the room. It was very clear that Cade had used his blade on Dion. There was the fresh smell of blood in the room. He'd been gutted, and Aleks's knees were soaked with the evidence of that.

"Turn to her and plead," Cade commanded.

Aleks didn't even hesitate. He pivoted to me immediately with tears in his eyes. "Please. Spare me. You'll make an enemy of the nation. Albania is mine. My family rules it. Think of your nation, how we could be allies. Please. *Please.*"

"Those were the words I used before Dion took my sobriety," I whispered, holding his gaze.

Dion was bleeding out on the floor already, the thick liquid flowing from his stomach as he rolled around in pain. I crumbled to the floor as I let the fear wash over me, the pain of the loss of my sobriety, and the relief that I could get out.

The man begged, and I tried my best to think beyond what I felt then, tried my best to understand that alliances would be broken if I acted with my gut and emotion. "Cade, you can do what's best for the nation."

Cade searched my eyes. Then he shook his head as his tattooed hand, the one that read CHAOS on it flexed hard.

The room faded away as he held my gaze, as he seemed to look in my soul, dig around and find my heart, my emotion, and my pain. He didn't blink or break eye contact, his eyes dark and haunted, as he slit the man's throat.

I turned away as Dante came to stand beside me and asked if I was okay. Cade was there a second later. He scooped me up even as I said, "I'm fine. I can walk."

"And I can carry you," he murmured into my neck. Then, he yelled for the guys to figure out this shit show we were leaving behind.

No words between us were exchanged as he set me gently into a black SUV and then we drove into the night silently.

I thought we were in the clear, that he'd come for me, and I'd figured out I loved him. We'd find a way to get over this and be together. I thought that everything was going to be okay.

Except Cade wasn't. That night altered something in his mind, something I wasn't sure I could ever get back.

CHAPTER 28

Cade

t was seeing her broken—the quiver in her voice, the bruises on her body, the blood from her mouth—that changed something in me. I'd pushed her buttons before, tortured her a little, fucked with her because she was mine, but this was different.

No one got to torture her but me.

No one got to mark her but me.

Izzy Hardy had been mine for a long time, but it took this kidnapping for me to realize it. My bracelet shined as if untouched on her wrist but it hadn't protected her. Nothing I'd done so far had protected her enough.

That was going to change.

"I'd corrupt the whole world for you. Have them bleed out and suffer for attempting to hurt you," I murmured as our driver turned a corner to make it back to my place. I couldn't take her home, where she needed to be, because they'd drugged her there, tainted the place she should have felt safe.

"I don't want the world corrupted," she replied. "I only need what you give me. A place to be free, a place to let go enough to be myself."

I pulled her close, grabbed her thighs, and had her straddle me so I could kiss her gently, so I could hug her and smooth my hands over her back, like I needed to check her and make sure she was really with me.

I barked at our driver to stop and get her some food, never letting her move from my lap. I hand-fed her without a word. She opened her mouth and chewed every bite, staring at me with tears in her eyes. She needed nourishment. I made a promise to myself, as her lips brushed my fingers with each bite, that I'd nourish her for the rest of my life.

When she'd finished eating, she nestled into my neck and was asleep in seconds. I told the driver to go until I said stop. How I hadn't given her love without fucking and torture before, I didn't know. Because there, in that SUV, I fell in love with loving her. I wanted to fuck her slow, with the night's city lights on her, and see how she melted into my gentle touch. I wanted her to feel safe and loved and treasured. I wanted to see the tears in her beautiful eyes. I wanted to see the love I felt for her right then in her eyes for me always.

After an hour or two had passed and she stirred, peering up at me. "I have to get home. My cat's probably scared and starving."

"Bug is fine." I cut her off. "She's at your parents' house. Does she always look at everyone like we're stupid?"

Izzy snickered. "Yes."

I readjusted my damn trousers because staring at her smiling, breathing her in, feeling her pussy so damn close, proved I couldn't resist her even in the worst of times.

When her hips rolled into me, though, I growled. I met her

gaze and found her biting her lip. "Izzy, don't fuck with me right now."

"I could have died, Cade. And if I'm starting over, maybe I'm not going to bury this feeling. Maybe I need to accept what I want right here and now."

"You want this?" I narrowed my eyes, trying to make sure she could handle it. "Now? Because I'm still on edge, Izzy. Someone fucked with what was mine."

"Show me I'm yours, then," she said, her gaze unwavering as she leaned to press the partition button on the door.

I didn't even wait for it to be all the way up. I couldn't. I grabbed some of her hair and pulled her head back to expose her neck. I licked and bit every part of it before making my way to her mouth. I tasted the blood on her lips still, and my dick got harder as she ground her pussy there, riding my lap like her control was about to snap. "This is never going to happen again, Izzy. You're my Untouchable, and I'll destroy the world before they come near you again."

She whispered *okay* over and over, but I was going to make her see. I spun her around so she was sitting on the seat, and I kneeled before her.

"Do you see me on my knees before you, dollface?" I rubbed my fingers over her and then I took my blade from my trousers. Opening it so that it pointed my way, I offered her the handle. "Hold it."

The dried blood there was another symbol of what we'd done, what we were, and what I'd do for her. She held it out to me, pointed at my heart, and then I guided her closed fist and the handle to her pussy. I pressed it against her opening.

"Do you see my life in your hands?" I whispered. "Do you want to take it, knowing I put yours at risk?"

She shook her head, and her eyes sparkled. "I can't take your life, Cade. Not when you gave me back mine."

She couldn't mean that. "I put you in danger."

"The only danger was because of them. And now I'm only in danger of myself." She said it softly, and I knew she didn't want to admit it, maybe didn't even want me to hear it.

"Dollface," I tightened her grip on the handle. "Do you feel that? The power you hold in your hands? In your soul?"

No woman would ever have me in her grasp the way she did. Tears formed in her eyes, and it felt like my damn heart broke when she said, "What if I can't be powerful enough, Cade? What if what they've done makes me relapse?"

I encircled her hand and moved the weapon's handle against her. She whimpered as I pushed my chest into the pointed tip until I felt the prick and blood started to bleed through my shirt. I grabbed her jaw with my other hand. "Watch how we work, Izzy. You see us together here, holding this. It's me making you feel everything, protecting you from the other side of destruction, and you holding my life in your hands. Me and you. We work."

She was panting, riding the handle, and losing herself in it until she was wet enough for me to know she was ready for me. I turned the blade and slid it between her pussy and the shorts to cut them, then up the side so that they fell, tattered to the floor. Then I pocketed the knife so I could have my way with drinking her in.

"Ride my face, baby. And don't stop until I tell you to." I grabbed her neck, needing to own her, needing to feel the control of her life in my hands again.

I cut off her oxygen, and her pussy gushed as though she needed it just as bad. She clawed at my head, at my back, and wrapped her legs around me. I clenched that neck harder, and she pulled me even closer, like she wanted me to take her life, like I was the only one who deserved it.

When she came on my tongue, I just barely remembered to release my hold from her so she could gasp in air. I saw how the marks left would bruise, and I was ashamed to find I wanted to put more there. I unzipped my trousers and pulled my cock from them.

She spread her legs, holding my gaze, and murmured, "Fuck me hard, Cade. Make me feel alive."

Her words caused something to break in me. I'd almost lost her, and it'd been my fault. I was supposed to be watching her every move. I was supposed to keep her safe, and she was only supposed to be in danger with me. Instead, my name, the company that I'd assigned her to, and the project I'd had her work on had almost taken her from me.

I thrust into her over and over again and emptied my seed inside her, hoping it'd never leave her body.

When we pulled up to my apartment, I tucked my suit jacket around her and swept her up like a baby to carry her into the building. Once we were inside, she walked around and took in the lack of decoration and interior design. It was an expensive place in a high-rise near Stonewood Enterprises with floor-to-ceiling windows onto the city. I didn't turn on the lights; I let the moonlight fall on us instead. Her in those damn T-shirts with my windows as her backdrop was all I needed to see for the rest of my life, anyway.

"Do I get a tour?" she asked softly as she dragged a hand over the island counter. Then she saw the roses on it. "Someone get those for you?"

"I've had them delivered daily since the cabin. I needed a reminder of you."

She hummed but didn't say much else.

"Let's get you cleaned up."

She stood there in that baggy shirt, dirt and dried blood splattered across it. "I'm a mess, huh?"

"I'd have you this way always if I could."

"Then have me again." She lifted a brow, and my dick jumped immediately. She needed rest, but I saw the hunger in her eyes, the way she was pushing herself to stay alive, to test her own limits.

"Let's go to the shower."

"You think I'm so fragile all of a sudden, Cade? You just killed a man in front of me, and I realized something during that time." She strode over to my window. "I wonder if the city will know it too. If my family will accept it. Will people see that if you hadn't slit his throat, I would have? That I have that in me? That I'm okay with having it in me all of a sudden? That I'm okay with every fucking emotion now?"

Jesus.

Hearing her say it out loud shouldn't have made my cock hard immediately. Yet I loved Izzy when she was mad, loved when she embraced what she really wanted—and if that was killing an asshole, I probably would have sat there watching and smiling the whole time.

I came to stand behind her and wrapped my arm around her waist. "Are you ashamed of that?"

She sighed as she stared out at the city. "I think I'm coming to terms with it. I'm not all good. I'm different and different's okay. It's what makes me who I am, and I need to be me."

I nestled into her neck. "I'll show you how good it will be for you, dollface. Let me take you to the shower."

She turned her head to look up at me, those hazel eyes vibrant and alive, searching my features. "Why? I want the world to see you taking me like this. Dirty and a mess. Raw and different and ready."

She took her time taking her tattered shirt off, sliding it inch by inch over her body before dropping it on the floor. The moonlight shone on her curves and had me memorizing every shadow and highlight.

I fucked her with the city as my backdrop and wondered if it'd be enough to show them that she belonged to me.

Then I fucked her slow into the night, made love to her, and told her she was mine forever. I meant it. I lay awake figuring out how to make it all right, how to make sure she was never taken again, how to make sure she'd always be mine.

Did I deserve for her to be mine when I knew deep down I'd always be some sort of danger to her? Someone would always have it out for me and my family.

I found that I loved her, and that meant I had to determine whether I loved her enough to let her go.

CHAPTER 29

Izzy

"**W**here are we going?"

Cade had somehow managed to get me to sleep in after showering and then fucking all night. And in that time, he'd had a suitcase of my belongings—including spray paint—sent over. I searched the bag and was able to pick out a pink T-shirt with Coolio on it and shorts. If my whole wardrobe wasn't a tribute to the nineties outside of work, I didn't want it.

He'd hurried me into his Tesla and told me nothing else until he murmured, looking out the window, "To your family's."

"Um . . ." I stuttered. "That's not a good idea. My brothers will—"

"Be happy to see me?" He chuckled and then cracked his knuckles. "I'm aware no one wants to see me right now."

Everyone knew the situation because Dante had told them. They'd all been texting me this morning. Gossip in my family traveled like wildfire. Dom was probably the most persistent, only because he was the oldest, and Lilah was already married to someone in the mob, so she'd given our family a good enough scare before.

> **Declan:** I'm at Mom and Dad's. I flew in. You'd better get here now.
>
> **Me:** Please don't start. We're already on the way.
>
> **Declan:** We? No.
>
> **Declan:** Don't bring him here. You need to rest and heal.
>
> **Me:** I am. I'm with Cade and safe.
>
> **Declan:** That's not possible if you're with him. What the fuck is wrong with you and Lilah? Pick normal men. Not the mob.
>
> **Me:** Oh shut up.

I shoved the phone into the cup holder. "I don't need to go to my family's."

"I'm going to be gone for a few days for work," Cade explained, but his voice was stilted, distant, not at all how it had sounded last night. "I don't want you to be by yourself, and you can't work, but the election is days away."

The reminder perked me up. "We need to get back to work. Not go to my parents'."

"You're on leave until further notice."

"Leave?" I leaned forward, and when he didn't respond, I snapped my fingers in front of his face to at least get him to glance my way. "I can't be on leave during the election, Cade. JUNIPER is my baby and—"

"You taught everyone everything they need to know. I've gotta be in DC, and then I'm heading out for work. You'll be back in the office in no time. Take a little—"

"I don't want time off work."

"Too damn bad." He slammed his hand on the steering wheel. "You're tired, Izzy. You work yourself to the ground. And you need rest. The fact that I'm not taking you to the damn hospital to get checked after a fucking kidnapping speaks volumes."

"Well, considering I slept with you all of last night, that probably proves I'm fine." I scoffed and tried not to smile at our bickering. Yet, this was what I was used to. We both enjoyed riling each other.

When we stopped at a red light, though, Cade looked at me, and his eyes were cavernous, full of regret. He took in my arms, legs, and neck. Every part of me that was exposed had some mark. Last night, he'd even left a bruises along my neck and bite marks across my chest. It was like he was trying to compete with the marks the Albanians had left there.

"Yes," he murmured. "You're going to be fine soon."

His comment made no sense, but I sighed and let him have it. "You know I'm fine now." I shrugged and stared out the window as my parents' home came into view. I saw the firepit out back and my niece's baby swing set up on a blanket, which meant Delilah and Dante must have been near.

We weren't going to get a chance to see them right away, though, because Declan sat out on the porch, a hat turned backward on his head. That look meant business, and so right when Cade parked, I swung open the door and got out in front of the situation.

"Declan Hardy in the flesh. You shouldn't have flown in for me."

He swooped me into his arms and pretty much swallowed me in a hug. My big brother was at least twice my size. He worked out way more than was needed and took his NFL career seriously. To most men, he would have been intimidating. Especially considering I knew he'd been one to fight off friends of his who'd tried to ask me out on dates.

He was overprotective, but it was always out of love.

So when Cade walked my suitcase over and stood in front of us, I tried to step between them.

"Cade Armanelli," Declan ground out, not extending a hand or any sort of warm greeting. "The reformed businessman in the flesh . . . or should I say reformed Mafia."

"We're businessmen," Cade corrected, narrowing his eyes.

"Either way, you come here to get your ass beat or to get your ass beat?" Declan asked and crossed his arms over his chest.

"Declan, get real." I patted his shoulder. "Everything's fine."

"From what I hear, everything's not fine. You got mixed up with this guy and almost died."

"Now, that's not—"

Cade cut me off. "That's correct. It's why I'm here. I already spoke to your parents." As if on cue, my parents stepped outside and waved at Cade. "Mr. and Mrs. Hardy, I appreciate this. Izzy needs a place to stay while I get an apartment squared away for her. I assure you she's safe now."

My mom squinted at him like she knew something we all didn't. "Cade, why don't you help Izzy up to her room. It'll be a good place for you to have a moment." She passed him the suitcase.

"A moment for what?" Declan growled. "They don't need a damn moment, Ma."

But Cade was already walking me to the door. He opened it and waited for me to step in, never meeting my eyes. I strode through and tried to call my cat over, but she was trotting toward my dad like she had a new best friend. I rolled my eyes and went to my bedroom, ushering Cade in. "Sorry about my brother. They all might be a bit weird for a while."

"Not weird. They're what you need." He set my suitcase on my bed and then took my face in his hands. "They're what you need, and I'm not, Izzy."

I froze. "What?"

"Lucas woke up, and he's coming here too. You're going to have all the people you need surrounding you."

"Surrounding me for what?"

"I'm leaving, dollface. You don't need me right now. You need them." He encircled my wrist and brought a key from his pocket. He unlocked the bracelet and put it in his pocket.

I didn't understand what he was saying or doing. "Sure I need them. I need you too. You're leaving for a few days, but you'll be back, right?"

He stared at me in silence, and then he took two steps back, away from me, and it might as well have been two fucking miles.

"You'll be back, right, Cade?" Why did my voice sound desperate?

"I don't think that's a good idea."

My heart stuttered, then it cracked, then it exploded into smithereens. "What?" I murmured.

"I think you'll be better off without me."

"Better off? *Better off*?" How could he possibly think that anyone could accept and love my shit show the way he did? "You just killed a man for me. I think you are the only thing I need in my life right now."

He fisted his hands. "All the more reason for me to leave you."

"What are you talking about?" I shook my head in disbelief.

"You're going to see the news in a few minutes. The country is breaking alliances with Albania. The world is going to feel the tsunami wave of chaos I just caused. I can't be involved with you right now, Izzy."

"You're leaving me?" The tears didn't even hesitate to fall from my cheeks almost immediately. Then I whispered what I couldn't hold onto anymore, "But I love you, Cade. And it's more than I ever thought I could love again."

"Baby doll, give it some time, okay?"

"Time?" I screeched. "You think time is going to heal me from losing you? I can barely fucking breathe with what you're telling me."

He shook his head and started backstepping away from me, out of my room, out of my life. "I'm leaving now, before I take you on your bed for doing something crazy like throwing something at me."

He was damn right. I lunged for the spray paint, but he was out the door before I chucked it.

CHAPTER 30

Izzy

One whole stupid month.

He disappeared on me for a whole fucking month.

And it had been a big month too. The news went wild with our nation breaking alliances off with Albania. We couldn't ship there, operate businesses there, fly there. It was probably in everyone's best interest to not even utter their nation's name.

Cade had done that. Yet, the Armanellis apologized for nothing. The president commended them and Stonewood Enterprises for finding the hack, for unearthing more, and for their patriotism in the nation. I was never mentioned, but Cade seemed to be mentioned everywhere, except in my life.

He didn't call, didn't text, didn't email.

But every day, he sent roses. And the one and only message had come attached to them the first day. *You get roses for the rest of your life, dollface. You deserve them for what I put you through.*

My mother wouldn't let me throw them in the trash.

That first week, the election went off without a hitch, but I wasn't allowed to go back to work to be a part of it.

Lucas called me screaming about how our president was back in office, how we'd done it. It was one good blip in a sea of darkness. I tried to be happy our system went off without a hitch, that there was hacking of the election. Yet, I couldn't celebrate without him.

Cade had left me. And nothing felt whole when he wasn't there.

The few days at home with my family came and went. I wanted to get back into my apartment; I wanted to get back to work and establish my routine. I needed to get back to normal. Yet, that same night, the apartment company emailed to say they were sorry I was canceling my lease but they completely understood.

I called the next day. "But I'm not canceling."

"Oh, we received your email and signature. We've already accepted the payment, Ms. Hardy, and we've been blessed with a few applications for your unit already."

"That fast?" I said in disbelief, but I knew what was happening. Fucking Cade.

"We really appreciate the generous lump sum you provided—"

I hung up. That's when I started the voicemails to him. I smashed his number into my phone and waited for him to not pick up so I could leave a message.

"Listen, you dick, you don't want to be a part of my life, then stop meddling in it. I told you I loved you and you left. That means that's it. And stop sending me flowers. Technically, you're sending them to my mom because all of them would be in the trash if it weren't for her." I sighed and tried not to cry. "I need to go back to my apartment. I'm . . . I freaking miss you, and my heart is breaking, and I can't do that here. I don't want to break down in front of my family. It's not fair to them."

He didn't call back.

And, of course, I broke down in front of my sister and my mom.

They held me as I cried. We ate ice cream and watched the *Real Housewives,* and Lucas even drove over to watch it with us. It was terrible and gross and exactly what I needed.

The next day, I got another email saying my penthouse apartment in the city was ready.

I called him again and left another nasty voicemail telling him I didn't want it. But Lilah and Lucas wanted it for me, and they pretty much packed my suitcase and dragged me there.

I walked in, and on the island counter were more roses. Outrageous amounts.

But no Cade.

Lucas told me not to dwell and to just enjoy the damn penthouse. So I made him come with me to move in my belongings. Not much was needed though. Beautiful leather furniture had been placed throughout with expensive paintings on the walls, lush carpets, and a walk in closet that held a whole wardrobe of pencil skirts and freaking nineties t-shirts. My heart hurt when I saw a folded pile of *Edward Scissorhands, Men in Black*, and *Pulp Fiction* graphics. Another pile though had Harley Quinn on each shirt. He was making additions to my freaking life, like he wanted to be in it, like he still knew me and wanted me.

I fumed to Lucas and made him stay over night after night to keep me company.

We talked about our sobriety. I told him I was scared, and he held my hand while we both cried. I think we decided then that it was best for me to go back to work, to find purpose without Cade, and to move on.

Yet, when I tried, Jett Stonewood met me in the lobby of the damn building with his wife.

He informed me that Cade really wanted me to take some time off. I tried to temper my anger and my hand went to my wrist to twist the bracelet that wasn't there anymore.

Fury flew through me at the thought that he'd taken that too. He'd taken my heart, the bracelet, and his love from me.

So, want to know what I told the owner of Stonewood Enterprises?

"You can fuck right off, too, Jett," I growled, because I was so done with all of them.

His wife was this beautiful tall blonde, and she looked up at him and said, "Well, she's right. You're all assholes."

"Vick." He sighed, but he was looking at her like she was the sun, the moon, and the stars.

"Come with me, Izzy." She looped her arm in mine and didn't wait another second to be told to stay put.

She led me to the elevators and then to my desk, talking the whole time. "They think they're smart, but they're so dumb. Just ignore them and do all the work here that you want. If they try to lock you out of your office, here's my number. Cade's being idiotic. He'll be back."

"I don't want him back," I seethed like an upset child.

"Right. My husband told me he left after a hiccup with the election system?"

I narrowed my eyes at her, and she narrowed her honey eyes back at me. "I'm not sure we should be talking."

"Oh." She tapped her chin. "You don't trust me yet, but I can assure you, I know pretty much everything that goes on around here. And because I know everything, I can say without a shadow of a doubt that you have a right to be mad."

"Okay." I dragged out the word, unsure what else to say.

She smiled wide and told me to follow her. She wore the brightest pink dress that matched the bright-pink purse on her arm, and she waved to a few of my coworkers as we walked to Cade's office. Then, she opened the door for me and shut it tight behind her before fogging the windows so no one could see in.

Then, without saying a word, she rummaged in her purse and pulled out a red spray can. "You used this on one ex before, right?"

I cleared my throat. "That was a—"

"Well," she hesitated only a moment. "There was the bed at the retreat, too, right?"

"I'm going to pay them back for—"

She uncapped the spray paint and shook it in her hands. "Do you think he likes his computers in here?"

"Sure." I shrugged.

"Good." She walked over to one screen and grabbed my arm to pull me over with her. Then she handed me the can.

"I personally think you should write *coward* on them. He's being a baby and isn't sure how to handle his love for you, but he's been a complete dick, so it might be a good idea to just write that on there."

The woman was a little off. Maybe even a lot off. But I liked her.

I liked her a lot. And I smiled the whole time I wrote *dick* on each one of his screens. Vick applauded me and told me she'd take care of her husband, that I should come to work every day I wanted to.

So for the remainder of that week, I worked alongside my team.

For every day I was in the office, candy canes and subs were delivered. It was always paid for at the same time and without a note. The team rejoiced, saying they knew it was Cade.

I got madder.

The next week, I still couldn't get through to him on the phone. I couldn't see him at work because he never came to the office. And when I checked my bank account one night, I saw extra zeros behind my balance. More zeros than I'd ever seen in my life.

I called him again. No answer.

I couldn't even track his location because he blocked me every time I tried to hack something that led me to his IP address, which proved to me that he was alive, which pissed me off more.

But I felt my fury this time. I felt it with every bone in my body.

He'd made love to me the night after rescuing me. He'd told me I held the power, and I felt it.

Felt how it swallowed me up and consumed me.

I probably went a little crazy. In all fairness, he'd told me to embrace every emotion, and I really had. Lucas told me I looked deranged during that second and third week.

By the fourth, I'd snapped at just about everyone, and then went home to wallow in the pain of being mad at him but missing him too.

Gerald continued texting me and hounding me for one meeting even if it would be our last. He seemed desperate and willing to take whatever he could get from me. I agreed mostly just to spite Cade. I'd give Gerald the closure that Cade wasn't giving me at all.

The day was beautiful, the late fall breeze blew in through the windows I'd opened, and the trees rustled with their last lingering leaves as the sun shined through the shade right into my penthouse. I texted Gerald the address and told him to make his way over.

But guess who showed up ten minutes later?

He didn't even knock. He had a fucking key and unlocked the door to walk right in.

I didn't move from the cozy furniture that had been placed there for me before I moved in. "Get out, Cade," I murmured without looking up from my phone.

I heard him walk over and then heard him sit down in the leather chair across from the couch. I wouldn't look at him. I couldn't. He was the man I'd mourned for a month, even though he wasn't dead. He'd just left me for no reason.

"I'll say it again, and calmly, one last time. Please leave. I have nothing to say to you."

"Well, we don't have to talk," he said casually, as if it was completely normal for him to stroll into my home after leaving me for a month.

"Get the fuck out," I screamed and threw my phone before whipping my head up to see him. I gasped at his appearance. He was thinner, with dark circles under his eyes like he hadn't been sleeping, but he was just as formidable, maybe even more so.

And he didn't move a muscle or flinch when I screamed.

I pushed up from the couch and stomped toward him, the wrath radiating off me. I felt the heat, the pain, the waves of vitriol running through my head that I wanted to spew at him. "Did you hear me?"

He frowned at me without moving a single inch. I could see love and remorse in his gaze but I hated it now.

The only feeling I would have died for a month ago, I now

wanted nothing to do with. The hole he'd made in my heart was cavernous. So dark I couldn't find a step to stand on to save me, to help me climb out. I'd instead dug a hole in it and made a home. I was staying there. Staying away from him.

"I don't want you here. I don't want to see your face. I don't want to hear your voice. Or feel your goddamn presence. Or smell your fucking smell!" My voice shook. "Get out."

"Izzy, I think I'm going to stay," he said as if he'd considered all options and this was his best bet.

"Gerald's coming." I threw up my hands. "He's coming to say sorry and take me out for a drink. Can you imagine . . . a sorry?"

"Seems a bit ridiculous," he had the audacity to say.

"You would think so, considering you can send a million dozen roses and not ever utter an apology to me."

"What would I be sorry for?" he inquired, and I considered whether I could choke him out and win the fight with the rage that pumped through my veins.

"Do you really want to be here when he comes? He was hurt by your text. Not that it really matters. He can be hurt all he wants, but he's also mad. For all I know, honestly, he might punch you. Quite frankly, I hope he does," I threw out, trying to get him to leave. God, I was childish.

"I hope he does too." Cade smiled at me, like he wanted to unleash something. And my body instantly buzzed to life.

I spun around, furious that I still reacted to him at all. I knew this wasn't right. I hated how much I loved him. How much I always would. "I'm trying here, Cade. I'm moving on like you told me to."

"I didn't tell you that. I said to give it some time," he murmured.

"Yes. And we can all assume—"

"Do you always assume things, Izzy? Because I never told you I hated you when we first met either, but you imagined that too."

"Cade," I took a deep breath in warning and paced away from him toward the kitchen. He got up to follow and leaned his hip on the counter as I pointed a finger at him. "You told me to move on."

"But neither of us can."

Those five words, said with such conviction, had me turning around like the girl from *The Exorcist*. If my head could have spun a full 360 degrees, it would have. Instead, on one heel, I made that turn, so slow and full of fury that I knew he'd better listen. "Take it back right now, Cade Armanelli. I *am* moving on."

"Shit, baby." He cracked his knuckles as he looked me up and down. "You look more pissed than I've ever seen, and I've seen you pretty mad. I'm trying not to be turned on, but don't come near me or I'll fold."

The fact that he hadn't answered my calls and had ignored my voicemails, then waltzed in here like nothing was wrong, had me seeing a red so bright I might have been blinded by it.

"You'll— Are you kidding me right now?" I stopped, not willing to walk any closer. I couldn't risk my heart wanting him when my mind knew better.

But both of us halted when there was a knock at the door. I was about to brush past Cade to answer it, but he grabbed my arm to say in a low voice, "I'll be nice if I have to, Izzy, but I can only take so much."

I ripped my arm from his grasp and glared at him. "You'll take whatever I want—even if it means Gerald and I getting back together—considering we're not even dating."

That Armanelli man had the audacity to grumble like a little boy as he stomped over to the kitchen island stool and took a seat. "We could go back to being enemies, and I still wouldn't allow that shit. He'd be a dead man walking."

CHAPTER 31

Izzy

I rolled my eyes, furious but also more alive than I'd been in weeks. Cade was back, we were sparring, and I was feeling so much more like myself that my heart ached at finding what I felt had been lost to me: myself and the love of my life.

I tried not to focus on that, though, and swung open the door. There stood my ex, his hair slicked back, a suit and freaking tie pressed perfectly for whatever show he was about to put on, and a small smile of hope on his face. He pulled me in for a hug, and we both turned as Cade growled from the countertop.

"Izzy, I didn't know you had company," Gerald ground out.

"Yes, well, he came unannounced."

I saw how Gerald's lips pulled back, how the distaste showed in his face. "I really wanted to speak to you privately."

I took a deep breath. "Gerald, if it's important, you can say it here and now, because I'm not quite sure I have any patience left at this point. I was clear when I left you—"

He nodded vigorously and held up his hands. "You're right.

You're right. I'm sorry for even insinuating I deserve more of your time. I just"—he glanced at Cade and cleared his throat—"I really meant what I said when I called you to tell you I missed you. I've done a lot of soul-searching without you. And with my father's business about to go bankrupt, I've really found it hard to cope without you because—"

Cade snorted and strolled over to my fridge like he owned the freaking place. He opened it up and grabbed a water bottle, then lifted a brow at both of us watching him. "Go on. We're listening, Gerald."

The way he sneered the man's name had me wide-eyeing him, but he shrugged like he didn't care. Quite frankly, I shouldn't have cared either. Gerald had cheated and then handled it terribly by texting me constantly for a month after. Yet, he'd been silent since Cade threatening him until today's text. It was a thoughtful one asking for forgiveness and for me to hear his side.

"Look, the only reason I'm here is for you. I know I fucked up, and I'm so thankful you're letting me come over to tell you that. It shows that we still care about each other, right, baby?" He flicked his gaze to Cade like he wanted Cade to understand that too.

I sighed and combed a hand through my hair. "Honestly, Gerald, no. I've recently been left to wonder why a certain relationship of mine ended as well. I didn't get it. I felt like you, texting that person, bothering them, leaving them voicemails. So I figured I owed you the same courtesy I would have liked."

Gerald's cheeks reddened and he started to sweat. I wasn't sure if it was the suit, Cade staring at him, or if he was just overwhelmed, but it wasn't even hot in here. Did he love me that much that he'd sweat over this?

"Okay, okay. That's fair." Then he did the most ridiculous thing ever. He kneeled down in front of me and pulled a ring out of his pocket. He gripped my hand, and I let him because I was in such shock. "I need you to forgive me. I need a second chance. I'll be yours forever. No cheating, no straying. You're it."

My freaking jaw dropped. And he was so dense, he took it as a sign to shove the diamond ring on my finger.

"Gerald." I shook my head. I grabbed him by the biceps and yanked him up. "No. What are you even thinking?"

"I love you, and we're meant to be together. I'll even tell him. I saw him with you, and I realized I needed to clean up my act. I needed to show you how much I cared."

"Gerald," Cade said his name quietly but with a firmness that made us both stop and listen to him as he walked over slowly. That small smile on his face held no happiness as he looked my ex-boyfriend up and down. "I did warn you about coming near Izzy and talking with her again, didn't I?"

"We-well . . ." he stuttered as Cade took another step toward him. Both men stared at each other. "I-I think it's best we let Izzy choose what she wants. Even if you're all businessmen now, we know that you're really . . ."

Gerald didn't have the balls to finish that sentence, but Cade waited as he slid his knuckles down the bicep of my outstretched arm which Gerald still held. I couldn't control how the trail of his skin touching mine left a wake of goose bumps or that I shivered when his hand encircled my wrist to slowly pull my fingers from Gerald's grip.

Gerald let me go and watched as Cade brought my hand to his mouth. He rubbed my fingertips over his lips as he murmured to us both, "Go on, Gerald. Finish your sentence."

"I just think she should choose who she wants."

The man I'd so desperately tried to get over for the last month smiled at me, and my whole body vibrated with need. He didn't stop there, though. He took his time dipping my ring finger in his mouth and swirled his tongue over every part of my skin before his teeth clenched around the engagement ring. Dragging it centimeter by centimeter off my finger, he held my gaze. I saw every part of Cade in his amber eyes at that moment. The anger at Gerald even considering that we would be apart, the pain that he'd given me the notion we could be, the humor in how I was mad at him right now but the knowledge that I wouldn't be forever.

"Cade," I whispered, but it came out a whimper, "what are you doing?"

He held the ring between his teeth, and it was so damn seductive that I had to clench my thighs together. I'd lost all awareness of Gerald at this point. It was me and the love of my life in that room. I wished to God that the damn ring he held between his teeth was from him to me.

"Take it," Cade commanded, and when I did, he said, "Hand him back the ring before I put it down the garbage disposal."

I extended my hand with the ring in it and Gerald's face fell as I shoved it into his hand. Then, Cade snatched my hand fast and threaded his fingers through it, turning to face Gerald like we were a united front against him.

"Gerald, Cade's right. I don't want this from you. You need to move on."

His face curled in disgust. "You want it with *him*, Izzy? You can't. I'm the one you need. If you think spreading your legs for a guy in the mob is going to get you a penthouse for the rest of your—"

Cade grabbed Gerald's neck so quickly, I didn't have time to stop it. "Should I kill you fast now, or slowly later?"

He lifted my ex off the ground and shoved him back into the wall, showing his strength, his fury, and his lack of hesitation to kill. Cade was a man born from power and he had no problem exerting it.

Some might have been frightened, but I found I wasn't at all afraid. I sighed and grabbed him by the elbow. "Cade don't kill him. Please. I like my penthouse, and I don't want the memory of him dying here."

Gerald looked at me like I was deranged. Surly, I must have been a little bit. I really didn't care about him at all. He'd cheated on me. He'd antagonized me for a long time, and he was a virus to women. It showed in the way he lashed out immediately when I turned him down.

"If I wasn't here to make you happy today, dollface, he'd be dead." He yanked open the door to the apartment and threw Gerald out by his neck. He crumpled to the floor, wheezing. "Your name is this close to being on a hit list, Gerald. And my family doesn't miss. Keep in mind, your company is about to go bankrupt. It will be by the end of the day. Go worry about that and forget my future wife exists. Forever."

Gerald might have tried to say something but Cade slammed the door and roared at it in frustration. Then he whipped around and grabbed me by the hips, shoving me up against the island counter and stepping between my legs. "Izzy, I swear to God, he comes back here or texts you again, I'm killing him."

Chewing my cheek, I tried my hardest not to give in and kiss him right then. "Did you do something to his father's company?"

"Of course I did something to his company," Cade bellowed. "I hacked their systems and exposed his infidelities to most of his clients. I've also had calls with his biggest investors questioning how well they can operate when I so easily am able to infiltrate their finances. He's finished."

"But why?" I whispered. "We didn't get along then and—"

"He cheated on you. He *hurt* you. Do you not understand the consequences of when someone does that? No one is allowed to fuck with you but me, don't you understand? You cried, Izzy. I had to see tears streaming down your face. For that, he's lost his company, his savings, his whole career. And if he dares go near you again, he *will* lose his life."

"Cade, you can't do those types of things for me." I murmured, but my heart was healing, being pieced back together by each of his confessions.

"I can do whatever I want. I will always do that for you. You deserve it and more." He tried to steady himself by taking a breath. "Don't ever text him again. Matter of fact, I'll be blocking him from all your devices. An ex texting my future wife is ridiculous anyway."

I almost forgave him right then, my insides warming to the word wife, but he had much more explaining to do. "People can come visit me, Cade. I'm single and not the future wife of anyone."

His eyes narrowed as he placed his hands on either side of me on the island counter. "You're fucking *mine*."

I shook my head and lifted my chin higher, ready to fight him about it this time. "You left me. And I've moved on."

"Bullshit." He grabbed my wrist and clamped his gold bracelet back on quickly. He fought me to lock it and then winked when he overpowered me as it latched into place.

"Are you kidding me?" I yanked at it and shoved him, but he didn't back up even an inch. "It's not bullshit. You can't leave and come back like I'm some mistress you call up every now and then. Maybe you were with other women, or maybe you got sick of me but want another taste now. It's not happening."

"Baby"—his forehead fell to mine—"you can't believe that."

"Why can't I?" I said, tears suddenly in my eyes. "I was broken, and you left. You left me to handle it all on my own."

"And you did," he growled out. "You had it in you. You needed to be without me."

"So you want me to be without you but not with anyone else either."

"Look, I thought I would be okay with you being with someone else, just not Gerald, but then I knew that wouldn't work. It's selfish of me, because I'll always have a target on my back and you'll always be in danger. But I flew around the world to try to make sure that, instead, I've made you as safe as possible." he admitted, and it cut me deep. He was standing so close. I could feel the love radiating off him, and I knew he felt it too. "Honestly, you're still better off without me."

He had to feel my rage at his words. How could he think that? How would I be safe from myself, from heartbreak, from feeling so lost, I couldn't see which way was up without him. He had to know his words would act as the last straw. "Don't you dare say that again," I whispered.

"Baby doll, you know it's true. Your world would be easier—"

he started, but I'd had enough.

My hand whipped out, and I swung at his face. The sound was so deafening I swear it echoed through the room, like we were in an empty cave that amplified our noise.

Cade didn't flinch, nor did his face turn to the side. I wish I could say he didn't lean into it, but I swear that man saw it coming from a mile away and wanted the pain of it.

"Again, Harley Quinn, and make it hurt this time."

The noise I made as I reared back was animalistic. Tearing this man apart would be a job well done by me, I figured. No one should be subjected to the type of pain I felt when I wasn't with him, to him coming back into my life and trying to lay claim to certain parts of me. "If you want the devil from me, you're going to get it."

He lifted an eyebrow, so damn cocky in his desire to ruin me. No part of me was right then. All the normal, calm parts of me disbursed and twisted. I was an algorithm ruined, I truly was glitching, falling apart, disassembling into nonsense, causing destruction as I did so. My hand didn't just meet his face this time, but the muscle I put behind it did too.

One slap, two slaps, and probably ten more. Cade let me wail on him until I tired.

I shoved him back and screamed, "I hate you. You've ruined me. You've ruined everything."

"Any more anger, dollface?" He smirked, nestling into my neck like this was normal, loving behavior between us.

"There's something wrong with you. I really think you need help," I warned him. He needed someone to tell him.

"Maybe. But there's something wrong with everybody." His hands went from the counter to my hips. "If you want me to, I can find the problem in anyone for you. Nobody's perfect."

"Don't come here and call me those names, like we have something, like you think the last month didn't happen."

"Oh, it happened," he ground out. "I had to live through it without the person I love in my life. The person who makes my heart beat."

"How can you say that after you told me you would let me go and let me be with someone else?"

"I still counted the days, the hours, the minutes, the seconds without you." He admitted it as if that made everything better.

The tears that streamed down my face were ugly reminders that I couldn't bottle up my feelings with him. "How could you leave me after that night? We . . . I thought you loved me, or at least liked me enough to stay. I fell in love with you, Cade. I fucking bled for you, showed you the inside of me and didn't shine it up at all. I gave you every raw part of me, only for you to leave the very next day."

"Izzy, I was trying to protect you." He shook his head, his own dark eyes glistening. "I thought it was right."

"And now?"

"Well, now I'm sure."

"Sure of what?" I asked even though it didn't matter.

"Sure that I've changed the world enough. I'm sure that every family knows who you are." He dragged a finger over the bracelet and I looked down to see *Untouchable* etched on the gold now. "You're safe, you're an Untouchable, and you're getting the best life you can."

"What does that even mean?" I threw up my hands in frustration. "I was safe with you here!"

"No." He shook his head. "How can you think that? You know

my family. You know people will always be out to get me. They kidnapped you, Izzy. They—" He took a shaky breath and then paced away from me, only to pace back again. "You could have died there. That would have been on me."

"No, it wouldn't have! I hacked their files. Me. Not you." I hit my chest in frustration, trying to make him understand.

"I should have been watching you! I should have protected you. Don't you see?" He dragged one of his tattooed hands down his face, and I saw the pain there, the fear. "I could have lost you."

"That wouldn't have been your fault, Cade." I didn't know why I was consoling him, but I had to. He looked broken, tired, and just as depressed as me.

He pulled at his thick dark hair. "It would have been my fault, dollface. I was so consumed with you that I let my guard down. I let shit slip through the cracks. I wasn't going to let that happen again. This country has made changes since then."

I glanced at the television. We all saw the news. "You created a lot of havoc."

"They should be happy I didn't create more. And I had to leave you for a while to make sure that in that time, you were safe. I visited every family in the world that's important. I've had conversations with them all. I've hacked every one of their bank accounts just to show them exactly what I'm capable of, to show them your value to me. They all know now."

"Know what?" I asked with a hand on my hip.

"You're mine. And if they even breathe an ounce of foul air in your direction, I will burn their country to the ground."

"Why didn't you just tell me you were doing that, Cade? Why make me believe you'd left? Why cut me off?" He needed a better excuse than wanting to protect me.

"Tell you?" He shrugged. "Until I was sure I could solidify your safety, Izzy, I couldn't have you clouding my judgment. I love you too much. You were better off without me around and I needed my full attention on the priority, keeping you safe."

I was furious he couldn't have just shared his plan with me, so I shrugged and went for the jugular. "Maybe I still *am* better off. I don't want a man who's in and out of my life. It's not like we ever established you would be. We were just having fun—"

"Is 'fun' me claiming you around the world?"

I poked his shoulder. "You can un-claim me."

"Is it *fun* that you have half my savings in your bank account?"

My stomach dropped. I wasn't sure if he'd been moving numbers around on accounts because he could or what. I didn't think that was *half* of anything. "Half?" I squeaked. There were more than eight zeros behind my normal balance.

"Sure, baby. I'll make more if you want, though." He leaned in to lick my neck, and I shivered. I couldn't deny him. My heart was beating too fast, my world suddenly stood still with him at the center of it, and the inkling of hope was bleeding out to become a huge puddle I couldn't overlook.

"So what? I'm supposed to just forgive you?" I didn't know how I would say no to him though, and the way my hands had crept up to smooth his shirt, to feel his warmth under me, to feel the love of my life there when I thought I lost him. It wasn't something I would let go of. I might have been emotional before, tried to hide who and what I was, but I couldn't hide from this.

"Of course. I can tie you up if you want to fight about it. It'll be more fun for me that way anyway, but we're doing this, dollface."

"I think I want to kill you," I admitted. For the whiplash he'd given me at the very least. "The pain you've caused me . . . It's either I die or you do."

He laughed. The beautiful, cruel man who I loved cackled at my turmoil. "Baby, look how mad you got at me this month. But didn't you feel alive?"

I hated that I did, that Cade made me feel every damn thing. He dragged his finger across my rib cage where he knew my tattoo was and then rubbed back and forth. "You need to change this 'Addict' tattoo of yours and put under it, 'Of life and Of Cade.' I deserve it."

"You don't deserve anything," I grumbled.

"Fine. Should I grovel more?" He smirked like he had a fucking sense of humor all of a sudden.

"More?"

"Well, you have half my savings, a new penthouse, roses every day that you throw away, and the title of an Untouchable. I didn't stop caring for you even if I was gone, dollface. Even if I let you go, I was still going to feed you every day—"

I rolled my eyes but did have to tell him, "The office team thanks you for the subs, by the way."

He chuckled. "But do you thank me?"

"No," I sneered, trying not to laugh with him. "You're a dick."

"I know. You wrote it on my computer screens at work."

"Yeah, well, maybe you should get that tattooed on you to match the one I got after what you called me."

He glanced up as if he was considering it. "Would that count as part of my groveling?"

"Oh my God." I shoved him to try to hide how having any of

my words tattooed on him would turn me on.

He didn't move at all. He leaned in and whispered, "I see that blush on your cheeks, pretty girl. Means me getting tattoos for you makes you wet, huh?"

"There's something wrong with us. I shouldn't even want to be near you right now."

"We're fucking volatile. And spontaneous and chaotic. It doesn't make us bad or wrong, dollface."

"It makes us hard to deal with, Cade."

"Life without chaos would be boring, Izzy. Life without glitches and your bursts of anger and me seeing you go off . . . it's unbearable."

"Everyone's working out the glitches for a smooth life!"

"Are you?" He cocked his head. "Or do you come to work every day looking for them, wanting to conquer them, wanting to wrangle them, and then you enjoy when they get out of control again and challenge you?"

"We're not stable."

"Of course we aren't." He shrugged and dragged a finger across my neck. "You want your stability with Gerald?"

"I don't know." I crossed my arms, just to piss him off. "Maybe he could give me that."

"Yeah." Then he bent at the knee and kneeled before me. "He'd wipe out your emotion, your beauty, your *you*."

"What I feel isn't always pretty, Cade. It had me wasted for a long time."

He nodded as he said, softly and almost like he was mourning the thought, "Would you be happy if you could feel them?"

I took in a breath, and it was shaky, so damn shaky that I knew he saw my chest quivering. The fact that I didn't hide it from him spoke volumes. "I'd try to be, and everyone would be happy for me."

"When you fight those feelings the way you do, your body explodes into doing dumb shit, because a fireball isn't made to be contained. Let the real you breathe so everyone else can witness it."

"I can't lose you and experience that pain, Cade. Not again," I whispered.

"You won't," he promised. "You never did. I was always watching. I may have thought I let you go but I couldn't. I won't. Never, Ms. Hardy. You're my future wife."

I laughed with tears in my eyes. "Not until you propose."

He hummed low, and then he slid his hands under my shirt to slip my shorts and panties off. "I can't do that for a while. I need to grovel some more first."

And then his mouth was on me. I sobbed out with need for him.

"Just so we're clear," I moaned, "I want a lot of groveling. Right now, I still hate you."

He chuckled into my pussy. "And I still love the way you hate me, dollface."

EPILOGUE

Cade

I knew she needed time, and so did I when I left.

If I could have changed the world's damn clocks, I would have. I contemplated fucking with the daylight savings and time zones. Like it would have mattered.

Instead, I did what I could for us, or for her.

She deserved the world, and I'd thought it would be better for her if I wasn't in it.

I claim to be good at the dark web, not knowing a woman's mind.

I'd spend the rest of my life making it up to her. I knew afterward I should never have left.

There were still days I wondered if she was better off without me, if somehow I still put her in danger by being tied to her. Yet, I did know better than to leave again. Izzy Hardy would always be my weakness, the girl I couldn't look away from or leave behind, even if I tried.

I had tried. Yet, in the month I was gone, I'd also checked on her every day. I'd hacked her text messages, listened to her voice mails repeatedly, watched the security cameras to see her face over and over again.

I knew what people meant when they said a person could die of a broken heart. Without her, I would have died, and I think she felt the same.

Every morning, I saw the way she looked at me—with a smile so wide on her face that I hoped the world would never be without it, I heard the way she moaned out that she loved me or hated me (dependent on the day).

Izzy was living.

Living her life to the fullest.

So, I intended to lock her down and make sure she would be mine, living exactly that way for the rest of her life, by buying a ruby the same color as the roses she now *wanted* every day.

We were at her parents' celebrating her brother's birthday just months after getting back together, and I knew I had to pull her father aside to discuss his daughter's hand in marriage.

Instead, all the guys hovered around the grill while Izzy grabbed her niece and tossed her up in the air before disappearing inside with her mother and Delilah.

Mr. Hardy flipped some of the steaks and let his sons all glare at me as I stood there in a suit while they wore gym shorts and baseball caps that didn't match their T-shirts at all.

"You like your steak rare or what?" Mr. Hardy asked. It was the first thing any of them had said to me since Izzy brought me home and announced, "Cade and I are together now. Get over or under it, but I'm not dealing with the bickering. He's mine and I'm his. Take him or leave him." Then she winked at me and ran off to play with her niece.

"Rare is fine," I answered.

When I slid my hands into my pockets and stared at Mr. Hardy's son, Declan stared right back at me. I knew he was the one I had to win over. And for once, I couldn't intimidate someone. He had nothing for me to hold over his head to gain his respect. Respect was all I wanted, not fear or coercion. I was good at getting those two things.

"You plan on sticking around this time?" Declan asked, menace in his voice.

"I never left."

"She said you did. For a whole month."

"I watched her, made sure she was safe, and confirmed the world knew she was an Untouchable. I needed to make sure—"

"You know about her first love?"

I nodded.

"She can't lose someone like that again."

I rubbed my chin. Her family, although they loved her . . . I don't believe they understood her strength. "She could. She'd be fine." Declan narrowed his eyes at me. "She's stronger than you give her credit for."

"Are you questioning how well I know my sister?" He tilted his head.

Dom, on his brother's right, bulked up like he was ready to fight.

"I'm just correcting you on my fiancée's resilience."

"Fiancée?" Mr. Hardy perked up at that and scratched his flannel-covered belly. "You propose yet?"

"I intend to tonight. It's why I'm standing out here trying to make small talk when I'd rather be on my phone working."

Her dad chuckled like he was happy with my candor. Her brothers practically growled in unison. But Mr. Hardy plucked the steaks off the grill and handed one of the plates full of meat to Dex. "Go on. Take the food in. And Dimitri, find your mother and tell her it's ready."

Good. He was helping even the odds. Now it was just three against one.

He squared up with his two boys, and they all sized me up. "What are you gonna do if we say no, Cade? Respect our decision?"

"Respectfully, no. I'm not even going to respect her decision if she says no. But I'm giving you the courtesy of bringing it to your attention."

Declan grumbled a "What the fuck" when his father let out a belly laugh and slapped his son's shoulder a few times. "See, that's the same thing I would have said about your mother to anyone who told me no. He's fine, boys. She'll give him enough hell as it is." Then he walked up to me and patted my cheek twice like I was a five-year-old. "Enjoy married life. Going at the world alone is too damn lonely anyway."

I think all our jaws were on the floor at how easily Mr. Hardy accepted me.

"We also need Bug back, Mr. Hardy. The cat's hers." I figured I'd drop all the bombs at once.

He actually hesitated with that. "Fine, but I want visitation hours then," He grumbled before he meandered away, probably to go cuddle the cat before we took him home.

"Dad's lost his marbles," Dom murmured.

"Fuck me," Declan groaned. Then his brow furrowed when his phone went off and he looked at the screen. "Oh no. She's not."

He stomped away as he punched buttons on the cell like they were the enemy. It seemed the man had some issues to deal with of his own as he bellowed once someone picked up his call, "You're not going to his place. If you do, you can bet your ass, I'll come get you to drag you out of there myself."

Dom and I glanced at one another before we heard him whisper with fury, "Babe, I swear to God, I'm not playing."

A second later, he held his phone out to see whoever was on the other side of the call had hung up on him. "Fuck," he grumbled.

Dom looked him up and down as he walked back up to us. "What's got your panties in a bunch?"

"She never listens." He glanced at me and slapped that glare on his face that he thought would drum up fear. "I need your jet."

"What?" I squinted at him. Was he kidding?

He combed a hand through his dark hair and I saw the crazy sort of love a man has in his eyes right before he walks off the edge of sane to fall over the cliff into insanity. He didn't know it yet, but he was about to find that the woman he was going after already owned him. "I need to get somewhere quick. So, you're loaning it to me. Or I'm beating your ass for hooking up with my sister."

"You think I can't take you?" I challenged.

Of course, Dom stepped up to his brother's side. "You really want Izzy coming outside to see us all wrestling?"

I guess I couldn't kill her brothers. "Fine. You can have the jet for a day."

"I'll take the jet for as long as I need it. And, Cade, you hurt her, and I don't care who you are, I'll kill you." Declan stared me down, no fear in his eyes at all.

"You seem to think I wouldn't kill myself for that very reason?

If I've hurt her, I'm already dead inside, you get me?"

His jaw worked up and down, up and down. "I got you."

Izzy bounced out of the house with her niece on her hip. "Are you guys coming to eat? We're hungry!" She snuggled into the little girl's face. "Aren't we?"

Them giggling together as we walked back inside had me murmuring next to her, "Careful. You'll make me want something I never thought I would."

She narrowed her eyes like she didn't understand.

Later that night, when we got home, she would finally get it.

"Cade." She came out of the bathroom in just a towel, wringing her hair with another one as she studied me. "Have you seen my birth control?"

"I have," I admitted, looking over an email from the Pentagon.

"Can you tell me where?" she asked in a condescending tone.

I pushed my glasses up on my nose but didn't look up as I said, "I saw them in the toilet right before I flushed them."

"You what?" she screeched. "What's wrong with you?"

"What's wrong is you made me want to have a baby at your family's. So we're having one."

"I'm not having a freaking baby with you." She waited a beat. "Are you insane? Stop working and look at me."

I set my laptop to the side of the bed and gave her my full attention. "I'm not insane, dollface. I'm in love. So fucking in love with you that I want to make copies of you mixed with me and see if we can duplicate our coding in a way that doesn't have as many problems as we do."

"We're not even married. And we've been together for not even—"

"For long enough." I got out of the bed to walk up to her and pull her hips close to mine. She whimpered at my hard cock against her stomach. "Want me to fuck you bare to remind you how good it'll feel every time I try to fill you up with my baby?"

"Jesus, Cade." Her hazel eyes squeezed shut before she stepped back and said, "I need to show you something."

Right then, after I'd told her I wanted her to have my babies? She wanted to show me something?

She hurried out of the room, and I readjusted my pants. The woman was going to make me work for this proposal, I guess.

When she returned, she had a piece of paper in her hand. "Remember when you told me to rewrite Vincent's letter?"

I cracked my knuckles and tried not to imagine Izzy broken, how he'd done that, how a man I'd never met took advantage of her love and then left her in ruin to pick up the pieces.

It hadn't been my place to pass judgment on him but I still felt the anger for her then as much as I did now. "I remember and I remember thinking a few choice things about him too."

She scoffed. "You'd think that about anyone who slept with me."

"Damn right I would." I pulled her close so I could at least hold her while she confessed whatever she was about to, my hand rubbing her back and trying to provide what support I could now for a tragedy she'd experienced on her own before.

"So, anyway, I didn't rewrite it like you said, because he solidified his own fate." She shrugged and took a deep breath. It was still something she'd always struggle with, but I'd be there to support her though it now. "But I wrote back to him because you made me strong enough to do so."

When she held out the letter in front of my face, I stared at it. "You want me to read it?"

She shook the paper in front of me. "Why else would I be holding it out to you?"

I searched her face fast, not sure if this was a lapse in judgment of hers. If she thought I'd be happy about her professing her love for her dead boyfriend, she'd be mistaken.

Fuck. I wasn't sure I wanted to read it all. Suddenly, my palms sweat like I wouldn't be able to handle if she did love him.

What if she loved him more than me? I mean, he was gone, but could I live with that?

I'd have to. I still wouldn't let her go for shit. With a lot more fear slithering through my veins about my proposal now, I snatched the letter from her hands.

Line 1: I won't say this is a love letter, because it's not.

Line 2: But if I were to have written one, it wouldn't have been about you.

Line 3: You left me, and you promised you wouldn't.

Line 4: You promised to love me forever. But you didn't.

Line 5: Don't ask me if you were weak or strong.

Line 6: Even though I've moved on, I still don't know what's right or wrong.

Line 7: I do know you lost so much good when you threw away the bad.

Line 8: I do know I'm older, smarter, and know you could have had a better life than you had.

Line 9: I wish you could have seen how to fight.

Line 10: That someone gave you the strength and love to see the light.

Line 11: Can you see that I found a love that wrecks me but still makes me whole?

Line 12: I feel the pain, the wreckage but also the love deep in my soul.
Line 12: So, I won't thank you for what you did, but I'll thank you for leaving me.
Line 13: It led me to him and to see I could be the person I wanted to be.
Line 14: I'm sorry you got lost in your mess.
Line 15: But thank you for showing me I should never let go.

"Jesus," I murmured and let out the long breath I'd been holding.

She loved me. And it wrecked me and put me back together too. I felt it while reading that letter, how my stomach twisted at thinking she may love him, how it uncoiled when I realized she didn't, and how it felt like electricity zinging through my system when it read like she was ready to be with me forever.

"What?" she asked quietly, like she was suddenly embarrassed.

"I'm ashamed to say I was fucking nervous you were still going to love him more than me in this damn letter."

"You're kidding me, right?" She guffawed and tried to grab the note fast from me.

I recoiled quickly enough that she couldn't reach it though. Then, I placed my other palm on her face gently. "It's beautiful, Izzy. Painful and raw too. It's you. Someone he didn't deserve and I don't deserve either."

"Oh, you deserve me. I'm going to make your life hell for the rest of it."

"Better believe it."

I got on my knees right then and there to pull the ruby ring from my pocket. "Say yes to hating that you love me for the rest of your life, Izzy Hardy."

"Cade? Seriously?" she whispered, staring at the ring and then staring at me as tears streamed down her face.

"Serious that I love you? That I love your attitude, the fact that you might still spray paint a line down our bed, that I currently owe Stonewood Enterprises for those computers and for the wall and bed on that retreat, that I wouldn't have it any other way?"

"I'll pay for that." She shook her head.

"You won't pay for a damn thing ever again, dollface. Say yes so I can tell your brothers and your father that I won't have to fight you over it."

"You asked them?"

"I did, and then when they said 'Well, what if we say no?' I told them it wouldn't matter."

"What if I say no?" She smirked.

"Doesn't matter if you say no either."

She laughed and then hiccupped, tears streaming down her face. "I'm still a mess. I still have to stay sober, and I still have to—"

"You're my mess. The one I want. Every fucking part of you, Izzy. Now, listen to your boss and say yes."

She sighed and continued to give me hell like the brat she was as she chewed her cheek. "You're still a dick, Cade."

"I know. Last time I'll tell you—say yes so I can fill you with our first of many babies."

"Fine," she giggled. "Yes."

The End

Want to see where Cade got his tattoo for Izzy? Get the bonus scene here: www.shainrose.com/newsletter

Want to read Dante and Delilah's Story, check out **Fractured Freedom.**

ALSO BY SHAIN ROSE

Standalone Broken Mafia Men Romances

Shattered Vows-Order Now

A *standalone arranged marriage romance where Bastian, a grumpy mafia boss, will wed a free-spirited surf girl and make sparks fly.*

Fractured Freedom

A brother's best friend romance full of steam and emotion where Dante will pine of Delilah as she checks off her bucket list.

ABOUT SHAIN ROSE

Shain Rose writes romance with an edge. Her books are filled with angst, steam, and emotional rollercoasters that lead to happily ever afters.

She lives where the weather is always changing with a family that she hopes will never change. When she isn't writing, she's reading and loving life.

35034632R00210